"Fascinating storyl?
My kind of book, I'm alre...,
– Wallace Czekalski, Real Estate Appraiser

"Forever Man draws you into its web in the first chapter and won't let you go. The thriller spins its twists and turns that you never see coming that continue until the end, and maybe beyond. The book combines the fast pace and suspense of a John Grisham work with the horror and evil of a Stephen King novel. It grabs you by the throat and just won't let go. A thriller that you just can't put down."
–Attorney, James P. Shields

"Spell binding.
Couldn't put it down.
Would make a great movie.
Keeps your interest all the way through.
Looking forward to a sequel.
– Dr. Roy H. Schmitt, Chiropractic Physician

The Forever Man ...
"Excitement abounds with every turn of the page.
The writer keeps you guessing until the last page.
The book is captivating from the very first page.
Save a block of time to read this book because
you will not want to put it down until you've
solved the murders!"
– Eleanor A. Windows, President of
Pittsburgh Anodizing Company

The Forever Man

C. William Davis III

Word Association Publishers
www.wordassociation.com

Edited by Theresa Doerfler
Author Photograph by Nicole Raymond
Cover design by James Baird
Interior design by Julie Csizmadia

Printed in the United States of America.

ISBN 10: 1-59571-156-2
ISBN 13: 978-1-59571-156-4

Library of Congress Control Number: 2006933909

Word Association Publishers
205 Fifth Avenue
Tarentum, Pennsylvania 15084
www.wordassociation.com
1-800-827-7903

DEDICATION

For
Linda, Michelle, and Shane
Chris and Becky
Shelby and Shane Paul
and our little Maddie

With all my love,
C. W. D. III

Acknowledgements

For your support and keeping the faith.

Brooks and Diane Paxton
Chuck and Linda Rosenberger
Dave and Nancy MCardle
Joe Lucchino
Jim and Kathy Geary
Lester Fortney

FORWORD

The basement room was dark and damp and smelled of old rags and mildew. The only light was a thin dim sliver from under the rusted iron door. Water dripped in a constant tick, like a clock, into a large chipped white porcelain bowl, from a copper tube and valve on one wall.

In the dark shadows in the corner across the room from the door, was the sound of low raspy breathing, as if someone was in deep sleep. The floor was covered with dirty straw and the only furniture was an old gray steel cot and a rocking chair. From outside the door footsteps came down a flight of stairs. The figure inside drew in a deep breath as he moved on the cot away from the light. The footsteps stopped just outside the door. There was the snap of a bolt lock, and a sliding window opened just above the center of the door, exposing six eight-inch steel bars. The open window allowed more light to enter, and the filthy room was now partially lit except for the corner where the cot remained dark and shadowy. There was the sound of a second bolt and a small door opened at the base. A hand pushed a large gray pewter mug into the room through the opening. Once the mug was inside the room, the small door closed again and was bolted.

Through the open barred window the person inside could see the neck and part of the hairy chest of a figure standing just outside the door. The person was wearing a white shirt opened at the neck, with a loosened tie. Sweat ran down his neck and onto his chest, and the open shirt exposed a small gold chain. The pendant at the base of the chain was one word in small gold letters: "Forever."

From inside the room, a sound of a chain clanking on the steel frame of the cot was heard as the figure began to move. Suddenly, from out of the darkened shadow into a portion of the light came one large bloodshot eye, and part of a forehead covered with curly dark hair. The window snapped shut once again, and the person outside ascended the stairs.

CHAPTER 1

Thursday, June 10, 10:30 p .m.

A county sheriff's car sat in the rain along the curb near the junction of Fourth and Main Streets in Smith Falls, PA. Across the street from the car was the lighted window of Miller's Boutique. Jody Miller, owner of this very popular dress shop, was just finishing up the inventory of stock and was finally preparing to go home. Taking inventory was a job she disliked, but necessary before the upcoming holiday sale on the Fourth of July. She had dismissed her help for the day at about nine o'clock and stayed on to finish the last of the paperwork. At twenty-seven, Jody was already a very successful businesswoman. She had graduated from high school in Smith Falls but had forgone college, preferring to attend business school in the city. After graduation, she had returned to her hometown and with the financial aid of her well-to-do parents, had opened the shop. It was a dream she had always had, and after just a few short years in business, she had made quite a respected name for herself in the community. As a cheerleader in high school and a member of the honor society, she had always been popular. She had passed on several offers of marriage, preferring the single life. About five feet, four inches tall, with blonde hair and blue eyes, she was exquisitely beautiful and the fashion business fit her perfectly.

Jody closed the books that were scattered across her desk, placed them in the top drawer, closed and locked it. She reached up and turned out the light on the desk, then retrieved her coat and umbrella from the rack beside her. Outside at the curb, the sheriff's car sat with the motor running and the windshield wipers pulsing slowly. The officer inside sat and watched the storefront across the street as he sipped on a coffee and puffed on the last of a cigar. Jody checked the timer on the coffee pot for the next morning, then slipped on her coat and picked up her briefcase next to the door. The officer in the car watched her through the rain-beaded side window of his car until the lights of the store went out. He put the car in drive and slowly pulled away from the curb with his lights off, then turned off Fourth Avenue and down Main Street, just as Jody closed and locked the front door of the store.

Jody placed her case on the sidewalk beside her and then peeked out from under the canvas awning on the storefront. The misty rain sprayed into her face and she felt chilled all over. She opened her umbrella, picked up her case, and started down the darkened street toward the parking area in the adjacent alley. She moved slowly down the deserted street as a breeze blew rain and mist up under her umbrella into her face. She stopped and took several pieces of tissue out of her coat pocket and wiped her face. Jody placed the tissue back into her coat pocket and was about to continue toward the lot when she thought she heard the sound of footsteps behind her. She stopped again and turned, her eyes searching, but the street and sidewalk behind her were deserted. She could hear only the sound of rain dripping from the storefront awnings. The wet concrete glistened in the glow from the streetlights and all was quiet.

Jody smiled and once again started toward the lot. Only a few steps further, she heard what sounded like a tin can, or some type of container, being kicked or dropped. She quickly spun around again. She thought she saw a shadow move near one of the storefronts. Standing motionless for a moment, she whispered, "What the hell?" There it was again—the shadow. A chill ran through her and she quickly turned and headed again for the car—only now at a faster pace. She moved faster the farther she walked, constantly looking over her shoulder. She turned the corner to the alley and there, half a block ahead, was her car sitting alone in the corner of the lot. Just the sight of the car made her feel a little better, as she fumbled for the keys in the pocket of her coat.

Suddenly, not twenty feet from the car, she heard a loud noise. It was the sound of a trash can that had been turned over. She spun around in her tracks in the middle of the alley, just as the lone can rolled out to the center and stopped. Jody was frozen, unable to move. Seconds later, darting out of the shadow near the can ran a large cat, followed by an even larger dog. They raced past her down the alley, as if she weren't there. She took in a deep breath, then placed her hand on her chest and let out a sigh of relief. She turned her head to the wet pavement and whispered, "Wow." She raised her head again and smiled, then turned back to the car. When she reached the car, she unlocked the door, closed her umbrella, and placed it on the floor in the back. She noticed that the rear tire was flat. She put her briefcase on the ground beside the tire, and reached inside to the glove box between the seats and took out a flashlight. Bending down on one knee, she examined the tire. A six-inch slice in the side wall was immediately visible. Touching the gaping hole she whispered, "Son of a _____." Slowly, the glow from the streetlight was darkened, as a huge shadow passed over her. She did not turn, but reached for the handle of her briefcase. Once the case was in hand, she jumped up and swung the case with a backhand motion. The case hit something solid and bounced back. For an instant, there was a large silhouette before her. The last thing Jody saw was the huge, dark hand that grasped her face.

Friday, June 11, 3:30 a.m.

Roscoe Black, local town drunk and vagrant, was sound asleep in a weeded ditch along the railroad tracks between the fairgrounds and Wilson Creek. Roscoe Black was sixty-five years old, about five feet four inches tall, with straight brownish gray hair and brown eyes. He was dressed in his regular attire: old worn herringbone sports coat and a felt fedora hat. He had no job and no particular place he called home. He slept most anywhere. Even a wet ditch under a sheet of plastic could be home if he had had enough to drink. His favorite hangout was Posey's Bar, where he begged for drinks if he didn't have the cash from the few odd jobs he could find. The owner of Posey's even fed him at times when he was sober enough to help clean up the bar. If he wasn't at the bar you could usually find him at the fairgrounds under one of the shelters or in the drunk tanks at the town or county police stations.

Roscoe's chosen bed for this night was a ditch along the tracks that ran through the south end of town to a small switching yard near the main rail lines of the Norfolk and Southern right-of-way. He was awakened from his fitful stupor by the sound of a car motor. He rose up on one elbow just above the weeds and rubbed his face. Through his bloodshot, misted eyes and the fog hanging in and around the creek, he saw a large, dark or black vehicle with only parking lights stopping along the tracks. He put his aching head back to the ground, when he heard a car door slam. He once again raised his head, and then sat up. He half yelled in the direction of the car, "Can't get any sleep, anywhere around here." Suddenly, the headlights came on high beam. The brilliant light hitting his eyes knocked him back to the ground in pain. He rolled several feet down the hill, almost to the creek and stopped. Mad and wet, he staggered to his feet and half crawled to the ditch at the top of the bank. His intention was to tell those suckers at the top a thing or two about a man's privacy. When he reached the top, the car was gone. He rubbed his eyes and his head, and then staggered across the tracks in the direction of the fairgrounds.

Friday, June 11, 5:15 a.m.

Hank Bower, railroad brakeman, and his work buddy, Dave Smith, engineer, were switching freight cars off the main Norfolk and Southern Lines along the extension track near the fairgrounds to the yards up the tracks. It was still misty but the rain had stopped hours before. Hank was walking along a line of boxcars to the next switch to move two of the cars to another siding. As he passed the last car he thought he saw something in the tall grass in a ditch along the tracks. He motioned for Dave to hold position while he investigated. Hank stepped off the rail bed and started into the weeds when he saw in the light of his lantern two bloody bare feet. He jumped back to the gravel then began to yell at Dave and run down the tracks in the direction of the engine. Dave Smith jumped from the train and ran toward Hank. When Dave met Hank a few feet down the tracks, Hank was almost speechless.

"What the hell," Dave said as he stopped Hank.

"A... a... a... body in the weeds."

"Where?" Dave yelled.

"Down there in the weeds," Hank gasped. "I'll call the police." Hank pulled away from Dave and headed down the tracks. Dave slowly walked to the last car and stopped, holding his lantern out in the direction of the weeds. The thick creek mist shrouded almost everything. He moved into the edge of the weeds and reached down and pulled some of the thick underbrush back. He held his lantern close to the top of the weeds and looked deep inside. Suddenly, Dave let out a yell, dropped his lantern and fell back onto the roadbed. He staggered to his feet, then to the boxcar. He placed both hands flat on the side of the car, then slid to the ground, moaned and vomited on the stones at his knees.

Friday, June 11, 6:05 a.m.

The police radio at the side of Clive Aliston's bed came to life with a loud crackle. "Sheriff. Sheriff," the female voice at the other end yelled. Clive rolled onto his back with one eye open and stared at the ceiling. "Clive Aliston," the voice blasted from the radio speaker. Clive rolled quickly to his right in a panic and knocked beer cans, an ashtray, and the radio to the floor beside his bed.

He reached for his service revolver hanging on his bedpost and yelled, "What? What?" He sat up, gun in hand, and scanned the bedroom in a daze.

The voice, now coming from under the bed, called again. "Clive, pick up the radio." He rubbed his eyes, then put the gun on the bed beside him. He glanced at the clock, then got down on his knees, and searched under the bed for the handset. The voice once again called. "Clive, please."

"All right. All right," he said as he finally pulled the radio out from under the bed. "Alice, what the hell do you want? It's six a.m."

"Sorry, Sheriff, but you got a big problem down here."

"What? Somebody's dog run away?" he said sarcastically as he sat against the bed in his underwear, rubbing his head.

"No, Clive, there ain't a lost dog," Alice said at the other end.

"What, then?" he snapped back.

"I think you better call me by phone. I don't think it's a good idea to handle this one by radio. Never know who's listening."

"What?" he said again.

"Yeah, the phone," Alice snapped back.

"Oh. Oh, hold on a minute. I'll call. I'll call." He threw the mike to the floor, then got up and placed his gun in its holster, and walked to the kitchen to the refrigerator. He pulled out a quart bottle of orange juice, then walked to the living room and sat in the chair beside the phone. He opened the juice and took a long drink, then put his head against the back of the chair and closed his eyes.

Clive Aliston was a county sheriff in southwestern Pennsylvania. He was forty-nine years old, with blonde hair and blue eyes. At six foot three, two hundred thirty-five pounds, he was a big, barrel-chested man. A no-nonsense, by-the-book lawman, Clive only broke the rules when he felt there was a better fit. He had a lot of compassion for the right people, but took no abuse from anyone. He was not corruptible and detested anyone who was. His motto: "Praise God, always have your gun loaded, and keep your ears and eyes open." He was tough, but fair, and would help anyone. Suddenly, the phone rang and he jumped again, spilling the juice on his boxer shorts. "Shit," he yelled as he grabbed for the phone. "Alice, what the hell?" he started to say, then paused, as he was about to take another drink. Slowly, he put the juice down on the table as he listened to Alice's voice on the other end of the line. His eyes opened wide as he sat straight up in the chair. "Yeah, I'll be right there as soon as I get dressed. Tell them no one touches anything. You hear? No one." He put the phone down slowly then stood up and wiped his face with both hands. "Damn," was all he said as he walked to the bathroom.

Friday, June 11, 6:55 a.m.

There were three other county sheriff's cars and two local cars, plus a contingent of the press at the tracks near the fairgrounds when Clive arrived. As he got out of the car, he was met by Alvin Richards. Alvin was the Smith Falls police chief. He was the son of a local magistrate, now retired. He was forty-three years old, with prematurely gray hair and blue eyes. Not a big man at five feet seven and a hundred fifty-five pounds, he was the new chief, having served in that position for only a little over a year. He had been on the force for the last fifteen years. Richards spoke first, "Clive, I'm glad you're here. This is a real mess. I've never seen anything like this, not around here."

"Where is she?" was all Clive said as he walked with Richards across the tracks. The mist and fog were slowly lifting but the clouds still hung low over the town.

Clive was met by Bob Anderson of the local *Smith Falls Gazette*, just on the other side of the tracks. "Hey, Clive, who is it? Got any leads? What's going on?"

Clive stopped, then put his index finger on Bob's chest. "I don't know. I just got here. Now stay out of my hair till I get some answers."

"But…" was all Bob got to say as Clive turned to Richards.

"Get him and the rest of the press back on the other side of the tracks," Clive said. Then he looked at Anderson. "No story till I say there's a story. You break the rules and you and your friends are out of here." He turned back to Richards. "Has anyone called the coroner?"

"Yeah," Richards said. "About half an hour ago. They'll be here about eight."

Clive turned back to Anderson, who was still standing there, pad and pen in hand. "This isn't the side of the tracks you're supposed to be on. Now move it."

"Okay. Okay," Anderson said as he backed up, tripping over the rails. Clive and Richards walked over to the weeds along the tracks and stopped. A sheet covered a section of the weed patch about ten feet away. Clive turned to Richards, then back to the sheet, then back to Richards.

Alvin Richards put both hands, palms up, toward Clive. "You go ahead. Look. I've seen enough."

Clive turned again to the weeds and walked the ten paces to the sheet. He removed his hat, then bent down on one knee. Everyone standing around was silent. Clive reached and grasped the sheet, then took a deep breath. He raised the sheet, then quickly placed it back, and turned away. "My God," was all he said. He composed himself, then raised the sheet and looked again. There on the ground was the once-beautiful Jody Miller. Her misted-over blue eyes stared up at nothing. Her face was bruised and marked with scratches. Her mouth was taped closed with duct tape. Her throat had been slashed from ear to ear so deeply that the vertebrae were visible at the back of her neck. She was fully clothed, but her blouse was soaked with blood from her neck to her waist.

Richards spoke from his position on the tracks. "Clive check out her forehead." Clive brushed back her once-beautiful blonde hair, now matted with blood and dirt. What he saw left him speechless. Cut into her forehead, almost to the bone, was the single word: FOREVER.

CHAPTER 2

Friday, June 11, 8:30 a.m.

Clive parked in front of the county sheriff's station on Route 55 just outside of Smith Falls. It had begun raining again and was now a steady downpour. Clive ran from his car and up the front steps and into the front lobby of the station. Once inside, he removed his hat and raincoat and shook off the remaining water. He hung them on a hook and wiped the water from his face with his hand. He opened the door to the main station office and was immediately met by two of his officers, Bret Collins and Jack Duff. Bret Collins was thirty-five years old, about five foot eight, with brown hair, brown eyes, and a medium build. Jack Duff was ten years older than Bret and stood six feet tall, with a slender build and reddish-blonde hair.

Jack spoke first, "Clive, we found her car. It's still in the lot around the corner from Miller's Boutique."

Bret followed with, "We were at the shop but it's locked. We'll need a key to get in."

Then they both spoke in unison. "What did the Coroner

say?"

"Whoa," Clive said. "Hold on a minute. Let me get to my office." He left the two officers standing in the main office looking at each other and headed for his office.

As he passed his secretary's desk she spoke, "Clive is it true? Was it Jody?"

Clive stopped in front of his office door and looked into her eyes. "Yes, I'm afraid it was. She was your friend wasn't she?"

Alice Shearer was Clive's secretary and a member of the county sheriff's department. She stood five feet ten, with a slender build, black hair and brown eyes. Alice shook her head and closed her eyes "Yes, for a long time."

Clive walked to her side and put his hand on her shoulder. "Sorry hon, losing a good friend ain't easy. Especially that way. I know. I've lost quite a few."

Alice raised her head and wiped one lone tear from her face. "Why did she have to die that way?"

"Why Jody?" Clive said. "I don't know why or by who, but by damned we're going to find out. Has anyone contacted her parents yet?"

"No," Alice answered. "I guess I, we, were hoping it wasn't her." There was a moment of silence, then Alice spoke again. "I figure you want to decide how to handle this."

"Yeah, I guess," Clive said as he pulled his handkerchief from his pocket and wiped the remaining rain from his face. "Get me a coffee, will you dear? And bring it into my office. No calls or visitors till I get organized, okay? And no press."

"I'll brew a new pot, be ready in a few minutes," Alice said as she got up and headed for the small lunchroom in the rear of the office. Clive entered his office to the right of Alice's desk and closed the door. He walked to his desk, turned on the small reading lamp on the corner, and dropped into the high-backed, black leather chair behind the desk. He leaned on the desk with both elbows, put his face in his hands and sighed. After a moment or two he sat back in the chair and ran his fingers through his short blonde hair, then shook more rainwater from his hand. He reached for a pad and pen on the desk and whispered, "Yeah, the parents." On the pad he wrote: June 11, Friday, J. Miller, Wilson Creek Siding, Fair Grounds, Time of Death? Forever. Forever? He turned in his chair and looked out the window as the rain beat against the glass. There was a low rumble of thunder in the distance and a branch of the tree next to the window made a scraping sound on the masonry outside. Seconds later there was a soft knock at his office door and Alice Shearer entered with a freshly brewed cup of coffee. She placed the coffee on Clive's desk and then just stood there for a moment. Clive turned back to his desk, picked up the coffee and took a sip. He then looked up at Alice, "Would you accompany me to Jody's parents place? It might be a help if they knew someone."

"I was going to ask you anyway," she said as she sat down in the chair in front of his desk. For a second they just stared at each other. Alice took in a deep breath then spoke, "When I got the message just before I called you on the radio this morning, I just couldn't believe what I heard. Even when they found her car with the doors open and her briefcase, I just wanted to believe it was someone else. It's like I'm still dreaming, like a nightmare. Things just don't happen like this. Not around here and not to Jody."

Clive just stared at Alice then looked back at his pad and underlined the last "forever" three times. He put the pencil down and stood up. "Alice call the coroner and tell him I want whatever he's got and as soon as possible. The info gets to me and me only. Tell Bret and Jack to come in here with whatever they have up to this point and, okay, yeah, get someone to put gas in my car. I didn't have time this morning." Alice got up and turned to leave the room when Clive spoke again as he looked at his watch. "Alice, what time do you have?"

"It's 8:50," she said as she stopped at the door.

"I want to leave for the Miller house at 9:15. Can you be ready?"

"Yeah, I'll have Rose take my desk and the radio while I'm gone. I'll be ready." She turned and left Clive's office. Clive again turned his attention to his desk, opening the top drawer, retrieving a cigar from a box inside, and removing the wrapper. He put the cigar in his lips and picked up and lit the lighter on his desk. He was about to light the cigar when the door to his office opened and Collins and Duff stepped into the room. Clive did not light the cigar. He placed it in an ashtray then leaned forward in his chair and placed both hands on his desk. He pointed to the chairs in front of his desk. "Have a seat. Well, what do we have at this point? Anything at all?"

Duff spoke first. "As I, we, said earlier, we found her car in the alley lot near her store. The door was opened and her briefcase was on the pavement under the car."

Collins then added, "Her keys are nowhere around and, oh yeah, the rear tire was sliced a good six inches at the side wall. There was a trash can lying in the middle of the alley about thirty feet from the car. I don't know if it means anything."

"Did you check around the area of the cans?" Clive asked.

"Yeah," answered Duff. "We found these between some other cans and the dumpster unit next to the store wall."

Jack put a plastic bag containing two large brown plastic buttons on Clive's desk. "I don't know if it's anything but they were on the ground near the cans. Funny they are both the same, like maybe from the same coat. A piece of material attached to one of them."

"Anything else?" Clive asked again as he examined the buttons. Before both officers could answer Clive raised the bag and pointed. "What's this stuff on the one button— looks like Crisco or grease or something?" He handed the bag back to Duff and both officers took a look.

Collins said to Duff, "I didn't notice that earlier, did

you?" Duff just shrugged his shoulders and shook his head.

"Well, is there anything else?" Clive asked again.

"No, not much," Duff answered.

"How about in the car? Anything interesting there?"

"No, just the usual, Kleenex, some fashion magazines and receipts for clothing from her suppliers, I guess—and an umbrella," Duff said still looking at the buttons.

"Could you tell if she had been in the car?"

"I don't know," Collins added.

"Was the umbrella wet?" Clive asked, taking the button bag back from Duff.

"Come to think of it, it was. I noticed it when I picked it up," Collins said, looking a bit puzzled.

After a few seconds Collins cleared his throat and spoke again. "Do you think the buttons mean anything? And what about the umbrella?"

Clive just shrugged his shoulders and shook his head. "I don't know, I just don't know."

"What's next?" Collins asked.

"Well, I don't think you'll find anything in the store, but look anyway. I would guess by now the employees are wondering why the store is not open. See if one of them has a key. No business there today. Send them home after you get the keys. If you can't get in, call me. Maybe I can get a set from her parents." Collins and Duff just sat still looking puzzled. Clive handed the bag back to Duff. "Was the car forced entry or unlocked?"

"Unlocked as far as I could see," Duff answered. Clive sat back in his chair.

"Well," Clive said with a pause. "I'm thinking the attack happened at the car. It wasn't raining Friday morning when she went to work. It started a light drizzle at around noon. I say she left the store sometime last night—check with the employees on that—and used the umbrella because of the rain. She must have been at the car when whatever happened, happened. I don't think her abduction or attack happened first. I think it was at the car. I don't think the car being open and not trashed and the briefcase being left tells me it was robbery. Was the briefcase open?" he asked.

"No," Duff said, "Still locked."

"Yeah," was all Clive said as he cracked the fingers on his right hand, then left. "Those buttons could be nothing," Clive said, pointing at the bag. "But could be from a raincoat, maybe hers. Take the buttons to the crime lab and have them checked out. I want to know what the white stuff is and whether they are from the same coat. When this is done I want them back. Maybe her parents can identify them. When you've finished at the lab and the store, check the area around the cans again—and good. Have the car towed to the lab also and checked out—and not Buzz's Auto. I want the damn thing there in one piece. Call Carl Dan's. Have him tow. I'm going with Alice to her parents' in a few minutes. Don't want them to find out from the media."

Duff and Collins stood up and Collins said, "Don't envy you that job, Clive."

Clive also stood up and picked up the cigar as if to light it, then changed his mind. "Yeah," was all he said as he reached for his coffee cup. Duff and Collins turned to leave and Clive spoke again. "Hey, where the hell is Brian? He off today or something?"

"Don't think so," Duff said as they left the room.

Clive walked to the doorway and spoke to Alice. "Well dear, I guess we better get moving. You ready?"

"Yeah," was all she said as she got up. Clive looked over at the next desk to Rose Bodin. Rose Bodin was the office secretary. She was thirty-two years old, five feet three inches tall, and slightly heavy, with light brown hair and eyes.

Clive, now looking around the station office, asked. "Where's Brian?" Rose just looked puzzled and shook her head. Clive and Alice put on their coats and were leaving when Clive turned again to Rose and said, "No press, not yet, especially that damn Bob Anderson. Tell them they get the news when I have news to give them, and I better not see any unauthorized info in the paper today. If you need me, call on the radio but I'll call you back by phone. Don't need any big ears listening." With that Clive and Alice left the station and headed for Jody's parents' home.

The ride to the Miller house seemed to take forever, but when they arrived Clive was glad to see no other cars from the press in the area. They met with Jody's mother and father for about an hour. It was an hour Clive and Alice wished they could have avoided. To see those two people in shock, then denial, and finally reduced to agonizing sorrow almost brought Clive and Alice to tears themselves. Before they left they suggested that Mr. Miller call the family doctor and explain what had happened because of Mrs. Miller's heart condition. They asked a few questions about Jody but decided to leave the rest for a later date. Clive gave Mr. Miller his card and told him if he needed anything, please call. George Miller, his sorrow now slowly turning to anger just said, "Find the son of a bitch."

When they got to the car, Clive asked Alice to drive so he could take some notes and make a couple of calls. For the first few minutes they said nothing to each other. Alice finally spoke, "You know Clive, I always thought of the Millers as really tough hard liners, you know, big business people. I guess who you are and what you have really doesn't mean much when you really get down to it."

"Yeah," Clive said, looking over at Alice. "Money, power. It all seems like the place to be, you know, the brass ring. But what can it all buy now?" Alice didn't respond; she just continued to drive in silence. About five minutes later the silence was broken when Rose called on the radio for Clive. He answered then told her he would call by phone. When he reached her she told him the preliminary coroner's report was in and Jack and Bret had gotten into the store but no report yet. Clive asked Rose if Brian had come in. She told him he had called and said he would be late and that he wasn't feeling well. Clive just said okay and that he would call him at home.

After talking to Rose, Clive looked at Alice and said, "Brian's sick again."

Alice just looked at Clive, shook her head, and said, "Posey's again?"

"I don't know," Clive said. "I'll try him at home. I hope it's not that place. That damn bar is going to undo that boy." Clive called Brian at his home but got no answer.

As Clive went back to his notes, Alice said, "I wonder if he knows about Jody? You know they were an item at one time?"

"So I've heard," Clive said. "But that hasn't been for a long time—what maybe nine or ten years?"

"I guess that would be about right," Alice said. "I think he still has a place for her somewhere in that tough front he puts on."

Just then Clive noticed Brian's patrol car at the diner on Route 55 just outside of town. "Hey, Alice there's his car. Pull in, pull in." Alice quickly slowed the cruiser and made a quick left turn into the diner parking lot.

As they started to get out of the car, Alice said, "Clive, don't be too hard on him. We don't know if he knows or how he's feeling if he does."

Clive just looked over the car roof at Alice and said, "Take it easy, Alice. I'm not the heartless bastard some people think I am."

Alice started to say, "Clive I didn't mean…"

Clive interrupted, "Yeah, I know. I know." They entered the diner and saw Brian seated at the far end in a booth by himself. He was in uniform but his shirt was open and his tie loosened. He sat motionless in front of a cup of coffee, with his face buried in his hands. He didn't notice Clive and Alice walk up.

Clive said, "Well, good morning Mr. Lasiter. And how are we this morning?"

Brian raised his head from his hands quickly, and with a surprised but sick look on his face responded, "Oh. Oh, not so good, Clive."

Clive just stared at him for a brief moment then asked, "Do you mind some company?" and pointed to the opposite side of the booth. Brian started to button his uniform shirt and pull his tie up, and said, "No, be my guest."

With that, Clive and Alice slid into the booth just as the waitress stopped and asked if they wanted anything. They both ordered coffee. Clive pulled out a cigar from his pocket and looked at both Brian and Alice and said, "Do you mind?" Brian just shrugged his shoulders and shook his head. Alice looked at Clive and sneered as if to say, well if you must. Clive shook his head and put the cigar back into his pocket.

Brian Lasiter was Clive's second-in-command, a lieutenant with the county sheriff's department. At six feet tall and a hundred ninety-five pounds, with light brown hair, blue eyes and an athletic physique, he was quite handsome. He was highly intelligent and in great physical condition. He was the son of the local funeral director but had never had much interest in the business. He had attended college on both scholastic and athletic scholarships, graduating with a degree in criminology. At the age of twenty-eight, he had moved up the ladder quickly. He became second seat at the station when Clive was promoted to sheriff a couple of years before, when the last chief, Dan Walters, died suddenly of a heart attack. Brian was a good officer but he had a passion for billiards and played often after hours until late into the night. Billiards was not the problem though. It was the booze that came with them. Brian loved rum and most times a glass sat on the edge of the pool table with a game in progress. He was an emotional man—one minute smiling, the next sullen or angry. He was missing something in his life that the job, the billiards and the rum couldn't supply.

Clive stared at Brian for a moment longer and was about to speak when Alice spoke first. "Do you know about what happened? I mean about Jody?"

Brian turned his face away from them to the windows of the diner as tears filled his eyes. He quickly brushed them away and whispered, "Yes." He paused, then continued, "I heard about it this morning on the radio."

Clive, also looking out the window, asked, "You okay? You called in this morning that you were sick. Are you?"

Brian turned and looked at Clive and started to say, "I, I, didn't know what to do. I couldn't believe what I was hearing. If I had only not chickened out last night and had the balls to talk to her, she might be alive today."

"What the hell are you talking about?" Clive said, a surprised look on his face. "What do you mean she would be alive? Were you with her last night?"

"No," Brian answered as he placed his face back in his hands. Alice reached over to him and placed her hand on the side of his face. "Brian take it easy, take it slow, tell us what happened."

He paused for a moment then raised his head again and looked at Clive. "As you know, I worked the daylight shift yesterday and you sent me into the city at around two o'clock with that drug evidence. I was there till well after six, and I stopped to eat on the way home. As I was eating I began to think about Jody and me. You see, we had been talking again, not exactly seeing each other—but that was what I was hoping for. You know we were very close at one time."

Clive just said, "Yeah, I know."

"Well I guess I thought I had the nerve built up to see her and ask if she felt the same way I think she did. By the time I got to her apartment it was near nine, but she wasn't there so I figured she must be working late so I went to the store. I arrived around nine-thirty p.m. and was parked outside the store, when I guess I lost my nerve. I kept thinking what do I do if she says no. I wanted to be with her so bad and I guess I was afraid she didn't feel the same. I sat there in the rain for nearly an hour; I just couldn't find the balls to see her. When I saw her leaving the store I was afraid she would see me and I guess I just drove off. I couldn't go home. I just didn't know what to do so I drove around for a while then I..."

Clive interrupted, "Went to Posey's?"

"Yeah," was Brian's response as he looked at Alice. Alice smiled and said, "Brian, she knew and she did want to begin again. I talked to her last week. Why didn't you talk to her?"

Brian just shook his head as tears filled his eyes again.

There was a moment of silence, then Clive spoke. "What time did you get home Brian?"

He wiped his face and said, shaking his head, "I don't know, maybe three or four o'clock."

Clive took in a deep breath then said, "Son, I think maybe taking the day off is probably a good idea. Go home, get some sleep, and don't stop at Posey's. We'll talk in the morning."

Brian spoke up loudly at first, one word, "No." Then recomposed himself. "Clive, I can't go home, I can't sleep and I won't go to Posey's. I need to be at the office or wherever you need me. I want to help, I need to help and don't tell me no."

Alice looked at Clive with an expression as if to say, "Well."

Clive looked out the window again and thought for a second, then said, "Okay, you want to work? Don't go to the office, go to the crime lab and find out all you can about her car and the other items we had shipped there. I'll get in touch with Duff and Collins and see what they found at the store and the alley. Get back to me ASAP, maybe they will get on it a little faster if we are on them. Remember one thing Brian; this goes against my better judgment—having you on this case. I think you're too close to it. I'll be watching you very closely. If you can't handle it, you're off.

You got it?"

"Yeah, thanks boss."

Clive took a last sip of his coffee and said to Alice. "Come on girl. Let's get back to the office."

"Okay, Clive, okay," was all she said as she slid out of the booth.

They both stood up and Clive, looking back at Brian, said, "Remember, do the job right. Don't make it personal, no matter how personal it is. I'll be watching." With that, they both left the diner, leaving Brian still sitting at his coffee.

When they got out to the car, Alice spoke up, "Could you have been a little harder on him Clive?"

Clive glared at Alice and responded, "Alice, I don't like this—not one bit. You can't tell me he can be objective about the job in his condition."

"But Clive," was all Alice got to say, as Clive interrupted.

"Alice, I said I'd let it go for now but if I see it's not going per the book he's off and then you can deal with me by yourself."

"Me?" was how Alice responded as they both slid into the car, Alice behind the wheel. "Why me?"

"Well you practically talked me into it Alice."

Alice just forced a laugh and said, "I talked you into it and I suppose you had nothing to do with it? Clive Aliston, if you were in his place what would you want to do?"

There was a moment or two of complete silence then Clive just looked at Alice and said, "Yeah." Alice started the car and they drove off to the station.

CHAPTER 3

Not much happened the remainder of that first day. Investigation continued well into the night but not much came back from the crime lab or the coroner's office. Saturday, June 12, and Sunday, June 13, came and went with no progress, with most of the crime offices and labs closed down fifty percent on the weekend. It wasn't until Monday, June 14, that Clive received some preliminary information. Clive, Brian, Alice, Duff and Collins met in Clive's office in the early afternoon on Monday and went over the evidence that they had. The crime lab had concluded that the car wasn't broken into and neither was the store. Jody's briefcase had not been forced open and all that was inside was papers pertaining to the business. They did find some hair and what appeared to be skin on the edge of the briefcase corner. The lab was still processing that. The buttons they had sent over were from the same coat and the white substance was a form of grease that was used in the lubrication of door locks and hinges on newer cars. The lab was checking on the type and make of the grease.

The coroner had also called with his basic but limited information on Jody. She had been bruised extensively around her face and neck. Marks on her wrists and ankles indicated she had been bound and her mouth had been taped closed with standard duct tape. Cause of death was a sliced throat causing, almost-immediate death. She had not been raped. The word "Forever" cut into her forehead was a mystery. After the meeting, Duff and Collins began interviewing the employees from Jody's store about any chance they knew of someone who had a grudge against Jody or any suspicious customer that had been around over the last few weeks. Alice began gathering items to be placed into the case file. Brian went to see Jody's parents and asked them the questions that had been held back on that first day. They had gotten the buttons from the lab and her parents confirmed that they could be from her coat.

Clive put together his notes and tried to form a picture of what they believed happened that night. He also made several phone calls to the crime lab and the coroner and also instructed Rose Bodin to organize a meeting with the press for Tuesday morning. There had been a small story in some of the papers about the murder with little info being reported. Clive thought that before the press started to create trouble, it was probably a good idea to at least meet with them. All seemed quiet for now.

CHAPTER 4

The small door at the bottom of the large iron door opened and a hand reached into the room and retrieved the large mug sitting on the straw-covered floor. In the corner of the room at the cot, was heavy breathing. The bolt on the large iron door snapped as it was unlocked. The door slowly swung open and a soft voice spoke just outside the room, "Come now. It is time."

Monday, June 14, 11:00 p .m.

Wesley Dans, son of Carl Dans, owner of Dans Towing, Auto Wreckers and Used Parts, drove into the dark lot in front of his father's business office at the auto wreck yard. He did not park in front of the office, but instead parked at the side of the building in the shadows. He turned off the ignition and walked around the front of the building into the dim light from the large red sign at the top of the building roof. He fumbled with his keys as he looked around in all directions. He found the right key and opened the door. He moved inside, quickly closing the door behind him, not turning on the lights but instead using a flashlight to move through the front office to the door to his father's office.

Wesley Dans was twenty-seven years old, five feet eight inches tall, one hundred sixty-five pounds, with red curly hair and brown eyes. He was a partner in his father's auto wrecking business—a job he hated. But after a failed attempt at college and numerous other endeavors he had had to settle for this, as he called it, "junk life." He was intelligent but lacked the common sense to make anything of himself. He was an addicted gambler. If he could bet on it, he would: football, baseball, hockey, basketball, the horses—anything. He was always in some kind of trouble with the bookies and bet takers and had been bailed out of trouble on more than one occasion by his father. For the last several years he had been padding the books at his father's business and skimming off the money he needed for his addiction. This was just one of many trips to the office late at night to obtain money for a debt. Wesley was in fair physical condition, considering the stress he placed on his body, just trying to stay alive. He had one problem—a bad limp from a slightly shortened leg, a result of a bad auto accident in his high school years.

After Wesley entered his father's office he quickly moved to the floor safe at the back of the room. He bent down on one knee and spun the combination dial back and forth till the handle he had a hold of clicked and he opened the door. He reached inside and from a box in the back retrieved a large stack of hundred dollar bills. He peeled off ten of them and replaced the rest of the bundle. As he recounted the ten bills, he felt a cool breeze on the back of his neck and stood up and looked around. To his right he noticed that the window was wide open. It was a large, picture window that was hinged in the middle and the glass pane was pulled to a horizontal position completely open. He walked to the window leaned down under the glass pane and looked outside. He shined the flashlight around and saw nothing but the trees in the back of the building. He backed up from under the glass window then slowly closed it. He stood there for a moment then shook his head with a puzzled look on his face. He started to count the cash again as he slowly turned around.

He stopped suddenly when he heard a noise across the room. He raised the flashlight in the general direction of the noise. His eyes opened wide and his mouth dropped open as he tried to yell or scream, but nothing came out. He quickly backed up two paces into the window behind him. When he hit the glass something hit his hand and the flashlight flew across the room. The money he was holding flew like confetti in all directions. He stepped forward in an attempt to run but was hit by a crashing blow to his chest that sent him through the glass window to the ground outside. He lay there motionless, trying to get his breath for a few seconds. His mind, temporarily in a fog, began slowly to clear. He rolled over to his stomach and then to his knees. He got up and ran to the side of the building where his car was parked. As he turned the corner he was met by a huge silhouette between him and his car. He stopped and changed directions and ran back behind the building and around the other side and out into the opening to the junkyard. He looked back and again saw the large silhouette behind him. He ran as fast as he could, half dragging his bad leg behind him and looking over his shoulders at every step. He had gone about one hundred feet when he was blinded by car headlights set to high beam directly in his path. He stopped, frozen in place, trying to shield his eyes from the glaring light. He turned to go back the other way but never moved. He just looked up and screamed at the top of his lungs. The scream came to an abrupt end as a huge shadowy hand slammed against the side of his head. The lights went out and the yard went silent.

Tuesday, June 15, 8:30 a.m.

Clive had decided to call a meeting with the press at the station conference room at 8:30 a.m., Tuesday. He entered the room crowded with press from all the local papers and the city. Duff and Collins sat at the back of the room and Alice and Brian stood off to the left of the podium. Seated at the front of the room in the center of the row was Bob Anderson of the *Smith Falls Gazette*. Clive turned his back to the crowd and walked up to the green chalkboard on the wall behind the podium. He picked up a piece of chalk and in fairly large letters he wrote, "No questions until requested." He then turned back and placed several sheets of paper on the podium, as the room grew silent. He was about to speak when Bob Anderson stood up and spoke first. "Do you have any idea who could have done this, and for what reason?" Clive just glared at Anderson and pointed back to the chalkboard.

Anderson started to speak again but Clive interrupted him with, "What is it you don't understand about no questions, Bob?" Bob Anderson was the lead reporter for the *Smith Falls Gazette*. He was an overzealous, overbearing news hound that could drive most anyone crazy if they let him. Bob's idea of reporting was when it comes to news there are no rules. He was not a big man but at five-eleven, and very thin, he seemed taller than he was. He was always seen with a charcoal gray trench coat no matter the weather—winter or summer, dry or wet—and his pad and pens were never far from his hands.

Clive just stared at Bob for a moment longer and Bob tried to speak again but was again interrupted by Clive, "Anderson, sit down and button it." He looked to the back of the room to Duff and Collins and said, "He sits or he's gone." Clive just stood there staring at him and Bob turned to look back at Collins and Duff who were now moving toward the front of the room.

Anderson turned back to Clive and raising his hands palms up toward Clive said, "Okay, okay," and sat down.

Duff and Collins looked at Clive, who then directed them to the back of the room again. With that, he shuffled his papers and began to speak. "First of all we are requesting that you print nothing except what we give you here today. This investigation is in its early stages and we don't want anything to get out that could jeopardize this situation. The wrong message could cause untold harm and diminish our chances of catching the perpetrator of this horrible crime. On the early morning of June 10, the body of Jody Miller was found along a siding of the Norfolk and Southern railroad near the fairgrounds and Wilson Creek. She had been there for a very short time and from what we have been able to ascertain she was not killed there. Her car was found in the parking lot near her place of business. Because of the condition of that vehicle, her personal items, and her place of business—Miller's Boutique—we don't believe that the motive was robbery. We have been conducting an on-going investigation since the discovery and are working closely with other law enforcement and the crime lab. We have instructed the railroad and the employees at her place of business, her family and all others involved to forward questions from anyone to us. What that means is no news unless it comes from this station. I hope that is very clear. We will keep you informed of any new developments that we can release as they come up. You can use the line we have set up for that purpose. Just ask Alice here for the details at the conclusion of this meeting. We are not trying to withhold news that needs to be reported but we will not, as I said, release anything we feel will have a negative impact on this case. With that, I now open the floor to any questions."

Bob Anderson's hand shot up first but Clive looked over his head and began taking questions from some of the other reporters. About two or three minutes into the questions, Rose Bodin came into the room and passed a slip of paper to Brian and then left the room. Brian read the note then stepped to Clive's side and whispered in his ear. Clive then spoke to the crowd and asked to hold up one moment. He motioned for Duff to come to the front. Clive and Duff turned their backs to the crowd and Clive spoke, "Jack, there has been an apparent break-in at Dans Auto Yard. You want to take a look at it, please?" Jack Duff nodded, and left the room.

Clive once again turned to the podium and started to respond to the last question when Bob Anderson interrupted and asked, "Was that more news about the case?"

Clive said, "No, it was not," and attempted to continue when Anderson interrupted again.

"Come on Clive, this is bullshit. What have you told us we don't already know?"

Clive moved from behind the podium and was about to step down from the raised stage floor but changed his mind. He instead asked the entire crowd if they wanted to continue the questions. They all answered with resounding yes's. Clive looked at Anderson and smiled, "Well Bob, I guess you're overruled. Are there anymore questions?" The conference went on for another twenty minutes, then Clive abruptly called an end to it and all the reporters left, most not happy with the entire process. Bob Anderson left the station and after speaking to several other reporters in front of the station steps he drove across the street to a coffee shop. He ordered a cup of coffee and sat in a seat at the front window facing the station. Clive returned to his office and had Alice get him a cup of coffee and started some other paperwork he had been pushing aside for far too long.

Tuesday, June 15, 9:30 a.m.

Duff arrived at Dans Auto Yard and proceeded to look the situation over and ask questions of Carl Dans and several of the employees. After each employee was questioned, he or she was sent on to work and told that he or she may be needed again. The first employee to be questioned was Dean Jackson, the crane operator. After several minutes with Duff he was sent off to work. Dean picked up his lunch bag and two-liter bottle of Mountain

Dew and headed out the door and toward the back of the yard where he had been working the day before. Duff sat at Carl Dans' desk and took notes as Carl started to check on what—if anything—was missing. He explained about the money all over the floor and of course the broken window. He told Duff about the flashlight on the floor, still on, but dim, and that he had picked it up with gloves on so as not to ruin any prints.

Dean Jackson continued on to the back of the yard, winding his way up and down rows of junk cars and stacks of flattened cars from the auto press. It was like walking up and down steel-walled canyons, some as much as thirty feet high. As he made the last turn and walked into a large open area at the back of the yard near the auto press, he noticed that his crane was swung out over the middle of the yard. Hung from the clam bucket some twenty feet in the air was a car. He stopped just below the car and just stared up at it. "Who the hell's been pissing around?" he mumbled to himself.

He walked to a small wooden shanty near the press and placed his lunch bag and the bottle of Mountain Dew on the top of a wooden icebox that sat next to the shanty. He opened his lunch bag and retrieved a sandwich then opened the Mountain Dew and took a long drink. He recapped the bottle, placed the wax paper wrapped sandwich in his teeth and lifted the lid of the icebox and placed the bag and bottle on a shelf inside next to a half-melted ice block. He replaced the lid and unwrapped the sandwich halfway and took a bite. He entered the shed and walked to an old dilapidated desk and chair to one side and got a pencil out of the top drawer. He took a clipboard from a nail on the wall that held a stack of work sheets and then turned and left the shed. He stopped again and just stared at the car hung over the middle of the yard and whispered, "Shit, I'm gonna have one hell of a time climbing into that damn cab with it parked that way. Shit," he yelled as he walked to the main body of the large red crane housing behind the shed. He took several minutes to climb the three ladders to the cab, his job being more difficult with the housing not being aligned properly as in the parked position. As he moved the last half of the sandwich hung from his mouth. He opened the cab door and started the crane motor. The diesel motor coughed and sputtered then came to life with a large cloud of dark smoke coming from the stack.

Dean sat in the operator chair and stuffed the remaining sandwich into his mouth and placed the clipboard on a hook on the cab wall. He took the controls in his hands and the crane began to swing toward the auto press to the right. As he reached the press he noticed for the first time that the car still had a license plate on the rear. He also began to realize that the car was fairly new and it also looked very familiar. He stopped the crane over the press and started to mumble, his mouth full of sandwich, "What in the hell is this shit?" He stood up and opened the front window of the crane and leaned out to get a better look at the car. The car was still swinging back and forth and it began to rotate around to the left, the driver's door toward him. Then he thought he saw something or someone in the car in the front seat.

He placed his hand above his eyes to shade them and strained to see. For a moment he just stared, then said to himself, "What the hell?" He moved the crane to the center of the yard and lowered the car to the ground. He released the clam bucket and swung the crane to its resting point and shut off the engine. He climbed down the ladder to the ground and walked slowly to the car. He could see what looked like someone in the front seat but the sun was in his eyes as it rose over the wall of cars surrounding the yard. He was about five feet from the car when the wall of cars behind finally blocked out the sun. The inside of the car became instantly clear. Dean's eyes opened wide and he yelled out loud as he stumbled backward and fell down in the dirt of the yard. He sat there for just a moment then slowly stood up and took another look. There, seated in the front seat with his seatbelt fastened, was Wesley Dans. His throat was cut from ear to ear, his chest was covered in blood, and his head lay back against the top of the seat. He was staring white-faced and open-eyed at the roof of the car. Dean yelled again, "Shit. Shit. Shit," as he turned and fell, then got up and ran toward the front of the yard to the office.

Tuesday, June 15, 11:00 a.m.

Clive sat in his office going over the last of the papers that he had let go for days. He was on his third cup of coffee and had taken a cigar out of his desk and had it between the fingers of his left hand while writing with his right. He stopped and picked up the lighter on his desk and placed the cigar in his mouth when the intercom buzzed on his desk. He pushed the talk button, removed the cigar from his mouth, placed the lighter back on the desk, and answered, "Yes, Alice."

There was a pause then Alice responded, "Clive, Duff is on the phone, line two." Clive just sat back in his chair for a second and sighed then leaned forward again. "Alice tell him to make out a report, I'll talk to him later."

Alice responded, "Clive, I think you better take this now. Line two."

Clive placed the cigar in his mouth, bit down on the end showing his teeth, picked up the phone, and pushed line two. "What's up Duff?" was all he said, the cigar still clamped in his teeth. He listened intently for several seconds then slowly removed the cigar from his mouth and placed it in the still-clean ashtray on his desk. He sat back in the chair and continued to listen. After a few more seconds he spoke. "Duff, I'll be right there. You know the drill. No one touches anything, no one leaves, and no one enters the place. You got that?" and he hung up the phone.

He sat and just stared for a second or two then leaned forward and called Alice on the intercom, "Alice, I'm going down there. Inform Brian about this but tell him to finish what he's doing then come down to Dans." With that Clive put on his hat, readjusted his gun belt, and left his office. He stopped at Alice's desk and told her to call the coroner and find Collins and tell him to do whatever he is doing but we may need him later.

Clive left the station and got into his patrol car that was parked out front and drove out to the highway to Dans Auto Yard. Bob Anderson was still seated at the coffee shop window as Clive pulled out of the parking space at the station. Bob finished his coffee, threw some money on the table and ran for the door and to his car in the shop lot. He threw it into reverse then turned out onto the highway just as Clive's patrol car disappeared over the low rise in front of him. When Clive reached the auto yard he was greeted by one of the employees who told him where to park his car, then led him through the yard toward the location of Wesley's car.

About two or three minutes after Clive arrived, Bob Anderson pulled off the highway into a grove of trees across the road from the auto yard—just in time to see Clive and another person enter one of the aisles that led deep into the yard. He got out of the car quickly, locked the door, and ran across the road and into the yard. He stopped behind a trash dumpster, scanned the area and saw no one. He ran in the same direction that he had seen Clive going just a few minutes before.

When Clive reached the auto press yard he saw Carl Dans sitting on a box, his face buried in his hands, surrounded by several of his employees. Clive walked to Carl and placed his hand on his shoulders as Carl looked up at him, his face wet with tears. Clive shook his head and said, "I'm sorry, Carl." Carl started to sob again and returned his face to his hands. The employee who had been with Clive joined the group around Carl and tried to help console him. Standing about ten feet from the car and facing Clive was Duff and Dean, the crane operator.

Duff, his hat in his hand and looking ash white even at fifty paces from Clive, spoke, "Clive you better have a look." Clive turned and looked back at Carl Dans, took a deep breath, turned back to Duff and started to walk slowly in that direction. When he got to the two men, Duff was still fumbling with his hat and looking half sick.

Clive looked at Duff and asked, "You okay?"

"Yeah, I guess so," Duff responded as he put his hat back on his head.

Clive looked at the car again, walked slowly to the driver's door, and bent down to look inside. What he saw brought back instant flashbacks of Jody Miller's face and he turned his face to the ground and closed his eyes. Seconds later Duff spoke, "Clive take a look at the hood." Clive stood up and turned to the front of the car. There on the hood in the now-bright sunlight was a single word scratched in the paint to the metal: "Forever."

CHAPTER 5

Tuesday, June 15, Noon

Bob Anderson wove his way up and down the aisles of cars trying to figure out what direction Clive had taken. At each turn he would stop and look around the corner, trying to make sure he wasn't seen. He moved quickly but he kept looking behind him and in all directions, up and down each adjoining aisle. He stopped at one corner after he thought he heard voices ahead. He leaned out around the pile of cars and saw Carl Dans on a box and several of his employees standing around him. They were talking among themselves and pointing out ahead of them in a direction that Bob couldn't see. He waited for all of them to be looking away from his direction and he ran across the opening to the other side of the aisle. He walked down the side of the aisle up close to the cars and in the direction the employees were looking. He figured if he could crawl up on the flattened cars he might be able to see what was going on. About fifty feet down the aisle he found a good place to try and climb up the twenty feet of flattened metal.

He moved up slowly trying not to make any noise. He reached the top then moved about ten feet to a place where he could see the open area near the car press and crane.

Standing beside a car in the middle of the open area were Clive Aliston, Jack Duff and Dean Jackson. Jackson was next to the rear of the car and was explaining something to Duff, who was taking notes. Clive was looking in the passenger side of the car around the dash. Anderson could tell he was wearing gloves as he retrieved what looked like a wallet and cards from the glove box. Anderson, now lying on his stomach, reached into his coat pocket, retrieved his note pad and pen, and began to take notes. He would write, then listen to try and hear what was being said. After about five minutes he reached into his other pocket and pulled out a small 35 mm camera with zoom lens and focused it on the car in the middle of the yard. He took a picture of the entire area with the car as the focal point, then a picture of the car itself. As he clicked the shutter the second time, he thought he could see someone sitting in the front seat on the driver's side. It appeared that he or she was looking up at the roof but not moving. He adjusted the zoom out to full magnification to try to get a better look, but the light reflecting off the windshield made it impossible to see clearly. He moved the camera from the shot of the windshield slowly down to the hood. There in the center of the hood he could make out, in large letters, scratched into the paint, the word, "Forever." He snapped the shot and then took several more pictures of the car, the hood and the entire area. He placed the camera back into his pocket and continued to write more notes in his pad. He was finishing a note when he heard Clive call Duff and motion for him to follow to the side of the yard near the cars right under the area where Anderson was laying. For a second Anderson stopped writing and put his head down on the smashed metal. He listened as Clive and Duff, unaware of his presence, discussed the scene and what Clive wanted Duff to do.

In the several minutes that the conversation lasted, Anderson was able to hear that Wesley Dans was dead and that the manner of death appeared to be the same as Jody Miller. He raised his head ever so slightly off the metal and then began to take more notes as the conversation continued. The last thing he heard as they walked back to the car was that the coroner would be there soon and that Brian Lasiter was probably on his way to the scene.

Bob Anderson, satisfied that he had enough information and pictures, decided not to push his luck. He slowly slid backwards to the other side of the pile with the intention of climbing down, when, from his perch, he saw off in the distance a police car with lights flashing pull into the auto yard entrance. He realized that it must be Brian Lasiter and that his escape route was now probably blocked. Knowing that he would more than likely be caught, his main concern was to keep the information and pictures a secret. He climbed down the other side of the pile of cars to the ground, walked to the next aisle, looked around the corner and when no one was looking ran to the other side and concealed himself. He got down on one knee and took his camera out of his pocket and rewound the film. He placed the film on the ground and put in a new roll and adjusted the film to the first picture. He pulled a handkerchief out of his pocket and laid it out on the ground. In it he placed the roll of film and his note pad. He tied them both lightly in the handkerchief and stuffed them into his coat pocket. He pulled a second blank tablet from his pocket and with camera and pad in hand started to make his way back toward the auto yard office.

Not far from the front of the yard he looked around a corner to see Brian Lasiter coming in his direction across the lot. He reached into his pocket and retrieved the knotted handkerchief and looked for a spot in the tangled metal near where he was standing. He found a small hole in the twisted mess and stuffed the handkerchief and its contents into the hole. He then turned back down the aisle toward the auto press again. He stopped at the last corner and again looked around it to see Carl Dans now standing with his employees talking to Clive. He looked back in the direction he had just come from, where he expected to see Brian Lasiter at any second. Brian was not there yet so he stuffed the camera into his pocket and held the pad and pen up as if he was going to write. Seconds later he heard footsteps behind him but he did not turn around; he just kept looking around the corner at Clive, pen and pad in his hand. A voice from behind and now very close called out, "Bob Anderson, just what the hell do you think you're doing?" Two seconds later Brian Lasiter pushed his open hand against the right side of Anderson's back, spinning him around. Bob faked a trip while spinning and ended up on one knee looking up at Brian. Just as Bob Anderson got up and went face to face with Brian, Clive and Duff hearing the commotion, came around the corner followed by Dean Jackson, Carl Dans and the rest of the employees.

Clive jumped between Brian and Bob and yelled, "Just hold it." For a second there was silence, then Clive looked first at Brian then at Bob, clenched his teeth and went nose to nose with Bob Anderson. "Just what exactly do you think you are doing here?"

Bob, unable to back up, just raised his hands with the pad and pen in one of them and said, "My job." Clive's face turned beet red and he reached up and ripped the pad out of Bob's hands and passed it to Brian without taking his eyes off of Bob.

Clive backed up one step and put out his hand and spoke one word, "Camera."

Bob Anderson responded, "As you can see, I don't have my camera."

Clive looked at Brian and said, "Cuff him."

Brian started to reach for his cuffs when Bob said again, "As you can see, I don't have my camera."

Clive stepped forward again, this time closer to Bob's face and said, "The camera. Not the press camera. Your camera, the small one, now." Bob reached into his pocket and retrieved the 35 mm as Clive backed up again and grabbed it from Bob's hand. Without looking at Brian, Clive said, "Take this," and showed the camera to Brian. He continued to stare at Bob, then said to Brian, "Check them out, what's he got?"

Brian checked the blank pad and quickly leafed through it. He looked at the top of the camera at the exposure number window, which now showed the number one. He looked at Clive and shook his head. "Looks like nothing here."

Clive, still staring at Bob, said, "Rewind and take the film."

Bob Anderson spoke up and said, "You can't take that. It's good, unused film. You don't have the right to." He was stopped in mid-sentence as Carl Dans leaped between Clive and Bob Anderson, sending Clive off balance sideways into Brian.

Carl grabbed Bob around the neck with both hands and started to scream, "You son-of-a-bitch, my son is out there dead and you want a story, I'll give you a damn story."

Clive jumped into the struggle, pulled Carl off Bob, shoved him toward his employees, and yelled, "Keep him back." Brian grabbed Bob and pinned him against the metal pile.

Clive then moved Brian out of the way and once again went face-to-face with Anderson. "You want the film you can put in a bill to the office for a replacement and same goes for the pad and pencil."

Clive backed up again and Bob Anderson, rubbing his throat, stepped forward and said, "First, I'm accosted by your lieutenant and pushed to the ground then you let me be attacked and now you take my personal items with no warrant. Who the hell's wrong here?"

Clive, still red-faced and beaded with sweat, looked at Brian and said, "Search him for anything else." Brian spun Anderson around and searched him and found nothing.

Anderson started to speak again but Clive spoke first. "Brian, get him out of here and on his way. Anderson, I could arrest you now but I won't. You'll get your personal items back tomorrow and as for the mistreatment, call it even." Anderson started to speak again but was again interrupted by Clive. "Last chance or the deal's off, you go to jail. We have enough witnesses here to prove our side of the story. Brian, get him out of here before I change my mind." Brian moved Anderson out into the aisle and headed him in the direction of the office. Clive turned to Carl Dans, now sobbing again, and tried to calm him down. Brian walked Anderson to the office and asked him where his car was. He pointed it out and watched as Bob walked to the car, got in, and drove away. Brian turned and headed into the auto yard office.

Bob drove up the road about a quarter of a mile, turned off onto a side road that overlooked the auto yard, then pulled over and parked. He rolled down the side window and watched the yard for about half an hour. At about 1:30 p.m., the coroner's vehicle pulled into the yard and Brian walked out of the office and got into the vehicle and drove off with the coroner to the back of the yard. Bob Anderson waited and watched for about ten minutes then turned around on the road and drove back to the auto yard and parked near the entrance aisle way and got out. He ran to where he had hidden his handkerchief and retrieved it from the hole, then raced back to the car and drove out of the yard and onto the road headed back to town.

CHAPTER 6

Clive and Brian spent most of the rest of the day at the yard with the coroner and some of the crime lab people. Clive sent Duff back to the office with his notes for Alice and told him to cover until he and Brian could come back. It was about 5:30 p.m. when Clive returned to the office. He checked in with the night shift people, headed to the diner on Rt. 55 for dinner, then went home to try to get some rest, but all he did was go over and over the details of the case. He made several phone calls, one to Alice at home to go over a few things, then he spent about an hour reviewing his notes and writing more. He called the station and told the desk sergeant if anything new about the case came in to call no matter what time it was. He was in bed at about 9:30 p.m. and fell asleep quickly, but he was awake at 12:30 a.m. and again at four. Finally, after lying awake for almost an hour, he got up at about five, showered and ate some breakfast. He sat in his lounge chair and again reviewed his notes and made some revisions, and then at about 6:45 he dressed and headed for the station.

Wednesday, June 16

He arrived at about 7:30 a.m., spoke to the night crew, and was sitting at his desk when Alice arrived for work at 8:00. She went to her desk and then to the lunchroom, returning with two coffees. She once again stopped at her desk and put her coffee down and picked up the newspaper she had just brought in. She walked to Clive's office and softly knocked on the door. Without raising his head from his paperwork, Clive motioned for her to enter. She walked in, closed the door behind her and placed the coffee on his desk in front of him and then stood there silently. Several seconds passed before Clive realized she was still there. He looked up and saw her with the newspaper tucked under her left arm, staring down at him. Looking somewhat puzzled he asked, "Yes, Alice, you need me for something?" She sat down in one of the front chairs and then asked if he had anything strong to put in the coffee she had just brought him. He didn't answer but just continued to look puzzled.

She continued, "Well, if you don't, I'll bet after you see this you'll wish you did." She placed the newspaper, still folded, on top of the papers he was working on and sat back in the chair and waited. Clive put his pen down and flipped the paper open to the front page. The headline of the *Smith Falls Gazette* jumped off the page like a strong kick to the gut: "Forever Killer Strikes Again." Clive's face grew a deep red as he continued to read. The article went on to tell about how Wesley Dans had been murdered and the similarities to Jody Miller's murder. It told that the police had very little to go on and that the investigation appeared to be stalled. He skipped over several more paragraphs and then continued to follow the column to the bottom of the page. Near the bottom of the page was the note: "Photos on Page A5." Clive ripped the paper open and was met by color photos of the auto yard, the car with Clive and the others standing around. In the center, a large picture showed a close-up of the hood and the word

"Forever" scratched into the paint. The caption under the photo read, "Killer's note baffles police." The article went on to ask whether local police could handle this situation or needed outside help.

Clive did not finish the article but instead stood up, smashed the paper into a ball, threw it across the room, and whispered, "Damn him." Alice rose from her chair and silently waited. Clive turned and walked to the window behind his desk and looked outside. There was silence for almost a minute, then as Clive turned back to Alice they both tried to speak at the same time. They both hesitated then Clive, now appearing to be calmer, spoke first, "Alice, put in a call to the paper, I want to speak to the editor."

Alice stood there for a second then said, "You know that the other papers will get a hold of this. You also realize that the whole thing is beyond the county limits now."

Clive didn't answer but instead turned back to the window. Alice turned and started out the door when Clive, still looking out the window, spoke, "Alice, we can deal with this. It's going to complicate things but maybe we can use this. When Brian and Duff and Collins get in send them to me right away. If anyone from any of the other papers calls, just take the message." He turned back to Alice and calmly said, "Now, could you get the *Gazette* please."

Clive returned to his paperwork and about five minutes later Duff and Collins arrived and entered Clive's office. Alice made several calls to the *Gazette* but was put on hold or repeatedly told that Don Creavy, the editor, was not available. Clive and the two patrolmen had just started to talk about the situation when Brian Lasiter stormed into the station with a rolled up newspaper in his hand. He did not stop at Alice's desk but raced into Clive's office and closed the door with a slam. Alice and Rose Bodin stopped what they were doing and just stared at the windows in front of Clive's office. They couldn't hear exactly what was being said but they could see Brian pacing back and forth behind Duff and Collins, who were still seated in the chairs in front of Clive's desk. He was waving the paper up and down, obviously agitated and angry. He continued for at least five minutes and to Alice and Rose's surprise Clive just sat in his chair and calmly listened. Brian finally stopped and then dropped into one of the chairs along the side wall of Clive's office. Duff and Collins said nothing but just sat quietly and tried to look invisible.

Clive sat quietly for a moment then took the cigar out of the ashtray and rolled it between his thumb and forefinger and said to Brian, "You feel better now?" Brian sat forward in the chair and started again when Clive interrupted. "You've had your turn Brian, now calm down." Brian stopped in mid-sentence then slid back in the chair and tossed the paper into the trash can at the side of Clive's desk.

Clive put the cigar in his mouth but did not attempt to light it. He bit down on the end and pushed the intercom button, "Alice, did you get the *Gazette* yet?"

Alice responded, "No, all I get is put on hold or told that Don is not available."

Clive said, "Okay, what's the number?" Alice gave him the phone number as Clive dialed it. Once dialed he sat back in his chair and took the cigar out of his mouth and waited. After several rings, Don Creavy's secretary answered and Clive asked for Don. He was told that Mr. Creavy was not available at this time. As the secretary continued, Clive interrupted, "Tell Don this is Clive and ask him if he really wants me to come over there. I have the time." There was a moment of silence then Duff, Collins and Brian sat forward in their chairs as Clive pushed the speaker button, and put the receiver back into its cradle.

A few moments later the speaker clicked and Don Creavy at the other end began to speak, "Hey, Clive how you doing, sorry about the delay but..."

That was all Creavy got to say as Clive interrupted him. "Don, I got a few things to say. Don't talk just listen. What you let happen here today there is no excuse for." Don tried to cut in but was cut off again. "Don cut the crap and listen. I've always treated you and your paper better than I've treated most of the others. As much as I don't like the press I've made an exception with you. I've always been fair and up front and you know how many times you got the jump on a story because of my department. Well consider that as history, the honeymoon is over, you just got booted to the bottom of the who-needs-to-know list. That's right. You are now lower than whale shit on the scoop position. I've told you before that idiot Anderson was not an asset but a liability. I guess I was right. Been nice talking to you, Don, have a nice day." With that, Clive pushed the "end call" button and then sat back in his chair and put the cigar back in his mouth.

Alice and Rose were still watching the conversation from the main office. They saw Brian get up and start again to pace back and forth and wave his arms. They watched as Clive rose from his chair, placed the cigar back in the ashtray and spoke to Duff and Collins who got up and left Clive's office. As Duff passed Alice's desk he just looked at her and rolled his eyes. Clive pointed to Brian to sit in one of the front chairs and then retrieved the paper Brian had thrown into the can and flipped it into Brian's lap. He then returned to his chair and sat down. They could see him speaking to Brian but could not hear what he was saying. After a few minutes Brian stood up and Clive leaned forward on his elbows and pointed to Brian three or four times while still speaking. He ended the conversation abruptly and started to work on his papers again.

Brian stood there for a few seconds then turned and left Clive's office. He did not look at or say anything to Alice or Rose as he left but as he passed the large trash can in the main office he threw the folded newspaper into the can with a thud. He walked quickly for the front door, placed his hat on his head and left the office, the door slamming behind him. All was quiet for several minutes then a call came in from the coroner for Clive. Alice paged Clive and he picked up the phone. It was Assistant Coroner, Bill Fry. "Clive, I would like you to come down here. There is something I need to show you."

Clive, looking somewhat disgusted, replied, "Can't we do this over the phone? I got all kinds of problems here."

"Yeah, I saw the paper," Bill replied. "I bet you got problems but I need you to see this. I'm getting ready to turn Jody's body over to her family I've got all I can get from her but you need to see this today. The funeral home is due here later today to get her body. I know you got more than you can handle but this has to be seen."

Clive took in a deep breath then said, "Okay, I'll be there, what time is it now?"

"It's about 10 a.m.," Bill replied. "How about 1 p.m., good for you?"

"Yeah, I guess," Clive answered. "See you then," and he hung up the phone. Clive put the papers in a pile on the corner of his desk and placed the cigar that was laying in the ashtray back into the desk drawer. He got up, took his hat and left the office. He stopped at Alice's desk for a moment, "Alice, I've got to go downtown to see Bill Fry, don't know what time I'll be back. If anything comes down let me know and tell the press nothing. They know too much now. Have Duff and Collins check in with me and tell Brian to have the report on my desk tomorrow on the Dans thing. I got a feeling we are going to get some major questions from the people who run this county now. Tell Brian to cool it, that I said cool it. Anger won't help now."

"Is Brian okay?" Alice said as she got up to copy something on the corner Xerox machine.

"Yeah, I think so," Clive said. "He feels like Anderson pulled one over on him and I think his armor is a little dented, ya know what I mean?"

"He'll be okay. I'd be a little pissed too. And I suppose you're not?" Alice said sarcastically.

Clive just sort of smirked, "Alice, your boys will be fine. Are you going to be fine?"

Alice just tossed the papers on her desk and replied, "Aliston, get out of here. You got an appointment remember."

Clive laughed and put on his hat and left the station. It was 12:30 p.m. when Clive pulled into a parking space on the fourth level of the city/county building parking garage. He walked up a ramp to the elevator in the corner of the garage and pushed the "down" button. When the elevator reached the fourth floor the door slid open and three teenagers—two girls and one boy—rushed out and head-on into Clive. He didn't move but just glared at them, especially the boy with the multicolored Mohawk hair cut. One of the girls said, "I'm sorry, excuse me," and they ran off, looking back at Clive and giggling and whispering to themselves.

As Clive entered the now-empty elevator, he whispered to himself, "Now there's some future cell block comedians." He pushed the button for the first floor and the doors slid closed. Clive wasn't happy with the city or any part of it. He was now and had always been more at home in the suburbs or out in the country. Cities felt confining to him and at times he almost felt smothered by the crowds and the lack of sky. He exited the elevator and crossed the lobby and out onto the street. A half block to the right and across the street was the city/county building—a seven-story, gray, granite monolith with large pillars and a long staircase in the front. He crossed at the intersection and walked to the front of the building and up the stairs that led between two of the huge gray pillars. He passed through one of the sets of revolving doors and on into the main lobby. Inside was an old worn but very shiny tile floor laid out in some old Mediterranean pattern. High above his head was a huge brass and crystal chandelier that looked older than the building. The lobby was dim and the only light was from the chandelier itself and a few sidelights.

Clive crossed the lobby to the opposite wall where the receptionist's cubicle was located. He asked if Bill Fry was in. She said he was still out to lunch but should be back soon. She asked if he wanted to wait in his office and Clive replied that he did. She started to explain the directions but Clive interrupted and told her he knew the way. He walked to the right and down a long hallway to the fourth office on the left side. The glass pane in the door read, William T. Fry, Assistant Coroner. He opened the door to an empty waiting room and looked around. No one was at the receptionist desk or in the office, behind which he could see through the door that was standing open. He found a seat and picked up a magazine and started to look through the pages when his stomach started to growl and he felt another hunger pain. He did not like the morgue and even though he was hungry the thought of food before this meeting was out of the question. He was only seated for about five or ten minutes when he heard voices in the outer hall. The door opened and Bill Fry and his receptionist entered the room. Bill Fry was a short, heavyset man of about fifty, five feet six inches tall and between a hundred eighty and a hundred ninety pounds, with a round face and no hair, except for a little above his ears. Clive got to his feet and Bill walked over to Clive and shook his hand and asked how he was doing. Before Clive could answer, Bill said. "You remember my receptionist Gail, don't you?"

Clive extended his hand in her direction while quickly removing his hat, which he had forgotten he had on. "Yes, I do remember. How are you, Gail?" he replied.

She smiled and said, "Okay, I guess, a lot better than you would be this morning." She was about forty years old, also short, five-four, dressed in a gray suit coat and pants.

Clive paused for a second and said, "I guess you saw the newspaper this morning?"

"The newspaper?" she said sarcastically, "You mean all the papers?"

Clive just looked at Bill and said, "All?"

"Yes, all," Bill replied.

"You mean it's front page?" Clive said, somewhat surprised.

"Bad news travel fast around here," Bill added.

Clive, looking a little unsettled, said, "Well, I guess we'll just have to handle it."

"Better you than me," Fry said as he started back toward the door. "Come on, Clive. Let's go to the lab. As I said, I've got something to show you."

Turning to Gail, Clive said, "Well, it was nice to see you again."

"You too," she responded and then added, "Good luck, Clive."

Clive just smiled and said, "Yeah, thanks," and turned to follow Bill into the hall. They walked out to the main lobby again and turned right to the long row of elevator doors. They stood there for several minutes not saying anything until the door of one of the elevators slid open. They entered and Clive put his hat back on his head and Bill pushed the button marked basement. When the door closed, Fry turned to Clive and began to go over the information that they already had about Jody's murder. The elevator reached the basement quickly and they both exited out into a long hall.

The tile floor, the walls and the ceilings were all white. Both sides of the hall were lined with white doors. The only color, the length of the hall, was the red fire extinguishers and the red fire alarm boxes staggered along the entire length. They turned right and walked to about the middle and entered a door marked with one word in black letters, "Morgue." Inside was another waiting room with about six or eight chairs and a coffee table in the center. Everything in the room was a shade of blue from the darker carpet to the light blue walls. There were no magazines lying around, like most waiting rooms and Clive thought to himself that most people who were waiting here didn't have much interest in what sports or fashion magazines had to say. They continued on through another door into a room with about four or five office cubicles, some occupied with lab techs. Fry yelled a "hello guys" and got several responses from different areas of the room. Fry asked Clive to hold up at the next door while he went to a cubicle and got a lab coat and lab skull cap and gloves and proceeded to put them on. When he had buttoned the coat, he and Clive continued onto another, shorter hallway. He walked to the first door and stopped before entering. He turned to Clive and asked if he had seen the report on the buttons from the coat. Clive responded that he had and Bill said they had double-checked the grease on the buttons and that it was definitely a GM product, one that had only been in use for two or three years. He also asked if he had seen the report on the skin and hair on the briefcase and Clive also responded that he had. Bill said they had still not been able to find a DNA match but they would continue to check other databases until they ran out of options.

Bill paused and asked Clive, "Now are you ready for this?"

Clive just stood there looking puzzled and then asked, "What?"

"What," Bill replied. "Well we found something strange about the DNA."

"What do you mean strange?" Clive asked.

"Well, it's not normal." Bill said.

"Not normal? What do you mean, not normal?" Clive asked.

Bill paused for a second then continued, "It's, well, the best way I can put it is genetically defective."

"What do you mean defective?" Clive asked, now even more confused.

Bill paused again, searching for a way to say it, then continued, "Clive, either the sample is messed up or the person it came from is not normal. I mean they were born with a major genetic problem. Let me put it this way; they wouldn't be exactly like you or me. By our standards they would be deficient or lacking, I guess, just messed up to put in street terms. I can't give you anymore than that, and please don't ask, I don't have any answers—at least not right now. I do know one thing. I certainly would like to see this person at least from a scientific point of view." Clive didn't respond but just stood there for a moment in silence. Bill then continued, "Well, I guess we better go in. There is still something I need to show you."

He opened the door and they both entered a large room, also mostly white, with sinks and tables, large gas bottles, instruments and chemicals that lined shelves along one wall. In the center of the room was a large drain that had several troughs leading away from it like spider legs in all directions. Each leg ended up at a table made of stainless steel. Above each table were hoses and power tools suspended from hooks in the white ceiling. The wall opposite the wall with the shelves was lined with stainless doors about four feet by four feet, with a latch handle like those on a meat cooler door. They walked to one of those doors near the back of the room and Bill hit a light switch that lit a quartz light above them. He motioned for Clive to back up a little and he reached for the door and opened it. The door swung in Clive's direction and he noticed a temporary tag in a slot on the door, Jody Miller. He pushed the door against the door next to it and was instructed by Bill to use the hook on the door to hold it back. Bill looked inside the cooler and pulled on a handle near the bottom. Out rolled a stainless flat drawer with a body on it covered with a sheet. All Clive could see was blonde hair at the top and pale gray feet at the other end. Bill looked at Clive and said, "Are you ready?" Clive nodded that he was and Bill pulled back the sheet to Jody's waist. Clive once again having forgotten his hat pulled it off quickly and then half turned away. Bill said, "You okay?"

Clive paused for a moment then turned back to the table. Before him was Jody Miller, her eyes closed, her body a grayish white. The word, forever, cut into her forehead seemed much smaller than when he first saw it at the tracks and her throat had been stitched closed. There were long incisions that had also been closed on her torso, one crisscrossed her chest and was from neck to waist. Her breasts and naval almost looked to Clive as if they were fashioned from wax. Without thinking, he grabbed the sheet and covered her chest again then let go of the sheet, the move being a surprise even to him.

Bill looked at Clive and softly said, "Clive, I don't think it matters to her anymore."

Clive paused then looked at Bill and said, "It matters to me."

They were both quiet for several seconds then Bill spoke, "Clive, this is what I wanted you to see." He pulled a chain on the overhead quartz light and brought it closer to Jody's face. "You see the bruises on her face?"

Clive leaned over for a closer look and said, "Yeah, they are all over her face."

"Yes," Bill replied. "That's the way it first appeared to me, but then later I noticed that the more prominent ones form a pattern." He pointed out four round bruises on the left side of her face spanning from just beside her ear to the back of her neck. He then showed Clive a single round bruise about twice the size of the others in the middle of the right side of her neck. He asked Clive, "Do you see the large round or oval-shaped bruise on her right chin?" It was not as clear as the others but it was still visible once pointed out. Clive studied them for a few seconds then looked up at Bill and shrugged his shoulders. Bill said, "Clive, look again, can't you see it?"

Clive looked again, studying each mark then he almost backed up a step. He looked at Bill Fry and from somewhere deep inside his chest he exclaimed, "My God, it's a hand print."

There was a pause and Fry then added, "Yeah, and it's huge." Clive just stared at Bill. Bill, looking intently at Clive, spoke in a very soft but determined voice, "With that DNA and this print, we have to be dealing with a Goliath."

CHAPTER 7

Clive and Bill spent an additional half hour in the morgue going over some of the other details before the funeral home arrived for the body. When they left, they went to Bill's office and sat for an additional hour going over theories on how the two murders were connected. Bill Fry told Clive all he knew at that point in time about Wesley Dans' murder. The results from the autopsy and the tests were not complete and Bill had not received anything but preliminary reports. It was 3:30 p.m. when Clive got up to leave. As much as he hated the city, he was feeling very comfortable in the chair in Bill Fry's office. It was kind of a break from the stress of the last couple of days and besides Bill Fry was a very easy person to be around. He was just a down-to-earth, nice guy.

It was about 3:50 p.m. when Clive left the city-county building, and as soon as he stepped onto the street that closed-in feeling returned. He walked to the intersection and was about to cross when he saw a black hearse coming around the corner. The sign on the door said, Lasiter

Funeral Home, Smith Falls, PA. He couldn't really see who was driving but he waved anyway, assuming it was Paul Lasiter, the owner and director and Brian's father. As he walked to the garage he couldn't get Jody Miller off his mind. What a terrible waste and the way it happened, he just couldn't seem to grasp that it was real. He just kept thinking that things like this were not meant to happen in a place like Smith Falls.

Once he got to his car he didn't waste much time getting out of the city. He had just left the city limits when his stomach let him know again that breakfast had been a long time ago. He drove for several more miles then called Alice to see about any messages. She told him several papers had called and that the county commissioner's secretary had called and left a message for him to call back as soon as possible. She said that the call did not seem urgent at the time so she did not call him.

He told her he was going to stop for supper on the way back and to let him know if anything important developed. He had just disconnected the phone when his stomach grumbled again. About that time he noticed a McDonald's sign about a quarter of a mile up the road and decided to stop. He was not much of a fast food person but somehow a Big Mac and fries sounded pretty good right about then. He decided to get take out and brought the bags back to an outside table near his car. He sat for about half an hour and ate his supper except for half the fries and half his coffee, which he took to the car when he left. He checked with Alice again and while he had her on the phone another line rang. When she got back to Clive she told him it was the commissioner's secretary again and she had asked why he had not returned the call. He told her to tell the secretary that he would call as soon as he got back to the office. She asked if he was sure he wanted to handle it that way and he said he wanted to collect his thoughts before he called and to make sure he had all the information on the case in front of him. When he hung up he knew that what he really wanted was to avoid what he knew was coming for as long as he could. Politicians had no place in police business and police had no place in theirs—but unfortunately it never worked out that way.

As he drove he started to think about all that had happened since the morning they had found Jody. He thought about all the evidence they had gathered and how unreal it all seemed. Nothing was making sense. What was the connection between Jody and Wesley? Why had they died the way they did? What was the significance of the slashed throats? Could there really be someone out there that was a Goliath, as Bill Fry had said? If it had been closer to the fourth of July and some of the carny people had been in the area for the holiday at the fairgrounds, he could possibly check there but none had been in the area. Why had the bodies been left where they were found, and most of all what the hell was FOREVER all about? He had just stuffed a handful of cold fries in his mouth when Alice called him on the radio. He picked up the mike and tried to respond but with his mouth full just unintelligible mumble came out. He tried to chew faster but Alice answered before he could finish. "Sounds like whatever supper is, it must be good," she said sarcastically. He didn't respond but just looked at the mike with a smirk on his face. Alice called again, "Clive, you okay or do I need to get someone who can do the Heimlich maneuver?"

Clive swallowed the last bite and took a drink of the now-cold coffee and then made an appropriate face. He pushed the mike button again and said, "Alice, you're real cute, just what do you need from me now?"

There was a pause then Alice continued, "Well, I don't know what you had for supper but this should give you a real good case of heartburn."

"Now what?" Clive responded.

Alice continued, "I just got a call from Pete Waters down at Posey's bar. He said Bob Anderson has Roscoe Black cornered in a booth and is feeding him booze trying to get some information out of him about the case."

"Roscoe Black?" Clive said. "Why Roscoe?"

"I don't know for sure," Alice said. "But Pete said Bob overheard Roscoe talking about being at the tracks at the time of Jody's murder; don't know anymore than that. I sent Collins to Posey's."

Clive sat and thought for a moment then said, "No, Alice. Call Collins back. I'll handle this myself." Clive continued up the same route for about five miles then cut off on a side road that he knew would shorten the trip by at least ten minutes. When he pulled the car into the lot at Posey's Bar and Restaurant there were not many parking spaces left open. It was 5:30 p.m. and the bar was obviously crowded with supper customers and the usual group of happy hour people. He parked at the side of the building and walked around to the front porch and up the four steps to the front door.

Posey's had been named for the original owner many years before. There had been so many owners over the years that most people couldn't say how long it had the name. It was probably the most popular bar and restaurant in that part of the county. It sat just outside the Smith Falls town limits along a two lane blacktop road that connected the town with the interstate about five miles up the road. It was located in a mix of farmland and small housing projects. It had wooded land on both sides and in the rear. It was a fairly large two-story aluminum-sided building. It had been recently remodeled and was a neat, clean gray color with burgundy trim. It had a porch on three sides lined with a wooden handrail and posts that were also painted burgundy. If not for the large sign that hung out over the wide wooden steps in the front it almost gave the appearance of a bed and breakfast nestled in the trees. It was about three quarters of a mile from the fairgrounds and Wilson Creek wound its way through the woods behind the building. Clive entered one side of the double doors in the front and moved quickly to the end of the bar to the right.

Posey's was made up of three large rooms: the bar, the game room, and the restaurant in the rear of the building. The bar ran about half the length of the right side of the room. The rest of the right wall was booths—about four or five that continued to the wall of the restaurant. On the left side were two cigarette machines and then a large doorway that led to the game room on the left side of the building. After the doorway was another row of booths—again four or five that ran along the left wall up to the front wall of the restrooms. They protruded out from the walls at about the center of the room to the front wall of the dining room. The walls were decorated with large, lighted paintings of forests and wildlife scenes and an occasional lighted beer sign. The walls were made of cedar planking run in a diagonal pattern from floor to ceiling. There was a row of ceiling fans down the middle of the room the length of the bar. The bar was dressed up with a slanted burgundy armrest pad and a brass foot rail. In front of the bar was a row of about fifteen armrest bar stools that matched the bar pad and the cedar walls. The floor was polished wood planking that ran the length of the bar and was covered with peanut shells from the many buckets of shelled peanuts that were always out on the bar and at each booth. The game room was about the same size as the bar but its walls were lined with pinball machines and video game machines and two electronic dartboards. There were four booths along the wall that the bar and game room shared. In the center were four large pool tables in four colors: green, red, blue and tan. Cue sticks lined the walls in several places and each table had a large fluorescent light hung above it. The back room was a dining area that was the width of the building and had ten or twelve round dinner tables, covered with red and white checked tablecloths. Each table was surrounded by six wooden barrel chairs. There was a swag light above each table and on the side wall was a large stone fireplace. The kitchen area was behind the dining room, an addition to the main building. The second floor was where Pete Waters' residence was.

Clive stood for a few minutes and let his eyes adjust to the room after coming in from the sunlight. After a minute or two he waved at Pete Waters who was behind the bar and serving drinks with the aid of one of the barmaids. Pete signaled that he would be right there in a minute or two. Clive stood and scanned the room looking for Bob Anderson and Roscoe. The bar was full of patrons and four of the five booths in the front were occupied with customers. In the last booth he saw Anderson and Black. Bob was facing the back of the room and Roscoe was on the opposite side, his head hung down over a half-empty glass of beer. Anderson appeared to be doing all the talking, moving his hands back and forth and tapping Roscoe on the arm every few minutes. Pete Waters walked up to Clive and motioned him to the access opening at the end of the bar.

Pete Waters was forty-five years old, with short brown hair and blue eyes. He was just short of six feet tall and weighed two hundred twenty-five pounds. He had been a local football hero in his younger days and he still appeared to be in excellent shape. He had been a police officer in Smith Falls for five years before he bought the bar fifteen years ago. When they were sure they were out of sight of Bob Anderson, blocked by the customers at the front of the bar, they started to talk. Clive spoke first, "Okay, Pete, what's going on here?"

Pete looked back again in Anderson's direction then back to Clive and said, "Roscoe, came in here earlier this afternoon and ordered a couple of beers. Who knows where he got the money. He sat at the bar and started talking about all kinds of things. You know what his gibberish can be like. He was on his second beer when Anderson came in and sat down about three or four chairs away. At first he didn't pay much attention to Roscoe; he just ordered a drink and was writing something on his pad. Roscoe then started to tell me that these murders were no mystery—he knew all about what was happening. He started to mumble about being there at the tracks the night Jody was murdered. That's when Anderson started to take notice. I told Roscoe that he shouldn't be talking about what he didn't really know anything about. But you know Roscoe, he just kept it up. I finally got him to change the subject when I asked him to bring in some supplies from my truck to the kitchen in the back of the building. I knew he probably hadn't eaten anything so I told him if he did the favor for me I'd give him his supper. He finished his beer and then walked out through the back door beside the kitchen and started to unload the truck. I walked him out there and when I got back to the bar Anderson was gone. He didn't even finish his drink, although, he did leave a tip."

Clive interrupted, "Well, how did they get back in here together?"

Pete looking back again in Anderson's direction for a second continued, "Well, I kind of got busy behind the bar with happy hour and dinner time coming up and forgot about Roscoe until about fifteen minutes later when they both came in through the front door. Anderson walked Roscoe to that booth and then ordered two drinks. Anderson still has the same drink in front of him now. I think Roscoe is on number seven. I sort of knew what was up so I tried to interrupt them and remind Roscoe that he had to eat. Anderson, the smart-ass bastard that he is told me in so many words to hit the road and that he would buy Roscoe any dinner he wanted. I proceeded to tell him that I owed Roscoe dinner and it was probably a good idea for him to eat it now. But you know Bob. You ain't gonna tell him much of anything. We argued for a minute more and I finally gave up. I let it go for a little longer than I should have I guess. That's when I decided to call and I talked to Alice."

Clive shook his head and said, "You did the right thing."

Pete then added, "I really don't want to cause any trouble but I was starting to get a little concerned, especially after the trouble I heard Anderson caused the other day."

Clive, looking somewhat surprised, said, "You heard about that already?"

Pete shrugged his shoulders and said, "Clive, it's a bar. What don't you hear?"

Clive shook his head and said, "Yeah, I guess." He looked at Pete and said, "I'll try to keep this as civil as possible." He turned and walked around the corner of the bar and in the direction of the last booth. As Clive slowly walked toward the booth he scanned the crowd that he could see. Some of the people he knew by name, others he recognized but did not know. Several of the people he did not recognize, but that was not unusual considering the popularity of the place and its proximity to the interstate. Some of those who recognized him waved and he nodded in response. When he reached the booth he just stood there silently, looking down at Anderson and waiting.

Bob Anderson was in mid sentence and once again pulling on Roscoe's arm to get his attention when he realized someone was standing there. He turned and looked up to see Clive standing, looking stone-faced back at him. His immediate reaction was one of surprise then almost guilt—as if he was a child who had been caught with his hand in the cookie jar. Clive stood and stared and said nothing. Anderson, regaining his composure, slid back against the wall of the booth and motioning for Clive to sit beside him, and said, "Well, Mr. Aliston, and how might you be today? Sit down. Have a drink. Join the conversation."

Clive stood there for a few seconds more then leaned over and placed both hands flat on the table. He started to speak but Roscoe raised his head from the beer he was hovering over and started to mumble. "Hey, Clive, old buddy, how are you? How are you?"

Clive looked over at Roscoe and then put his hand on top of Roscoe's and softly said, "I'm good, old Buddy, but I think you've had enough of this." He reached for the beer glass in front of Roscoe and slid it across the table to just in front of him.

Bob Anderson, reaching into his coat and retrieving his wallet, said to Clive, "Hey, Clive, I'll buy, you don't need to take old Roscoe's beer."

With that, Clive turned again to Anderson, only this time his face was red and if it was possible fire would have come out of eyes. For a second he composed himself then he spoke softly just as Anderson was about to. "Bob, I know what is going on here and it stops now."

Anderson came back with the immediate reply, "What's going on here? Nothing is going on but a good old conversation about current events."

Roscoe spoke again, "Yeah, Clive, we was just talking, you know, 'bout Jody."

Clive once again looked at Roscoe and said, "That's okay Roscoe, just hold on here one minute." He looked back at Anderson and continued, "I said I know what's coming down here and it goes no further. You won't do what you're doing to dig up more dirt?"

"Dirt? Anderson responded. "What I do is my job and I don't see that any law is being broken, so just what is your problem?"

Clive leaned closer to Anderson and almost started to grind his teeth as he spoke, "You're right Anderson, there is no legal law being broken but I can see one big moral one and I just became the moral sheriff and it stops now." Anderson turned to interrupt again but Clive continued, "You get your ass out of this booth and this bar or I will find something to arrest you for."

Anderson, now feeling somewhat angered, slid toward Clive and in a raised voice said, "You got no reason to arrest anyone—especially me."

Clive, now close to the explosion point, went nose to nose with Anderson and yelled, "Anderson, move it now or you're under arrest." With that he grabbed the shoulder of Anderson's coat and pulled him out of the booth and into a standing position. At that same second what seemed like the entire bar went silent. Anderson stood there with an amazed, almost fearful look on his face. Clive, realizing that the entire bar was now silent, looked around behind him to the booths in the back. Three of the five were occupied and he could see the people in two of them. In the third and closest booth was a single person now looking over their newspaper at the booth where Clive was standing. Clive could not see the face because it was in the shadows but it made him realize that all attention was on him. He quickly turned back to Anderson, who at the same moment pulled his coat out of Clive's hand and backed up a step or two. Anderson started to yell something about police brutality but never got to finish as Clive, now back in control but more determined than ever, reached for his handcuffs and said, "That's it. I've had enough of you. You're going to the station with me now."

Anderson, realizing that the conversing part of this confrontation was over, backed up several more steps, put his hands palms up toward Clive, and kept saying, "I'm going, I'm going, I'm going."

Just as Clive was turning to Roscoe to tell him to stay where he was, the door of the men's room opened and the sound caught Clive's attention for a second. The light from the men's room shone briefly on the once-dark booth where the lone figure with the newspaper was sitting. For just a split second the light glinted off something around the person's neck but the face was still not visible. Bob Anderson was still backing up and Roscoe was attempting to get out of the booth when Clive returned his attention to the situation. He looked over at Pete Waters behind the bar and asked him to take care of Roscoe for a second. As Pete started around the bar toward the booth, Clive started to walk toward Anderson. He pointed toward the door behind Anderson and said one word very forcefully, "Out." Anderson turned and left the bar with Clive hot on his trail. When Clive got to the door he turned to Pete and said,

"Pete, could you bring him outside for me?" Pete nodded, yes, and Clive opened the door and walked out to the porch. When he got outside Anderson was down the steps and on his way toward his car. Clive, trying to get his eyes adjusted to the sunlight, placed his hand above his eyes in an attempt to shade them and yelled at Anderson, "Just hold it there a second."

Anderson turned around while still backing up, and yelled, "I don't have to stop, I didn't do anything." At about that same time Brian Lasiter pulled his patrol car off the highway and into the lot. When he saw Clive coming down the steps and Bob Anderson rushing in a hurry toward his car, he quickly drove forward, cutting off Bob's route to his car. Bob stopped not five feet from the patrol car as it slid to a stop in the dirt parking lot. Brian got out of the car and as he did Bob started to turn around to go back the other way. He took two steps and was once again face-to-face with Clive. Clive started to walk Anderson backwards toward the patrol car as Brian stepped aside and stood beside Clive.

Bob backed up against the car then put his hands up again and said, "Hold it. Hold it."

Clive, calm but looking very determined, said, "Shut the hell up and just listen. You want to do your job, fine. You do it, but I catch you pulling something like this again and legal or not you and I will spend sometime together—and it won't be to socialize."

Anderson, scared but embarrassed, just couldn't let it go. He swallowed hard and started again back at Clive, "What are you so afraid I'll find out? Maybe it's you who has something to hide. Maybe the reason this whole case is going so slow is because you know more than you're letting on." Bob looked up toward the porch as Pete came out the door with Roscoe in tow and also noticed several customers looking out the window at the three of them.

Without taking his eyes off of Bob, Clive said, "Brian, would you get Roscoe and put him in your car?"

Brian turned to walk away and as he did Bob, realizing he had witnesses watching, spoke loud enough for all to hear, "Yeah, maybe he's protecting you, Lasiter."

Brian stopped in his tracks, turned around and said, "What's that supposed to mean?"

Clive, still not taking his eyes off of Bob said, "Brian just do what I asked, please."

Bob then continued, "How do we know you didn't have something to do with Jody's death. You had reason."

Brian stood his ground and responded, "Listen asshole."

Clive interrupted again, "Brian, please."

Bob, now almost leaning over to look around Clive, continued, "She dumped you a long time ago. Maybe you just couldn't deal with it anymore. What, was Wesley moving in on your turf?"

With that, Brian almost leaped the five steps to Bob and if it wasn't for Clive blocking his move he would have had his hands around Bob's neck. Clive went face-to-face with Brian, leaving Bob bending back against the car. He pushed Brian in the chest and yelled, "Now Brian, get Roscoe. Don't make me ask again."

Brian, now glaring at Bob, started to back up and then turned back to the bar to get Roscoe. Clive slowly turned back to Anderson, who was slowly standing up straight again. He moved a couple of steps closer and then leaned toward Anderson and not six inches from Bob's face whispered, "Forget the law, Bob. One more word and you go back to the newspaper in a box." Clive backed up again and just stared at Bob. Bob, now realizing more than ever that Clive had reached the end of his rope, said nothing else. He slid sideways down the side of the patrol car and around the front and then turned and headed in the direction of his car. Clive turned and walked back to the front porch as Brian was helping Pete get Roscoe down the steps.

Clive thanked Pete and told him he would be in touch.

Pete waved and then added, "Good luck," and went back into the bar. Clive and Brian walked Roscoe to Brian's car and they placed him in the backseat and closed the door.

Clive turned and leaned his back against the car then started to speak to Brian, but Brian interrupted, "Clive, I know I lost it there for a second but I'm okay now. I know you said if I couldn't handle it I was off the case but..."

Clive put his hand on Brian's shoulder and said, "Brian, forget it, I was ready to deck him. Why would I think you wouldn't be? Look can you take Roscoe wherever it is he wants to go?"

Just then Anderson, now in his car, stopped beside Clive and Brian long enough to yell at Clive, "You think the last headline was a good one? Wait till you see tomorrow's." He ran the window up and pulled out onto the highway.

Clive and Brian just stood silently and watched as he drove away. Clive looked at Brian and shook his head and said, "You know, I wonder if his mother ever liked him?"

Brian smiled and added, "Ya think he had a mother?"

Clive smiled again and then repeated, "Like I said, take Roscoe where he wants to go. I'll see you at the station tomorrow."

Brian started to get into the car then stopped and asked, "What did Anderson want with him anyway?"

Clive shrugged his shoulders and said, "Well all I got out of all this was that Roscoe claims he was at the tracks the night Jody was killed. Apparently, Anderson found out and was trying to milk him for the story."

"Do you think he was?" Brian asked.

Again, Clive shook his head and with a puzzled look on his face said, "I don't know. He's too drunk now to get much out of him. Better he sleeps it off. We'll pick him up in the morning and have a talk with him. I guess it can wait till then."

Brian got into the car and started it as Clive walked to his patrol car. When Clive was at his car, Brian pulled up beside him and rolled the window down. As Clive turned,

Brian said, "You know, I forgot all about what I was supposed to tell you with all the confusion. Before you go home you better call the commissioner and make an appointment, I think from what Alice said he's a little pissed at you for not calling back." Clive just closed his eyes for a second then said, "Oh hell, I forgot about it completely. I'll call when I get to the station. See you tomorrow." Brian pulled out of the lot and onto the highway toward the fairgrounds. Clive got into his car and headed in the opposite direction back to the station.

CHAPTER 8

Wednesday, June 16, 6:30 p.m.

Brian had asked Roscoe where he wanted to go for the night and Roscoe had told him the fairgrounds. He told Brian he had made an arrangement with the groundskeeper that he could stay in the shed next to the carousel if he kept the place clean and helped open the ride for the holidays and the fair. Brian pulled onto the grounds and parked the car along the road just below the carousel and the shed. He woke Roscoe, who had fallen asleep, and watched in the rearview mirror as he got out of the car and staggered to his side window. Roscoe thanked Brian and Brian asked if he would be alright. Roscoe just said, "Alright" and started to walk across the grass to the shed. Brian opened the glove box and pulled out a cigar and unwrapped it slowly. He continued to watch Roscoe as he put the cigar in his mouth and lit it. He watched Roscoe stagger to the shed and then he saw him lift the mat in front of the door, guessing it was for a key. Roscoe stood and fumbled for several minutes with the door as Brian sat in

the car and smoked the cigar and watched. After what
seemed like five minutes, Roscoe got the door open and
entered the shed, the door closing behind him. Brian sat
there watching the shed then unfastened his seatbelt and
opened the door and got out of the car. He didn't shut the
car off but instead closed the door, took a few more puffs
on the cigar and slowly walked up the slight grade through
the grass toward the shed.

Wednesday, June 16, 9:30 p .m.

Brian had returned to Posey's bar and decided to have
something to eat before he went to his apartment. After
eating he sat alone in a booth in the game room and started
on a series of drinks. For the best part of an hour he sat
quietly in a half trance, thinking, smoking a cigar. At about
eleven o'clock he started to play pool. Over the next half
hour he had several offers for games or partners from a few
of the regular clients, but he refused and continued to
practice and drink alone. Close to midnight, he was bent
over the table, setting up a rack of balls when he looked up
just as Bob Anderson came in the front door. Bob didn't see
him as he walked to the bar and sat in the third chair from
the end. Brian left the rack half-filled with balls, and with
the cue-stick still in his hand, walked slowly to the
doorway between the bar and the game room. He stopped
in the archway and leaned against one side and stared at
Bob Anderson's back.

Bob retrieved his wallet from his coat and was
thumbing through the money in it with the idea of buying
a beer. He looked up for several seconds after he put a five-
dollar bill on the bar. He scanned the bar and turned
slightly to the booths on the opposite wall then rose up
from the stool to try and see who was in the booths in the
back of the room. As he turned back facing the back of the
bar he saw Brian's reflection in the mirror. For a moment he
froze, staring at Brian still leaning against the side of the
archway holding a cue-stick, with his uniform shirt open,

his tie pulled down, smoking a cigar and smiling. He was about to spin around when Brian spoke, "Hey, Bob, he's not here. I took him home. Thought you might catch him alone again did you?" With that, Brian started to walk slowly toward Bob, who spun the bar stool around then stood up and started to move toward the door. Brian stopped for a moment as Bob slowly moved closer to the front door.

When he reached the door he said, "Look Lasiter, I don't want anymore trouble." Brian just continued to smile and puff slowly on the cigar. Pete Waters had seen what was happening and slowly walked to that end of the bar. Brian still had not said a word when Bob continued, "You're off duty now, you can't do a thing."

Still smiling, Brian removed the cigar from his mouth, leaned the cue-stick against the wall and said, "You're right Anderson. I am off duty."

Pete Waters, standing at the entrance to the back bar, spoke to both of them, "Look guys we don't need any trouble here tonight."

Brian looked at Pete and smiled, then placed the cigar back between his clenched teeth and said, "What trouble? I don't see there's any trouble." He again turned back to Anderson and just continued to smile. At that moment, Bob's nerves had had enough. He quickly turned without saying anything and left the bar, the door slamming shut behind him. Brian turned again to Pete, removed the cigar from his mouth, and pointed in the direction of the bar where Anderson had been sitting. "Big tipper, eh Pete?" referring to the five Bob had left on the bar.

Brian turned and picked up the cue stick and walked back to the game room. Pete walked to the bar and picked up the five and put it in his shirt pocket as he stared at Brian walking back into the game room. He shook his head then used the cloth he had in his hand to wipe the bar. As he turned and walked away he just said, "Damn."

Brian walked to one of the front windows and watched

Bob, still visible in the light from the sign above the bar. He stood there for several minutes just smoking the cigar until he saw Bob's taillights disappear as he turned out onto the highway. Brian put the cue-stick on the top of the table he was using, put on his hat and pulled his tie up. He walked to the booth he had been sitting in and picked up his drink and downed the last of it. He readjusted his hat and turned and left the room through the corner of the bar room. He went out the door without saying anything to anyone. Pete didn't even realize anyone had left until he looked up as the door was closing. Brian walked to his car parked along the darkened side of the building, pulled it out of the lot and headed in the direction of Smith Falls.

Thursday, June 17, 7:30 a.m.

Clive had stopped to pick up a newspaper on the way to the station and had it tucked under his arm when he stopped in front of Alice's desk. Alice and Rose Bodin were having coffee at their desks and carrying on a conversation before the start of their shift at 8 a.m. Clive stood there for a second and waited for Alice to finish what she was saying. When she had finished he asked her if she had seen the front page of the *Gazette*. She said she hadn't had time to pick one up, and why? Clive unfolded the paper and held it up in front of her and Rose. "Well girls, how do you like this one?" The headline read: "The Forever Man Killer Still At Large."

Alice took the paper from Clive and scanned the article then asked, "Clive, you read this yet?"

"Oh, yes, I've read it. You can have it. I've read all I need to. It's pretty much what I would expect from someone like Anderson."

Looking back at the paper, Alice asked, "What is it that the *Gazette* sees in Anderson's style of writing?"

Clive, looking somewhat calm about the whole thing, smiled and said, "It's what the people want to hear, I guess—or maybe it's what the newspaper thinks they want to hear. I guess they are frustrated and a little scared and looking for someone to strike out at, someone to blame. Guess it may as well be us." Alice dropped the paper on her desk and pushed it to the side with a disgusted look on her face. "With what little we have to go on since Jody was killed, what can they expect? Like to see what they could accomplish if it had been dropped in their laps."

Clive just smiled and said, "Yeah, I guess they think the shoe's on the other foot. Pretty easy to pick apart what you really don't know about or understand." Clive shook his head and turned toward his office. When he reached the door he turned back to Alice and asked, "Have you heard from Brian yet?"

"No, not yet," she said, looking at the paper again. "Do you want to talk to him when he gets in?"

"Yeah, I guess so. I need him to pick up Roscoe Black and bring him in for some questions."

"Roscoe Black?" Alice said with a surprised look on her face.

"Yeah, I guess he may have been in the area where Jody's body was found. Also could you get me a coffee and see if you can get Collins and Duff. I need them to refresh my memory on a few things before I see the commissioner this morning."

As he turned to enter his office, Alice said, "Oh yeah, almost forgot. The commissioner's secretary called and left a message at seven a.m. and said the meeting you had scheduled this morning has been changed."

"Changed to what?" Clive said as he turned back to Alice.

"What and where?" Alice said, handing him a slip of notepaper.

Clive stepped forward and took the note from Alice and read it. He looked at Alice a little puzzled and said, "Now he wants it at 1:30 p.m. at his home, not the office. That's a little strange. Oh well at least I don't have to go back to the city again."

They stared at each other for a second or two then Alice said, "Well, I'll get your coffee."

Clive turned and entered his office and took a seat in the chair behind his desk. He sat there for several minutes thinking, then he opened the drawer and took out the cigar he had placed there the day before. As he put the cigar in his mouth, Alice entered with the coffee, placed it on his desk and without saying anything turned and left the room. Clive picked up the coffee and then spun around in the chair and removed the cigar from his mouth and began to sip on the steaming brew while staring out the window. About five minutes passed before he turned again to his desk, placed the coffee down in front of him and once again put the cigar in this mouth and picked up the lighter. He had the flame inches from the cigar when the intercom buzzed. He put the lighter down, took the cigar out of his mouth and answered, "Yes Alice."

There was a pause, then Alice responded, "Clive you're not going to believe this one."

"I doubt that" Clive said sarcastically.

Alice continued, "I don't think you'll be talking to Roscoe Black this morning. The groundskeeper at the fairgrounds just found him dead."

Clive paused for a minute then asked, "Did he say how, was it a heart attack or something?"

"No," Alice said. "He acts like he's hysterical. At least that's what the 911 operator said. Looks like he's been murdered."

"What?" was all Clive said as he got up from his chair. He started around the desk then realized he still had the cigar in his hand and he turned and dropped it on the top of the desk. He left his office and stopped at Alice's desk and waited while she was on the phone. When she hung up she told him the 911 operator had contacted Collins by radio and he was headed there. Clive, now standing in front of Alice's desk, asked if she found out anything else.

"No, Clive. The 911 operator said he still had the

groundskeeper on the other line and that he was trying to calm him down."

Clive turned back to his office, stopped, paused for a second, then spoke, "Okay, I'm headed out there. Call Duff. Tell him to get here and cover for me. Where's Brian?"

Alice, still looking surprised, said, "I don't know, I haven't heard from him."

Clive entered his office, put on his hat, and strapped on his gun and then stopped at Alice's desk again, "Find Brian, tell him to meet me at the fairgrounds ASAP and call Collins back and tell him same as usual, no press and…"

Alice cut in as Clive was in mid-sentence, "Yeah, I know. No one touches anything. No one leaves. No one goes anywhere."

"Yeah," was all Clive said as he turned and left the station.

Thursday, June 17, 9 a.m.

When Clive arrived at the fairgrounds he parked his car just below the carousel, right behind Collins' patrol car. Collins and the groundskeeper, Harvey Logan, met him halfway to the ride. There didn't seem to be anyone else in the area at the time. Collins spoke first, "Clive, he was definitely killed. You'll see what I mean. Come on have a look." Clive, Collins and Logan started to walk the remaining distance to the carousel when Logan stopped. He had looked a little pale when Clive first saw him and now he bent over and then went down on one knee.

Clive stopped and walked back to him, as did Collins. Clive asked, "Harvey, you okay?"

Logan looked up at Clive and said, "No. Right now I don't think so. I feel a little dizzy and sick. I don't want to go up there again. I'll be okay if I can stay here. I ain't never seen a dead person before, not like that. He scared the hell out of me this morning when I first saw him. I'll stay here. I'll just stay here."

Clive asked him if he would be okay by himself and he

nodded yes. Clive and Collins turned and again headed to the carousel. They stepped up onto the carousel and wove their way along between the wooden horses now covered with canvas. When they reached the other side of the ride, Collins pointed to one of the bench seats between two rows of wooden horses. As Clive approached the bench from the rear he could see someone seated in the middle. He approached slowly, with Collins behind him. He paused for a second then walked around to face the front of the bench. Seated in the middle his head down and his felt fedora hat on his head was Roscoe Black. Clive moved closer to Roscoe and then saw the blood on the back of his neck and soaked into his jacket. He noticed silver duct tape on Roscoe's ear. He bent down and looked into Roscoe's face. Roscoe's eyes, mouth and ears were each covered with a strip of duct tape. Clive looked back at Collins and whispered, "What the hell?"

Collins shrugged his shoulders and said, "I don't know, Clive. I just don't know."

They walked around the area for a few minutes looking for any clues but found none. After several more minutes searching around the shed and carousel they returned to Logan who was now seated on the curb next to the patrol car.

Logan looked up at Clive and said, "Ain't that some shit? Like to crapped my pants when I saw that. Ain't never seen nothin' like that before."

Not saying a word, Clive sat in his patrol car and picked up the mike. He first turned to Collins and said, "How about you and Harvey go over this again and make as many notes as you can. I'm going to call Alice and have her call Bill Fry. Check out the inside of the shed but don't touch anything.

He was about to continue when Alice's voice interrupted him from the radio speaker, "Clive, are you there?"

Clive stopped in mid sentence and responded, "Yes

Alice, I'm here."

Alice continued, "Clive, I just got a call from Chief Richards in Smith Falls."

Clive cut in and said, "Alice, can we do this later? I'm in the thick of this now."

There was a pause then Alice responded, "Clive, he said they just found Bob Anderson in his car behind the *Gazette*. He's dead." There was several seconds of complete silence then Alice spoke again, "Clive, are you there?"

Clive just sat there and he and Collins stared at each other. Clive pushed the button on the mike and responded, "Alice, tell Alvin Richards I'll be there as soon as I can." He paused and then added, "Where's Brian?"

"He called in a few minutes ago, said he would be late. He don't sound too good Clive."

Clive sat there a second then whispered, "Damn it." He keyed the mike again and added, "Okay, tell him to head for the *Gazette* and do it now. I don't care how he feels. I'll be there soon and you tell him he knows the routine." Clive hung up the mike and just sat there for a minute thinking. He got out of the car and then said out loud but not to anyone in particular, "Roscoe then Anderson." He started to walk back to the carousel and then he looked back and called Collins to follow him. When they arrived back at the bench where Roscoe was seated, Clive stepped up and looked into Roscoe's face again. He stood up and turned to Collins with a surprised look on his face.

Collins, looking puzzled, said, "What?"

Clive, still looking surprised, said softly to Collins, "The tape, don't you get it?"

"Get what?" Collins said.

Clive turned and started to walk away then turned back to Collins. He looked at Collins and said, "See no evil, hear no evil, speak no evil." Clive turned again in the direction of the cars, leaving Collins bent over and looking into Roscoe's face.

Collins stood up, and looking at Clive as he disappeared

around the other side of the carousel, and said, "What, hear no evil, speak, see, what evil?" He bent over and looked again and then he straightened up and started to walk in the same direction that Clive had just taken. As he walked away he whispered, "Evil, where did he get evil?"

When Collins got back to the car, Clive was on the radio with Alice again. "Alice, also tell Brian to have Duff go to Anderson's house and notify his wife. We don't want her to find out from his paper or any other way. Call Bill Fry again and let him know that he's going to need more help. Is Brian there yet?"

"Yes," Alice responded, and, "I already called the coroner's office and talked to Bill. I figured you would want him to know ASAP."

Clive keyed the mike again and said, "Good job and tell Brian to help Richards keep those newspaper people away from Anderson. The newspaper parking lot isn't the best place to keep anything quiet. They probably touched too much already. We don't need any more evidence contaminated than we already have. Like I said, tell Brian and Alvin I'll be there soon. I'm going to leave Collins here to handle this end and, oh yeah, see if you can get anyone from the other shifts to come out here and help."

"Will do," was all that Alice said as Clive hung up the mike.

Clive got out of his car and was about to speak to Collins when he realized that Harvey Logan was still sitting there. "Harvey, could you do me a favor?"

Harvey stood up from his seat on the curb and said, "Sure Clive, whatever you want."

Clive walked to the trunk of his car, opened it, and retrieved a roll of yellow crime scene tape. He handed it to Harvey then asked, "Could you run this around the four light poles that surround the carousel and the shed? I want it clear of all people and that includes you, Harvey. I'm going to need your help. We are a little short right now but I can't let you back in there again. You did a good job but we need to keep it clear and clean for the crime lab people."

"Yeah, okay for sure," was all Harvey said as he took the tape and walked away.

Clive then turned to Collins, "Jack, I hate to leave you here alone but help should be here soon. I may even see if Alvin can spare a few men. When Harvey is finished with the tape, tell him to put the "Fairgrounds closed" sign at all the entrances. You keep an eye on this entrance. It's the only one I want used. There's too many ways in and out of the place. If anyone who is not authorized comes around, tell him or her it's off limits. Anyone gives you any crap, arrest him or her. I'm going into Smith Falls and see about the Anderson thing."

Clive started to get back into the car when Collins asked, "Clive, what's with the see no evil thing?"

"Well," Clive said pausing, "I didn't want to say anything in front of Logan but someone appears to be trying to say Roscoe knew too much."

"Uh huh," Collins said, then added, "Do you think he did?"

Clive put the key in the ignition then turned to Collins, "Well Anderson seemed to think so and now he's dead. Makes you wonder doesn't it? Oh, yeah, no more answers for Logan. He's an okay guy but he knows enough now. We got to try to keep some kind of a lid on this. It's not going to be easy but the more that gets out—well, you know." Clive started the car and said, "See ya in a while." He pulled out of the fairgrounds and headed for Smith Falls.

Thursday, June 17, 10:45 a.m.

When Clive arrived at the *Gazette* parking lot, there was a huge crowd around the area. Crime scene tape had been strung and Smith Falls Police and firemen kept the crowd back away from the lot. When he got out of his car Alvin Richards met him. "Well, Clive, I'm not going to ask you how you're doing. I can guess. I heard about Roscoe Black. Is it the same as the others?"

"No, not exactly," Clive said as he looked across the lot to where Anderson's car was parked.

"This one's not either," Richards said, "but it's kind of unique anyway."

"I'll bet," was all Clive said as he and Alvin started to walk to the car. Clive noticed Brian standing on the other side of the car with a note pad, talking to a young woman. As they reached the car Brian stopped his conversation to meet Clive and Alvin. Brian told Clive that the woman he was talking to was the first one who saw the car with Bob inside. He said that several other people had parked in the lot and went into the building without noticing. Alvin Richards saw the coroner's car pulling up to the lot and excused himself to meet them. When he was out of hearing range Clive looked at Brian and asked, "You okay? You look like shit."

"Yeah, yeah, I'm good," Brian said as he stuffed his note pad in his pocket.

Clive looked up under Brian's hat and with a disgusted look on his face said sarcastically, "You could have fooled me. You look like you're bleeding to death from your eyes. Some day that Old Captain Morgan's gonna get you boy."

Brian, looking at his shoelaces and acting a little embarrassed, whispered, "Okay, Clive, I got the point. I guess what Anderson said got to me a little last night."

Clive stood and stared at Brian as Brian raised his head again. "I thought you could handle it, remember," Clive said as he turned to the car door.

"I can, Clive, just give me a little room, okay?" Brian said as he turned and looked back to where Richards was talking on the other side of the lot.

"Okay, then handle it," Clive said as he leaned over to look into the car window. Inside, seated on the front seat behind the wheel, was Bob Anderson. His hands were at his sides and there was a pen between the thumb and forefinger of his right hand. His head was hung down facing his lap and there were blood stains from the back of his neck around and down the front of his shirt. It was not a large amount of blood and Clive noticed it seemed to come from the same area and the same type of wound as Roscoe Black. Placed on Bob's lap was his note pad. Just as Clive saw it, Alvin Richards who had just walked up with Bill Fry, spoke up, "Clive, look at what's on the note pad." Clive took his handkerchief out of his pocket and using it opened the door to get a better look. He leaned in and tilted his head to see the writing. Printed like stick men on the page was one line: "Local newsman found dead." It was underlined with a streak of Bob's blood.

CHAPTER 9

Thursday, June 17, 12:35 p .m.

It was well past noon when Clive, Brian and Alvin Richards finished what they could around the crime scene and turned it over to the crime lab. Alvin had sent two of his patrolmen to the fairgrounds to assist Collins. Clive had checked in with Alice and Duff but not much was happening at the station. As Clive was standing near Anderson's car talking to Brian, Bill Fry walked up and just stood there for a moment. When Clive had finished, Bill asked if Clive could join him at his vehicle across the lot. They both turned and walked slowly in that direction, leaving Brian standing there looking a little puzzled. About ten paces away from Anderson's car Clive turned around and spoke to Brian, "Brian, I will be leaving to go to that damn meeting with the commissioner in a short while. How about you finish up here and then go to the fairgrounds and see what's up. I'll talk to Alvin and ask for whatever help he can give you. Oh yeah, and I don't want anyone near any of the scenes until Bill's people are finished. Alvin told me he sent one of his people to see Mrs. Anderson so we won't need to do that. Don't give the press anything more than necessary and…"

Brian interrupted, "Clive, I got it. Go do what you need to do. I can deal with this. I've got a handle on it, remember?"

Clive answered, "Yeah, I'm sorry. I guess you're right. Carry on." Clive and Bill turned and continued across the lot to Bill's vehicle. They were met there by Alvin Richards. Clive looked at Bill and said, "Hold on one minute. Alvin, this one happened in your jurisdiction. I'm second seed here so whatever you need."

Alvin replied, "Clive, you know me. I'd rather work with you. We can accomplish more as a team –not as Smith Falls and the county."

"Okay, you're right about that. I guess I'm a little tired," Clive said as he leaned against Bill's vehicle.

"Tired?" Bill said cutting in. "You look exhausted, I think you need some time off."

"I agree," Alvin said. "You can't do it all. Let Brian take it for a few days. Take the weekend off. Brian, Bill and myself have worked together before."

Clive, putting his hands up, palms out as in a stopping motion, said, "Okay guys, I hear ya. I'll think about it, okay? Now can we get on with this, what was it you wanted to tell me, Bill?"

Bill looked around in all directions to check if anyone else was within hearing distance and when he was assured they were alone, he spoke. "Clive, I know you have a meeting with the commissioner this afternoon at his home—at 1:30 p.m., I believe?"

"And how did you know that?" Clive responded, looking a little surprised.

Bill was about to continue when Alvin cut in, "Hey, if this is private I'll just move back to help Brian, okay?"

"No," Clive said. "It's okay. Remember, we work together. Go ahead Bill, Alvin is in the need-to-know."

Bill started again, "All I want to tell you is watch your back."

"Watch my back?" Clive responded, looking surprised.

"Yeah," Bill said nodding the affirmative. "I overheard a conversation about the case this morning. Something's up and unfortunately I didn't get enough to know exactly what. It's something about the way the case is being handled and that you might need to have help or some such nonsense. There was also a mention of financial influence and the trouble it could cause. I don't know more. I wish I did; you know I hate that political bullshit as much as you do."

Clive, still looking somewhat puzzled, asked, "How did you overhear this?"

Bill looked around again then continued, "It's amazing what you can pick up if you decide to use the top brass's bathroom to take a shit. I overheard a conversation—or should I say part of a conversation—this morning. Those guys need to check out the stalls before they open up to someone. Never know who's listening. All I know is it was the commissioner and I believe someone from the state police. Don't know who for sure, didn't recognize the voice or see a face but I did see the uniform. Well anyway, I just wanted you to know." Bill paused for a second then looked at Alvin, "Alvin, you best keep an eye behind too. When it comes to politicians, who knows."

Alvin smiled and said, "Thanks Bill. I appreciate it."

Clive looked at Bill and then stuck out his hand and shook Bill's. "Thanks, buddy. Having people like you that I can call friend means a lot. I will watch my back, but they don't scare me much. I've gone a few rounds with them before."

"Yeah, you have, Clive," Bill said. "But you never had four murders in a little over a week before."

"He's right," Alvin said. "We need to be careful, maybe watch each other's backs, ya know."

"Yeah, okay. I know you're right," Clive responded.

"Well thanks again both of you."

"Sure, anytime," Bill said.

"Anytime," Alvin added.

There was a few seconds of silence then Clive said to Bill, "Can you give me anymore info on any of this before I go to that damn meeting?"

"Well," Bill said as he rubbed his jaw with his right hand. "You have all I gave you before on Jody Miller and Wesley Dans. Most of that hasn't changed but I can tell you now there is no doubt that the same weapon was used in both murders. Whatever it is it's sharp—like maybe a surgeon's tool, a scalpel, something like that. The cuts are clean—no marks like from a serrated edge, you know. Both Jody and Wesley bled out. I mean they knew what was happening at least for several seconds anyway. I talked to the guys at the fairgrounds and they tell me it appears that Roscoe died of a puncture to the left side of the neck near the spine. It's the same thing we have here with Anderson. Whatever the weapon was, it had a narrow thin blade about the size of a scalpel. It penetrated all the way to the spine. At least that's what we think now. Death was instantaneous with Roscoe and Anderson. They didn't bleed near as much as Jody and Wesley. There was, as you know, extensive bruising on Jody and Wesley but not on Roscoe and Anderson. Now, if you were to ask me if the same person killed all four, don't know for sure. Maybe after I get them to the lab I can tell you more. If you ask me my guess, I'd say Jody and Wesley were killed the same way for some reason. Roscoe and Bob, well, I think someone needed to shut them up. I'll bet we find that the weapon is the same—just used differently."

"Is that about it?" Clive asked.

Bill paused for a second then continued, "When I said for you both to watch your backs it's not just the politicians. Whoever we are dealing with knows exactly what they are doing. They are on top of this. The same as us, only they are several steps ahead. I can't tell you the reason anymore than you can tell me. What I can tell you is we are dealing with someone who has no conscience. They kill with no remorse, and believe me they are good at what they do. They leave no clues and not much in the way of evidence. I haven't seen crime scenes this immaculate in a long time. Sure there are some things we can go on but it's just bits and pieces. Whoever it is they are good at clean. If I can impress anything on you two it's this. This person is a calculating killer with no thought about whom they kill, whether it's for their unearthly objective or just to wipe someone out of the way. No one, not even you two, has immunity. So I say again, watch your back. Clive."

Alvin and Bill continued to talk for a few more minutes, then Clive, after looking at his watch, excused himself. He walked back to Brian who was talking to one of the crime lab people. "Brian, I've got to go to that meeting now. I'll stop at the station on the way out to the commissioner's house and check in with Alice. Do you need anything?"

Brian just shrugged his shoulders and said, "No Clive. I don't think so. Not at the moment."

Clive turned to walk away then turned back to Brian. "Oh yeah, I almost forgot. We need to get a list of names of the people who were at Posey's bar yesterday when we picked up Roscoe and ran off Bob. Someone heard or knew something about the two of them. I don't know what Roscoe knew if anything and I don't know what Bob got out of him but someone must have heard something and decided they needed to be silenced. Can you get that started for me? I can take over when I'm done with whatever the commissioner wants."

Brian said, "Sure, Clive, but how do we know that whoever killed them was connected to all of this or that they heard it at the bar?"

"Well," Clive said, pausing for a second. "I guess we don't know on both counts, at least not yet—but we may as well start there. We don't know who else Roscoe may have talked to or where. All we know according to Pete Waters is that Bob seemed to have first learned of whatever Roscoe knew there at the bar. Was Roscoe followed from somewhere else to the bar then Bob entered the picture? I don't know."

Brian agreed then added, "You know the bar was pretty crowded yesterday. I hope Pete can remember who was there, or maybe some of the waitresses might."

"Yeah, I hope so, Brian," Clive said, adding, "I was there and I didn't know some of the people myself. It may come to nothing but then again we may get lucky." Clive turned to leave again and almost ran into Bill Fry who had just walked up behind him.

"Hey Clive, I just got a call from my people at the fairgrounds. They say they're guessing Roscoe's time of death at about 7:30 p.m. yesterday, give or take an hour."

"7:30 p.m.," Clive repeated, looking at Brian. "That had to be just after you dropped him off wouldn't it?"

Brian, looking a little strange, said, "Yeah, well actually I'm not sure. May have been a little earlier than that. I don't know."

Bill Fry then added, "We put Anderson's time of death as close as we can between one-thirty and two o'clock this morning. That's maybe six or eight hours between. Whoever did this had time to think about it and carry it out—at least with Bob."

Clive repeated again that he had to go then thanked Bill and told Brian he would call him later. He left Brian at the car as the crime lab was removing the body and walked across the lot with Bill Fry. When they got to Clive's car, Clive told Bill to keep him and Alvin up to date as much as possible and thanked him again and left the scene headed for the station. He made a brief stop at his office to gather a few of his other notes and talk to Alice. It was close to 1:30 p.m. when he left and headed north on Route 55 toward the commissioner's house about ten miles from the Smith Falls township line. He radioed Alice and asked her to call the commissioner and tell him he would be a few minutes late.

He stopped at a mini-mart about five miles up the road and bought a small sandwich and a coffee, then drove the remaining five miles while eating his lunch. It was 2:00 p.m. when he pulled into the horseshoe driveway in front of the commissioner's house. It was a fairly large beautifully landscaped Tudor home with an attached three-car garage. It was just off Route 55, nestled against a backdrop of woods. When he parked the car he saw three other cars in the driveway: a state police car, a BMW, and a dark blue Lincoln Navigator with federal plates. He gathered some paperwork and rolled it together in a tube and placed a rubber band around it. As he got out of the car, still looking at the other three cars he whispered, "Now, just who do we have here?" He walked up the sidewalk and knocked on the door while looking back at the blue Navigator.

Several seconds later the door opened and he was greeted by the commissioner's wife, Ann. She was a short, thin, middle-aged woman, fairly good-looking and with meticulous silver hair. She smiled and said, "Well, hello Clive. It's been a while, come on in."

Clive stepped inside, removing his hat, and said, "Hello, Ann. Yes, it has been some time, and how are you?"

"Fine," she said. "No complaints. They are in Jack's study. Go ahead in. Can I take your hat?"

"No," Clive said. "I'll hang onto it. No problem." She excused herself and headed in the direction of the kitchen, but then turned and asked if he wanted anything to drink.

He told her just water would be fine and then he walked across the living room to a door at the other end that was just slightly opened. He could hear voices from inside as he stopped and gently knocked on the door. From inside a voice said, "Yes, come on in." Clive pushed the door open and entered. Seated behind a large oak desk across the room was Jack McCall, the county commissioner. To his left was the new state police captain for the district, Jim Terrell. Seated in two chairs to the right of the desk was George Miller, Jody's father. Next to him was a man Clive did not recognize. He appeared to be about six feet tall and had dark hair graying at the temples. He was dressed in a dark suit with a pale green shirt and perfectly tied tie.

Clive walked to the desk and Jack stood up and reached across to shake Clive's hand. As he did he introduced Terrell and Clive shook his hand. Terrell said, "Hi, we've met once before downtown. It's been a few years."

"Yes, I remember," Clive said.

Jack said, "Clive, of course you know George Miller." George Miller did not get up from his chair; he just looked at Clive and nodded. Then Jack said, "And I would like to introduce you to J.D. Ricketts of the F.B.I."

Ricketts slowly stood up and extended his hand to Clive. Staring Ricketts straight in the eyes, Clive said, "Yeah, I know who you are."

Ricketts responded with, "Yes, and I have heard of you."

Jack pointed to one of the chairs in front of the desk and said, "Have a seat, Clive." Terrell and Ricketts returned to their chairs. George Miller sat silently and stared at Clive. Jack spoke first, "Before we start gentlemen, I would like to know if what I heard a short time ago is true? Clive, was Bob Anderson found dead this morning?"

"Yes, unfortunately that is true," Clive said as he rolled the papers he had brought slowly through his fingers.

"Was he murdered or was it natural causes?" Jack said.

"It appears to be a murder," Clive responded.

George Miller sat forward in his chair and still staring at Clive said, "Now Bob Anderson. That's three. Oh you really got a handle on this one, Aliston."

Clive continued to sit calmly in the chair, then looking at Miller said, "No George, that isn't three. It's four. We also found Roscoe Black dead this morning, and yes, he was also murdered."

Terrell sat staring at Clive and whispered, "Four."

Jack McCall leaned forward on his desk and said, "My God Clive, four dead in ten days. What the hell is going on?"

"I'll tell you what the hell is going on," George Miller

said, still sitting on the edge of his seat. "What's going on is we need some professional help here. This is obviously too big for our local-yokel police force."

Jack turned to George. "George, calm down. I'm quite sure Clive is doing all he can."

George said, now looking angered at Jack, "If we had the right kind of police support in this county my little girl would be alive today. I'm surprised this hasn't happened before."

Terrell then spoke, "George, I've known Clive for quite some time. We don't work together but I know the quality work he has done here in the county."

"You're an ass, too," George said, now showing even more anger than before.

Ricketts, who had been sitting quietly, spoke. "George, sit back, take a break and calm down." George quickly turned and was about to chastise Ricketts when Ricketts said, "George, please."

George paused for a moment, then slid back in the chair and said, "Yeah, Yeah." Clive was still sitting quietly in the chair rolling the tube of paper in his hands.

Jack sat back in his chair and, slowly looking at each person, said, "Okay, I think we have vented enough anger here. We have a problem and we need cooler heads to prevail. We have four people who have lost their lives and…"

George jumped up from his chair and yelled, "I don't care about four people, I care about one—my daughter. I have to go to the funeral home tonight and look at a closed casket and all this sheriff tells us is we have two more dead and one's a drunk. Screw your news reporter, he was a dick and Roscoe—don't waste my time. Who killed my baby? I want answers. Now."

Jack McCall confronted George, "Sit down and calm down now."

"Don't tell me to sit down or calm down," George yelled. "If it wasn't for my support, you wouldn't even be in this cushy job, I practically."

"Practically, what?" Jack screamed back.

George was about to continue when Ricketts yelled over both of them. "Shut the hell up both of you." It took them both by surprise and they just stopped and stared at Ricketts. For a moment there was complete silence.

Jack and George both sat down as the study door opened and Mrs. McCall entered with a tray of drinks. They all remained silent as she passed drinks to each one of them. As she handed out each drink she said, "You're welcome." When the tray was empty she walked to the study door then turned and spoke. "Yes, you are all welcome for the drinks and now I'll just add one thing. Please, this is not Jack's office, it's our home. I trust you will act accordingly." She stood with the tray in her hand and stared at the group for a second or two, then turned and quietly left the room.

All five men sat silently for several seconds then Jack spoke, "Now, Clive, can you please tell us where we are in this investigation?" He turned to George. "George, as my wife said, please, let Clive answer." George didn't respond; he waved his hand in a go-ahead gesture.

Clive looked around at the four men while still rolling the papers in his hand. "What can I tell you now? We have four dead people: Jody Miller, Wesley Dans, Bob Anderson and Roscoe Black. Three were found dead within the county limits. The fourth, Bob, was found within the Smith Falls jurisdiction. The first three are my responsibility; the fourth is Alvin Richards'. They were all brutally murdered. My office, the crime lab and Alvin's office are working on it twenty-four/seven. They were all killed with some type of sharp instrument. At two of the four scenes we found— for whatever reason—the single word, "Forever." At this time we don't know what it means. We are moving in several directions with the investigation. For now that's all I can tell you."

George said sarcastically, "I got that much out of the

paper from that dick Bob Anderson. That's all you can tell us?"

Clive didn't look at George but instead stared at Jack. "Yes, that's all I can tell you right now. It's all I'm going to tell you as long as we have a civilian here at this meeting."

George jumped up again, "You son of a bitch, I have as much right to know what's going on as you do. My daughter is dead."

Before George could finish, Clive cut in, "Yes, George you do have the right and you will get to know after we catch the person responsible for these crimes. Anything we release too early may have a direct effect on the case. What I have is far too important to take a chance telling you or anyone who might tell someone else. As far as the four people now dead, they are all important: Jody, Wesley, Bob, and yes, even Roscoe." George's face was beet red.

Jack McCall spoke slowly and softly, "George, calm down."

George turned to Jack and clenching his teeth said, "No one, not even this tin badge sheriff tells me that some downtown drunk is as important as my Jody."

"Clive's right," Ricketts said as he sat in the chair staring at Clive.

Turning to Ricketts, George yelled, "What? I bring you here to get some professional help and you're going to side with Yosemite Sam."

Jim Terrell, breaking his silence, cut in before George could continue, "George, bringing all of us into this may help and it may not, but Clive and J.D. are right. We've got to keep this in-house. We can't afford to leak anything out. It can affect the way the person committing the crimes acts. It can change the flow of evidence. We let him or her know what we know and the whole picture changes. We can't allow that to happen."

George turned to Ricketts with a questioning look and said, "J.D."

Ricketts calmly said, "George, it's over. Go home. We'll

fill you in when we can."

George turned to McCall and Jack just shook his head. George started to walk toward the door then paused and turned back to the group. "Okay, you want to play games, play your games, but by God you better find out who's responsible for this. You don't and you all will wish you had picked a different profession. I don't play games." George turned and walked out the door. There were several moments of silence then they heard the BMW leave the driveway.

Jack McCall leaned forward and started to wring his hands, "Man, that guy is going to have a stroke one of these days."

Ricketts smiled and said, "He is a little pissed."

Clive looked at Ricketts and, using the paper tube, pointed at J.D., "And if it was your daughter, you wouldn't be?" Ricketts just shrugged his shoulders but didn't respond.

Jack McCall again asked Clive, "Okay, now what else do you have?"

Clive sat forward in the chair and handed Jack the tube of rolled papers. "It's all in there—at least what I can give you now."

Jack unrolled the papers and placed them on the desk and rolled them in the other direction to straighten them out. He got up and asked, "Do you mind if I copy these so we can all read them?"

"Not as long as I get all the copies back before I leave," Clive answered.

Jack walked to the corner to the copy machine and made two extra copies and handed one to Jim and the other to J.D. When all three of them had a copy they began to read, as Clive sat silently and sipped on his water. When they had finished Jack sat back in his chair and just whispered, "My God."

The meeting went on for another half hour. When they had discussed about all they could, Jack called for an end to the meeting and he gave his and Jim's copies back to Clive. As J.D. handed his copy to Clive he asked, "Don't I get to keep this?"

Clive took the papers and said, "If you need to see them stop by the station." J.D. just sat and smiled at him.

Jack asked Clive, "Is there anything you want to ask?"

Rolling the papers again, Clive said, "Yeah, just one question. What the hell are these two doing here?"

Jim Terrell slid forward in his seat and said, "Whoa, hold on Clive, I'm here only because I was asked. I'm not going to step on anyone's toes. You need my help, you got it—but only if you ask." Clive just nodded that the statement was accepted.

Jack spoke, "Clive, you've done a great job here since you've been in office but you haven't had to handle anything like this. I'm just a little concerned that..."

"That what?" Clive interrupted. "That, I'm not up to the job?"

"No of course not," Jack responded. "George and I just figured."

Clive cut in again, "Figured what, that this is too big for Yosemite Sam and his local yokels?" Before Jack could respond again, Clive stood up and placed his water on the edge of the desk. "I've been listening for the best part of two hours. Now it's my turn. First of all George has no place telling anyone in my department what's going to happen, money or no money. Second, I don't appreciate you bringing in anyone without talking to me first. Third, you cut my department twice and now when we need the help you bitch because we are moving too slow."

"But," was all Jack got to say.

"Fourth, if I need the state police or the FBI, I will be the first one to ask. When I need help, I ask for it. I don't need it shoved in my face. Number five, you appointed me to this job when Dan Walters died but I was elected in the last election just like you were. Like it or not the people said they wanted me here. If you want the FBI, the state police or any other agency involved, fine. I'll share information, I may even ask for help, but nobody, and I mean nobody, runs my investigation. If that's not good enough then you can have this gun and the badge and you can deal with the voters, not me. One more thing, the next time you want to call a meeting, you do it on county property by the book. I don't take to being leaned on or intimidated by money or power. Now, if that's all, I have more important things to attend to. That's unless you want to take me up on the gun and badge thing."

"No, no Clive, that's fine," Jack said as he stood up. "Go back to work. Calm down. I didn't mean to step on your toes. It's your investigation."

Clive turned and walked to the door of the study then turned back to Jack. "If you need to know anything else you know where to find me—on the job."

As Clive left the room, J.D. Ricketts got up, shook Jack's hand, then smiling said, "I'll handle him. Not to worry. I've dealt with guys like him before."

Jim Terrell stepped over to J.D., shook his hand and said, "Well, it's been interesting to say the least, and oh yeah— you haven't dealt with anyone like Clive. At least not yet." J.D. just laughed and walked to the door leaving Jack and Jim still talking.

When Clive got to his car he just sat there for a few minutes then he put the key in the ignition and whispered, "Politics."

Just as he started the car, J.D. Ricketts walked up to the car and leaned down to Clive's level and said, "You may be a tough old country boy but believe me, you're way out of your league on this one."

Clive looked at J.D. and smiled. "Yeah, city boy. You forgot one thing. You're in my country now."

CHAPTER 10

Thursday, June 17

It was close to 4:30 p.m. when Clive returned to the station. He stopped at Alice's desk and asked if Brian had come in. She told him he had started on a preliminary report but had left again to pick up some information from Pete Waters at Posey's Bar. As Clive walked away toward the men's room, Alice asked how the meeting went. Clive didn't even turn around; he just answered, "It sucked."

Several minutes later, when he returned from the men's room, Alice stopped him. Looking very puzzled, she said, "Clive, there is a woman on line two. She speaks with a kind of a southern accent and she says she wants to talk to you. She says her name is Kathryn Aliston."

Clive looked at Alice for a second then said, "Kathryn. I'll take it in my office. Hold on for a minute and no interruptions please."

"Okay," Alice said, still looking somewhat confused.

Clive entered his office and closed the door. He sat in his chair behind the desk and then just repeated, "Kathryn."

He pushed the button for line two and picked up the phone. "Hello, Kathryn?"

A woman's soft voice with a slight southern touch responded, "Hello, Clive. How are you doing?"

Clive paused for a second then responded, "I'm fine Kathryn, and how are you?"

She said, "I'm fine, but I don't think you are fine—at least not from what I've been reading in the papers here."

Clive sat back in his chair then asked. "You mean this story is in the papers all the way down to Mississippi?"

She responded with, "Yes, it's all over the news and in the papers. You really didn't think it would stay bottled up in that little backwoods town did you?"

"No, I guess not," Clive said. "I guess I just haven't had the time to think about it much. I've been kind of busy, if you know what I mean?"

"Yes, I can imagine," she said sarcastically. "And just how are you doing under all that pressure and don't tell me there is none. I know better. I was a cop's wife for a while remember?"

Clive smiled and said, "Yeah, I remember, and the pressure—well, I think I'll get by."

There was a pause then Kathryn continued, "You still try to put on that tough-guy no-one-can-push-my-buttons attitude, don't you? Well, I was your wife long enough to know the real Clive Aliston, and I know what really lies beneath that thick coat of Yankee armor you try to wear. Now, I'll ask you again, how are you doing?"

"I'm good, I mean, I've been better but I'm okay. I'm glad you called. It's good to hear your voice again. How's Amanda?"

Clive was on the phone for almost twenty minutes and when he finally hung up Alice buzzed him, "Clive, I'm leaving now, you need anything?"

"No, I'm good. See you tomorrow. Have a good night," he said, as he sat leaning on his elbows, his face half-buried in his hands.

When Alice got up to leave she stopped and knocked on his door. He looked up and motioned for her to enter. She walked to the front of his desk and said, "Clive you look tired. Go home and get to bed early. The night crew can handle things. You gotta get some rest."

"Yeah, I know. I've been told that before today," he said as he slid back into the chair again. "I think I will, I'll call Brian, Collins and Duff and then I'm out of here."

Alice asked, "The phone call. Are you okay, Clive?"

"Yeah, I'm okay, just a little unexpected," Clive said, smiling. "If you're wondering, it was my ex-wife, well actually, she's not my ex-wife. We never divorced."

Alice, now slowly backing up to the door, said, "Clive you don't owe me an explanation."

"Alice, it's okay," Clive said as he picked up the cigar he had placed on the desk earlier in the day. "Have a seat if you have a minute. Guess I could use someone to talk to right now."

Alice sat in one of the chairs in front of the desk then said, "Well, I have a few minutes, I guess. And what do you mean, wife? I never knew you were married. Well never mind, I shouldn't have asked. As I said, you don't owe me an explanation."

"It's okay," Clive said again. "I guess I just never said much to anyone. We were married about twenty-five years ago. I met her at a cop convention in Washington, DC. I was young and kind of gung ho about being in law enforcement. She was actually there with someone else, but as it turned out they weren't serious—or at least I didn't think they should be. We hit it off right away and before the weekend was over I guess I fell pretty hard."

Alice interrupted again, "Ah, Clive why are you telling me this? And why now?"

Clive paused for a moment as he rolled the cigar in his fingers. "Well I guess even old Clive Aliston has to get things aired out once in a while. I don't know why I never said anything. Guess sometimes it hurts a little more than I am willing to admit. Why now? I don't know why. I guess with all that's going on around here and now the phone call—I don't know, Alice. Sometimes I actually surprise myself. Jody Miller's murder kind of hit me hard. You see, I have a daughter about your age. You even remind me a lot of her."

"What's her name?" Alice asked.

"It's Amanda," Clive said, as he sat staring at the end of the cigar. "We, I mean me and Kathryn, dated for several months. I was working in Pennsylvania out near Philly on a local police force, and she was from Mississippi but she was working for a magazine in New York City. Well, Philly and the Big Apple, they're not too far apart. We dated whenever we could but then I got hired by the county police here and well you can guess the rest. I talked her into moving in with me, so we married. She got a job in Pittsburgh at one of the magazine offices right after that. Amanda was born about a year later and things went well for a while, then I almost got killed during a bank holdup. I think it scared the hell out of her. I think reality came knocking on the door. She was married to a cop and life could change in a matter of minutes. We stuck it out for another five years but she just couldn't be a cop's wife."

"Do you still love her?" Alice asked, now leaning forward in her chair.

"Yeah, I do Alice. I think I always will."

"Do you think she loves you?" Alice asked, smiling.

"Yeah, I think she does," Clive said, now smiling back at Alice. "She never remarried either. She became a businesswoman, a very prominent figure with the magazine. She and Amanda are back in Mississippi. I hear from them all the time and I see them once in a while. There are no hard feelings on either side. Kathryn explained it all to Amanda and we have a very good relationship, the three of us. Well as good as it can be seven hundred miles apart. I don't ever think about divorce and she's never asked. I guess it's the way it was meant to be. Maybe someday, who knows? Maybe we can get back together."

"What's Amanda do?" Alice asked. "She's a pharmacist-in-training I guess, don't know what they actually call it. She's happy, has a boyfriend. I met him; he's a really nice guy."

"Well," Alice said as she got up from the chair. "I guess I know now where you go when you disappear on those few vacations you take. I hope it all works out Clive."

"Thanks, Alice," Clive said as he slid forward in the chair. "As I said, maybe someday. Well I've kept you long enough. Thanks for letting me ramble on. I guess I talk too much sometimes."

Alice walked to the door then turned and said, "Clive, you're not only my boss, you're my friend. You need to talk, I'm here. I'm not Kathryn or Amanda but I can listen. Now get some rest. I'll see you tomorrow." She winked at him and smiled and left the office.

Clive picked up the lighter and was about to light the cigar then changed his mind and placed them back into the drawer. He watched as Alice walked away from her desk and out the door. He smiled and whispered, "Yeah, and I'm damn lucky to have a friend like you." Clive spent another half hour at his desk talking to Brian, then Duff and Collins. When he had finished he said goodnight to the evening crew and left the office. He went straight home, made a snack, and went to bed early, but sleep did not come easy. He rolled and tossed for almost an hour and when he finally got to sleep it was only for a few hours at a time. He just couldn't get the case off his mind. He also kept thinking about Kathryn and Amanda. He finally gave up at about four a.m., got up, made coffee and sat for a couple hours reading the crime lab information and the reports from Brian, Duff and Collins that he had brought home with him. It was six a.m. when he showered, dressed and headed back to the station.

Friday, June 18, 7:30 a.m.

When Clive arrived at the station he went straight to his office and checked for messages. Alice arrived with Rose about ten minutes later. He was reading over the partial report from Brian when Alice buzzed him. He answered, "Yes Alice, and good morning."

"Good morning, boss," Alice said, adding, "You sound a little better this morning. I'd guess you got some needed sleep last night?"

"No, as a matter of fact, I didn't," Clive responded. "Sleeping last night came in a close second to the suck meeting I had yesterday."

"Sorry I asked," Alice said sarcastically. "I got a note here on my desk from the night shift says you're to call Pete Waters at the bar as soon as you can. He has something he wants to tell you."

"Okay, Alice. Sorry I snapped at you," Clive said as he returned to his reading. About eight a.m. Clive left his office and stopped at Alice's desk. "Alice, I'm going to get some breakfast and then head over to Posey's to see Pete. When Brian comes in, have him call me please. There's a few things I want to ask him about."

As he turned to leave, Alice said, "Clive you forgot something."

"What?" Clive asked.

"The funeral. I assume you are going?"

Clive stood there for a moment with a blank stare on his face then said, "Yeah, I guess I did forget. Yes I'll be going. What about you?"

"I'm going, of course, and I thought I might go with you if you don't mind?"

"Of course not. What about Brian?" Clive asked.

Alice shook her head and said, "Clive, I don't know. I'll ask him when he gets in but he hasn't said a word. Maybe he won't or can't. I don't know where his mind is on that."

"Okay, what time?" Clive asked.

"We need to be at the church at one o'clock or just

before," Alice said.

Clive turned to walk away then stopped at the door, "Alice, if Brian is going, ask Collins to come in and handle the office. If not, then ask Brian to stay here."

Clive left the station, then drove to the diner on Route 55 and got some breakfast. At about 9:30 a.m. he arrived at Posey's bar and knocked on the front door but got no response. He walked around the side and rang the bell for Pete's apartment upstairs. About two or three minutes later, Pete Waters opened the door, looking like he just crawled out of bed. "Well Pete you look real good this morning," Clive said. "You fall out of bed or just have a little too much party last night?"

"Funny, Clive," Pete said sarcastically as he rubbed his head and eyes. "Come on up. I didn't expect you this early. Do you ever sleep?"

"Yes. From time to time," Clive said as he followed Pete up the steps.

When they got to Pete's kitchen he asked Clive if he wanted some coffee. As he poured them each a cup, Clive asked what it was that Pete wanted to tell him. "Well Clive, if I got this right, Bob Anderson was killed around two a.m. yesterday?"

"Yeah," Clive said. "And how did you find that out already?"

Pete looked at Clive over his coffee cup and said, "Clive, it's a bar like I said before. It's like the barbershop, or a beauty parlor; any and all news goes through here. Besides, it was mentioned in the paper."

"Okay, yeah, it was about two a.m.," Clive said. "Why?"

Pete sat down at the table then said, "Well, I actually wanted to give you a couple more names that I remembered after I talked to Brian yesterday. I have them written down. I'll give them to you before you leave. After I called the station last night I did remember one other thing and it sort of freaked me out."

"What would that be?" Clive asked.

"Well," Pete said, pausing to sip the coffee. "Bob was in the bar night before last at close to midnight. That couldn't have been more than two hours before he was killed. "Ain't that some shit?"

"Two hours before?" Clive repeated.

"Yeah," Pete said. "I'm surprised Brian didn't mention it to you."

"Mention it to me?" Clive said, now looking puzzled.

"Well, Brian was here when he came in," Pete added. "They almost got into it. I didn't exactly break anything up but I did say something."

"What happened?" Clive asked as he held his cup with both hands and took a sip.

"Well, Bob lit out of here like he was scared to death of Brian. Don't know where he headed," Pete said as he got up and picked up a slip of paper from the countertop.

"What did Brian do?" Clive asked.

"I guess he left several minutes later. I really didn't see him go but he was gone." Pete then handed Clive the list of names. "I just can't believe he was dead not two hours later. Man that does freak me out."

Clive and Pete talked for a few more minutes then Clive thanked Pete for the information and the coffee and went back to the car. After he started the car he pulled out to the edge of the lot and waited for traffic to pass. As he did he looked at the slip of paper Pete had given him, then placed it on the seat. As he pulled out onto the highway he whispered to himself, "Brian, Brian, Brian."

Clive didn't go back to the station right away. Instead he drove to the Smith Falls Police Station and talked to Alvin Richards for about half an hour. After they traded some information they discussed Jody's funeral, and how they would help each other handle the expected large crowd, and of course the press and the media that would undoubtedly be there. It was close to eleven a.m. when Clive left Smith Falls and drove back to the county station.

He parked in front then spoke to several of the night shift officers that had been called to help with the funeral. He had just finished talking to them in the parking lot and was walking up the front steps when Brian came out the door. He stopped on the top step and asked, "Brian where are you headed now?"

"Well I heard from Alice that Pete called and maybe had some other information. I was going to go over there and check it out," Brian said with a strange look on his face.

"And Alice didn't tell you I was already there?" Clive asked.

"Yeah, she did," Brian said, now sounding a little uncertain of himself. "I just, well I just…"

Clive interrupted, "You just what?"

Brian didn't say anything for several seconds; he just stood and stared off to his right. "Just what?" Clive said again sternly.

Brian turned back to Clive, now with a look of anger rather than uncertainty. "I just don't think I can do this. I mean I don't think I can go to the funeral. I don't know. Hell, I don't know what I mean."

"Calm down Brian," Clive said, with a little less forcefulness in his voice. "If you don't want to go then don't go. You can stay here and keep an eye on things. Personally, I think you will regret it if you don't go. But then that's just me talking. Whether you go or not you and I have something to talk about." Clive paused, then added, "Today."

"Now what?" Brian said, still looking somewhat unnerved. "It's about the night Bob Anderson died," Clive said as he started toward the front door.

"What about that night?" Brian asked.

Clive paused at the door, then said, "Brian let's go back inside and deal with this funeral thing first. We can talk later." Brian said nothing but just followed Clive into the station. When they got inside they stopped at Alice's desk and Clive asked Alice if she was ready to go. She said she was and then asked Brian if he was going. Brian said nothing, then Clive asked again, "Well, Brian do you want to go or not?" Brian again didn't answer he just half turned away from them both and shook his head.

Alice stepped out from behind her desk and walked to Brian's side. She could see tears welling up in his eyes as he looked away from them both. She said, "Brian…"

Brian interrupted, "Yeah, I know Alice. It will probably do me good to go. I should go, I know that, but I don't know if I can. It's more than just Jody. It's also my father. He's handling the funeral and you both know we don't talk much. He and I haven't had much to say since I left high school."

Clive interrupted, "Brian, Alice and I will go in my car. You follow in yours. I think you need to at least try to do this. If you get there and well, you can't, then at least you tried." Brian shook his head yes, reluctantly, then said he would wait outside and left the station. Alice asked Rose to take the radio calls and then she and Clive also left the station. When they got outside, Brian was already waiting in his car.

Alice stopped at the top of the steps and said, "Clive, this has to be hard on him. Jody's death has apparently affected him more than we thought and you and I both know that he and his father have had very little in the way of a relationship. Stop and think about it. How would you feel in his place?"

"Okay, Alice," Clive said. "I got you. You're right; I'll give him credit for even agreeing to go. But you and I both know it will be better for him if he faces up to this. I'm not trying to be hard on him; I guess I just have a few other things on my mind right now. Let's go and get this over with. Maybe it will be alright once we get there." They walked to Clive's car then left the station lot with Clive in the lead. They arrived at the First Baptist Church at just before one p.m. and the parking lot and the streets for blocks around were packed with cars. The city police waved them into a lot across the street from the church that had been set aside for the other police cars. As they started to cross the street they were met by the media and the press that had gathered on that side. Clive just waved them off, totally ignoring their questions and the flash of cameras. When they reached the other side of the street they were met by Alvin Richards. Clive spoke to Alvin for several seconds while pointing to the media on the other side of the street. They then walked to the front steps of the church and Clive stopped again to talk to one of the night crew people from his station. After several minutes the three of them entered the church. They walked through the foyer and entered the worship area.

Just inside, Brian stopped and said, "Clive, I'll be here in the back, you go ahead."

Clive just nodded, "Okay," and he and Alice moved to the first available seats near the center. Brian did not take a seat but instead stood in the back against the wall. Several minutes later, after the church was filled to capacity, the casket was rolled in by Paul Lasiter, followed by eight pallbearers. As they entered, Paul looked around and saw Brian standing in the back. Brian saw him at the same time. Brian stared at him and Paul nodded in recognition. The casket was moved to the front and was followed by George Miller, his wife, and several other members of the family. As they passed the section where Clive and Alice were seated, George Miller stared at Clive with an almost angry look on his face. As they passed, Clive realized that sitting almost across from them was J.D. Ricketts, who was also staring at Clive—only he was smiling. Clive diverted his attention to the front as the preacher stepped to the podium and began to speak. Several minutes later Clive turned to the back of the church to where Brian was standing, but he was gone.

After the service ended, Clive and Alice stopped outside again and talked to Alvin Richards for several minutes. While they were talking, Commissioner Jack McCall and

J.D. Ricketts walked past them and across the street and into the crowd of media and began to talk. Clive and Alice cut their conversation short and crossed the street to the lot, got into Clive's car and pulled out. Some of the media noticed that they were leaving and attempted to get Clive's attention but he ignored them and slowly drove up the street and back to the station.

When Alice and Clive arrived at the station they found Brian in the lunchroom, sitting with a cup of coffee and staring at the blank wall. Clive and Alice each got a cup of coffee and Alice went back to her desk. Clive asked Brian, "Are you okay?" Brian just nodded that he was and said nothing. As Clive turned to leave the room he said, "Brian, when you're ready, I need to see you in my office, please."

"Okay," Brian said as Clive walked away toward his office. Clive had been in his office for about ten minutes when Brian knocked on the door and entered.

"Have a seat," Clive said pointing to the chairs at the front of his desk. Brian sat down but said nothing. Clive sat back in his chair, paused for a second or two, then said, "Brian, I know this has been a bad day for you, I can imagine how you feel."

Clive was about to continue when Brian cut in, "Clive, I appreciate how you feel but there is no way you or anyone else knows how I feel."

"But," was all Clive got to say when Brian cut in again.

"First of all, as I said, Jody might not be dead if I had balls enough to talk to her that night. Second, we are no closer now to finding out who did this than we were the first day. Third, I feel like I'm treading water here. I guess the frustration is getting to me a little. That's why I guess I let Anderson get to me the other day. It's like this is my fault and I can't find any answers."

Brian paused for a minute and Clive cut in. "Brian, none of this is your fault and as far as the frustration, we are all feeling it. This is the first time any of us has dealt with a case like this. If you don't believe me just ask J.D. Ricketts.

He'll be more than glad to remind you."

Brian got up and started to pace back and forth. "It's not just Jody today. It's all of it. The thing with my dad; the whole deal."

Clive leaned forward in his chair and put his elbows on his desk, "Brian, sit down please. It's time we talk about all of this. What's on your mind beside Jody and this case? I'm not just your boss; I'm trying to be a friend. Sometimes people need someone to listen. Just ask Alice. She had to listen to me not too long ago."

Brian returned to his seat then took a deep breath. "Thanks, Clive," he said as he slid down into the chair. "Like I said, it's the thing with Jody, the case and the deal with my father. I guess sometimes we think we are tough but then we find ourselves alone with nowhere to turn. It's what I feel now. I've got no real family around other than my dad. As you know my mother died several years after my sister's birth. Some kind of complication related to another birth. I was too young to remember. Me and my dad never did hit it off much. He was always partial to Victoria, my sister, as you know. She died in an accident while in high school and I don't know why but it almost seems he blames that on me. I left home right after graduation. The thing that got me was when he decided to pay for my schooling. Maybe he felt guilty or some such thing. I don't know. He got in contact with me and set up the whole thing. I guess I thought he had changed but then after I came back from school it all went back to the way it was. I haven't been in that house in over five years. He lives there alone in that big place and there I am in an apartment not three miles away and we never talk. Sorry to lay all this on you Clive. I guess it's been coming for a long time."

"It's fine," Clive said. "We all need a friend to talk to now and then. Just don't let this interfere with your job. You're a good cop. You have a future here. I know family problems and the loss of someone close is a real bad deal, but don't throw away what you have. Stop and think about it this way, Jody wouldn't have wanted you to do that and if we asked your dad I doubt he would either."

Brian sat quietly for several seconds then said, "Yeah, I guess."

There was silence for a few seconds then Clive said, "And speaking of the job, I've got something I need to talk to you about. Why didn't you tell me you were at Posey's when Bob Anderson came in the night he died?"

"How did you find out about that?" Brian said as he sat up straight in the chair.

"I found out from Pete Waters this morning," Clive said. "And don't get the idea he was talking behind your back or anything like that. He just happened to mention it when he gave me the few extra names for the list of people in the bar the day before Roscoe and Bob died."

"Well, what exactly did he say?" Brian asked.

"He said you two didn't have a confrontation but that you scared the hell out of Bob and he left," Clive said as he opened the top drawer of his desk and retrieved a piece of paper. "What exactly came down, Brian?"

"Nothing came down, Clive," Brian said, looking a little frustrated.

"I mean I didn't do anything. I just realized he had come back to try and bleed Roscoe for more information. You should have seen him checking out the whole bar, trying to see if he was there."

"And what time was that Brian?" Clive asked.

"I don't know, Clive. Close to midnight I guess. I'm not sure," Brian said, still looking a bit nervous.

"Okay, Brian, tell me what happened after you left Roscoe. I may need to know this on down the road here," Clive said as he rolled the paper in his hand.

"Need to know? For what reason, Clive? Don't you trust me?" Brian asked as he slid to the edge of his seat.

"Brian, don't get excited. I'm not accusing you of anything. I just need to understand what came down here. Now, again what happened after you left with Roscoe?"

Brian paused for a minute to collect his thoughts. "I left with Roscoe and took him to the fairgrounds. That's where he wanted to go for the night. He said something about having a room there in the shed near the carousel. Some kind of deal he had with the groundskeeper or something. I took him there and watched him till he got to the shed and inside. He had trouble with the lock and he could hardly stand up so I went up to the shed and checked on him before I left. He was already on his bed and passed out by the time I walked from the car. He was fine when I left him."

"And how did you get back to Posey's?" Clive asked.

"Well, my shift was over and I decided to stop and get supper," Brian said, now looking a little more relaxed. "I got something to eat then decided to play pool and have a few drinks. And yeah, I know what you said before. I just needed to relax a little is all. I didn't really expect to stay as long as I did. I guess I just needed some time to think. I don't know."

"Well what about this Bob thing?" Clive asked.

"As I said, I was playing pool when I looked up and saw Bob come into the bar. Guess I should have just played the game but I didn't."

"And then?" Clive asked. "I noticed he was looking for someone," Brian said as he stared at Clive. "I just knew it had to be Roscoe. I guess it sort of pissed me off, that maggot reporter sneaking back after we left. Anyway, I didn't touch him. I just let him know that I knew what he was doing. I didn't think he would just take off like that— and Pete didn't break up anything. He just told us to cool it."

"Didn't say he did," Clive said.

"Well, after he left, I left," Brian said as he slid back into the chair. "I didn't follow him or anything. I just went home."

Clive sat for a few seconds just looking at Brian, then he said, "Brian do you see how this looks?"

"Looks, looks like what Clive?" Brian said, now

somewhat angered.

"Hold on Boy," Clive said. "Let me finish and then you think about it. You are, as far as we know, the last one to see Roscoe alive. Then you and Bob have this thing at Posey's in front of Pete and a few other people. He leaves, then you leave, and he's found dead the next morning. Come on Brian, how do you think that looks?"

"I didn't do anything," Brian said as he stared at Clive. "And for God's sake I wouldn't murder anyone."

Clive took a deep breath then continued, "Brian, I trust you and of course I believe you. I know you didn't murder anyone, but if you didn't have that badge, and you were me, how would it look to you? I mean, come on, you can't tell me this looks good. I didn't ask you any of this because you're a suspect or anything like that. I just needed to know what came down in case I'm asked. Like Pete says, next to a beauty salon or a barber shop the next best place to hear anything is a bar."

Brian looked away from Clive to the wall to the left and said nothing for a few seconds. He then turned back to Clive and asked. "You want me off the case?"

"No," Clive said. "I don't want you off the case. Some people might do it that way, but I don't. I'm just trying to get you to see, we are in the middle of the investigation of our lives here. We have four dead, very little in the way of good evidence, no suspects, and now the county commissioner and the public are on our backs. The people are scared and I don't blame them. The commissioners wants answers, the families want answers and now we got Mr. FBI hanging around. The last thing I—we—need is to give them something else to grab a hold of, like my second-in-command is now a suspect. Brian, you're a good cop. You do a good job. As I said, you have a future here but get used to the idea that on or off duty you're in the spotlight. Someday you may sit in this chair or one like it, and when you do and I'm quite sure you will, you'll see things from a whole different perspective. You've made mistakes, and

Lord knows I did too. The key is to recognize them then don't repeat. Remember, one thing about leadership, the only leaders qualified to lead are those who have learned to serve."

Brian said nothing. He looked down at the front of Clive's desk and took a deep breath. After a few seconds he looked back up at Clive. "You're right boss. I guess I messed up. I've been feeling a little too sorry for myself. That's going to stop. I'll make no excuses. That's a waste of my time and yours. No more kidding myself. This is more than personal. I will get my head screwed on right. Now if I'm still on the case, what's our next move?"

Clive handed Brian the slip of paper he was holding, then smiled and said, "You're still on the case. What's next, Well, that's the additional list of names from the bar that Pete gave me this morning. I think you and I should go over the entire list and eliminate anyone who couldn't possibly have committed the crimes due to age or whatever. Then I say we split the list three ways, you me and Duff or Collins and start to check these people out."

He was about to continue when Alice buzzed him and said that Jack McCall was on line two. "This should be good," Clive said sarcastically as he picked up the phone. "Hello Jack this is Clive, what can I do for you?" Clive didn't speak he just listened for several minutes then he said, "Okay Jack and thanks for that. But just remember what I told Ricketts. I'll work with anyone, but this is my investigation. I understand, just so you understand. Yes I will keep you informed. Thanks again; talk to you later." Clive hung up the phone and looked at Brian with a surprised look on his face.

Brian said, "What?"

Clive shook his head then said. "He just told me we are getting some help. They are bringing in some county boys from some of the other districts because he knows we are short-handed. I wonder who got on his back? All he wants to do is pinchpennies and now he's going to pay for additional help. Imagine that."

"What about the Ricketts part?" Brian asked.

"Guess we got to put up with him, but he says he understands about the investigation, that Ricketts will work with us. We'll see. Now let's go over this list and then we'll split up and cover as much as we can the rest of the day." Brian and Clive spent another half hour going over the entire list, and then got a message to Collins to meet them in the station lot to split up the list. It was three-thirty p.m. when they walked out the front door of the station house. They stopped for a second or two at the top of the steps.

Brian took one part of the list and Clive another. Brian looked out toward the lot looking for Collins when a large, dark blue car, a new Buick, pulled in and parked. It had a license plate bracket and sticker that read Enterprise Rental Car. Clive was still talking about the list and who would be home after work or at the bar when Brian's face went blank, almost as if turned to stone. His attention was now not on Clive, or what he had to say. It was as if he didn't hear anything Clive was saying. Clive, realizing Brian was looking elsewhere, turned toward the lot to see what Brian was intently studying. Brian's eyes were fixed on the man who had just gotten out of the car and was walking to the front steps of the station. He was tall, maybe six foot three, about two hundred twenty-five pounds, with light brown hair. When the man, dressed in an expensive gray business suit, was halfway up the steps, Brian stepped past Clive to the edge of the top step and with a surprised look on his face said, "Doc Watson, what the hell are you doing back in this town?"

CHAPTER 11

Doc stopped on the next to last step and stared directly into Brian's eyes, "Well, if it isn't Brian Lasiter, super cop. You still got your ass stuck in this backwoods hicktown. I'd of figured you'd be in D.C. or some such place. Would have bet you'd be some big FBI agent by the way you talked years ago. I guess small potatoes are always gonna be small potatoes, eh Lasiter?"

Brian didn't show any emotion; he just asked again, "What the hell are you doing back in Smith Falls?"

Clive didn't say a word. He just watched as Doc stepped up the last step. "Well Lasiter, I don't see how what I'm doing here is any of your business. It's just like the old days. Your business and mine don't belong on the same page."

Clive looked at Brian, expecting some type of reaction, but Brian remained calm and said, "Doc, once more, what are you doing here?"

Doc was about to answer again when Clive cut in. "Look guys, I see you know each other and first impression is, it ain't a good relationship."

Brian looked at Clive and said, "It's okay Clive. I'm cool."

Doc laughed and looked at Clive and asked, "Who the hell are you?"

Clive turned to face Doc and answered directly, "I'm the sheriff here, and Brian is my lieutenant, and when he asks a question I expect to get an answer. Now I'll ask. Who are you and what are you doing in Smith Falls?"

Doc, looking somewhat angered, said, "Look, Chief I haven't broken any of your laws here. I'm in town on business, personal business, and unless you got a legal reason, as I said, ain't none of your business."

Clive stopped Brian as he tried to speak, then continued. "First, I'm not a chief, but I am the law here and if Brian thinks he needs to know what's coming down then I suggest you answer."

Doc looked back at Brian then said, "Okay super cop, you want to know what I'm doing here, fine. I'm in town to take care of some of my mother's business and to sell the house. If you remember she died six months ago. I'm here to take care of the estate. That good enough? It still ain't none of your damn business."

Still looking quite calm, Brian said, "I heard about your mother and I am sorry. She was a good woman. If that's it, fine, but we don't need any of your other business here in this town. We've seen enough of that years ago."

"What the hell's that supposed to mean?" Doc said as he took a step toward Brian. Clive stepped forward almost between them.

Brian did not move but stared at Doc and said, "You know exactly what business I'm talking about, and don't use that tough guy bullshit here. It doesn't work. Or maybe you got that big boy with you. That big bodyguard that you keep chained to your side." Doc's face started to turn a light shade of red as Brian stood calmly and stared back at him.

Doc, now noticeably upset, said, "No, I don't have my big boy with me. I don't need him to take you. I didn't need him years ago to take your ass. Why would I need him now?"

Clive put up both hands toward Brian and Doc, "Okay guys that's it." He looked at Doc and said, "You got business here, fine. You go ahead, but I can see the sooner you're finished the better." Brian didn't say a word he just continued to calmly stare at Doc. "Is there something here at the station that I can help you with?" Clive asked, looking at Doc.

"No man, I don't need your help or his. I just need to get some information about my mother's deed. I was told I could find something out here at the annex. What I don't need is your harassment. Now, if it isn't too much trouble, it's getting late and I need to go."

Brian looked at Doc, smiled and said, "Go Doc, go."

Clive motioned Doc toward the front doors and said, "Go ahead." As Doc walked away toward the station doors he kept staring at Brian. Once he was inside the building, Clive turned to Brian and asked, "What the hell was that all about?"

Brian looked out toward the lot as Collins pulled his patrol car into a parking place, then said, "Come on, Clive. There's Collins. I got something to tell you about. I think we may just have our first break." Brian started down the steps followed by Clive, who had a puzzled look on his face. When they reached the patrol car, Collins had just gotten out. Brian looked at Collins and said, "Get back in." Brian told Clive to get into the back seat. He got into the front passenger seat. Brian turned in the seat so he could look at Clive. Collins was staring at Brian with a, "what-are-we-doing" look on his face.

Before Brian could speak, Clive asked again, "Brian what the hell was that all about?"

Brian said, "At first I couldn't believe who I saw coming up the steps. I haven't seen Doc in a couple of years"

"Who is he?" Clive asked.

"Who is he?" Brian repeated. "He's about the biggest drug dealer in the Chicago area."

"Drug dealer?" Clive said, surprised. "What's he doing here?"

"He lived here," Brian said. "I mean he was born here, and grew up here. He graduated from Smith Falls High School, same class as Jody and Wesley."

"You saw him a couple of years ago?" Clive asked.

"Yes, in Chicago," Brian said. "I was there to pick up a prisoner. Might have been three years ago. Before you took over. I'm not sure. I was there over a weekend and I ran into him at a club. It wasn't any better than our meeting today. He and I never did hit it off. I'm two, almost three years older than him and I dated Jody for about two years before he came into the picture."

"He came into the picture?" Clive asked.

"Yeah," Brian said, looking at Collins. I dated Jody for about, as I said, two years. Then we broke it off and he started to date her. Like I said, he is from her graduating class. It lasted maybe six months and then they split and I guess it was pretty ugly. I started dating Jody again right after that and that's when the trouble started between us. I guess when you're Davy Doc Watson's girl you don't dump him—especially for some future cop."

"Watson?" Clive said, surprised. "Not Agnes Watson's boy?"

"Yes, Agnes Watson's boy," Brian said, looking back at Clive.

"She was a great lady," Clive said, "And her husband George, I hear, was a prominent doctor in town."

"Yes, he was," Brian said. "He died about fifteen or twenty years ago, I don't remember. All I know was it was before we graduated."

"Well, you broke it off with Jody again didn't you?" Clive asked.

"Yeah, I did. Or should I say, we did," Brian said. "I

guess we drifted apart after I graduated and she was still in school. I hear Doc tried a couple of dates with her again but I guess nothing came of it. Why hell, he even tried to date my sister. That is, till my Dad found out. By that time he was ready to graduate. Just about everyone in town knew he was a minor league drug dealer. Well everyone except his mom, I guess. He was arrested here right after he graduated on drug charges, but was put on probation for a first offense. It almost cost him a chance at college."

"How did he get to Chicago?" Collins asked.

"That's where he went to school," Brian said, turning back to Collins. "He got in and did quite well for maybe a year. I heard he was planning on being a doctor. It may even have been two years, I don't really know. Anyway, I guess he never was that far from the drug culture even then. Wasn't long before he was in trouble again—only this time it landed him in jail for six months and they booted him out of college."

"How did you find all of this out?" Clive asked.

Brian, looking back at Clive, said, "Clive, like you said— what don't you hear in a bar? It's where I ran into him in Chicago. After we had our little confrontation I met one of his old girlfriends that he dumped. Had a long conversation with her over a couple of drinks. That's when I was warned about the bodyguard."

"Yeah, what about the bodyguard?" Clive asked.

"Well, I'll get to that, but first let me finish." Brian said. "I guess after he was released from prison he sort of disappeared for a while. When he showed up back on the scene he was in expensive suits and big cars, with lots of women and big money. I guess he found a way into the drug business in Chicago and he must have made the right connection or impressed somebody. I hear that with his good looks—the light hair and the year-round tan, he's called the surfer. Some nickname for a backwoods Pennsylvania boy, huh? He's been on the most-wanted lists of half a dozen law enforcement agencies. Trouble is he always seems to get off. His lawyer must be worth every penny he pays him. I also hear that a few people who got in his way have conveniently disappeared. Just can't seem to pin much on him. Don't think there's much small-town boy left in him. He got real big-town real fast. Hell, even Ricketts would like to nail this one. Be one big feather in his hat."

"And why do you think this is a break for us?" Collins asked.

"Yeah, why?" Clive asked. "And what about the bodyguard?"

"The bodyguard?" Brian said. "I saw the bodyguard when I was in Chicago. He's an ex-wrestler and man is he huge. I mean this guy is a proverbial mountain. He isn't much on smarts; guess he's a little slow. Some say he was always that way, that the promoter took advantage of him. I guess Doc rescued him from all that. That's if you want to call being with Doc rescued. He's been with Doc ever since. Right there by his side, ready to do whatever he wants."

Clive just shook his head and said, "Now, I see what you mean by a break."

"Yeah," Brian said. "You got Doc back in town. He knew Jody and, oh yeah, Wesley too. I forgot about that. Wesley was one of Doc's flunkies that followed him around all through high school. You add the big bodyguard; well, what's it sound like to you?"

There were several seconds of silence then Collins asked, "Well what do we do?"

"What do we do?" Clive repeated. "Well, first we can't just assume it's him even if it sounds this good. We have only a really good scenario. We have no proof. But you're right Brian, this is the most promising thing to come up so far. I think a change in plans is due. Forget the three of us tracking down the people on the bar list. We do need to cover that but not all three of us. Collins, you and me are going to split the list. We'll cover some of them tonight. Remember, anyone who doesn't have a good alibi for the night Roscoe and Bob were killed, I want called in for questioning. Brian you got a new assignment. That is—if you want it," Clive said, with a sort of half smile. "You got Doc, stay on him twenty-four/seven. I want to know his every move."

Brian smiled back, "You got it boss. Be my pleasure."

"Okay Brian, you need some sleep too," Clive said, adding, "Pick someone from the night shift to take your place when you're off. You pick whoever you want. We are getting help from some of the other stations, probably starting tomorrow. So things should loosen up here. Brian, just remember one thing. All past grievances with Doc aside. He's just a suspect like anyone else. Watch what you do. Like you said, he's got a good lawyer. We can't afford to screw up. Unfortunately he's still innocent until we find out otherwise. Now Brett, you start on your half of the list. If you need me, call—otherwise I'll see you in the morning. Brian, you follow Doc and stay on him. When you need replaced, call. I'm going to cover the other half of the list but first I need Alice to check out a few things about Doc. I'll see you two in the morning. You need anything, call. I don't care what time, just call." Clive got out of the car and headed back into the station.

Collins took his half of the list and left the station lot, headed for the first address. Brian left his marked patrol car in the lot and got into his personal car that was equipped with a radio. He left the lot and pulled across the road to the coffee shop parking lot and waited, watching the blue Buick still sitting in the station lot.

Clive asked Alice to work over for an hour or two to call the airlines and Enterprise Car Rental to check on Doc Watson. If he had flown into Pittsburgh and rented the car there, they would have a record of his time of arrival. Clive took his half of the list, left the station and drove to the first address. Clive and Brett covered several addresses and Brett stopped at Posey's and talked to some of the people who had gone there for happy hour. It was close to nine o'clock when Brett went home, and Clive was home at about ten o'clock.

Brian wasn't so lucky. He waited in the coffee shop lot until Doc came out, and followed his car into Smith Falls to the Bradley Funeral Home. He waited outside for about an hour until Doc came out with Mr. Bradley. They talked for several minutes outside, then Doc handed something to Mr. Bradley and they shook hands and Doc left. Brian followed Doc to Bartolli's Restaurant in Smith Falls. It was the most expensive eatery in town. Brian waited outside for nearly two hours while having a McDonald's burger and fries. When Doc left the restaurant he headed to the north end of town and up Tower Hill Road. The road was a windy two lane that led up hill to the highest point in town. Near the top, facing the lights of the town below was the Watson family home. It was a large, old masonry structure with an eerie, almost Gothic look. Doc turned up the long driveway that led off the road and up to the house near the top of the hill. Brian passed the driveway and parked about two hundred yards up the road at the edge of some trees where he could still look up and see the house. It was 9:30 p.m. and almost dark. The lights came on at the house and stayed on until about midnight then all went dark. Brian stuck it out till almost one o'clock but he needed sleep. He called for a replacement, and when he arrived, Brian went home.

Saturday, June 19, 7:00 a.m.

Clive, Brian and Brett met at the station for a few minutes to exchange notes, then Clive and Brett started out on the lists again and Brian went to relieve his night shift replacement. He arrived at the Watson stakeout at about eight a.m. and was told that nothing had happened all night. No one left or came to the house. He sat in his car until almost eleven a.m. The dark blue Buick came down the driveway out onto Tower Hill Road headed for town. Brian followed Doc to a small restaurant on Main Street: Patsy's. Doc was in the restaurant for about an hour. When he left, he walked to the cleaner's on the corner, and a few minutes later came out with several suits on hangers. He got in his car and then headed out of town toward the city, with Brian on his tail. Brian followed Doc all over the city, from the courthouse to restaurants, clothing stores and jewelers. It was 5:30 p.m. when Doc finally headed back to Smith Falls.

Clive had gone to Bradley's Funeral Home on the information Brian had given him. He found out that Doc had stopped to pay Mr. Bradley for the headstone and burial of his mother several months before. Doc had moved his mother to Chicago a year before, when she had become sick. She had died in Chicago and a memorial service was held there. Her body was sent home for burial in the family plot next to her husband. Doc did not accompany her body back and Mr. Bradley had just been paid for handling the arrangements. Late Saturday, Brett, Collins and Clive finished with their lists. Brian, still following Doc, got back into town about 6:30 p.m. Doc again stopped at Bartolli's for supper while Brian waited outside. While waiting, Brian called the station and asked if Bill Tomson had come in. Bill was the night shift officer Brian had picked to work with him on the Doc Watson tail and stakeout. Bill had been off the day before but was back on duty. Brian told him he would call if and when he needed him.

At about 8:30 p.m., Doc left Bartolli's and drove back to the house. Brian parked his car again just behind the trees, then, realizing how tired he was, called for Bill Tomson to come up and take over. It was about 9:30 p.m. when Bill arrived and Brian left for home. At ten o'clock, Bill saw lights coming down the driveway that turned out onto Tower Hill Road. He waited until the taillights disappeared around a bend in the road then began to follow. About halfway down Tower Hill Road was an intersection, a four-way. He watched as Doc's car stopped then continued on through toward town. Bill pulled up to the stop sign as he saw Doc's taillights disappear over the hill. He was about to pull out when a car stopped at about the same time from the left. He started to move and the other car did also. He jammed on his brakes and the other car swerved to the left. At the same instant a car came from the right at high speed and never stopped at the stop sign. It smashed into the car in front of him, spinning it around facing in the opposite direction. The other car veered off the road and drifted head-on into a tree. Bill pulled his car to the side of the road and called on the radio for an ambulance. He put the portable flashing light on top of the unmarked car and ran to the car in the middle of the road. Inside were two teenagers: a boy and a girl. Both seemed to be unhurt. He then ran to the car against the tree and found an unconscious pregnant woman. He checked her pulse then ran back to his car and called again for help. He called the station. The desk officer answered and he told him he had lost the tail on Doc and that he needed help.

Saturday, June 19, 10:00 p .m.

Bobby Rodgers had just arrived home from a long day at work in the computer store on Route 55, just outside of Smith Falls. Bobby was twenty-seven years old. He was a short man, maybe five foot four, and very thin with dark brown hair and brown eyes. He had always been into computers, starting back in high school. By most standards he was a computer genius. If it could be done he could do it. Bobby however had settled for a job with no pressure. He was a salesman and not much more. Bobby's interests besides computers were booze, internet porn and x-rated movies. He had received the name "Buzz" in high school because he was always high or drunk. He lived alone and never went to clubs or bars. He was by definition a closet drunk. He had stopped on his way home at the state store in Smith Falls then the adult bookstore just outside the township line.

He arrived at his house with two bags: a bottle of bourbon in one, and half a dozen x-rated movies in the other. He unlocked the door and as soon as he entered went straight to the TV. He put a tape in the VCR and put the bottle of bourbon on the table next to his lounge chair. He went to the kitchen and from the refrigerator got a bottle of beer and a large slice of pizza. He opened the beer and drank half the bottle in one gulp. He put the pizza on a paper plate from a stack on the countertop then finished the beer with a second and third gulp. He reached inside the refrigerator again and got a second bottle of beer then went back to the living room and sat in his chair. He cracked the seal on the bourbon and took a drink as he pushed "play" on the TV remote.

It was close to 11:30 p.m. when Bobby put the second tape in the VCR. Next to his chair were three empty beer bottles and at least a third of the bourbon was gone. He had just started the second tape when he thought he heard a noise on his front porch. He paused the tape and sat and listened for several seconds, but heard nothing. He started the tape and was about to take another drink from the bottle when he thought he heard it again—a noise like a scraping sound coming from the front porch area. He paused the tape again, took a drink and walked to the front door with bottle in hand. He opened the main door but kept the storm door locked. He turned the porch light on and looked to both ends of the porch and saw nothing. He put his hand against the glass to shade his eyes from the porch light and tried to see beyond the front steps to the yard. He stood there weaving back and forth for several minutes but he saw nothing. He switched the light off, closed the door and locked it. He slowly walked back to the chair and was about to sit down when he heard a loud noise coming from the back of the house. He stood there for several seconds then took another drink from the bottle of bourbon. There it was again, the same noise coming from the back of the house. He put the bottle on the table beside the chair then stood there and rubbed his eyes and face. Again, the sound came from the back of the house. Now anger started to fill his mind. Who was out there playing games? He yelled, "Damn it," and walked toward the kitchen, weaving back and forth as he moved.

He turned the light on above the back steps and then opened the back door. This time he unlatched the back storm door and stepped out onto the top step. He looked around the portion of the back yard that was in the reach of the light. Once again he saw nothing. He stood there for several minutes then yelled, "I've had enough. It ain't funny. Cut the shit." He stood there for two or three minutes more but there was complete silence. He turned and entered the house and as he did he yelled, "Assholes." He closed and locked both doors then walked to the refrigerator and got another bottle of beer. He wiped the bottle with a rag from the counter, twisted off the cap and threw it in the trash can. He was about to take a drink when he heard a scratching sound on the side of the house. It was just outside the window that was next to the refrigerator. He set the bottle on the windowsill, quickly unlatched the window and opened it. He placed his hands on the window ledge, leaned out and yelled, "Listen, assholes." He was about to yell again when the front of his shirt was grabbed and pulled with such force that he was dragged off his feet and out the window. There was the sound of thrashing in the bushes outside, then a thud and all went silent.

CHAPTER 12

Sunday, June 20, 1:00 a.m.

Bobby Rodgers started to come out of his unconscious state. He raised his head from his chest and opened his eyes. At first all seemed to be in mist or a fog. He could see light but it was in rainbows of color like looking through a rain-covered windshield. He shook his head, squeezed his eyelids tight and looked around. As his sight started to come back he realized he was in the center of a dimly-lit room. The corners of the room that he could see were dark and the only light was almost directly over his head. He tried to move his arms to wipe his face but they wouldn't do what he wanted. He looked down and realized he was sitting in a straight-backed wooden chair. Around his body and arms was duct tape that prevented him from moving and made breathing difficult. He tried to move his legs but realized that something was holding them to the chair also. His next thought was to speak or even better scream but his mouth was also held shut by something. He scanned the room on the three sides that he could see and at first saw nothing except walls. On his second scan he thought he saw someone seated on a chair in the shadows to his right. He squeezed his eyelids together trying to see if he could make out who it was, but the room was too dark. He continued to stare in that direction and tried again to speak but his lips were held fast in position and he could sense a sickening plastic taste. He looked down at his taped body again and realized his mouth must also be taped closed. He turned once again to the person seated in the dark and just stared, the fear now growing more and more intense. He tried again to scream but the sound only came from his throat—not from his mouth. He tried three more times and then he stopped and put his head back and looked at the light hanging from the ceiling.

He was about to scream again and tried to get up when he heard a voice come from the side of the room where he had seen a person sitting. "Bobby, how are you doing? Not so good I suspect." Bobby turned again to that side of the room and stared at the person in the dark for several seconds. The fear now burst from his chest like an explosion and the sound rose from his lungs in another scream that once again stopped at his lips. He tried again to stand up as he forgot the tape that held him fast. All he did was move the chair a few inches across the floor. He screamed again and bounced the chair up and down and tried to stand but he could not move. He paused for a second and once again he heard the voice. "Bobby, you cannot escape. You have done that for too long. Your time is up. All that's left for you now is the booze, the wonderful booze. It has been your place to escape and now it will be the judgment that you deserve."

Bobby was staring intently at the person seated along the wall when someone from behind grabbed his hair and pulled his head back. His eyes now saw nothing but the light and the ceiling above him. He tried to pull his head away but another hand seemed to grasp his throat up under his chin and pinned his head back even harder. As he was being held he saw another set of hands in front of his eyes. In one hand was a bottle of bourbon, in the other was an instrument that looked like a small thin knife or surgical scalpel. He saw the hand with the instrument move toward him and then he felt the tape on his mouth being cut. He realized that there was now an opening in the tape and he tried to scream but the open bottle was jammed into his mouth through the hole. He felt the bourbon filling his mouth. He tried to close his throat but it came too fast and all he could do was swallow and swallow and swallow.

Sunday, June 20, 2:00 a.m.

Bobby had been force-fed a full bottle of bourbon and had one poured all over his body. He was now in a semiconscious state. The light on the ceiling seemed as if it had become three and when he looked around the room spun and all seemed to be in motion. He felt sick to his stomach and his arms and legs felt numb. He heard a noise to the left and he slowly turned that way as the dark figure moved toward him. His head was again pulled back by the hair and he once again saw the ceiling. He saw a hand above him and then something long and shiny. He felt something like a pinch on his neck and then a burning sensation from ear to ear. His head was released and dropped to his chest. The last thing Bobby saw was the front of his shirt slowly turning red, and then all faded and went black.

Sunday, June 20, 8:00 a.m.

Clive drove to the station in his civilian clothes and stayed long enough to find out that Bill Tomson had lost Doc Watson the night before. He had talked to the officers on duty for the weekend and gotten what information he could from them. He checked his messages and then called Bill Fry at home. Bill told him that the weapon that had killed both Bob Anderson and Roscoe was the same—and in all likelihood was used to kill Jody and Wesley. He said he could not be absolutely sure but he would bet that was the case. He told Clive that, as he had reported before, the main difference was that Jody and Wesley bled out. He said that Bob and Roscoe had died instantly because the weapon cut the spinal cord. Bill discussed a few more details then said he would fax a report first thing Monday morning. Clive called Brian at his home but got no answer. Clive left the station at about nine o'clock and started again on the list of names from the bar. He called Brian on the car radio and to his surprise, Brian answered. They talked for several minutes and Brian told Clive he had been looking for Doc ever since he found out Bill Tomson had lost him. They decided to put out an all points bulletin to all police in the county area. They requested that if found, Doc would not be stopped but only followed until Brian or Clive could begin the tail again.

Clive spent the next few hours with the list, visiting people at their homes. When he had completed his half of the list he only had two people whose alibis required them to come into the station for further questioning. He checked with Collins, who had three. All five were requested to report Monday but Clive knew that none of them was suspicious enough to be considered a likely suspect. He knew that every lead must be followed, but in the back of his mind he—like Brian—seemed to be leaning toward Doc Watson. It was well past one o'clock when Clive was finished and decided to stop at the Smith Falls Police Station. He talked to several people at the station and was about to leave when Alvin Richards came in. He spent another hour talking to Alvin and then decided to head for home. He stopped at Posey's and ordered a take-out supper, drank one beer and called it a day.

Sunday, June 20th, 10:00 P.M.

Alvin Richards Senior got up from his chair, grabbed his

cane and slowly walked to the kitchen, his German Shepard, Casey, right behind him. He opened the refrigerator and got out what he needed to make a sandwich. He placed all the components on the countertop and then gave several pieces of lunch meat to the dog. Alvin Sr. was sixty-three years old, an average sized man at about five foot ten, with a full head of white hair. He had been a judge in the county court system for over thirty years. He had retired two years before after suffering a stroke that left him slightly paralyzed on one side. He lived in a house in Smith Falls about three blocks off of Main Street. He was the father of Alvin Richards, police chief of Smith Falls. He made the sandwich and placed it on a paper plate along with some potato chips and was about to return to the living room when Casey started to whine and scratch at the back door. He opened the door and let the dog out then picked up his plate and put it in a small basket that had a rope loop attached to it. He placed the loop over his head, which allowed the basket to hang in front of his chest. He opened the refrigerator again and replaced all the sandwich items and then got a can of cream soda and placed it in the basket. He closed the refrigerator door and then the back door and slowly walked back to the living room. He placed the basket on the stand beside his chair and then picked up the TV remote and raised the volume. He had been seated only a few minutes and had taken only two bites of his sandwich when he thought he heard a knock at the front door. He lowered the volume again and listened. After several seconds of hearing nothing he was about to raise the volume again when he heard it. It was a knock. He lowered the volume, put the sandwich back on the stand, got his cane and stood up. He slowly walked to the front door and looked out the peephole. He could see someone standing to the left of the door but he could not make out who it was. He called out, "Who is it?" but there was no response. He was about to call out again when the person knocked once more. He mumbled to himself that they must be harder of hearing than he was. He unlatched the door and opened it. As the door opened, and the person turned to face him, he got a look of recognition on his face as he said, "Oh, it's you, I got your note this afternoon. I must have been at the store when you left it in the door." He turned and picked the notepaper up from the stand beside the door. He turned back to the person and said, "I'm surprised that you would want me to look over any legal matters for you. You know I'm retired. I'm surprised that you would ask me anyway. Well come in," he said as he backed up. At that second the person stepped to the left out of the judges view. The judge stepped forward and said, "What are you doing?"

An instant later something came flying through the doorway and hit Judge Richards in the center of the chest. The impact sent him backwards about five feet and onto his back. He lay there for a few seconds trying to get his breath. He was about to try to get up when he realized something heavy was laying on his chest. He pushed it off with his good hand and then he saw blood. His hand and chest were covered with it. He turned and looked to the floor beside him and there in a pool of blood, nearly torn to pieces, was Casey. He tried to roll away as he yelled, "Oh my God, oh my God, Casey." He was stopped in his attempt to roll away and get up by someone now standing in front of him. He slowly looked up and saw a huge dark figure. He was about to scream when he was grabbed and picked up like he weighed nothing and tossed another ten feet into the room. He landed on his stomach and then he slowly rolled onto his back. He raised his head as the dark figure reached to the floor and grasped him again.

Monday, June 21, 7:30 a.m.

When Clive arrived at the station he stopped at Alice's desk. He was about to ask about Doc Watson when Alice pointed to his office and with a disgusted look said, "You have a visitor."

Clive turned and saw J.D. Ricketts in his chair behind the desk. His face started to turn a light shade of red as he leaned over toward Alice. "How long has he been here and what's he doing in my office?"

Alice said, "Clive, I didn't let him in. He's been here since seven o'clock—at least that's what the night desk said. They told me he came in and started to ask questions and when they referred him to you he entered your office and he's been seated there ever since. When I came in I told him we have a waiting room and that you wouldn't be too happy if he waited in your office. He just ignored me and made some asshole remark like, 'Don't I have something else I can do?' I asked him a second time to leave and he just smiled and said he would wait here."

Clive stood straight up again and looked toward his office then back to Alice. "What did you find out about Doc?"

Alice opened the top drawer of her desk and retrieved a tablet and read the notes, "Doc has been in town since June 8. That's two days before Jody was killed. I confirmed it from the airline ticket desk and the Enterprise Rental Car people."

Clive paused for a second then asked, "Was it a single ticket or did he have company?"

Alice said, "Apparently he was alone but I can't say if someone came in on another flight. I mean we don't have a name that we can match up with his. Maybe if we check with Brian he can give us the name of someone. He seems to know Doc better than anyone, better than me I think. I mean I know him from high school but I haven't seen him for years."

Clive just shook his head then turned again toward his office. He walked to the door then turned back to Alice and said, "When Brian comes in, tell him I need to see him. No, better yet, just find out what he knows about Doc's bodyguard, his name, anything at all." Clive turned and entered his office and walked slowly to the front of his desk. J.D. Ricketts just sat in Clive's chair and smiled.

There was a moment of silence then Ricketts spoke. "Well, good morning Mr. Aliston and just how might you be this fine morning?" Clive didn't say a word he just stood and stared at Ricketts. When Ricketts didn't get any response he moved the chair closer to the desk and then leaned on his elbows and said, "We need to talk. I've been doing some investigating on my own and I'd like to compare notes—that's if you don't mind. You know, in good cooperation between departments and all such stuff." Clive still didn't respond but just continued to stare at Ricketts. There was again several seconds of silence, then Ricketts spoke again. "Clive, come on. Work with me here. I mean like I said, this one is way out of your league. Just let me in on what you've got and I can give you the benefit of the experience I have on cases like this. I mean I'm here to help, old buddy."

He was about to continue when Clive put his hands flat on the top of the desk and leaned forward to within inches of Ricketts' face. "Ricketts, you got ten seconds to vacate that chair or the only benefit you're going to need is Blue Cross/Blue Shield." Ricketts sat straight up in the chair and started to speak but Clive interrupted again, "You heard me. When it comes to help you're the one who's going to need help. I ain't your old buddy, and you got about 3 seconds left." Again there was silence as they just stared at each other. Clive then slowly walked around the corner of the desk, stopped beside Ricketts and stared down at him.

Ricketts, realizing that this was not an idle threat, rolled the chair back and stood up. "Take it easy, Aliston, we are on the same side here. We got enough to deal with. We don't need any bad blood between agencies." Clive moved the chair and then sat down. Ricketts walked around to the front of the desk and took a seat in one of the chairs. Clive tested his top drawer to see if it was still locked. It was. Ricketts looked at Clive and laughed and said, "Jeez, man what the hell is your problem? I wouldn't get into your desk. I mean like I said we are on the same side here. I was..."

Clive interrupted again. "First, we may, as you said, be on the same side but I didn't ask for your help. The only reason you're here is because of the Miller money and influence. I can't stop you from joining in on this case, but as I said before, this is my investigation. You want to help fine, but you go by my rules. I don't really much care who called you in on this, George Miller or the commissioner. There's only one way to take over and that's the day I'm gone. One more thing, I find you in my office or behind my desk again and Blue Cross/Blue Shield will be the least of your worries."

"But..." Ricketts said.

Clive cut in. "I don't like you and I don't even know you that well. But there is one thing I do know and that is your reputation. You are a very successful agent. I will give you that, but you are also a headline grabber. You love to see your name in print."

"Hold on one minute," Ricketts said as he slid to the front of his chair.

Once again Clive stopped him mid-sentence. "This is my county and my jurisdiction and the people and what happens to them is personal to me. You're looking for a headline; I'm looking for a way to stop this carnage. Now you want to work that end and we'll get along as well as we can. You put the heroics up front and you'll have a real bad time—about as bad as you've ever had because I don't back down. You may think you're some hotshot big-city Fed boy, but like I said before, you're in my county now. This county boy will take great pleasure in kicking your ass."

Ricketts didn't even attempt to respond. He slid back into the chair, clasped his fingers together in front of his face and smiled. There was what seemed like several minutes of silence then Ricketts dropped his hands from in front of his face and said, "They told me you were tough. I guess they just didn't say how tough. Guess I just wanted to see for myself. Okay, it's your investigation and forget the money thing. Yeah, Miller called for me but it was the commissioner who put in the request. Nobody buys J.D. Ricketts. You're the boss. I'll work with you the best I can. Just don't close me out of the loop. Oh yeah, the lives of the people here are important to me too. Sure, I've made a few good headlines and I won't deny that I enjoyed it, but the job has always come first. Now that we got that out of the way, do you think we can compare notes here? I'd rather work with you so what's it going to be?"

Monday, June 21, 8:00 a.m.

Brett Collins had called into the station at about 7:45 a.m. and told Alice that he was going to make one stop for the last person on his half of the bar list. He had found that no one was home and was again driving through Smith Falls on his way to the station. He was about three blocks from Main Street and had just stopped at the stop sign in front of Alvin Richards Sr.'s home. As he pulled out, he happened to glance to the right and saw that the front door of the Richards' house was standing open. He crossed the intersection and was going to continue on when something told him to stop. He pulled the car to the curb, looked back at the house and watched the front door. After several minutes, still seeing no movement around the house he put the car in reverse and cautiously backed up across the intersection. He parked the car at the curb in front of the house and once again sat and watched. Several more minutes passed while the door stood open with no one in sight.

He put the patrol car in park and called Alice on the radio. "Alice this is Collins. I'm in Smith Falls, in front of Alvin Richards Sr.'s home. The door is standing open and it appears no one is around." Alice responded then Collins continued, "I'm going to check on this. I'm a little concerned, especially with the judge's medical condition. I'll call you back." He turned off the ignition, got out of the car and walked up the front sidewalk to the porch. When he reached the porch he stepped up to the deck and as he did he yelled, "Judge are you there? Are you okay?" There was no response—only total silence. He walked to the doorway and as he did he noticed something red smeared across the front door. He stopped and reached out and touched the red swath across the door. He placed his fingers in front of his face and rubbed the red substance between his thumb and forefinger. Suddenly he realized it was blood.

Collins unsnapped and drew his service revolver as he turned and backed up against the side of the house. He pulled the gun up close to his face and took in a deep breath. He spun and again faced the inside of the house—this time with the gun pointed out in front of him. He slowly moved inside the front door then spun first to the right and then to the left, checking the room on both sides. He was about to move further into the room when he saw the judge's dog, Casey, lying in a pool of blood. He stopped in his tracks and then began to slowly back out of the front door and onto the porch. He backed off the front porch while watching both sides of the house. When he stepped down to the sidewalk he quickly holstered his gun and ran to the patrol car and called the station.

Clive and J.D. Ricketts were still involved in a somewhat tense conversation when Alice buzzed him, "Clive, pick up line two. It's Collins. We got a problem." Clive looked out the window at Alice. She was standing up, holding the phone and pointing at the receiver with an unusual look on her face.

Clive said to J.D., "Hold on," and picked up the phone. He sat intently listening for several seconds then said, "Brett, do not enter that house. Wait for back up. Stay there. I'll be down as quick as I can. Don't call the Smith Falls station, I'll do that on the way." He hung up the phone and stood up and J.D. did the same. He looked at J.D. and said, "You want to help, well you got your chance. Something has just come down at Judge Richards' house."

CHAPTER 13

Monday, June 21, 8:45 a.m.

Clive and J.D. left the station and headed to Smith Falls in separate cars. On the way Clive called the Smith Falls Police Station and asked for Chief Richards. He was told that he was on his way into the city to the courthouse. Clive explained the situation and asked for backup from the township police. He was told that help would be there and that they would get Chief Richards turned around and headed back to Smith Falls.

When Clive arrived at Judge Richards house, Brett Collins was standing behind his patrol car with his weapon drawn and ready. Clive and J.D. Ricketts parked across the street and ran to Brett's car. Just as they got to where Brett Collins was standing, two Smith Falls police cars came around the corner and parked in the middle of the street— one at each end of the block. At almost the same time, Brian Lasiter came around the other corner in his unmarked car, slid to a stop, got out, and ran to Clive's position. Clive asked the Smith Falls officers to cover the back of the house and was told that there was another township car already there in the street behind Judge Richards' garage. Brian told Clive that he had heard the call on the radio, that he had been on the Watson stakeout and had left to come there. He said he still had not seen Doc Watson either at the house or anywhere else around town.

J.D. Ricketts looked at Brian and asked, "Who the hell is Doc Watson?"

Clive looked at J.D. and said, "I'll fill you in later." He looked at Brian and asked him to cover the back of the house and to watch the left side of the house where the cellar door was. Brian nodded an okay, ran back to his car and drove around to the back of the house. When he was in position with the other Smith Falls police officers he called and confirmed that they were ready. Clive asked the two Smith Falls officers with him to stay in the front and cover that area. He looked at J.D. and said, "Well you wanted to help. Are you ready?"

J.D. just drew his weapon and said, "Let's do it." Clive, J.D. and Collins, all with weapons drawn, moved around the car and ran across the front yard one at a time to the porch then against the front wall of the house. Clive and Collins were on one side of the door and J.D. on the other. On Clive's count Collins moved into the front door and to the left and once again scanned the room gun drawn. He was followed by Clive, who moved to the right and then J.D., who moved in right behind him. They checked that room and then Clive slowly moved to the living room. J.D. stood for a second and looked down at what was left of the dog, then he and Collins followed behind Clive. As they moved into that room, Collins walked backward, still scanning the entry room and covering their backs. The living room was empty, but the TV was still on, and there was a partially-eaten sandwich and chips on the table beside the judge's lounge chair. Once that room was secure they moved back to the entry room, then on to the kitchen in the back of the house. Once again they found nothing.

Clive called on the radio and asked the two Smith Falls officers to move up to the house and to come inside. Clive also called Brian and had him check the cellar door, but it was still locked. Brian left the one township officer outside to cover the back of the house and then entered the back door after Clive unlocked it. One of the two township officers remained out on the porch to cover the front and the other entered and then, joined by Collins, checked the two bedrooms off the hallway that led from the living room. The two officers returned from the bedrooms and told Clive all was clear.

Clive sent Collins and the other officers to cover the cellar, and then returned to the entry room with Brian and J.D. He moved slowly and stepped over the dog's body, looking at the blood on the door. As he did, J.D. noticed several drops of blood leading to the last door on the right side of the entry room. He whispered to Clive and Brian, pointed to the blood, then realized that there was a cane on the floor against the door where the blood trail disappeared. They all moved slowly toward that door, Clive and J.D. on one side and Brian on the other. The door was closed and the blood trail disappeared behind it. Clive used his foot and slid the cane back out of the way then looked at J.D. and Brian as if to say, "Are you ready?" He turned and faced the door and with his gun pointed out in front of him, staring for a second at the letters on the door: "Judge's Chamber, Judge Alvin Richards Sr." He raised his leg and with one quick movement kicked the door and swung it open. He moved quickly into the room followed first by J.D. then Brian. His intention was to scan the room quickly but what he saw first froze him in his tracks.

Directly across the room from the door, seated behind a large elevated desk, was Judge Richards in his long black judge's robe. Directly in front of him was a brass model of the scales of justice. His right hand was placed on the right side of the scale, and it was tilted down to that side. His head was back against the chair he was seated in and his throat was cut almost from ear to ear. His eyes were wide open and his mouth contorted as if in a frozen scream. Brian, Clive and J.D. all slowly lowered their weapons and walked to the front of the desk. Behind the Judge smeared in blood on the wall was the single word, "Forever."

Once the house and the grounds were searched and secure, Clive called Alice and told her to call the coroner's office and crime lab. They were all out on the front porch when Alvin Richards' police car came around the corner, wove between the other police cars, and slid to a stop, the lights still flashing. Clive and Brian stepped off the porch and headed toward the car as Alvin got out leaving the car door open and started to walk slowly toward the house. They met him about midway up the sidewalk. He looked at Clive and just said, "Dad?"

Clive put his hand on his shoulder and just shook his head, "Yes."

Alvin tried to go around Clive but Brian stepped in his way and said, "No Alvin! Don't go in there now."

Clive reached for Alvin's arm but he pulled away and once again Brian blocked his path. Alvin stared at Brian for several seconds then said, "Brian, please."

Brian looked at Clive then Clive said to Alvin, "Wait till the crime lab gets here, Alvin. You don't want to see him like that."

Alvin continued to stare at Brian then removed his hat and his gun belt and handed them to Clive. He was still looking at Brian when he repeated, "Brian, please." Brian lowered his head and slowly moved out of the way. Alvin looked up at the house with the police officers standing all around the porch. He started to walk slowly to the porch and as he did each officer stepped out of the way. He moved slowly up onto the porch and walked to the front door. J.D. Ricketts was standing in front of the door and paused for a second then he too stepped out of the way. Alvin looked at J.D. then entered the house.

Clive and Brian walked to the police car at the curb and

Clive put one elbow on the car roof, then pushed his hat back and just held his forehead and whispered, "Damn it." For about five minutes the officers on the scene were talking in whispers, then all went silent. Clive and Brian looked toward the house as Alvin stepped onto the porch. His face was pale, and he had no real expression—only a cold stare. He walked across the porch and down the steps to the sidewalk as the group of officers in front of him parted. He left the sidewalk and crossed the yard to a large tree then just stood there for several seconds. He placed both hands on the tree then slowly slid to the ground to his knees. Clive and Brian walked quickly to his side as he turned his face to the ground and the tears began to flow. He said nothing. He just stared at the ground and quietly cried. Clive and Brian stayed at his side for some time, then Clive heard a commotion up the street.

He looked around the tree and saw a TV van and a few cars parking on the other side of the yellow police ribbon. He looked at Collins who was seated at the edge of the porch and waved him in that direction. As Collins got up to move, Clive silently put his hand over his mouth in a gesture as if to say, "Say nothing," then pointed to the TV van. Collins shook his head that he understood and he and one of the Smith Falls officers headed in that direction.

Clive and Brian stayed with Alvin for a few more minutes then Clive heard one of the Smith Falls officers call him from one of the cars. He walked to the car leaving Brian with Alvin. When he got to the car the officer told him he was to call Alice at the station now. He went to his car and called. Brian stood with Alvin and watched Clive as he talked for several minutes. When Clive was finished Brian saw him turn to the police car, remove his hat and slap it on the roof of the car. Brian stood beside Alvin, still on his knees, and watched Clive with a puzzled look on his face. Clive stood with both elbows on the roof of the car, facing away from Brian and running his fingers through his hair. Brian could see the frustration even at that distance.

Several seconds later, Clive put his hat back on his head, turned to Brian and motioned for him to come to the car. Brian called one of the Smith Falls officers to take his place beside Alvin, then walked to Clive, sitting in the front seat of his car with the door standing open. When he reached the car Clive looked up at him and said, "I just talked to Alice. We got another one."

"What?" Brian said. "Another what?"

Clive took a deep breath then said, "Another body. They just found Bobby Rodgers in a dumpster behind the liquor store in Smith Falls."

Monday, June 21, 10:00 a.m.

Clive sent Brian to tell Collins to handle the Richards crime scene while he and Brian went to the Rodgers scene. To Brian's surprise Clive also asked him to ask J.D. Ricketts to accompany them. The three left in separate cars and drove to the liquor store at the opposite end of town. When they arrived at the parking and unloading area behind the store they were met by Jim Terrell of the state police. Jim walked to their cars as they parked and got out. There was a large crowd around the area and the usual press and TV representation. They were all being held back by several state troopers who were also stringing out yellow crime scene tape. "How you doing Clive?" was the first thing Jim Terrell said as he extended his hand to Clive.

"Oh, I'm sure I've had better days," Clive responded as he shook Jim's hand.

Jim also greeted Brian and J.D. then turned back to Clive. "I heard about what was going on at Judge Richards' house, and then I heard about this from the Smith Falls station. I thought you could use some help. I also took the liberty of sending a couple men to the Richards scene. I hope you don't take this wrong. I figured you could use them. I don't want to step on any toes, Clive."

"Thank you," Clive said as they all started to walk across the lot to the back of the liquor store. "Right now

Jim, I appreciate all anyone can do to help." Brian was surprised to hear that coming from Clive but he was also beginning to feel the frustration. J.D. Ricketts was also surprising Brian for he had said next to nothing most of the morning. As they walked slowly across the lot Clive looked up at several news helicopters that hovered over his head. They walked to the back wall of the store near a loading dock and stopped at a red dumpster that rested against the wall. The lid was standing open and the first thing Clive noticed was a human hand hanging out over the front side of the box. One of the state police officers moved a small step stool from the store to the front of the box just in front of Clive. Clive stepped up the one step and looked inside.

Lying on his back mixed in with some of the trash was Bobby Rodgers. His eyes were open wide, as was his mouth. He stared up at nothing and blood covered the entire front of his shirt. His throat was slashed from ear to ear—the same as the others. Jim Terrell said, "Clive, look at the bottle around his neck." Clive saw an empty bourbon bottle tied loosely around Bobby's neck with brown twine. Inside the bottle was a small piece of paper that had one word printed on it: "Forever."

As Clive stepped down from the stool, J.D. Ricketts stepped up and took a look. He remained there for several minutes just scanning the inside of the box then he stepped down and Brian stepped up. J.D. was about to say something to Clive when a man in the crowd about thirty feet away yelled, "Hey Aliston you gonna stop pissing around and catch this guy, or are you just interested in the coffee and doughnut perks on that job?" Clive stepped away from the box and looked in the direction that the voice had come from. As he did a large man in a pair of bib overalls and t-shirt yelled again. "Maybe you're just good at playing cop. When it comes to the real job, you suck. Why don't you let the FBI do your job, maybe they can show you what real cops do."

There were several other people in the crowd that joined

in with "Yeah," and, "Get some real cops."

Clive started to walk in the direction of the hecklers when J.D. stepped in front of him. He just smiled and said softly, "Let me handle this one."

Clive, looking somewhat surprised, said, "Be my guest." J.D. turned and slowly walked to the crowd as Brian followed. When J.D. reached the crime scene tape, he smiled at the heckler, who was at least a head taller and a hundred pounds heavier.

The big man looked down at him and said, "Who are you, his mouthpiece?"

Brian felt his face grow warm and flushed as he began to speak but was interrupted by J.D. "That's okay Brian. I'll handle this." J.D. just stood and continued to smile.

The big man leaned down very close to J.D.'s face and said again, "Who are you little man, Aliston's police dog?" J.D. said nothing; he just continued to smile. The big man now with three or four other men behind him looked up and down J.D.'s body then added, "Pretty suit. Aliston buy you that?" He moved his face a little closer to J.D. then sniffed and said, "And you smell pretty too." Brian was about to explode when he saw one quick movement from J.D. His hand flew forward to the big man's crotch and he grasped his testicles and squeezed and twisted. The big guy's face froze as if it had been turned to stone, and then began to turn a bright shade of red as he gasped for breath. J.D. squeezed and twisted again and the big man went to his knees. He tried to yell but nothing came out. Brian placed his hand on his weapon as the three or four men behind the big man started to step forward. When they saw the move they stopped and stepped back several steps. Brian then looked down at J.D. who was now to the side of the big man but still clamped tightly to his crotch. The big man was on his hands and knees and J.D. was right there beside him.

He leaned over to the big man's ear and asked. "And what might your name be, old buddy?"

The man couldn't do anything but whisper, "Bert, my name is Bert."

J.D. whispered in his ear again. "Well Bert, I might smell good to you but you smell like booze to me and with that attitude I'd say we just might have a drunk and disorderly. Now, I'm going to let you go, so I suggest you be a real good boy, and maybe all you get out of this is a day and night in jail." J.D. squeezed again then said as the big man's face went to the pavement. "And who am I? Well, I'm that FBI agent you asked for." J.D. left go of the man and Brian and two other officers stepped in and cuffed him and pushed the crowd back. J.D. stood up and brushed off his suit, then looked at Brian who was standing holding the man's arm with an amazed look on his face.

J.D. smiled at Brian then walked back to where Clive was standing. When he got to Clive he said, "Now can we get on with this, I think the distraction has found other interests."

Clive shook his head and said, "Maybe, I might be glad I didn't butt heads with you Ricketts."

J.D. smiled and said, "Don't sell yourself short Sheriff, I think I know a good man when I see one too."

Jim Terrell spoke up, "Well guys, if we have all our fur and feathers tucked back in place I guess Mr. Rodgers needs our attention." Clive, Jim and J.D. covered the scene and then Brian joined a few minutes later. A call was put into the crime lab and they sent another crew to the liquor store. Clive spoke on the radio with Bill Fry who was at the Richards' house. He requested that Bill meet the four of them at the county station later in the day. When Clive, Jim, J.D. and Brian had finished what they could Clive sent Brian back to the Richards' home.

Clive, J.D. and Jim drove to the county station. Upon arrival Clive asked Alice to call the commissioner and ask him to meet them there at about two p.m. He also instructed Alice to call Brian and tell him to ask Bill Fry if two o'clock was okay and if not would three o'clock do.

The final time of the meeting was set at two-thirty. J.D., Jim and Clive spent the rest of the morning in Clive's office going over their notes, and trying to rehash the evidence from the previous murders. All parties requested to be there were in the station well before two-thirty. They all had coffee and talked. The actual meeting began at close to three o'clock in the conference room. Just before the meeting started, Clive gave Alice a list of names from the media and asked her to call them to the station if and when he requested it.

CHAPTER 14

Monday, June 21, 3:00 p.m.

Those called for the meeting began to file into the station conference room just after 3:00 p.m. They included Jack McCall, Bill Fry, J.D. Ricketts, Jim Terrell, Brian Lasiter, Alice Shearer, Tim Dockens, a lieutenant with the Smith Falls police, filling in for Alvin Richards, and to everyone's surprise, Wade Philips, the actual sheriff and number-one man in the sheriff's department. He had been on sick leave with heart problems and each station commander had taken care of his own district. Each person met him one at a time with handshakes and well wishes. Before the meeting began, Clive pulled J.D. Ricketts aside and, as promised, filled him in on the Doc Watson information.

It was about 3:25 p.m. when Clive stood up at the end of the long table and called the meeting to order. "Gentlemen, first I want to thank you all for coming here on short notice. Especially you, Wade. It's good to see you up and with us again." Wade just nodded and smiled. "First, I want to apologize for the delay in calling this meeting. It should have been done several days ago."

Jack McCall spoke up and said, "Clive, you'll not take the blame for that. We are all in a state of shock over the speed that this thing has taken. Anyone of us could have called for this action and didn't. What we need now is not hindsight but a plan of action."

All agreed and Clive continued, "Several days ago I was confronted with a meeting that I must admit pissed me off. I felt that I was able to handle this situation even though I have never dealt with anything like this before. After that meeting Mr. Ricketts and I had a bit of a confrontation. He told me in straightforward up-front terms that this was out of my league. I told him that he was in my county now and that big-city police tactics won't work here. Well he was right and so was I. As Jack McCall said, we don't need hindsight we need a plan. J.D. said out of my league. Yes it is, and I need his help and I asked for it. It's also out of his city turf and he needs me. Bill Fry said to me several days ago that he didn't envy me the job I had ahead or the people I had to deal with. Bill was right. What started out as a single murder has grown into a huge snowball and it's on a downhill run moving faster than any of us could ever have imagined. At this point in time I have certain leads and information that my station has gathered. Most of what I have has been supplied by ongoing and lengthy investigation, and information supplied by Bill Fry and the crime lab.

"Even with the hours and effort spent we have little but disjointed information and dead ends. We have a possible suspect and I say again, only possible. There is no evidence pointing a finger at this person. He has a past record and is from this area originally. He showed up in town several days before the murders began. I will fill you in on the info we have on this at the conclusion of this meeting. I also know the Smith Falls police, state police and Mr. Ricketts have information that may or may not be the same.

"What I am getting to is that this has become bigger

than any of us. We can no longer fight this evil as single departments. We need to put down our interdepartmental problems and in some cases our pride and work together. I don't have the authority to form a task force nor do I have the experience to try. I know what we need and I think you all do also. I am now asking for your help to form a united front. We can't let this go on. We owe it to those who have died and especially the ones they have left behind to stop it now. City, county, local, federal—none of it means anything. We need us and we need to get this maniac before anymore die or before his evil plan is finished and he disappears—to quote him, Forever."

Wade Phillips then spoke up, "Clive, I don't have anymore experience than you or any of the other departments and I'm quite sure they will admit to that. The only person in this room that has dealt with this type of case is Mr. Ricketts. If we are to form a task force—and believe me I agree we need to—he is the man to head it." All in the room agreed, including Clive—although somewhat reluctantly.

J.D. sat for a moment with his hands clasped in front of his face, then sat back in the chair and spoke. "Well, gentlemen, I thank you for your vote of confidence but before I go on I would like to get a few things off my chest also. I came here at the request of one of the victim's families and your commissioner, Jack McCall. I'm quite sure he and I know that the family's influence—not only here but also in many other places—had a lot to do with that first meeting. I must admit that I felt I was the man to run this investigation and I'll be the first to admit also that the headlines it would get had me quite interested. Now that I've been here and had the chance to meet a lot of you and see your dedication to this thing my attitude has changed.

"You may not have the experience that I and my department have, but I must admit to you something I lost some years ago: that desire to stop what is evil for that reason and that reason alone. I guess after you are faced with this each and every day you become hardened to the horror of it all. It is no longer the oath you took or the pure desire to do good. It is no longer the plain simple idea to do your job. It is no longer the ideals you had when you took this job fresh out of the academy. Routine becomes the worst enemy a criminologist can face. Maybe I needed to come here to remember that. Clive's right. I'm in his county now and maybe it's a place where you can remember what you actually took this job for. Do I have the experience you need? Maybe I do, but experience needs heart and over the years on that count I fall short. If this man can pull off his armor and admit what he lacks then so can I. Maybe if we work together we can not only stop this but come out the better for it. We need to create a solid unit and work together under the proper guidance. No special people or agendas. A task force. You're damn right. I'm in, but as for me I follow this man." J.D. just looked at Clive and nodded.

Clive thanked J.D., then said, "I'm not sure I'm the one to be taking this job." All of those present then spoke up at one time and agreed with J.D. For a moment there was silence then Clive took in a deep breath and said, "Okay, I guess I'll give this a shot, but one thing I make plain now. If I'm not doing the job well I expect to be replaced. I also want and need any suggestions and help any of you can provide."

He was about to continue when Rose Bodin, who had taken Alice's place so she could take notes, knocked on the door and entered the room. She motioned to Clive to come to the door but Clive said, "Rose, what is it?"

She said, "You have a call you might want to take out here."

Clive said, "No Rose, if it's about this case it's now for all to hear."

Rose paused for a second then looking a little surprised said, "It's the governor's office calling."

Everyone in the room turned to Rose then back to Clive.

Clive stood silent for a few seconds then looked at Jack McCall and said, "Maybe you want to take this?"

Jack said, "First, I didn't call him." Everyone else in the room said the same. "If he wants to talk to you, Clive, take it," Jack said.

Clive paused again for a second then turned to the desk behind him and picked up the phone and pushed line one. He said, "This is Clive Aliston, yes I'll wait a second." There were about ten seconds of silence as all in the room waited. "Yes Sir, this is Clive Aliston," Clive said again. "And how are you today Sir?" he added as if in response to the same. He stood and listened for several seconds then said, "Yes, Sir," then paused again for several minutes and said, "Yes, Sir" again. There was another pause of several minutes, then Clive said, "Yes Sir, and thank you very much. I will, Sir. Yes I will tell him. Thank you again and I will keep you informed. Yes, Sir and goodbye to you, Sir."

Clive dropped the phone to his shoulder and just stared at the wall for a few seconds. He hung up the phone and turned back to the table. All eyes were on him. He stood silent for a few seconds, then said, "He just told me whatever I need to make a list and let him know. He told me to tell Jim Terrell that he said hello."

He looked at Jim who sat forward in his seat and said, "I ran into one of his aides a day or two ago and happened to mention what you were up against. I didn't think he would call, himself. I hope it's okay, I didn't..."

Clive interrupted. "It is okay Jim. You are right we need help and if he's offering we are taking." Clive looked at his watch and said, "It's 4:30 p.m. and I think we need to start to put some of this together. If all of you can stay I'll have Rose order food. I think it's going to be a long night." All agreed to stay and even Alice remained to take notes on Clive's request. The meeting lasted until close to eleven o'clock as they compared notes and set up the task force.

Bill Fry was put in charge of the crime lab work and was to be supplied by the state, local and federal with whatever he needed. Jack McCall was to be the liaison between all the different government agencies. J.D. Ricketts was in charge of the FBI end of the plan and requested more men and material. Smith Falls police would handle all of the crime scenes to keep out the press and the people who didn't belong. They and the sheriff's department would follow up on all the interviews with everyone directly or indirectly involved since day one. The state police, headed by Jim Terrell, were to patrol all areas of the town and the county that could not be covered by the normal police force due to the workload. Jim Terrell was to keep in touch with the governor's office and make the formal requests for whatever was needed. Requests were put in to all departments for the additional personnel and the overtime pay required to cover them. A list of equipment was made up. Chalkboards, communications, computers, file cabinets—anything that maybe needed. Alice made calls to various places for sleeping arrangements and rooms for the out-of-town personnel. By eleven fifteen, most of the plans were pulled together and Clive set up a meeting the next day with certain members of the press and media. It had been decided to let a certain amount of information out to the press to try and quell the fear that the town and county people must be feeling. By midnight, all those who attended the meeting had left and Clive locked his office and headed for home to get a few hours' sleep. He had asked Brian to continue with the search for Doc Watson and to request any help needed to maintain twenty-four hour coverage. If Watson was found he was to be brought in for questioning.

Tuesday, June 22, 7:30 a.m.

Clive was at the station and behind his desk shortly after 7:30 a.m. He had made several phone calls and placed a small pile of notes on Alice's desk. She arrived at about 7:50 a.m. He stopped at her desk on his way to the lunchroom for coffee, and asked her to make the phone calls to the press and media from the list he gave her the day before. He set up the meeting for 1:00 p.m. in the main conference room and told her: "The list names only." He spent the rest of the morning on the phone with members of the task force, the crime lab, the State Police, and FBI. He set up a notebook with the breakdown of the agencies and their parts in the task force, and with Alice's help set up the notes for the one o'clock press conference. It was 12:45 p.m. when the members of the task force and the press and media started to arrive at the station. Clive was about to leave his office to join the others for the conference when George Miller, Carl Dans, Bob Anderson's wife, Bobby Rodgers' mother and father and Bart James, a wealthy and influential friend of George Miller, entered the station. Clive met them in the hallway as Alice was telling them that they must be on the meeting list to attend. Clive interrupted her and said, "I'll allow this, but this is an informative meeting—not a debate. You're here to listen. If you have questions about anything Alice and I will be glad to talk to you later after the meeting."

George Miller immediately spoke up, "We have a right to know what's coming down and now, not tomorrow or tonight in the press or on TV. You and your department have kept this quiet for too long. I want answers and now." Bart James tried to calm George but without much success.

Clive said calmly, "George, I already said you'll get your answers when we are finished and not before. I understand your frustration, but as I said before we need to handle this a certain way, and we will not vary from that procedure."

George took two steps toward Clive as Bart James tried to intervene. "Aliston," was all he got to say as a voice down the hall interrupted him.

It was J.D. Ricketts. "George! You heard the man. You get your time when the meeting is over. Now, if you want to attend, I suggest you shut up and take a seat in the back of the room."

George, now turning his attention away from Clive

walked to the doorway of the conference room and stopped in front of J.D. "I called for your help and now you're in his little basket with him. I thought you were a better man than that Ricketts. Guess I was wrong."

Ricketts stared at George and Bart, who was standing beside him, and said, "Yeah, you called and I came because I thought I could help. You know what, I can help. But it's going to be here—not in your back pocket." George tried to interrupt but J.D. continued, "You have been allowed to come to a meeting that you were not invited to. Personally, if it was up to me you would wait, but if Clive okays it then you stay. Now I suggest you take your seat before the offer is withdrawn." George, his face now red, was pushed through the door by Bart and Carl Dans before he could speak again. J.D. just looked at Clive and shook his head then reentered the room.

Clive and Alice stopped just outside of the conference room and were talking when Rose called Clive back to the office. When he reached Rose's desk she told him Brian had called in. He had found Doc Watson. Clive called Brian on the phone rather than the radio. "Brian, Rose said you found Doc. Where?"

"I was at the main intersection in Smith Falls and he drove right past in front of me. I mean we've been looking for several days and wham, there he is out of the blue," Brian said.

"Where is he now?" Clive asked.

"I'm sitting outside Bartolli's Restaurant. He's inside, I guess for lunch," Brian said.

Clive paused a second then said, "I'm in that press conference now. I'll send backup. I want him brought in for questioning. If he resists, arrest him."

"On what charge?" Brian asked.

"I don't care," Clive responded. "Ask him to come in now. If he gives you trouble, get him on resisting arrest, interfering with an investigation, a parking violation, whatever. I just want him here."

"Okay," Brian said. "Will do."

Clive hung up then told Rose to check the airlines and rental car companies again to see if he had left town and come back. He told her that when Brian brought him in to put them in the small conference room at the other end of the building. He did not want the press or anyone else to see or question him. He told Rose that he wanted to be told when Brian arrived with Doc—but to tell only him. Clive then left Rose and walked to the large conference room at the end of the hall and entered.

Tuesday, June 22, 1:00 p.m.

When Clive entered, all of the task force members were at a table across the front of the room. Behind the table was a blank green chalkboard. In front of the table were several rows of chairs that were filled with members of the various newspapers and TV stations. Each station had its mobile recording and video equipment around the sides and back of the room. In the last row of chairs were the families of the victims and many of the media people were talking to them. When Clive walked to the seat behind the table the room grew silent, as the press that were in the back of the room returned to their seats. Clive sat down and placed his paperwork in front of him. As he did so several state police, Smith Falls and county police officers entered and spaced themselves at various points around the room. The members of the task force leaned forward and talked among themselves back and forth for several minutes, then they all sat back as Jack McCall stood up and walked to a podium on one side of the table. He carried several pieces of paper in his hands and as he looked up to speak, several members of the media raised their hands and started to yell, "Jack... Jack..." asking questions.

Jack stood and raised his hand palm open and out in a gesture that he wanted silence. It took several seconds for the room to become silent again. When all was quiet Jack spoke. "First, I want to welcome you all here for this meeting." He had no sooner said that than the hands went up again and the questions started to fly. Once again, he raised his hand and waited. When all was quiet he continued, "There will be no questions, and no statements made by anyone except the task force until such time that we deem it necessary. This is an informational meeting intended to let you know where we are in our ongoing investigation. All information will not be divulged, for we cannot take a chance on damaging this case. If you have any questions we may ask you to see a designated person after the meeting. If we feel we can take some questions at the end of these proceedings we will. If not, we won't. Any disruption of this meeting will be met with immediate dismissal."

He was about to continue when George Miller jumped up and screamed. "Dismissal! This ain't no grade school. This is a murder investigation, you asshole." Bart James and Carl Dans tried to pull George back into his chair but he pushed them away. He started to walk away from his chair toward the front of the room when two of the officers started toward him. They met him in the center aisle about the middle of the room. He tried to push his way through as Bart and Carl tried to pull him back. He was screaming, "I want that murderer caught. I'm sick of your rules and all the delays. Someone has to do something."

While he was screaming, one of the press people from the *Smith Falls Gazette* stood up and yelled, "Yeah, what about the delays? What's the cover-up all about?" The screaming was abruptly ended when a loud, pounding noise was heard from the front corner of the room. All attention turned to that corner.

There, standing with a large law book in his hand, slamming it on a desk was J.D. Ricketts. No one had seen him get up or move in that direction. All eyes had been on Jack McCall. The room grew totally silent as Jack and the rest of the members were turned in that direction—as was most of the crowd. J.D. set the book down and then said,

"Enough." He walked to the podium then looked at Clive and asked, "You mind?"

"No," Clive said. "Go right ahead."

J.D. first looked at George and said, "You return to your seat now. We'll give you a break only because you lost someone and we are trying to accommodate. But this is your last warning. One word and I'll have you escorted out. And George, we don't care who you are, you're gone." He then turned to the *Gazette* reporter and said, "And you, you're out of here now." He motioned for two of the officers to take him out. The reporter protested but was led out and the door closed. J.D. then turned again to George who was still standing there and said, "Well, make up your mind." Bart and Carl walked to George's side and whispered to him. He pulled away and then slowly returned to his seat. Once the room was silent again, J.D. looked out over the crowd and repeated, "One more time." Then he smiled at Jack and returned to his seat. Jack stepped to the podium again and continued. The conference went on for over an hour. All that could be explained was, and then some questions were taken. Each task force member took a turn at the questions, then the last one to take the podium was Clive.

Clive walked to the podium with his papers in hand and adjusted the microphone. "Good afternoon," he said, then pausing for a second he turned to the other members of the task force. "Thank you, gentlemen for your time and the information you have put together." He looked back at the press and media people. "The information we have given you is all we can afford to release at this time. We cannot take a chance on giving you more for fear that the killer will use it to escape—or worse." As he spoke, the door opened and Rose Bodin looked in. She motioned to Clive that Brian had arrived with Doc Watson. Clive acknowledged her then continued. He added a few more pieces of information then told the press that they would take questions for a few more minutes.

As the press asked their questions, Jack McCall got up, spoke to Alice, and handed her a piece of paper. Alice stopped taking notes then walked to the chalkboard behind the table. She took a piece of chalk and started to write: 1. Task force commander, 2. Liaison between departments, 3. FBI director of operations, 4. Crime lab director, 5. Local police commander, 6. Sheriff's department commander, 7. State police commander and Governor's office contact. Once the list of positions was written she started to fill in the names: 1. Clive Aliston, 2. Jack McCall. She was about to write, 3. J.D. Ricketts, when George Miller screamed from the back of the room. "You assholes put Aliston in charge of this investigation. You have got to be kidding me. You have the FBI and the state police here and you give it to Deputy Dog, the donut commando. Are you people nuts? He couldn't investigate his way out of the men's room."

He was about to continue when Jack McCall cut him off. "George take your seat and shut up. Letting you in here was a mistake but we can correct it very quickly."

Instead of listening, George continued to scream as he once again left his seat and started down the center aisle. Clive got up from his seat and was about to walk around the table when another voice was heard from the conference room doorway. "George Miller, for once in your life shut the hell up." All attention was suddenly on the man standing in the doorway. It was Alvin Richards. He was not in his uniform but in a plain black suit. The entire room was silent as he slowly walked to the front of the room and stopped in front of the table. He pulled down his tie and unbuttoned the top button of his shirt, then slowly walked toward George Miller in the center aisle. "George you are not the only one that has lost someone through this nightmare. I just came from the crime lab, the funeral home and the church. I can understand your anger, but what you are doing here will not help. Your daughter was the first victim. You are also a victim and if anyone knows that to be true it's me. I feel the same loss as you. These other people feel the same loss as both of us, yet I do not hear them the way I hear you. We all feel the same pain or at least understand the pain. The only difference is you have money and apparently a mouth to go with it. These men at the table can only imagine what you and I and the rest are going through, but they are dedicated to finding the killer. It has nothing to do with power or money for them. Each life that was taken is important to them. Your daughter, my father and yes even Roscoe Black. You can buy your way into almost anywhere, but not here George. Here you are just one of us. One of the unfortunate few that has lost something precious to this evil. An evil that these men are trying with the utmost effort to stop. And as for Clive Aliston, I would have voted for him also. In all my years on the force I can say I have never met a more dedicated cop. I have never met a more honest cop. I have never had the pleasure of knowing a man like Clive Aliston. His salary is mere pocket change to you, and yet he will pursue this killer until he is either captured or one of them is dead. Now George, take yourself and your pain home. Take your money and your power, put them away, they have no place here. The innocent blood spilled was more than just Miller blood. Stop causing these good men problems and let them do their job." George tried to speak again, but Alvin stepped forward to within inches of George's face. "George, damn you, go home. Your wife needs you; she has lost a daughter too. Or have you forgotten?"

George was silent as tears ran down his face. He stood in front of Alvin and sobbed. Alvin took his arm and walked him to Carl Dans and Bart James who had started down the aisle toward George. The three men then slowly and silently left the room followed by the rest of the family members. When all was quiet again Alvin took a seat where he was standing, put his face in his hands, and sat silently. Alice continued to fill in the names: 3. J.D. Ricketts, 4. Bill Fry, 5. Tim Dockins, 6. Brian Lasiter, 7. Jim Terrell.

When the list was finished Clive added that Wade Phillips would be assisting him on a limited basis due to his medical condition.

Clive was about to call an end to the meeting when Alvin Richards spoke up, "Gentlemen as soon as I can I would like to join this task force. I can assist Tim Dockins if Tim does not mind." Tim agreed, as did all the members of the task force. The conference was called to an end and the press and media began to file out. Alvin Richards remained seated in his chair in the center of the room as the members of the task force started to form a group around him to talk and console him.

Clive was the last person to walk up to the group. He stood and listened for several minutes, then spoke to Alvin. "Alvin, if there is anything I or my department can do please do not hesitate to ask. I am here for you and thank you for being there for me. It meant a lot—a lot more than you know."

Alvin stood up and shook his hand then put one arm around Clive and hugged him for a brief second. He looked at Clive and said, "I meant every word. You lead and we'll follow." They all talked for several more minutes then began to file out one at a time to get started on their assignments. The last two left were J.D. Ricketts and Alvin Richards.

Clive looked at both of them then asked, "You two have a few minutes? That suspect I told you about—we got him. He's here now. I'd like you to watch this from the viewing room off our small conference room. I don't know what, if anything, he may have to do with this but I got several questions I want to throw at him. I'd like you two to give me an opinion." The two agreed and Clive asked Alice to get a tape recorder and meet him in the conference room.

CHAPTER 15

Tuesday, June 22, 3:00 p .m.

J.D. and Alvin entered the viewing room to the side of the small conference room. They seated themselves in two chairs behind the two-way mirror that hung on the conference room wall. In the conference room, seated at opposite ends of the table, were Brian and Doc Watson. Clive and Alice were still in the office getting tablets, pens and the recorder when Rose told Clive that Bill Fry was on line one, calling from his car. Clive told Alice to wait as he picked up the phone on her desk and pushed line one. "Hello Bill. This is Clive. What can I do for you?" Clive listened for several minutes and only said, "Okay," several times. He asked, "Are they sure?" There was a pause, then he said, "And what about the prints?" He listened again then said, "Okay, Bill. Thanks for the information. Stay in touch if anything else changes. I'll see you soon. I believe we will be calling another meeting in a day or two. See you buddy."

He hung up the phone then looked at Alice with

disappointment showing on his face. "What was that about?" Alice asked.

Clive paused for a second then said, "Well, it may be nothing, but you remember the buttons we found that may be from Jody's coat. They had grease on them that the lab originally said was a new GM product used on newer vehicles for door latches, hinges and such. Well, now they say they also found traces of an old style of grease that was also present and dried. As if it had been there for a while."

"What does that change?" Alice asked.

"Well," Clive said with a sigh. "We have been thinking of and looking for a newer-type vehicle. One like the Buick that Doc is driving, you know the rental car? Now this may indicate that the vehicle used may not be new but an older, and I say much older year. It may not change anything but this may mean that if the buttons and the grease came from Jody's coat and the car the killer used it may be a vintage vehicle. As for the rest, I guess the only prints they found on Bob Anderson's car that matched the other crime scenes was from the same person that we had found before and we have nothing to match it to. They also said they found evidence that someone else was present but was wearing some type of latex gloves."

Alice stood and thought for a few minutes then said, "I guess we can't just assume then that the car could be Doc's. It's new, I mean this year's model."

"Yeah," Clive said, looking down at the floor. "It does not rule him out, but if there's an old car involved, where does it fit in with him? He rented a car. I mean he doesn't even live here. Where would an old car come into this picture?"

Alice, still thinking intently, asked, "Well Clive, what about his mother? I mean she had a car—or at least I would think she did."

Clive looked up from the floor, smiled at Alice and said, "Good point. When we've finished with Doc how about you check that one out?" They made several more comments as they walked slowly to the conference room.

Clive and Alice entered the room and Clive took a seat to one side of the table and Alice the other. Doc Watson sat back in the chair with a slight smile on his face and his hands clasped across his stomach. Clive spoke first. "Mr. Watson, if you remember I am Clive Aliston, a county sheriff and this is Alice. She will be taking some notes and—if you don't mind—recording this interview."

Doc sat forward in his chair, placed his elbows on the tabletop, and spoke while still smiling. "Before we start this little party of yours, I don't remember being read my rights—or have we stopped doing that here in this little dump of a town? And I haven't been allowed to call my lawyer yet. Am I going to need a lawyer?"

Clive put up his hand in a gesture to slow down, then said, "Mr. Watson."

Doc interrupted, "It's Doc, just call me Doc. Don't make me feel like I'm as old as you, Pops."

Clive, with a disgusted look on his face, paused then calmly said, "Okay, it's Doc and you can call me Clive and we don't need to read your rights and you don't need a lawyer. You are not under arrest. We brought you here because we thought you could help us with the murder investigation that we have underway."

"Murder?" Doc said. "I heard all about your murder— or should I say murders. Don't try and pin this one on me. I'm not in the business of killing people."

"What business exactly are you in?" Brian asked.

"None of your damn business, Lasiter. I wasn't talking to you, Supercop." Brian's face started to turn red but he didn't move or show any other emotion.

Clive once again put up his hand and said, "Okay Doc, we don't need any disrespect or trouble here. We didn't accuse you of any crime in anyway and yes; your business is your business. We don't care what you do for a living here, or in Chicago. We just want to ask you a few questions about your whereabouts since you got into town."

Doc turned to Clive and said, "If I'm not under arrest why do you think it's any of your business where I've been, or how long I've been in town. As for your notes and that tape recorder, go ahead. I could care less. I did nothing and I have nothing to hide." He sat back in the chair, placed his elbows on the arms and clasped his hands in front of his face and forced a smile at Clive. Clive was about to speak again when Doc interrupted. "Oh yeah, and tell whoever you've got behind that mirror I could care less what they hear or who they are. I'm not in fear here. I've done nothing and this is bullshit."

Clive paused for several seconds then continued. "Doc we are not saying you are guilty or anything. We just need to know when you got into town, with who and where you have been since you got here. You're not the only person who is being questioned. When we have a case like this we need to check out anything unusual, and you being here in town after so many years is a bit unusual. Don't feel that you're being made a special case. You're not. A lot of people have been, and will be questioned about their whereabouts over the last couple of weeks."

"When you have a case like this," Doc said. "You ain't never had a case like this in this shit town. I'm surprised they even let you two toy cops run this show. You couldn't find your asses with both hands." Brian, completely red-faced, started to stand up when Clive motioned for him to be seated.

Clive sat forward in his chair, then slowly got up and walked to the large mirror on the side wall. Looking into the mirror he calmly said, "Okay Doc, you want your lawyer, you call him. You want your rights; we'll read them to you. You want to play hardball we can play that game too." He slowly turned and walked to the side of Doc's chair then continued. "You can be out of here in twenty minutes and on your way, or we can hold you on whatever charges are deemed necessary. And don't forget, if we hold you I get a warrant to search car, house, luggage you name it. You want to play; we can play. We not only know the rules we made 'em. Now, Mr. Smartass, what's it going to be? Answer the simple questions or move on to a holding cell. The choice is up to you." Clive slowly walked back to his chair and sat down. He clasped his hands in front of his face and forced a smile back at Doc.

There was silence for several seconds then Doc spoke. "Well Lasiter, I see one thing. Your boss has more balls than you. You might want to listen when he talks cause the one thing you don't have is a big set." Brian didn't respond. He just sat back in his chair and forced a smile at Doc.

After several more seconds Clive said, "Okay Doc, what's it going to be?"

Doc looked at Clive and said, "Okay what the hell do you want to know?"

Clive once again sat forward in his chair, "When did you get into town and for what reasons?"

Doc just sat, now smiling again. "Two days before Jody Miller died. You already knew that. You checked it out already. Why? Because, as I said the other day when I ran into you and supercop outside, my mother's estate needed to be taken care of. You think I'd be back here in hicktown for the fun of it?"

Clive asked, "Where have you been staying?"

Still smiling, Doc said, "At my mothers old home and you already knew that too. You've had me tailed for the last few days. You know where I eat out and what laundry I use. You think I can't spot one of your local yokel cops tailing me? You best send them boys back to school. They ain't done learning yet. What else do you want?"

Clive said, "Okay Doc, where were you over the weekend? This last weekend from Friday night till today."

"Ya lost me didn't you?" Doc said with a laugh.

"Just answer the question," Clive said.

Doc leaned forward, placing his elbows on the tabletop again. "And maybe I don't want to say where I was. There are friends of mine that I don't want to get involved with this."

"Answer the question," Clive said again.

"And if I don't?" Doc said.

"Then call your lawyer, and Alice, call the judge for the warrant," Clive said as he stood up again.

Doc paused for a second as Alice got up to leave. He then said, "Okay, okay. I was in Pittsburgh to see some friends and an old girlfriend. I guess you want names and numbers, right Sheriff?" Clive motioned for Alice to sit again then he replied, "Yeah, names, numbers and times. See how easy this can be when you decide to be a good boy and help?" The questioning went on for another ten to fifteen minutes, then Clive told Doc that was enough. He was free to go but not to leave town unless he called and told them.

Doc complained, but added that he still had enough of his mother's business to take care of and that he would be around for a few more days. Just before he left, Clive asked if his big friend had come with him. Doc acted dumb and said, "What big friend? I came alone." Doc left the station at about 3:45 p.m., followed, on Clive's order, by one of the night shift officers who had come out early.

Clive, Brian, J.D. and Alvin gathered in Clive's office and went over what they had heard. Alice started on the list of names and numbers that Doc had provided and also called the DMV to see if she could find out whether Mrs. Watson had owned an older car that might still be around. It was well past five o'clock when the meeting in Clive's office broke up and everyone left. Clive stopped to eat on the way home, then made several calls from his home phone that lasted till late in the evening. The next couple of days went by without much happening. Alice had contacted all of the people on the list that Doc had given them and to everyone's surprise Doc's story seemed to check out. Out-of-town personnel from the various departments began to arrive and check into the rooms that had been provided. There was another meeting called for Thursday afternoon with all the members of the task force—the originals and the new personnel that had arrived. Schedules were set up and officers from the various departments were placed on the previously decided assignments.

Thursday, June 24

By Thursday evening the town of Smith Falls and the surrounding county area was flooded with personnel from every department and agency. Even though Doc's story seemed to check out they had decided to keep the tail on him for the time being. Most of the names he had given as friends were people who had been in trouble with the law before. The so-called girlfriend turned out to be a high-class hooker that he had once dated in high school before she had taken up her present profession. All of the people seemed to back up his story but how much could be believed? The tail on Doc was set up in three eight to ten hour shifts that started at odd times of the day so as not to create a routine that could be figured out by Doc then used to avoid the tail.

It was Thursday evening at seven o'clock when Brian Lasiter took over the tail on Doc. He was in charge of the sheriff's department portion of the task force to fill in for Clive who was task force commander. Even with the workload that had been added he still wanted to take a turn at the tail on Doc. He was convinced that Doc had something to do with the case and being confined to the station office was not cutting it for him. Alice had received the report from the DMV, which confirmed that Mrs. Watson did indeed own an older model car, a 1976 Cadillac. It had been transferred to her son, and was now titled in the state of Illinois. Apparently, Doc had kept the car because of its mint condition and low mileage. Brian had taken over the tail once again at Bartolli's Restaurant in Smith Falls. He had hidden the unmarked car well and had watched Doc leave the restaurant at about 7:45 p.m. He had been watching from across the street in the front room of a pizza parlor. When Doc left Bartolli's, Brian had seen him act somewhat surprised when he did not see any type of police car parked in the area. Brian had posted another unmarked car on a side road off of Tower Hill Road. Once Doc drove away from the restaurant he was picked up by a third car and followed at some distance to the bottom of Tower Hill Road. When he turned up that road headed in the direction of home the third car called the one on up the road and warned that he was coming. When Doc passed the second car on the side road it also followed until Doc turned up the driveway to his mother's house. The second car continued on down the road but did not stop. Brian was told when Doc arrived at home then he drove his car to the secluded area behind the trees just down the road from the house driveway.

Thursday, June 24, 6:00 p.m.

J.D. Ricketts and Ed Cane, one of the newly-arrived FBI agents, had just finished supper at their motel. They were in a discussion about the case and had just entered J.D.'s room. J.D. had just gone inside the bathroom when the phone rang. He told Ed to answer it. When he opened the bathroom door he saw Ed sitting on the end of the bed holding the phone with his hand cupped tightly over the mouthpiece. He pointed to the phone and whispered, "It's our boss and he wants to speak to you, now!"

J.D. looked at Ed with a half-forced smile and took the phone. He took in a deep breath then said, "Yes, this is J.D." Ed motioned that he was going to leave, but J.D. pointed to one of the chairs and put his hand over the phone and whispered, "Sit down, hang around." J.D. then continued, "Yes, sir. Cane said you wanted to speak to me?" Ed sat and listened to the half of the conversation that he could hear. J.D. continued, "Yes, sir. I know why I was sent here. No sir, it was not to take control of the situation, it was to evaluate the case and then make that decision. From what I have learned I do not feel that I need to exert any pressure on anyone at this point in time. Yes sir, I am aware that Sheriff Aliston is not a qualified agent. I know he lacks experience in a case like this but there are some aspects of this case that I need input on also. No sir, I am not doubting my ability to run this case. I am not doubting it because I am not as I said in charge of this case. I have developed the fullest respect for and have the utmost confidence in Sheriff Aliston. Look sir," J.D. said more forcefully. "You and I know why I was sent here. It was because of the money and the political influence. I am not in your normal big city arena and believe me—not after your run-of-the-mill serial killer. I have never seen a case that is as clean as this when it comes to clues. I am not as attuned to this type of out-of-town atmosphere. You're dealing with a totally different breed of people here. This isn't, as I said, the city." J.D. listened for several minutes then continued, "Sir, I feel that as much progress has been made and is being made as can be expected. We are working as a team and it's a good team I might add. If you are not happy with my evaluation of this or the setup of the task force then I am prepared to return to my home office. You always have the option of replacing me." J.D. stopped then listened again. As he did, he looked at Ed and shook his head.

After several minutes, J.D. continued, "Yes, sir. I am confident in the team here. Yes, sir. I will monitor all that happens and if necessary take control, but only if I feel that is necessary. Sir, I can't make it any more plain than I have. I have confidence in all members and departments of this task force. Yes sir. I understand that the integrity of the bureau must be maintained. Sir, do you want me here or not?"

J.D., looking angered, took the phone from his ear and held it out at about two feet from his head, looked at Ed again, and showed his teeth as if grinding them together. He returned the phone to his ear, then continued. "Ok, then if you want me here and have confidence in me then also have confidence in my assessment of this situation. Yes sir, I will keep you as informed as I can. Yes sir, I am convinced that Sheriff Aliston can do this. Yes, sir, I will keep in touch. Yes sir, if I need anything else I will call. Thank you very much, sir. Goodbye, sir." J.D. placed the phone on the receiver and then stood for a few seconds and just stared at it. He then looked up at Ed, who was sitting quietly with a smile on his face. "Cane, don't ever mix politics with crime work no matter how far up you get in the line of promotions. The two don't mix well, like oil and water, and those who try to mix them, well they just generally suck. Come on. After that I need a drink."

They both left the room and headed for the motel bar.

Thursday, June 24, 11:00 p .m.

Brian had been in the car watching the house for at least two and half hours when he noticed that several lights had come on in what seemed to be the basement of the house. There had been little to no traffic on the road over the course of the evening so he parked the car into a small cut in the trees and decided to walk to the house for a closer look. He used a small mag-light flashlight to navigate his way through the trees and bushes on the hillside below the house. When he reached the last of the trees he was still about fifty yards from the edge of the yard at the side of the house. He made his way keeping low in the tall weeds that covered the space from the tree line to the yard. When he reached the open grass of the yard he lay down on his stomach and watched for several minutes. He wasn't there long when the back door opened and he saw Doc on the porch with something in his hands. He watched as Doc placed whatever it was in one of the large garbage cans at the edge of the porch. He remained there until Doc once again entered the house. When he heard the back screen door slam closed he got up and ran to the side of the house. He positioned himself against the house between a set of horizontal cellar doors and a cellar window. He remained there for several minutes in a crouched position, his back against the foundation of the house, and listened.

When all seemed quiet he slowly turned and cautiously looked into the lighted cellar window. The window was at the bottom of the cellar steps and he could see about a third of the cellar on one end of the house. He could make out two doors on the right side of the cellar wall. Both doors were closed and appeared to be old rusted metal. The door closest to him looked old—almost medieval and had a large bolt lock and what appeared to be a small window near the middle. He could see what appeared to be a small table on the opposite side of the room but he could not make out what was on it. He put his face close to the glass and used his hands to shade the light from the sides to get a better look. He was intently focusing on the table when someone passed right in front of him down the steps to the bottom. It was Doc. Brian quickly backed away from the window almost falling backward as he did. He quickly regained his balance and then once again leaned his back against the foundation wall. He remained there for several seconds then slowly leaned to the right to the window again and looked inside. He kept his face several feet from the window as he watched Doc unlock and enter the door closest to him. He waited for several minutes and was about to move in for a closer look, when Doc walked back out of the room with an armful of what appeared to be rags or old clothes. He watched as Doc dropped the rags to the floor in a pile, then walked to the table across the room and retrieved a large box. He brought the box to where the rags were, then opened the box and placed the rags inside. He once again entered the room and was out of sight for several more minutes.

Brian was about to move closer for a better look when Doc came out of the room again with another bundle of rags or clothes. There was something different about this load though. The rags appeared to be covered in something red that could have been paint, rust or maybe blood. He watched as Doc placed that bundle in the box and then he saw in Doc's right hand a large object that appeared to be a large blade knife. It also was covered in something red. Doc placed the knife in one of the rags and wrapped it up tightly then took another rag and wiped his hands. He entered the room one more time and came out with more rags and placed them in the box. He took one of the rags from the box and once again wiped his hands. He walked back to the table, opened a can, reached inside and retrieved something, and then began to rub his hands together. He walked back to the box and got out another rag and wiped his hands again. When he was finished he closed the box and picked it up and walked toward the side of the cellar that Brian could not see. Brian put his face against the right side of the glass trying to see back into the cellar to the left but could see nothing. He pulled back away from the glass and whispered, "Shit." He was about to move to a more comfortable position when he heard what sounded like a lock snap on the inside of the double horizontal cellar doors. Realizing that someone was coming out he made the only move he could, a roll to the left up against the cement base that the cellar doors rested on. Seconds later the two doors opened and were pushed up and to both sides. The door came down on his side and partially covered him except for his lower legs. He quickly pulled his legs up to his body and at the same time unsnapped his weapon, drew it, and held it up close to his chest as he snapped off the safety. He heard someone come up the steps from the basement, then saw feet walk past the bottom of the door in front of him. He watched as Doc, now carrying the box, walked to a fire pit just off the back porch. Doc placed the box in the fire pit then walked to the porch as Brian watched from under the cellar door. Doc returned from the porch with what appeared to be a gas can and poured something on the box. He returned the can to the porch then took a piece of rag from his pocket and used a lighter to light the rag. Once the rag was ignited he threw it onto the box. It burst into flames and the entire back and side yard was bathed in a yellow-orange glow.

Brian could see Doc's dark silhouette in front of the growing fire and also realized that the light had now totally illuminated the underside of the door he was hiding under. He knew he must make a move and make it now. He watched Doc intently for several seconds and when he was sure Doc's attention was on the fire he made his move. He rolled out from under the right side door and moved low to the ground around the front of the steps and under the left side of the door, pulled in his legs and waited. Several minutes later he heard footsteps approach then move down the steps to the cellar. The doors on each side were pulled up and then closed and locked. Brian straightened his legs out on the ground, laid the gun on his chest, took in a long breath, and then slowly let it out. He remained there for several minutes and listened in the dark. The only light was the remaining glow from the now-slowing fire. When all that remained was embers Brian slowly got up and started back across the yard to the high weeds. When he reached the weeds he turned back to the house and watched for several minutes. He saw the cellar lights go out and then saw Doc in the kitchen area and then that light went out. He stayed until all the first floor lights were out and the second floor bedroom light came on. He turned and moved low through the weeds and into the trees and bushes toward the road. As he moved he realized what he had seen. It could have been evidence that Doc had placed in the fire. It could have blown the case wide open but what could he do under the circumstances? He had no warrant and he was on private property. What he saw could not be used in a court of law. He knew what had started out as a closer look at a suspect was now the closest thing they had to solving the case. Right or wrong he had to get to the car and let someone know what he had seen.

CHAPTER 16

Friday, June 25, 12:40 a.m.

Brian returned to the car and called in a short report. He also asked for a replacement at the house. He wanted to return to the station and fill out a complete report on what he had seen. The sooner he had it on paper the sooner they could get a search warrant to check out the house, and save what evidence that might be left. His replacement showed up about thirty minutes later at 1:15 a.m., and to his surprise it was Jack Duff. He had volunteered for some of the night duty, and when he heard about Brian's call he wanted to fill in for him. Brian talked to Jack for about ten minutes and went into a little more detail on what he had seen and done.

Brian got in his car and headed back to the station at about 1:30 a.m. Jack parked his car in the same spot as Brian's, giving him a good view of the house and the driveway through the trees. He opened a thermos of coffee and poured himself a cup, then took one of several sandwiches out of a brown bag and started to eat. He was trying to get comfortable for what he knew was going to be a long night. Brian entered the station at about 1:55 a.m. and reported to the night desk sergeant, and then went to his office and started on the report. He told the sergeant to put in a call to Clive no later than 6:30 a.m. When the sergeant reached Clive he was to tell Brian and connect him. At close to 2:30 a.m. Jack Duff was still seated in his patrol car in the trees below the Watson's house. He had poured a second cup of coffee and was sitting quietly watching a storm move in from the south end of Smith Falls. Lightning was all over the sky and he knew they were in for a good old-fashioned summer night storm. He was actually beginning to enjoy the fireworks display that had not reached his location, when he saw a car coming up Tower Hill Road in his direction.

It was 2:35 a.m. and Brian was still working on his report in his office. He had heard the thunder for close to half an hour now, and he could tell the storm was almost over Smith Falls. He stopped what he was writing, turned his chair to the window, opened the blinds and looked outside. The window glass was just beginning to show spots of water from a fine mist that had started to fall. He was looking out at one of the parking lot lights that had a rainbow of mist around it, when a bolt of lightning crossed the sky followed by an almost immediate crash of thunder. It took him by surprise and he jumped in his chair and yelled, "Wow." He shook his head then looked out the window again. It was beginning to rain harder and he saw the trees in the parking area being whipped back and forth wildly. He closed the blinds and turned again to his desk. He read the last line that he had written and was about to start again when the entire office seemed to be bathed in intense white light that lasted for a split second. The light was followed by a thunderous crash, and sparks flew from the florescent fixture over his desk. He instinctively covered his head and backed up just as the tubes fell from the fixture and crashed to his desk. All the building lights flickered several times, then all went black and the fire alarm sounded.

Jack Duff watched as the car he had seen still headed slowly in his direction. He could almost make out the silhouette of the front of the vehicle as each flash of lightning crossed the sky. As the car reached the driveway to the Watson's house he realized that the headlights were single and round. A thought went through his mind as the car slowly turned up the driveway. At the last briefing they had been told that the vehicle used in the crimes was maybe an older vehicle, not a new one as they had originally been told. He also remembered that they were actually looking for possibly two suspects. One of them very large. The car moved slowly up the driveway toward the house as another streak of lightning crossed the sky. Jack could for an instant see the full side silhouette of the vehicle. It was fairly large and appeared to be an older model. His mind went once again back to his last briefing. Possibly two suspects. An older model car. Doc Watson had a large bodyguard who may or may not have accompanied him on this trip. A fine mist sprayed across the windshield and he turned on the wipers and strained his eyes to see the car again but it was gone. He sat for a few seconds and sipped his coffee again as thoughts raced through his mind.

With what Brian had seen and now what he had seen he needed to call the station and report. This could be the break they had waited for. He keyed the radio mike and waited for a response and got nothing but static. He waited several seconds and called again, and again nothing but static. He placed his coffee on the dashboard, looked out at the stormy sky and whispered, "What the hell?" Again he called, and again he got static. He waited for at least thirty seconds, then called to any unit that could hear him. Again there was nothing but static. He placed the mike back in the cradle then reached for his cell phone. He dialed the station number and listened. His phone started to beep and the display read re-dial. He dialed again, and once more got a beep and re-dial. He looked at the phone then tried the radio and again got static. He tried the phone again and this time it rang. After seven or eight rings he heard the desk sergeant answer, "County sheriff's office, hold on please," then the phone went dead and there was a beep and the phone display once again said re-dial.

Jack realized then that the storm must have affected all communications. He also realized he couldn't miss what might be the chance to help end this case. It was against his better judgment, but he decided to do what Brian had done. He had to see for himself who was the person or persons in the car that had just gone up the Watson driveway at three o'clock in the morning. He left the car and locked the doors, then went to the trunk and got out his rain poncho. It had stopped raining for the moment but he knew that because the wind was picking up that the worst was yet to come. He put on the poncho then checked his service revolver and tested his mag-light. He closed the trunk and headed into the trees in the same direction that Brian had gone hours earlier. The wind was growing more and more intense and the trees and bushes around him moved back and forth in his flashlight beam. They almost appeared to be covered in wet silver as his light bounced off their wet leaves. He moved through the trees, the branches slapping his shoulders and hat as he wove his way toward the field of weeds. Several minutes later he was in the open in waist high weeds. He bent down for a second on one knee and studied the dark house as the wind whipped the tall grass all around him. He scanned the top of the driveway but at that distance in the dark he could see nothing. There was a bright flash of lightning overhead and behind the house that illuminated everything. He could see for an instant the silhouette of the house and a large car at the top of the driveway.

As he started to move through the weeds the thought crossed his mind that this would make a perfect scene for a horror movie. He kept low to the top of the weeds as the wind came from all directions. It was strange. It was wet but not raining. The lightning was almost constant and the wind seemed to come in swirls from everywhere. He reached the edge of the yard and kept low in the weeds. He remained there for several minutes then he made his move toward the house, flashlight off. He ran to almost the same place that Brian had earlier and stopped and watched and waited. When he had seen the entire area in the light from the constant flashes of lightning, he moved toward the front of the house and the car parked at the top of the driveway. He moved slowly with his back against the side of the house until he reached the corner of the front porch. He could see the car in the darkness about a hundred feet away, but he could not make out what it was. The wind became even more intense and the lightning was coming from everywhere. It was starting to rain again and within seconds the water was coming in sheets.

Even with the sound of the wind, rain, and thunder he thought he heard something close. He reached for his service revolver and with both hands pulled it up in front of his face then waited. Several seconds later he turned and looked around the corner of the front porch. In the distance in a flash of lightning he saw a man on the front sidewalk facing him. He wiped the rain from his eyes and tried to see who it was. He then felt an overwhelming feeling that someone was close behind him. He squeezed the grips of his revolver and turned in the direction he had just come from. Suddenly, there in front of him was a large dark silhouette that towered over him. He tried to make a move with his revolver but it was knocked from his hands. Lightning flashed and for an instant he thought he saw a face. But was it a face? There was no time to think. In a second there came a crashing blow to his shoulder and neck that slammed him against the house. He hit the brick side of the house and slid to the ground. Almost paralyzed he felt his body being pulled by his feet out to the front of the house, then rolled onto his back. The rain pelted down on his face and filled his eyes as he looked up trying to see. There was another flash of lightning directly overhead and he saw the huge silhouette now hovering over him. He wanted to move but he couldn't. A large hand grasped his poncho at the chest and lifted him several feet from the ground. He heard a voice from behind, "No. He is not one of the guilty. He must not die." He was held for several more seconds then dropped to the ground. There was another flash of lightning and he could see two silhouettes standing over him. One seemed normal; the other was huge. The rain was pouring into his eyes and he tried to see and move but he could not. He then felt someone pick him up from the ground and almost place him on his feet. He saw in another flash of light a huge hand draw back, then he felt for an instant a crashing blow to his face and all went black.

Friday, June 25, 4:30 a.m.

The rain had stopped and the storm was off in the distance. Only an occasional rumble of thunder could be heard over Smith Falls. The station was alive with activity. The parking lot was filled with fire and emergency vehicles and temporary bright floodlights were trained on the building from all directions. There were police from the county, state, and town all either in the station or outside, trying to keep the small group of media and spectators away. There was a group of repair people on the roof of the station and also inside the first floor and the basement. The storm had done its work at the station in Smith Falls, and all over the county. Lightning had struck the radio antennae and the electrical entrance at the station, knocking out all communications and power. Three quarters of Smith Falls was without power and the county did not fare much better. There were even several reports of tornadoes touching down just east of town.

Clive had been awakened by the fire department at

C. William Davis III

around 3:15 a.m. and had arrived at about 4 a.m. He was joined by both J.D. Ricketts and Jim Terrell at about 4:10 a.m. They had been notified by the fire department also at their rooms at the motel. The three of them and Brian were in Clive's office, talking in the dim light from the emergency lighting system, when Alvin Richards stepped into Clive's office. Brian stopped in midsentence when the door opened. "Hello gentlemen. Quite a night I guess," Richards said as he closed the door behind him.

"Hi Alvin," Clive said as he sat back in his chair. "I see they got you up too."

"No," Alvin said as he sat in one of the empty chairs. "The storm got me up. Oh hell, I really wasn't asleep anyway. I heard about the damage to the station from some of my guys. Just came down to see if I could help. As I said I wasn't asleep."

J.D. and Jim both said hello, as did Brian. "What can I do?" Alvin asked.

"Well," Clive said, pausing, "You are much the same as us when it comes to the damage here. We are probably best to leave it to the people who know what they are doing. I don't know about you but I know I'd be in the way more than help."

"You're probably right," Alvin said. "What else is going on?"

Clive smiled and said, "Well Alvin, I'm glad you're here. You'll be very interested in what Brian has to say about his tail on Doc Watson." Just then the lights flickered on, then off, then on, then off again.

They all sat quietly for several seconds then J.D. spoke up, "Well, I guess the problem isn't fixed quite yet. While we wait Brian, why don't you start again on what you were telling us before Alvin came in?"

"I agree," Clive said. "Start at the beginning." As Brian started over on what he had seen, Clive saw Alice come into the office holding a box in her arms. He got up and told Brian to continue as he went to the door and opened it.

Alice came into the room and set the box on Clive's desk. Brian stopped again but Clive told him continue up to where Alvin had come in.

Alice whispered to Clive, "I heard about what happened so I made some coffee. I still have power at my place. There's some breakfast rolls in there too. I figured you would all be here and I thought you might be hungry. Besides I couldn't..."

Clive interrupted, "Yeah, I know. You couldn't sleep either." She looked at him kind of puzzled and said, "What?"

"Never mind," Clive said. "It appears none of us were asleep. Well, anyway, thank you. Have you eaten?" he asked.

"Yes," she said, "Before I came in. You guys eat. I'll be out here if you need me." She was about to leave the room and everyone was thanking her when the lights came on again, and this time they stayed on.

"Alright," Clive said, "That's half the trouble. Now if we can get the radios up again." Alice went out to her desk and Clive, J.D., Jim, Brian, and Alvin got coffee and rolls then Brian continued on his report.

They had been listening to Brian and talking for about twenty minutes when Alice called on the intercom. "Clive, sorry to interrupt but the radio is back up again. Thought you would want to know." Clive gave her a thumbs up then was about to continue in the conversation when he saw Bret Collins come into the station. He excused himself and went out to the main office.

Bret was talking to Alice when Clive came out. "Hi Boss," Bret said. "I just came from the east end of town. We got damage everywhere. Lines down, roofs torn off, trees blown over. I don't think I've seen one this bad in a long time."

Clive looked at Bret, then at his watch and asked, "What are you doing out at this time of day?"

"Well," Bret said, "I couldn't..."

Clive interrupted again, "Yeah, you couldn't sleep either."

"What?" Bret asked, looking a little strange.

"Never mind," Clive said. "What we gonna need out there?"

"Well," Bret said, "We could use a few more officers to take care of traffic and emergency vehicle access. Other than that the fire departments and the Smith Falls boys have it pretty much under control."

"Was anyone hurt?" Clive asked.

"No," Bret said. "It appears that everyone is okay but we are gonna have one hell of a clean up for awhile." Clive said he would send some help out and asked if Bret could take over that part of the problem. He wanted to remain at the station until all was up and running, and he wanted to continue with the meeting on Brian's report about Doc. They talked for several more minutes then Bret left and Clive went back to his office.

When Clive was seated the meeting continued. J.D. Ricketts felt that what Brian had seen was more than enough reason to get a warrant issued before any more evidence, if that's what it was, was destroyed. Like J.D. said, even if they were wrong about Doc all they would do is piss him off, and when it came to Doc, who cared? The meeting went on for several more minutes as each one asked Brian more questions.

Friday, June 25, 5:00 a.m.

Jack Duff slowly opened his eyes, but all he could see was blackness. He knew he was on his back but he couldn't figure out if he was at home in bed or somewhere else. He lay there for several more minutes passing in and out of consciousness. After what seemed to him like hours he opened his eyes again and all still seemed dark. He tried to raise his right arm to wipe his eyes but there was a sudden intense pain in his right shoulder. He moaned and put his right arm back at his side. The pain seemed to awaken him more and then he started to remember: the car, the house, the storm, and the huge silhouette. His eyes opened wide and he quickly tried to sit up but waves of pain passed through his shoulder and head. He managed to rise about a foot off the ground but quickly fell back. He lay there as the pain began to subside again. After several more minutes he tried his left arm and it moved with no pain. He raised his left hand to his face and tried to wipe his eyes. As he did, he touched his nose and a burning pain seemed to spread all across the top of his face. He lay there several more minutes as the burning passed. The next thing he remembered was the huge arm drawing back just before all went black. His eyes opened again and slowly raised his left arm and carefully wiped his eyes, trying not to touch his nose. He moved his head slowly from side to side and then he tried his legs. All seemed to work but the pain in his shoulder, neck and face was turning into a constant throbbing, burning pain. He slowly moved his right hand to where his service revolver should be, but it was gone. He then moved his left arm to his belt where his cell phone was clipped, and it also was gone.

He lay there for several more minutes and just listened, but all he heard was the sound of water dripping off the roof and onto the horizontal cellar doors near his position. When he was sure that he could hear no one near him he sat up and then rolled to his left, and looked around slowly in all directions. As he turned his head the pain in his shoulder, face and neck returned with a burning vengeance. He put his head down on the ground and breathed in slow, long breaths. As he lay there it was finally starting to sink in that he was badly injured. He needed to get back to the car and call for help, but could he make it? As he lay there he also realized that he needed to report what he had seen. He had to try and try now. He used his left arm and pushed himself to his knees then paused again as the pain increased then subsided. He slowly got to his feet but his knees seemed weak and he staggered to his left several feet until he ran into the side of the house. He reached for his back pocket and retrieved his handkerchief, folded it with his left hand and stuffed it into his mouth and bit down hard. He looked around again and when he was sure all was clear he took in a deep breath and started to walk across the yard to the high weeds. When he reached the weeds he fell to his knees in pain and screamed, but the handkerchief clinched tightly in his teeth muffled the sound. He leaned forward on his left hand, then back into a sitting position, and then removed the handkerchief and took in long breaths through his mouth as waves of pain and nausea moved over him.

Several minutes later he got back to his feet and started toward the woods line with the handkerchief in his mouth again. He fell several times in the weed field, his feet becoming tangled in the twisted mass of wet undergrowth. Each time he hit the ground he let out a muffled scream and stopped to catch his breath. When he reached the tree line he backed up against a large dark tree trunk and slid to the ground in a sitting position. He pulled the handkerchief from his mouth, moaned slightly, then turned and vomited on the ground next to him. Waves of pain moved over his shoulder, head and face, and he began to get lightheaded and dizzy. He knew he was going to pass out and he started to take in deep breaths through his mouth and with each exhale he repeated, "No, no, no." After what seemed like a lifetime the pain started to subside again and the dizziness passed. He sat against the tree in the wet forest and looked back toward the house. The sky was beginning to slowly light up and the house appeared as an ominous dark silhouette on the crest of the hill.

He looked for the car. There against the orange-gray sky was the large dark vehicle. Its outline made the house look even more sinister. It was then that he realized what he had seen. He sat there for several more minutes as the clouds in the eastern sky started to glow a dull pink-orange. He realized the sun was not far behind and that he must have been unconscious for a long time. He needed to make that call, pain or no pain. He must get to his car now. He had to report. He placed the handkerchief back in his mouth and slowly got to his feet. He turned and headed into the woods in the direction of the car. He was within sight of the car and was trying to walk faster when his foot caught on the root of a tree and he fell forward into a large hole filled with water and mud. He landed face first in the pool, his right shoulder slamming against a small tree as he hit the ground. The pain was like nothing he had felt before. He rolled to his back; the mud caked on his face and upper body. He spit out the handkerchief and let out a long scream that came from somewhere deep inside of him. The scream seemed to echo through the still dark and wet forest as if it would never stop. He felt as if he would pass out again, then realized if he did he might drown. It took all the strength he had, but he rolled to his stomach and then got to his knees. He wiped the mud and water from his face, took several deep breaths, and staggered to his feet. He stood there weaving back and forth then finally grabbed a tree next to him. He took in another deep breath and started again for the car.

When he reached the vehicle he put his hand on the side, then rolled to his back and slid to the ground. He started a slow search of his pockets for the keys but he could not find them. He always put things in his right shirt pocket but they were not there. After several minutes he moved around the car to the driver's door and tried it, hoping it was open but in his mind knowing he had locked it. He stopped, put his aching head on the roof of the car and just breathed.

After several seconds he looked around the area near the car and saw a rather large rock in the ditch on the side of the road. He bent down and tried to pick it up but his muddy left hand could not grasp it. He wiped his hand on the trunk of the car to pick up some of the water then wiped his hands on his pants and tried again. This time he had it. He moved back to the driver's door and with a half swing hit the window but the rock only bounced off and hit the ground at his feet. He slowly bent down and picked it up again and this time he gave it all he had. The window only cracked and the stone fell to the ground again. He placed his head on the roof of the car again and just breathed. He looked down at the rock again and then bent to pick it up and as he did the keys fell out from somewhere under his poncho and hit the ground in front of him. He didn't know whether to be glad or mad. He picked up the keys and tried to put them in the door lock. After several tries the key went in and he heard the lock snap. He opened the door and fell into the front seat on his face. He just lay there for several seconds then he sat up and put the keys in the ignition and started the car. He picked up the mike and held it close to his face and once again paused to take in air. He was feeling dizzy again and waves of pain continued to roll over him. He knew he was going to pass out. He keyed the mike and forced the message out, "Hello. Can anyone hear me? This is Officer Duff. I'm at the Watson house and badly injured. I repeat, officer down."

CHAPTER 17

Friday, June 25, 5:35 a.m.

Clive, J.D., Brian, Jim Terrell and Alvin were still in Clive's office, and Alice was at her desk working when the radio cracked and came to life. Alice listened as Jack Duff's voice came over the speaker. She couldn't believe what she had heard, but the last statement leaped out of the radio at her, "I repeat, officer down."

Clive was in the middle of a discussion with J.D. when he saw through the window of his office, Alice jump up with the radio mike in her hand. He stopped in mid-sentence. He could see by her expression she was panicked or distressed. He slowly stood up staring out the window as the last word trailed off his lips. The other four men stared at Clive then turned to look out at Alice also. Clive had just put a cigar in his mouth and had been intending to light it, but instead took the cigar out of his mouth and placed it on the desk. He started out around his desk, as Alice, forgetting the intercom, came around her desk on a run to his office. They both reached his office door at the same time. She opened the door, almost hitting Clive in the face, and began to yell incoherently something about Jack Duff.

Clive said, somewhat sternly, "Alice, calm down. Start over. What happened?"

She took a quick breath then said, "Jack Duff just called from the Watson house. He said, 'Officer down.' He's hurt, Clive—maybe bad, and I can't raise him now. I tried several times. No response. He sounded bad, I mean really bad."

Clive paused for a second as the other four men all stood up almost in unison, "Damn," Clive said, then quickly, "Alice, call all available units. Tell them to meet me at the bottom of Tower Hill Road, ASAP." He turned to the other four and said, "Well guys, let's get moving now. I want the place covered totally. No one gets out. Alice call for an ambulance, I want it there three minutes ago, the bottom of Tower Hill Road."

Brian cut in on Clive, as he was about to continue, "Clive, I know that area and well, there's an old dirt road behind the house. It hasn't been used in years but we need to cover that. It comes out onto the main road about three quarters of a mile away. We have to cut that off. It's one of the only two good ways off the property."

Clive looked at J.D. and said, "How about you going with Brian. Cover that road. We can't let anyone slip out the back—that's if they haven't already done that. Alvin, Jim, you two are with me. We'll hit the place from the front. Alice, as I said all available cars even if they have to cut something short for now, and I want that ambulance." Alice didn't wait for anyone; she ran back to her desk and started to put out the calls.

Clive turned to the four as he took his weapon and belt off the cabinet behind his desk and checked them. "Gentlemen, if it's Doc Watson or not I want him or them alive if possible. I need answers and I can't get them from dead men. If you must shoot, try and wound them. Just don't put your lives on the line. If lethal force is the only way then so be it." They all left Clive's office and Clive stopped at Alice's desk, "Have you raised Jack?" he asked.

Alice looked up and said, "No, I've tried several times. I get nothing. God, Clive I'm worried. He sounded like he was, well, in real bad shape." Brian and J.D. had already left for their cars and Clive motioned to Alvin and Jim to hold up. He turned again to Alice and said, "Get me warrants to search everything at the house and I don't care how you get them or who we owe for it. Just get them." He quickly turned and the three raced out of the office headed for Clive's car.

When Clive, Alvin and Jim reached Clive's car he yelled across the lot to Brian to get his walkie-talkies out of his trunk. He told him to use Channel 3 unless otherwise notified. Both cars left the lot, lights and sirens on, and headed to the bottom of Tower Hill Road. When they arrived at the intersection at the bottom of Tower Hill, seven other cars, Smith Falls, county, and state were there, as well as FBI vehicles and the ambulance. Clive got out and quickly instructed all vehicles to follow him to the Watson house. He told Brian and J.D. once again to cover the road at the rear of the house. The remaining cars were to be dispersed along the front road and to block the intersection below the house. The ambulance was to proceed to where they figured Jack's car had been parked. All personnel were instructed to use walkie-talkies on Channel 3 and that if possible any and all suspects were to be taken into custody. All the vehicles left, with Clive's car in the lead followed by Brian's. The ambulance took up the last position in the line up. The procession traveled up the road with the lights on and sirens off. When they reached the intersection below the house, Brian's car cut to the left, headed to the dirt road three quarters of a mile away. Two vehicles stayed at the intersection to stop all traffic and check cars. Clive, the ambulance, the FBI vehicles and several others continued to the bottom of the driveway to the house. An FBI vehicle blocked the bottom of the driveway and the rest—except for Clive and the ambulance—positioned themselves along the lower road.

Clive and the ambulance continued on to where Jack's car was parked. When Clive saw the patrol car at the side of the road the first thing he noticed was the driver's door ajar and what looked like a foot hanging out of the opening. He brought his car to a sliding stop in the center of the road as the ambulance stopped behind him. He, Alvin and Jim jumped out and headed for the car, guns drawn. It was now almost light and they all looked around and made sure the area was secure before they motioned for the ambulance crew to get out. When Clive was satisfied that all was clear he went directly to Jack's car. He looked inside and saw Jack lying across the front seat, the radio mike still in his hand. He opened the car door and with Alvin and Jim looking on, climbed partway inside. He looked close into Jack's face, still covered in mud, called his name twice and touched his shoulder. There was no response. He called again and this time Jack started to move his head.

Clive looked back at Alvin and Jack and said, "Thank God, he's alive." He put his hand on Jack's head and whispered, "The guys are here to help you now. You'll be okay. You'll be okay."

Jack opened his eyes and said, "Hi boss, what took you so long?"

Clive answered, "You scared us big time old buddy. You'll be okay."

Clive moved to get out so the ambulance crew could get in but Jack grabbed his arm and pulled him close. He whispered slowly and so low Clive had to put his ear next to Jack's head. "Clive, I saw them. Both of them—the big guy too. He's a monster boss, a monster. I tried but he hit me so hard. I saw the car, the old car, but... I'm sorry boss, I'm sorry."

Clive whispered back, "It's okay, Jack you did good. You

did good. We'll take it from here. You must rest now, just rest." Clive got out of the car and the ambulance crew got to their work. Clive walked to the center of the road and spoke to Alvin and Jim. "He's alive but just barely. He's hurt bad."

Jim said, "Is he going to make it?"

Clive shook his head and said, "Lord, I hope so."

One of the ambulance crew walked to Clive and said, "He's probably got a bad concussion and I'm sure a broken nose and a possible fractured cheekbone. He may also have something wrong with his shoulder and arm but I'm not sure. We'll stabilize him then move him to County Memorial, ASAP."

Alvin asked, "Will he make it?" The ambulance driver said he thought so but they would know more when they got to the hospital. Alvin then turned to Clive and Jim and said, "Let's do this."

Clive called on the walkie-talkies and checked with the cars at the intersection and the bottom of the driveway. All were prepared for the move to the house. He then called to Brian and J.D. on the back road. They had parked their car across the side road and were making their way up the back road to the house. Clive told Brian to hold up until he, Alvin and Jim were in place. He then turned to Alvin and Jim and said, "We are all in place. Let's move up to the house before we give the green light to go." They all checked their weapons then started into the woods. The three moved into the woods in the direction of the house. It was 6:45 a.m. and full daylight. They worked their way through the woods about twenty-five yards apart until they reached the field of weeds. They formed a line at the edge of the woods about fifty yards apart then Clive called all units to start toward the house. Brian and J.D. covered the back road while the FBI unit closed off the driveway and sent two agents up the driveway to the house. The cars at the intersection below the house remained at their position and the remainder of the units moved up the hill,

spaced at fifty-yard intervals. Clive, Alvin and Jim Terrell
moved through the field of weeds to the edge of the yard.
When they reached the yard they called all the other units
and made sure everyone was in place.

Clive noticed that the large car that Jack had seen was
nowhere in sight. All that stood before him was the old
house at the crest of the hill. He made a last radio check
with Alvin and Jim on his side of the house and Brian and
J.D. in the back. He called the FBI unit at the top of the
driveway and the remaining units that had moved up the
hill at various positions. The house was now completely
encircled. If Doc and his accomplice were still there, they
had no possible escape. Clive waited for several more
minutes then gave the command, "Go slow, but go now."
He added, "Do not enter the house until told to do so." He,
Alvin and Jim moved across the yard and then quickly up
against the wall of the house on the lower side. He scanned
the area but heard and saw nothing. He checked again
with all units then told Jim to circle the house to the right,
while he and Alvin moved to the left. Clive and Alvin
moved around the front porch, leaving the FBI agents to
cover the other side of the driveway. Once the front door
and porch were checked he stationed Alvin on the front
porch along with another Smith Falls officer with a
shotgun. He then moved around to the back of the house.
When he reached the side of the back door and the small
porch he called Brian and J.D., who had just come into
view along the woods line at the back of the house. He
asked Brian to remain at the top of the road, and asked one
of the county officers with a high-powered rifle and scope
to join him. He asked J.D. to cross the open area behind the
house to his position. J.D. moved in a zigzag pattern from
the edge of the woods to a large shed behind the house,
then moved across the open back yard to Clive's position.
Jim Terrell had come around the house from the opposite
direction and positioned himself on the other side of the
porch.

Clive called all units, "Is everyone ready?" He got an "okay" from most units but had to wait several minutes for the rest of the county, city and state units to get into position. When he had an "okay" from all units he looked at J.D. and said, "You ready to go?"

J.D. responded, "If you're ready, I'm ready."

Clive called Alvin on the front porch and told him, "On three, take out the door and go." He told all units to move up and told Brian and the sharpshooter, "No one gets out the back." He looked at J.D. then Jim on the opposite side of the porch. He nodded his head then spoke slowly into the radio, "One, two, three." On two, Jim Terrell opened the screen door. Clive and J.D. put their shoulders into the back door on three. Alvin and the other officers did the same on the front porch but met major resistance from the door. A third officer joined them to break it down. Clive and J.D. flew through the back door, which was only closed, and almost fell into the kitchen.

Within several seconds the front door was forced open and Alvin and the two other officers were inside the house. With the force of their push J.D. and Clive and now Jim were in the center of the kitchen. Alvin called and confirmed they were inside.

For an instant Clive, J.D. and Jim stopped and looked at the kitchen floor. Blood was splattered in several areas and a revolver was lying in the center of the floor. Two or three seconds later Alvin and the other two officers came into the kitchen from the front room. Alvin's entrance was so quick that J.D., Clive and Jim almost pulled up their weapons toward them as they entered the room. When they recognized each other at opposite ends of the room they lowered their weapons, and Clive motioned to Alvin and the other officers to cover the rest of the house. Clive, J.D. and Jim stood in the center of the kitchen looking at the blood and the gun. Clive looked up at J.D. and said, "What the hell?"

J.D. shrugged his shoulders and whispered, "You got

me man." Clive whispered to Jim to pick up the gun and check it.

Jim looked around the room then picked up a pencil on the sink counter and scooped up the gun by the trigger guard. He looked at the cylinder and said, "Fully loaded." He smelled the barrel and shook his head, then said to Clive, "Not been fired." He set the gun back on the floor then looked at Clive and J.D. and whispered, "What the hell is going on?"

Clive, looking as puzzled as J.D., shook his head and whispered, "The cellar." J.D. and Clive moved to the cellar and Jim motioned to them that he would cover the remainder of the house with Alvin and the other two officers. Clive and J.D. spent the next ten minutes in the cellar and found next to nothing. When they returned to the kitchen they were met by Jim Terrell, Alvin and the two other officers. They conferred for several minutes then Clive called for more officers to make a more thorough check of the house. Clive, Alvin and J.D. moved out to the back porch, then called the remainder of the crew to fill them in on what they saw. They told all officers to move up to the house except for the cars and the officers at the intersection and the bottom of the driveway. Those officers were told to check all cars that came through and to hold everyone. Clive told one of the county cars to call and check with the hospital on Jack Duff's condition.

They were all out on the back porch talking and trying to figure out what they had seen when Brian came around the back side of the shed. He slowly walked from the shed door to the porch with his head turned to the ground. He was intently studying something and when he reached the porch steps he stopped and looked up at Clive. "What is it?" Clive asked. Brian turned and looked back at the shed then looked back at Clive, J.D. and Jim. Brian raised his gun to the front of his face then turned back toward the shed and motioned for Clive, J.D. and Jim to follow. As he slowly walked, he pointed to the ground, never taking his eyes off the shed. Clive looked down at the ground as he moved behind Brian and noticed the dark splatter of blood on the ground and grass.

Clive silently motioned to J.D. and Jim, who raised their weapons up in ready positions. All four moved slowly toward the shed, with Brian in the lead. The officer with the high-powered rifle and the other with the shotgun got down on one knee and covered the shed from two different directions. The remaining officers in the immediate area, all as if programmed, got into ready positions, guns drawn and ready. The four moved slowly across the yard to the shed, until they were within five feet of the door. Brian cocked his weapon and pulled it close to his face. He took two steps toward the door. As he reached for the door handle he saw a piece of paper rolled in a tube and stuffed into the door latch. He took one hand away from his weapon and pulled the paper out of the latch. The door did not move. Without opening the paper he handed it back to Clive. He then returned to a ready position and waited as Clive pulled a handkerchief out of his pocket and used it to unroll the paper. When Clive unrolled the small notebook sheet he saw printed and smeared in red the single word, "Forever." He dropped the paper to the ground and then moved ahead of Brian. He looked back at the other three men to see if they understood, nodded, and reached for the door latch. He lifted the latch and as the door swung open, they saw the word, "Forever," painted in red on the inside wall. As the morning light entered the shed, it shone on the back wall.

There, sitting on the floor in his boxer shorts and nothing else, was Doc Watson. Both arms were at his sides and in each arm at the inside of the elbow in the vein was a hypodermic needle. His face was turned to the ground and his chest was covered in blood from his neck to his crotch. Clive and Brian entered the shed, moved to either side of the door, and quickly checked out the interior. There was no one inside except for Doc and all seemed to be normal. J.D. and Jim followed them inside, and as they all lowered their weapons, Clive moved to Doc's body and bent down on one knee as he holstered his weapon. Clive took his handkerchief again, grasped a handful of Doc's hair, and lifted his head. His head tilted to the side at a right angle and Clive quickly let go and jumped back. He whispered, "Damn," as he backed up into J.D. Doc's head rested on his shoulder like it had been served on a plate. His throat had been cut from ear to ear, almost decapitating him.

CHAPTER 18

Friday, June 25, 1:00 p.m.

They had all been at the house now for hours. The crime lab people and Bill Fry had arrived at about 9:00 a.m. The blood in the kitchen was proven to be Doc's. The gun had been checked and was thought also to be Doc's. Doc, being a convicted felon, was not permitted to carry a weapon. A check of the serial number found it to have been stolen in the Chicago area. Prints were lifted from the gun and from all areas of the house. What Brian had seen in the cellar the night he had been watching Doc turned out to be just old rags covered in rust and paint, some of which had been left in the cellar. The fire pit was checked and the remains of burnt rags and the handle-less knife were found. They had been in the flames and hot embers for so long that any evidence was gone. They checked Doc's body and found indications that he had been hit in the face several times. His nose appeared to be broken and several teeth had been knocked out, which probably accounted for the blood in the kitchen and the trail of blood out to the shed. Bill Fry had checked both hypodermic needles in Doc's arms and found the balance of what appeared to be heroin.

Clive, J.D., Jim and Alvin were on the back porch talking and Brian was leaning against the house near the porch, not saying anything. He had been quiet ever since Doc's body had been found. Bill Fry walked out of the shed and across the back yard and stepped up onto the back porch with his clipboard in hand. "Well gentlemen, here's what I think. Come down if you're ready to listen." They all said "yes" almost in unison as Bill looked over at Brian, now slouched down in an almost sitting position against the house. He was staring at the ground and fingering several stones almost as if he were in a trance. Bill looked at Clive and said, "What about him?"

Clive said, "I don't know. He's been quiet for hours now." Clive walked to the porch rail and called to Brian. There was no response. He called again, "Brian."

This time Brian seemed to wake up, then quickly stood up, turned to Clive and said, "Yes, Boss."

Clive looked at him and asked, "You okay?" Brian didn't answer. He just nodded that he was. Clive said, "Bill wants to talk to us. You mind coming up here?"

"Ah, yeah," he answered as he walked to the porch and joined the group.

When he stepped up onto the porch Clive put his hand on his shoulder and asked again, "You sure you're okay?"

Brian said, "Yeah, I'm fine boss, I'm fine. Bill, go ahead." Bill looked at his notes on the clipboard then started. "Okay, first understand that this is all just preliminary—not to be taken as factual until we get back to the crime lab. Here's what appears to have happened. First, as I said before, the rags and knife that Brian saw appear to have nothing to do with any of the crimes. It's all just trash but we will try to check what's left of the knife for evidence. I doubt we'll find much. It appears that Doc was asleep, the bed is unmade and the nightstand drawer was open. I think it's probably where the gun was kept. I think he was awakened by whoever got into the house. He must have come downstairs and into the kitchen. I believe that was where the confrontation took place. Whatever happened, Doc never got off a shot. His nose and possibly his cheekbone are broken and three teeth are knocked out. We found them under the kitchen table. Whatever hit him hit him hard. I think he was taken out quickly. He then appears to have been dragged out to the shed. It looks like the heroin, if that's what it is, was administered there."

"Was he dead when his throat was cut?" J.D. asked.

"No, I don't believe so," Bill said. "But with two doses of heroin in him I doubt he could do much but see and breathe. He was alive when the final cut came. The note and the paint on the door could have been out there before or after the murder. I can't say." They continued to talk among themselves for another ten or fifteen minutes. Brian stood and listened and said nothing.

After about five minutes, J.D. Ricketts excused himself, walked to the driveway, bent down and looked at the ground. He slowly got up and walked down the driveway, stopping every few feet and bending down each time he stopped. After several minutes he called to one of the crime lab people to come over to him. Then the group on the porch really took note of what he was doing. They all left the porch except for Brian and walked to J.D.'s position. When Clive walked up to J.D. and the lab technician who was taking pictures of something on the ground he asked, "What is it?"

J.D. pointed to the tire tracks on the dirt road that had been pushed into the soft mud. "You see the tracks?" he said.

"Yes," Bill Fry said. "We looked at them before."

"Yeah," J.D. said. "But did you notice the odd thing about the right tire mark? I saw it before myself but it didn't click with me until just a few minutes ago." Brian walked off the porch and slowly over to the group. J.D. continued, "There appears to be a chunk of rubber missing from the side of that tire. It's not large, and it may be more of a defect than damage, but it is there and that makes it a significant find. If you follow the tracks you pick it up every so many feet."

Bill Fry bent down and touched the tread mark and whispered, "Damn, how did we miss that?"

J.D. remarked, "Hey, I almost missed it too. Don't know why I just thought of it now. Can't see the forest for the trees—you know what I mean?"

Bill Fry stood up, looked at Clive and said, "Okay, for now, I'd guess we got a large, possibly heavy older car with new tires and a defect in one of the right tires, most likely the front. It's more than we had." Brian, who had been listening, turned and slowly walked back to the porch steps and sat down.

Clive watched him as the others talked, then excused himself and walked over to Brian and said, "Brian, what is it? What's on your mind?"

Brian looked up at him nervously and said, "I'm okay boss, honest, I'm okay."

"Bullshit," Clive said. "You're not okay. What is it?" Brian shook his head then Clive added, "Is it Jack Duff?"

Brian looked away for a second or two then turned back and said, "Yeah Clive. It's Jack, okay? He took my place. Now look where he's at."

Clive sat down beside Brian and said, "Jack's going to be fine. He's tough and he'll be fine. What else is it? Something else is bothering you."

Brian stood up, turned to Clive and said, "Clive, that's it. It's just Jack. Nothing else. Nothing else." Then he turned and walked to the center of the back yard and stared at the shed.

Bill Fry and J.D. walked over to Clive and Bill asked, "What's going on? What's his problem?"

Clive stood up, looked at Bill and said, "He says he's worried about Jack but I don't think that's all of it. He won't say. I'll let it ride for now. Maybe I can get it out of him later."

J.D. looked over at Brian then turned back to Clive and said, "Whatever it is I hope he gets over it soon, we need everyone on this, and I mean everyone in sharp, crisp condition."

Bill Fry looked at J.D. then asked, "And what's your problem? You're usually Mister Cool, calm, nose-to-the-ground, true-blue FBI."

J.D. paused for a moment then said, "When I came here I figured this would be my case. I mean, this is what I do. But this, I never seen anything quite like this. In all my time in this field I never have had a case that didn't follow some kind of a profile. We got a dandy here. We got very few clues, little in the way of evidence, and not even a motive. We've received no notes or requests for ransom asking for money to pay whoever it is to stop. Most serial killers want to be caught and will leave clues for you to figure out. Some will play with you leaving just enough to test your intelligence. Are you smarter than them? Some are abused people who then become abusers. Some hate men, some hate women, some get their sexual kicks from killing." He took a long breath, turned away for a second, then turned back to Bill. "There's no profile here, there's just a mass of puzzle pieces and no way to start to put them into a pattern. Every road is a dead end. I thought we had him when we had Doc. Now I can't even begin to guess. There's no sense in my telling you otherwise. I don't have a clue what we have here. This is virgin ground for me and I tell you I don't like it, not one bit. We're lost, and I mean lost." He shook his head, turned and walked away.

Bill looked at Clive, held his clipboard against his chest, then said, "Well, even Mr. Crimebuster is baffled. Now I don't feel so bad." Bill just smiled at Clive, Jim and Alvin and also turned and walked away.

Friday, June 25, 4:00 p.m.

Clive called the hospital and got a report on Jack, then

decided to go there to see for himself. J.D. and Brian went with him. Jim Terrell, Bill Fry and Alvin stayed at the house for a while longer with the crime lab. When Clive arrived at the hospital he went to the desk and checked on the room number and then he, Brian and J.D. went to the room. When they turned the corner on the second floor hallway they saw Alice leaning against the wall next to the door of Jack's room.

Clive walked up and said, "Alice, I didn't expect to see you here. How's he doing?"

Alice shook her head and said, "Not good. He's got two fractured vertebrae in his neck, a separated shoulder, a broken nose and cheekbone and a major concussion. They are very concerned about the concussion. He keeps fading in and out of consciousness."

"Has he said anything?" J.D. asked.

"No," Alice said as she turned and looked into the room. "He mumbles a lot like he's trying to tell us something, but we can't make out what it is. The doctor left for a few minutes and he said they want no visitors for now. If you want to see him you better get in there before he comes back, 'cause my guess is he'll tell us to leave." The four of them entered the room. Alice, Clive and J.D. walked up to the bed. Brian stayed back at the doorway as if he didn't want to get too close. Jack was bandaged and swollen and in a neck brace. His arm was taped to his side and one eye was swollen badly. There were all types of monitors, and several IVs ran into his arms.

Clive leaned down to Jack and whispered, "Hi buddy. It's Clive, just came to check on you. You'll be fine; you're a tough cop like old J.D. here. Too tough to let them get you."

J.D. leaned over close and said, "Jack, it's J.D. I'm here too and Clive's right. You'll be fine. Me, Clive, Alice and Brian just wanted to make sure they were treating you right here at this hotel." Jack slowly started to open his eyes and looked first at Clive and then to J.D. and tried to speak.

Alice moved in beside Clive and whispered, "Don't talk, Jack. Just rest. You can talk later." Jack's eyes moved to Alice and he again tried to speak but nothing came out. Alice then said to Brian, "Come on over and say hello." Brian moved a little closer then stopped just short of the bed. Jack opened his eyes again and tried to raise his head but couldn't.

Clive said, "Brian, move in. I think he wants to see you." Brian hesitated then moved to the side of the bed.

Alice said to Jack, "See Jack, Brian's here to see you too." Jack opened his eyes and when he saw Brian there was an immediate change in his expression. His eyes became wide and he tried hard to speak but all he could do was mumble. The monitor began to make a sound as his heart rate and blood pressure increased.

Clive put his hand gently on his chest and said, "Jack, calm down. It's okay. It's okay. It's only Brian and he's okay." Brian backed up several steps out of Jack's view and just stood there. Jack would not quiet down and continued to try to talk.

Alice said to Clive, "I think he's trying to tell you something."

Clive put his ear close to Jack's face and listened as Jack whispered. He rose up and looked at Jack and said, "I didn't get that, old buddy. Say it again." He got even closer and listened again. Several seconds later the doctor entered the room just as Clive raised up from Jack's bed with a strange look on his face.

The doctor, as Alice had warned, was not happy with the four of them in the room. He looked at the monitor then told Jack to calm down. He turned to the four of them and said, "You will have to come back later. I know he's your friend. We will take good care of him but you must leave now." Before the doctor had finished, Brian was gone. Clive, Alice and J.D. left the room and went into the hall. Brian was standing at the corner of the hall several feet away, looking at the floor and nervously playing with his hat.

The doctor came out and Clive asked, "Is he going to be okay?"

The doctor took several minutes to explain Jack's condition, repeated, "No visitation until notified," and walked away.

When the doctor was gone, J.D. asked Clive, "What did Jack say?"

Clive took a deep breath and, looking puzzled, said, "I'm not sure. He was very hard to understand, but I swear I heard him say, 'Death travels with him. Death travels with him.'" Clive looked down the hall at Brian then walked slowly to him, followed by J.D. and Alice. He looked at Brian and said, "You okay?"

Brian said, "Yeah, Boss, I'm fine. What did Jack say?"

Clive said "Does 'Death travels with him' mean anything to you?"

"No," Brian said as he looked down at his hat. "No, Boss. It means nothing to me. What else did he say?"

Clive looked at Brian and said, "That was it, that's all he said." Clive continued to look at Brian and asked again, "Are you okay?"

"Yeah boss, I told you I'm fine. I'm fine. It's Jack we need to be worried about, not me."

Alice then said to Brian, "Why do you think he got so upset when he saw you?"

Brian shook his head and said, "I don't know. Maybe it's because he took my place and it should have been me. I don't know."

Brian looked at Clive and said, "We going back to the station or what?"

Clive said, "No. Our main suspect is dead and we are pretty much at an impasse now. We can't do much until the lab is done and there's not much sense in going over old material. Much as I hate to say it, I think we all need a few hours rest. What do you think, J.D.?" J.D. agreed and then suggested that they all meet the next day and see what they could put together. J.D. said if they needed him he would be at his motel room or at the restaurant there and to call.

him on his cell phone if something changed. Brian said he was going to get some supper and go home then they all realized that three of them had come in the same car. They decided that Clive would take J.D. to his motel then check in at the station and go home for the night. Alice would take Brian back to the station to get his car, then continue home from there.

As they were leaving the hospital, Alice asked Clive, "Did you get the note I put on your desk yesterday? I would like to know if it's okay?"

"If what's okay?" Clive asked.

Alice looked at Clive and said, "Well, I guess you didn't read the note. I know this is not a good time but I was wondering if you absolutely needed me this weekend. It's my parents' anniversary and we wanted to have it at our camp. It's their favorite place to be. We wanted to throw a surprise party for them and with this case I haven't been able to do anything. I'm supposed to get help from my friend, Sally, to set it up. But if you need me…"

Clive thought for a second then said, "Alice, go ahead and take care of it. Take the weekend off. You've been here twenty-four/seven and this is important to you, so I'll see you Monday a.m. Rose can fill in—and if not, I'll get one of the others to take it." He looked at J.D. and Brian and they both nodded in agreement.

Alice looked at Clive then gave him a hug and said, "Thanks Clive, but are you sure it's okay?"

Clive said, "Alice, we are at a dead end for now. We've got nowhere to go on this. All we can do is rehash the old clues. If there was a good time to take off I guess now is the time." She hugged Clive again, and to J.D.'s surprise, hugged him also. She and Brian got into her car and headed toward the station. Clive and J.D. drove to his motel.

On the way to the station Brian said very little but Alice could tell something was on his mind. When they got to the station, she asked him, "Brian what's wrong?"

Brian looked into her eyes and said, "I told you and Clive it's nothing. I'll be fine. Stop worrying. I'll be fine."

"Okay," she said, then added, "If you need me, call my cell phone. The phone at camp is not connected."

He got out of the car, then leaned down and said, "You'll be at camp then? Well have a good time and tell your folks congratulations. I'll see you Monday. Have fun." He closed the door and watched as she pulled out of the lot and headed in the direction of her home. Brian pulled down his tie and unbuttoned his shirt, then unlocked his car and sat inside. He closed the door, started the car, put on the air conditioning, then pulled the rearview mirror toward him so he could see himself. He wiped the sweat from his face and neck then whispered, "Death travels with him." He put the car in drive, pulled out of the lot, and headed in the direction of Posey's Bar.

CHAPTER 19

Friday, June 25, 8:00 p .m.

Just before 8:00 p.m., Alice left her home and headed out Route 5 toward the family camp. She had packed a few clothes and some items for the party decorations, and made a last minute call to her friend Sally Evans, confirming that she would be at camp Saturday morning to help set up. She had left her patrol car at home and packed everything in her yellow Jeep. As she packed the Jeep she looked behind her several times. She had an odd feeling— a feeling as if someone was watching her. When she finished she looked around again then dismissed it as nerves. She stopped at a MAC machine on the way out of town and then at a gas station to fill up. It was 8:20 p.m. when she was on the road again with the windows down and the radio on loud.

Friday, June 25, 8:30 p .m.

Brian had been at Posey's Bar for only a short time but

had already consumed three beers and asked for a fourth. Pete Waters was behind the bar and when he brought the beer he asked Brian if he was okay. Brian just took the bottle, pushed the money toward Pete, and said, "I'll be fine," as he got up off the stool and walked to the poolroom. He didn't notice anyone in the room. As a matter of fact the bar was not crowded at all—especially for a Friday night. He didn't play pool. He just sat on the edge of one of the tables and stared out at the bar while sipping his beer. He was there for about ten minutes in deep thought, when a good-looking young girl walked in, picked up a cue stick, and asked if he wanted to play. He slid off the table, gave her a quick look, and said, "No hon, keep your money. You can't afford to play me."

He smiled and walked away as the girl said, "And don't we think we are some hot-shot cop?"

Brian ignored her statement. As he walked into the bar again he whispered to himself, "Death travels with him." He put the now-empty bottle on the bar and asked for another. As he did, he heard the door open. A young boy came in with the early edition of the Saturday *Smith Falls Gazette*. He waited till the boy left, then he went to the machine and bought a paper.

When he returned to his seat, Pete put the bottle on the bar and said, "Brian, am I going to have to call you a ride? That's number five and you ain't been here an hour. How about some food to go with that beer?"

Brian picked up the bottle, took a drink, looked at Pete, and said, "I don't need any food, and right now Pete, I don't think I need any advice either."

Pete put his hands up in a gesture that said, "Okay. Sorry I asked," then wiped the bar and walked away. Brian sat the bottle down, then read the headlines. "Serial Killer: Forever Man Strikes Again." The article went on to say that Doc Watson, who was from Smith Falls, but lived in Chicago, was found dead Friday morning at his mother's home. Brian took the front section of the paper and placed

the rest on the bar. He continued to read
sweat ran from his forehead and neck. W.
put the paper down, took his handkerchiei
face and neck. As he did, he looked at the
second section of the paper. He picked up his .
was in the middle of a long drink when suddenly he
the bottle from his mouth and stared intently at the be
of the second section. He slowly set the bottle down a.
picked up the front page again. He read part of it then he
put it down and picked up the second section and read it
again. He put the paper down, stared into the mirror
behind the bar and whispered, "Death travels with him."
He slowly got up, never taking his eyes off his reflection in
the mirror. Several seconds later Pete Waters heard the
door to the bar close and looked up from the cooler he was
filling; Brian was gone. He walked to where Brian had been
sitting and found the paper, the half-empty bottle and the
rest of his money. He picked up the money and walked to
the door. When he got out to the front porch all he saw was
Brian's car headed out of the lot and onto the highway. He
returned to the bar and began to clean up the paper, when
he noticed that the article at the bottom of the second
section had been ripped out.

Brian drove to his apartment and when he entered he
saw a package on the floor that had apparently been
pushed through the mail slot. It was flat, rectangular in
shape, wrapped in brown wrapping paper, and tied with
brown twine. He walked to the refrigerator and retrieved
a beer from inside then returned to the door and picked up
the package. He placed the beer on the table in the kitchen,
sat down, and started to untie the twine.

Friday, June 25, 9:30 p .m.

Alice had driven all but five miles of the trip to camp,
then decided to stop at an all-night grocery to pick up more
of the items she would need for the party and breakfast the
next morning. It was 9:30 p.m. when she entered the store

d said hello to the clerks on duty. There were only three r four customers in the store as she took a cart and started up the first aisle.

Friday, June 25, 10:00 p.m.

Clive dropped J.D. off at his motel, where they had talked for a while, then Clive went to the station. He checked in with the night crew and checked to see if there were any messages from Bill Fry. There were none. He contacted Rose Bodin and asked her to fill in for Alice on the weekend and she agreed. When he left he told the desk sergeant that if anything came up to call him at home. It was ten p.m. when he arrived at home. He had stopped at the restaurant on Route 5 and had them make a take-out sandwich, which he had almost finished. He was tired and all he wanted was bed. He finished the sandwich, drank a small bottle of water, and got into the shower at about 10:55 p.m.

Friday, June 25, 11:00 p.m.

Alice finished her shopping and unloaded the bags into the back of her Jeep. She had parked at the side of the store because of the other cars in front. When she finished she took the cart back to the store. As she left she picked up the early edition of the *Gazette*, paid for it, and went to the car. She opened the door, threw the paper on the seat and slid inside. She was about to start the car when she looked at the headlines and instead picked up the paper. She put her keys on the seat beside her and in the light from the dome she started to read. She read the entire article then took the front section, laid the rest on the seat and opened the paper. Inside was an additional article about the killings, with a list of the people killed, along with times and places. She read it slowly through one time. When she finished she was about to put the paper back together when she noticed the article at the bottom of the second section. She put the front section on her lap and read the second section article. When she finished, she stared out the window for a few seconds, then looked at the article again. She slowly put down the second section, then picked up the front section and opened it again. In a low whisper she read the names aloud to herself: Jody Miller, Wesley Dans—she skipped over Roscoe Black and Bob Anderson—Bobby Rodgers, Judge Alvin Richards and Doc Watson. She stopped and stared out the window again, then picked up the second section and read it again. Suddenly her eyes were wide open and she took a deep breath, "Oh my God..." came from somewhere deep inside. Then again, "Oh my God..."

Alice sat frozen for several seconds, then reached inside her purse and looked for her cell phone. She couldn't find it. She fumbled around for it for several more seconds then dumped the entire purse on the seat. She found the phone and dialed the station. She got a beep, beep, beep and when she looked at the phone it said redial. She checked the antenna and had only one bar. She got out of the car and ran to the front of the store and checked again—no bars. She ran back to the car and opened the door then looked at the phone again: one bar; no, two; no, one. She opened the door, stepped up on the car's running board and looked at the phone again: a solid two bars. She dialed the station number again and this time the desk sergeant answered, "Hello, County Sheriff's Department. Can I help you?"

Alice started out speaking so fast the sergeant interrupted her and said to slow down—that she couldn't understand her. Alice took in a breath, calmed herself and said, "This is Alice Shearer, I need to talk to Clive, now." The sergeant explained that he had gone home, and did she want her to call him on the radio. Alice said, "No, no. I'll call him at home," and hung up. Alice stepped down from the car and took a minute to catch her breath. She picked up the paper again and looked at the second section. She made a face that almost looked painful then said again, "Oh, my God." She took a black marker pen from the pile of items on the seat and circled the article on the second page and then put the paper back together and laid it on the seat. She whispered to herself, "If I had taken the other car I'd have the radio. Damn it." She got up on the running board again, checked the antenna and got two bars. She dialed Clive's house but got a beep, beep, beep and the word redial on the phone again. She hung up then got down and was about to try the pay phone when she decided to try her phone again. She got up again on the running board and had two bars of antenna. She quickly dialed Clive's number and the phone rang. It rang once, twice, three times, and Alice said, "Come on Clive, pick up, pick up."

It was 11:05 p.m. and Clive was still in the shower enjoying the warm soothing water as the phone rang in the bedroom. It rang a forth, fifth and sixth time but Clive heard nothing over the sound of the shower. Alice heard the phone ring for the eighth time and the answering machine picked up. "Hello, this is Sheriff Aliston. I am unable to come to the phone. Please leave a message at the beep."

Alice almost yelled out loud, "Damn it," as the beep sounded. She calmed herself and started to speak, "Clive, this is Alice. It's just after eleven p.m. Friday. I need you to call my cell phone, now. Clive, I know who it is. I know who's been doing it and why. We have to act fast. There are only two of us left. Clive, it's..." She was grabbed from behind and pulled away from the car. Her cell phone dropped to the ground and a huge foot smashed it into the pavement. She was spun around and for an instant she saw a huge silhouette in front of her. She was slammed into the side of the car and fell to the ground. She tried to get up but was pinned down from behind. She opened her mouth to scream but a foul-smelling piece of cloth was pushed into her face. She tried again to scream and get up but she could not. She took in a breath then dizziness came over her. She tried to move again, then she felt numb and all went black.

Friday, June 25, 11:30 p.m.

Clive had finished his shower and was thinking about going to the kitchen for more food. He walked from his bedroom down the hall and was about to enter the living room on his way to the kitchen when he abruptly changed his mind. He turned and started back toward his bedroom, and as he did he whispered, "Just too tired, too tired." He reentered his bedroom and then quickly crawled into bed. He was asleep in minutes. In the living room next to his chair the answering machine light continued to blink red.

Saturday, June 26, 2:00a.m.

Alice slowly started to wake up. She had a hard time opening her eyes and she tried to lift her head up from her chest but each time she did she felt as if she was spinning around. She tried to move her arms but they felt as if they were pinned down somehow. She just sat as her mind went from fog to clear and back again. Several minutes passed, then she was finally able to lift her head from her chest and she let it fall backwards. She opened her eyes and at first all was as if in a mist. Slowly, her vision began to clear. She was looking at what appeared to be a ceiling above her. She saw something hanging directly over her head but couldn't quite make out what it was. She closed her eyes again and moaned softly. She reopened her eyes then tried hard to focus. As her eyes cleared she realized it was a chandelier in the center of a plaster and wood beam ceiling. As her vision grew clearer she could see that the chandelier was made up of deer antlers, and had six candle-shaped lights that were not lit. Something looked familiar. She lowered her head slowly and looked out at what was in front of her.

It was a large picture window that was made up of small individual panes of glass. At each side of the window was a curtain that appeared to be red or dark burgundy. As she looked out the window, her head weaving back and forth, she saw from the outside a flash of light in the sky that made a tree line visible. It was apparently a storm off in the distance. She lowered her head again to her chest, took a deep breath and squeezed her eyelids together. She raised her head again and shook it back and forth, trying to get the cobwebs out of her brain. When she opened her eyes again she saw the sky in front of her light up again. She realized then that there was a source of light in the room—but very dim. She turned to the corner of the room to the right and saw a small lamp on a stand next to the door. She looked left and saw what appeared to be a fireplace in the shadows.

It suddenly became clear to her. She was sitting in the front room of her family camp. She lowered her head again and once more squeezed her eyelids together and shook her head. She raised her head, then as all became more clear she looked around the room. Yes, it was the camp. She tried again to raise her arms and then realized she was seated in a wooden chair and she was tied to it. Her arms were behind the chair and fastened tightly. She tried to move her legs but they were also pinned down. She had flashes of thought go through her mind in a rapid machine gun effect. She saw her Jeep, the grocery store, and the cell phone. She remembered trying to call Clive, and the redial on her phone. She remembered being slammed against the car, then, as if it leaped out at her, the newspaper article. Fear shot through her like the lightning in the sky outside.

She drew in a deep breath and screamed as loud and long as she could. When that scream was finished she tried to get up to move, but she could not. She screamed again, and again, and again, as she tried to free herself. After several minutes she was exhausted and a wave of dizziness came over her again. She stopped and lowered her head to her chest and sat motionless, breathing hard. As her breathing slowed she sat with her eyes closed and the dizziness faded. From somewhere in the room came the sound of music being played, at first very low. As the sound started to grow louder she raised her head again and tried to identify where it was coming from. As she twisted and turned, the sound got louder and louder. It was coming from behind her, from the stereo she knew was there. Now she recognized the song—it was "Vehicle" by the seventies group, The Ides of March, and it grew louder and louder. It became so loud that it hurt her ears; she again tried to raise her arms but could not. The music became a terrible noise that made the panes of glass rattle in the picture window in front of her. She raised her head to the ceiling again and screamed a scream she never would have thought she could make. It came from deep inside her, from a place where sound had never come before. She held the scream for what seemed like forever, then realized most of the sound was now coming from her. She stopped as abruptly as she started, and let her head fall to her chest again. She sat breathing hard as she realized the song was still playing, but at a level that was almost quiet.

She sat for several minutes, her chin on her chest, just breathing, and listening to the words of the song: "I'm the friendly stranger in the black sedan, won't you step inside my car." She was about to raise her head again when she was grabbed by the hair from the back. Her head was pulled to an upright position facing out toward the window. There was another flash of lightning in the distant sky, and several seconds later it was followed by a low rumble. She tried to tear away from the hold on her, but the hand that held her hair became two, that now clamped on each side of her face like a vise. It held her head straight out toward the window. She tried again to tear away but she could not escape the grip on her head.

She screamed again, then thought she heard a voice from behind. She stopped screaming and listened. She heard a soft, almost soothing voice say, "Let her go. She can do nothing."

She felt the iron grip on her head slowly let up and finally the hands were taken away. She tried to look behind her but she could not. She thought she saw movement to her left, near the fireplace. She turned and strained her eyes to see, as the figure started to come closer. She sat watching in the almost-dark room, with the storm coming closer and the music playing in the background. The dark silhouette came closer and closer in the dim light. The sky outside lit up again and for an instant she saw a face. She took in a deep breath and whispered, "You." The figure stopped just at the edge of the light as the sky lit up again from behind him. Alice strained here eyes to see and as she did she said, "Why are you doing this? This can't change anything. The past cannot be changed. How can you hate so much?"

There was a moment of silence as the figure started to move slowly around her chair. Then the voice spoke again, "Alice, no matter how hard we try to forget, our past is real. Our sins affect others. Just like scars remind us of the wrong we do to ourselves, the past reminds us of the innocence taken and the blood we spill. I do what I must, for I am the instrument for truth and justice that must be appeased."

Alice screamed, "You can't make it disappear, it happened. It was wrong and terrible but this will not make it right."

The voice, coming from behind but still moving, continued. "What was taken was pure and clean. What was done was dirty and evil."

Alice, trying again to see behind her, screamed, "How can you hate so much? The hate will not cleanse the sin."

As the figure moved again into the light to her left, he spoke again. "This is not about the hate. It is about a balance that must be restored. What was taken cannot be returned, but those of the taking must now also be taken."

Alice began to scream and fought against the ropes that held her fast. She screamed and bounced the chair across the floor, trying with all she had to get away. The figure moved in front of her as Alice, her strength gone, just sat and stared at him. The voice came again as another flash appeared in the sky behind him. "For you and the others the end can only be the same. The retribution is not about hate. It is about the collection of a ticket for a debt owed. This is not hate. It is about the fear, all about the fear. Now the others call to you from that dark place and you must join them. Your ticket is now redeemed." The hands came from behind again like the vise that had her before. They grasped the sides of her head and held her fast. The dark figure moved toward her till she could see the face that she had recognized. He raised his hand and something glinted silver in the dim light. Her head was snapped back and the ceiling once again came into view. She felt a strange sensation at her throat that seemed like the cold touch of ice, then followed by a burning pain, then a kind of numbing sensation. The hands that held her were taken away and her head was pushed forward to her chest again. The last thing she saw was a flash of light from the lightning outside and a dark red stain that moved down her stomach to her lap. There was a rumble of thunder as the music became loud again. Then all became dim and the sound faded into nothingness.

Saturday, June 26, 3:00 a.m.

The dark car in front of the cabin started and the headlights came on. As the vehicle turned to leave the driveway, raindrops fell in the beams of light. There was a flash of lightning across the sky followed by a loud rumble. As the car turned, the lights shone on the front of the cabin. Splashed across the front door, in red letters running to the floor, was the single word, "Forever." The car pulled out of the driveway and started slowly down the dirt road. The red taillights glimmered for several minutes, then disappeared over the hill and all was dark.

CHAPTER 20

Saturday, June 26, 7:15 a.m.

Clive was sound asleep when the phone rang. It was the fifth or sixth ring when he finally picked it up. "Yeah? I mean Clive, or, uh, Sheriff Aliston. Can I help you?"

There was a pause then Rose Bodin spoke from the other end, "Clive, this is Rose. Are you awake?"

Clive lifted his head off the pillow and squinted to see the digital clock radio. When his vision cleared somewhat he saw the time. It jumped right off the face of the radio like a hammer hitting him in the center of the forehead. He sat straight up on the edge of the bed and said, "Rose, oh Rose, yeah this is Clive. I must have slept in. I'll be there in thirty minutes."

He was going to set the phone down when he heard Rose say, "Hold on a minute, Clive."

He put the phone back to his ear and said, "I'll be there. I'll be there."

Rose continued, "Clive, I've got a note from the night desk. Something about Alice calling you last night at about eleven p.m."

Clive thought for a minute then said, "Eleven p.m. She called me at the station at eleven p.m.?"

Rose said, "Just a minute till I get the note." There was a pause then Rose said, "Yes, the note says she called and asked for you then said she would try you at home."

"What else did she say?" Clive asked.

"That's all I have, Clive," Rose said, then added, "The desk sergeant said she sounded excited or frustrated but okay. Did you get a call?"

Clive paused for a second then said, "No, no calls from anyone last night, Rose. I'll check my answering machine. I'm getting ready; I'll be in, in half an hour, forty-five minutes at most. I'll check my machine and call at camp or on her cell. See you in a few."

He hung up the phone and sat there for several seconds just rubbing his face and running his fingers through his hair. He looked at the clock again then whispered, "You idiot, you forgot to set the alarm." He slowly got up then started to walk out of the bedroom to the hall. As he did, he whispered to himself, "Too tired just too tired." He went to the bathroom and splashed water on his face and brushed his teeth. He was putting on deodorant when he remembered the answering machine. He left the bathroom, walked to his chair in the living room and sat down. He looked at the red light flashing on the machine then whispered to himself, "Yes, Alice. I'll come to the party."

He was about to push the button on the phone when it rang again. He picked it up; it was Rose again only this time she sounded different, "Clive, we got some kind of trouble. It's Alice."

Clive paused for a second then said, "Alice, what about Alice?"

Rose, sounding really upset, continued, "Clive, we just got a call from the state police. They were contacted by an all-night grocery store not far from Alice's family camp. I guess they found Alice's jeep abandoned at the side of their building early this morning. She's nowhere around and the owner of the store says the driver's door is open and her cell phone is smashed on the pavement next to the car."

Clive sat forward in his chair and asked, "Was there a sign of a struggle?"

Rose said, "I don't know. The police unit is not there yet. What we have is from the storeowner or an employee. It's kind of sketchy right now.

Clive took a deep breath and said, "Rose, call Brian, J.D. and Jim Terrell—also Alvin if you can get him."

"And tell them what?" Rose asked.

Clive paused again trying to gather his thoughts. "Tell Brian and J.D. to meet me at the store. I know where it is, do you know?"

Rose answered, "Yes, I do. I'll explain."

Clive continued, "Ask Jim and Alvin to stay in touch with you or me until I know more. I'm leaving now." He hung up the phone and was about to get up when he remembered the answering machine. He sat back in the chair and pushed the button. The voice on the machine said, "You have one message at 11:05 p.m., Friday."

There was a pause then Alice's voice came on. "Clive, this is Alice. It's just after eleven Friday. I need you to call my cell phone now." As the message continued, Clive could feel the fear in her trembling voice. "Clive, I know who it is. I know who's been doing it and why." Clive sat forward in the chair again and stared hard at the machine. "We have to act fast. There are only two of us left. Clive, it's..." The message abruptly ended and Clive could hear what sounded like rustling noises in the background then there was a thud sound and the phone went dead.

Clive jumped to his feet and yelled, "Shit." He ran to his bedroom, pulled out civilian clothes and practically jumped into them. There was no time for his uniform. He put on a blue, lightweight, sheriff's department jacket over his blue shirt and then reached into his cupboard shelf for a sheriff's department ball cap. He remembered his weapon and as he pulled the coat off again he yelled, "Damn it." He put on his shoulder holster and fastened it, then reached back on the top shelf of the same cupboard, got a wooden box and placed it on the bed. He unlocked it and retrieved his Glock 40 and two clips already loaded. He opened the slide of the weapon and checked the chamber. He placed one clip in the handle of the weapon and then pulled the slide again, chambering one round. He put the safety on and put the blue jacket on again. He put the second clip in his jacket pocket and ran for the front door. Within seconds he was in his patrol car, lights on and siren howling, headed toward the grocery store.

Saturday, June 26, 7:35 a.m.

Alice's friend Sally Evans drove her car up the dirt road to the camp and turned into the driveway. When she could see the back yard of camp and the rest of the driveway, she realized that Alice's Jeep was nowhere around. She smiled as she parked her car and said to herself, "Went to the store I'll bet. She's going to be really surprised to see me here already. Alice, I bet you figured you had plenty of time to make breakfast. Old Sally is always late. Well, I got you this time." She got out of her car then removed four or five bags of items for the party from the trunk. She took all the bags and started across the yard toward the porch.

Sally was a petite and quite pretty blonde. She was humming a song as she walked to the porch, her head turned to the ground. When she got to the steps she stopped humming. Still looking at the ground, she said, "I'll just wait on the porch and surprise you, girl." She started humming again as she walked up the steps, then looked up as she reached the top step. She stopped dead in her tracks and dropped all the bags, some of them bouncing down the steps, spilling their contents in all directions. There in front of her on the door in dark red with run lines to the floor was the large word, "Forever." She was gripped by paralyzing fear, unable to move. She stood frozen for almost a minute as she whispered, "Alice," once very low then again, louder, "Alice." She began to move toward the door, looking around in all directions.

When she reached the door she put out her hand slowly to grasp the door, trying not to touch the ugly red mess in front of her. She tried the door but it appeared to be locked. She backed up several steps and looked around again. No one was there. She started to call, "Alice, where are you? Alice. Alice." There was nothing but complete silence. She moved toward the picture window and tried to look inside, but the outside glare made it nearly impossible. She looked around again then leaned forward and cupped both hands around her face to shade her eyes and looked inside. A split second later she let out a loud scream and quickly backed up to the handrail at the edge of the porch, almost flipping over it backwards. She fell to her knees while still screaming and almost vomited on the floor. She tried to get to her feet again and fell again. Her legs were like rubber. She took a deep breath and finally got up and turned to go back down the steps. She was ashen white and trying to catch her breath again. She took one step down and her legs gave out. She tumbled down the remaining three steps to the ground, tearing her jeans and splitting her knee as she fell. She landed on the ground in the mud, face down, within inches of a puddle. She lay there for several seconds then slowly got back to her feet and stumbled to the car. She was crying uncontrollably as she reached inside for her cell phone and dialed 911.

Saturday, June 26, 7:55 a.m.

Clive's car flew down the highway, weaving in and out of traffic. He had been in contact with 911 and the state police car that was dispatched to the grocery store. Rose had contacted J.D., who was now on his way to the store also. The state police had contacted Jim Terrell, and Rose was going to call Alvin to inform him. Rose had told Clive that she had tried without success to get in contact with Brian. She had called his apartment, his car and most anywhere else but he was nowhere to be found. Clive told Rose to keep trying for Brian and that he would talk to Jim Terrell personally.

Clive was about five minutes from the store when Rose came over the radio again, "Clive, this is Rose again. I just got a call from 911 and another from the state police officer at the store. Call me on your cell phone, now. I'm not sure you want this over the air."

Clive said, "Rose, the hell with that. What is it?"

There was a short pause then Rose continued, "A woman who gave her name as Sally Evans just called 911 and they called the state police. The call was transferred to the car at the store and he called me. Clive, Sally is Alice's friend. She says she's at Alice's family camp and she needs police and an ambulance now. I guess she is hysterical."

Clive stopped and thought for a few seconds then asked, "What is the officer at the store going to do?"

"I guess he is going to stay there," Rose said. He said if you're close to continue there yourself, he will handle that end. He said all he has is the car. No sign of Alice."

"Okay. Okay," Clive said, "I'm on my way. I'll call J.D. I want him there with me. Did you find Brian?"

"No," Rose said. "I have no clue where he is. No one has seen or heard from him since last night."

"Okay," Clive said. "Get everyone you can except for J.D. and send them to the store, and call an ambulance."

"I already did," Rose said. "Five minutes ago. They are on the way there now."

"Good, good," Clive said. "And also call Bill Fry and the lab. Get them to the car ASAP. I want answers, and I don't care if they're at work or home, just get me some answers." He paused for a few seconds as he passed the grocery store on his left. He saw a small crowd of people and the state police car with the lights still flashing. He also saw Alice's yellow jeep near the back side of the building. He keyed the mike again and said, "I just passed the store, the state boy is there. I'm on my way to the camp. Should be there in several minutes. Patch me into J.D. and find Brian." Clive waited several more minutes as his car moved down the highway at close to eighty miles an hour.

J.D.'s voice came over the radio, "Clive, it's J.D. I'm on the highway about twenty minutes or so behind you. Jim Terrell is behind me by a few minutes. Alvin is going to the store. I just talked to him. How close are you?"

Clive saw the back road coming up on his left and slowed to make the turn. "I'm a minute, maybe less. Do you know where to turn off?"

"Yes, Rose explained," J.D. said, then added, "Clive, I'm ten minutes behind. Remember, ten minutes. You be careful."

Clive responded, "I got you man, just get here." Clive threw the mike onto the seat as he made the turn, fishtailing back and forth in the wet dirt road. As he moved up the road through the thick forest, mist rose from the trees and drops of water fell off the branches overhead from the night's rain. There were patches of ground fog in every low area and for an instant it reminded him of the morning they found Jody Miller. A shiver went through him and he whispered, "Alice, Alice." In what seemed like just a few seconds he saw the entrance to the camp driveway at the crest of the hill. He slowed and then whipped the car to the left and down the driveway to the camp. He drove the car into the back yard and slid sideways to a stop. As he did he saw a car parked just beyond where he stopped. As he got out he drew his weapon and held it toward the sky. The door of the car opened and he saw a young blonde woman covered in mud get out. He walked around his car toward her while looking back several times toward the cabin. When he got to her she was leaning against her car crying almost uncontrollably. He placed himself between her and the cabin then asked, "Sally?"

She had a hard time talking but finally got the words out, "Oh God, help. Please help. She's in there. Please help. I couldn't get in. I think she's hurt bad, maybe dead. Oh God, please help."

Clive put his hand on her shoulder and turned to calm her, then moved her back into the front seat of her car. He bent down and looked at her and said, "You'll be okay. Just stay here. Whatever happens, just stay here. More help is coming." He turned and faced the cabin, then slowly moved back to his car and stood behind it for a few seconds. He checked out the entire area around the cabin then slid the safety of the Glock 40 off and started around the car toward the cabin. He moved slowly as he continued to scan the cabin trying to see any movement inside. He reached the steps then stopped and checked the area all around him. When he felt it was clear he moved slowly up one step at a time. When he reached the top step he saw on the door the dark red "Forever," and a chill ran through him again.

He moved to the space between the door and the picture window and put his back against the wall. He paused then turned to his left and tried to see inside. He moved back, put the Glock in his left hand and reached down and tried the door handle with his right. As Sally had told him, it appeared to be locked. He put his weapon back in both hands, stared for a moment out at Sally in the car, then took a deep breath. He stepped away from the wall and turned and faced the door. He took one more deep breath, raised his right leg, and kicked at the door. It moved, but not enough. He quickly backed up and kicked again and the door flew open. His weapon came down into his line of sight directly in front of him and he slowly moved into the cabin.

Several minutes passed as Sally watched the front of the cabin from inside her car. She waited a while longer then slowly slid out and stood up. She was about to move toward the cabin when she saw Clive slowly come out the door. He had his head down to his chest. His gun was at his side and he slowly shuffled to the top step of the porch. He grasped the porch post with his left hand, placed his forehead against the post, and stood there swaying back and forth. After several minutes Sally saw him step down one step then slowly sit down on the porch. His head was hung low; he moved the weapon to his lap and just sat there, not moving. Sally, as if she realized what was happening, slid back into the car's front seat and began to cry again. There was a low rumble of thunder in the distance as large raindrops began to fall all around. In a matter of minutes it had turned into a heavy downpour. Clive never moved. He just sat in the rain, with his weapon in his lap and his head turned down to the ground. Sally never closed her door. She just sat and cried. The rain came harder and harder but Clive never moved. He was soaked in minutes but he didn't seem to care. Water poured from the gutters and off the roof, as the wind blew the rain in sheets. Rain ran from his ball cap and off his nose but it didn't matter. For Clive, nothing seemed to matter.

Saturday, June 26, 8:30 a.m.

The rain was still coming down so heavily it seemed like fog. J.D. Ricketts drove to the top of the hill and stopped at the driveway he thought led to the camp. He tried to see out the side window but the rain made it impossible. He ran the window down and rain splashed inside as he strained his eyes. Off in the distance he saw flashing lights and he turned the car and sped quickly down and into the yard, coming to a stop next to Clive's car. He slowly got out and looked at Sally's car as she slid out and pointed to the cabin. He took his weapon out of his shoulder holster from under his FBI jacket and turned toward the cabin. The rain had him soaked in seconds as he scanned the cabin across the yard. He could see Clive sitting on the steps of the front porch. He walked slowly toward the porch, his weapon in a ready position as he looked to the right and left. When he reached the porch, he looked up and saw the door standing half-open with the large red lettering scrawled across it. He moved up two of the steps, leaned down and put his hand on Clive's shoulder, and spoke his name, "Clive." There was no response. He squeezed his shoulder then repeated, "Clive." Clive slowly lifted his face into the rain and J.D. could see the intense pain that seemed to flow from his expression. Clive stared blankly at J.D. then lowered his head again. J.D. squeezed his shoulder again then moved slowly up the last two steps to the porch. He paused for a second then holstered his weapon and walked to the door. He wiped the rain from his face, took a deep breath, and entered. J.D. was inside less than three minutes when he came out again. He stepped out the door, leaned against the cabin wall, and lowered his head to his chest. Sally was still in the car crying, Clive was sitting motionless on the front steps and J.D. just stood and looked at the floor as the rain poured and the thunder rumbled in the distance.

Several minutes later, Jim Terrell came down the driveway, followed by the ambulance. He slid to a stop between the other cars and the cabin and quickly stepped out, his weapon drawn. The ambulance stopped behind him and he motioned for the paramedics to stay inside the vehicle. When he saw Clive on the steps and J.D. on the porch, Jim lowered his weapon and slowly walked to the cabin. When he reached the bottom of the steps he holstered his weapon and stared at Clive. He slowly moved up the steps, not stopping to speak to Clive but pausing for a second or two and looking down at him. He walked to J.D. and spoke to him. Their conversation was short; J.D. walked to the railing at the end of the porch. He placed his hands on the rail and lowered his head. Jim walked to the door but did not enter. He looked inside then walked to the front rail and called to the ambulance crew to come out. When the two EMTs got up to the porch, he directed one of them inside and the other out to Sally's car. He stood holding onto the rail next to Clive and stared out at the rain.

During the next hour, the yard was filled with police vehicles from all departments. The crime lab came to the store to check out the car, and to the cabin.

Clive remained seated on the front step in the rain for almost half an hour. No one talked to him; they just left him alone. J.D. and Jim handled what needed to be done. After the rain began to slow, J.D. walked from his car and up the two steps to Clive. He did not speak to Clive but instead removed his weapon from his lap, dropped the clip from the handle and ejected the round in the chamber. He placed the single round back into the clip, put the clip back in the weapon and spoke to Clive. "Clive, are you okay?" Clive looked up slowly and stared at J.D. J.D. spoke again, "Clive, are you going to be okay?"

Clive slowly stood up and said, "Yeah, okay." J.D. handed him his weapon and Clive slowly holstered it then walked to his car. J.D. followed him, not saying any more. When they reached the car Clive opened the door and sat inside. J.D. just stood beside the open door not saying anything until Jim walked up to them. J.D. and Jim began talking when they heard Clive call Rose on the radio, "Rose, this is Clive."

There was a pause, then Rose answered, "Yes, Clive. I'm here." Clive sat motionless for several seconds as Rose responded again, "Clive, are you there?"

He did not answer her question but instead asked, "Did you find Brian?" He sat and waited for several seconds then asked again, "Rose, did you find Brian?"

"No," was the answer. There was a pause then she added, "Clive, I, we, have looked everywhere. We can't find him." Clive sat staring out the window for several more seconds and Rose spoke again, "Clive, did you hear me?"

Clive came out of his trance and said, "Yes, Alice, I mean Rose. I heard you. Keep looking, please. Call me if you find out anything." He threw the mike onto the seat, stood up and moved between J.D. and Jim, then walked to the back of the lot to the woods line and stared into the forest in front of him.

J.D. and Jim spoke for several more minutes then Jim walked to the cabin as Bill Fry's car came down the driveway. J.D. walked to the ambulance as they were loading Sally inside. Bill Fry got out of his car and walked to Jim, pausing for a second to look at Clive along the tree line. Bill Fry and Jim entered the cabin. J.D. talked to Sally for several minutes then told one of the county officers to accompany her to the hospital. As soon as she was checked out he was to get a statement. Clive stood at the end of the property and said nothing. The rain had stopped but thunder could still be heard from every direction. Half an hour later Bill Fry and Jim came out of the cabin as Alice's body was being removed. J.D., who had been sitting in Clive's car talking on the radio, looked up as the body was being moved down the front steps to the coroner's vehicle. He turned to speak to Clive, but as he did he saw Clive coming toward the cabin. He joined Clive and they walked to the coroner's vehicle together.

When Alice's body was at the vehicle, Bill Fry told the two attendants to hold up. All stood quietly as Clive walked up to the black zipped bag on the gurney. He stood silently looking down at the body for several minutes, then removed his wet ball cap and placed it on the bag. He slowly unzipped the bag several feet, exposing Alice's face. Except for the blood at her neck she almost appeared to be in a peaceful sleep. Clive said nothing for a while, then bent down and kissed her forehead. He slowly zipped the bag back up and turned and walked to his car as all watched him. When he reached his car he put both arms on the roof and lowered his face to his arms. He was there for several seconds then J.D., Jim and Bill Fry walked up to him. He heard them coming but said nothing. He raised his head, took the ball cap that was in one hand, turned and threw it toward the woods. He turned to the three and Bill spoke first, "Clive, I have all material from the store and we are covering this place now. This is the only job we are working on; this is top priority. We will get answers."

Clive had almost no expression. He looked at J.D., then Jim, and said, "I gotta go now. I gotta go now." He started to walk away then turned and said, "Please, I need you two to do this. I'll be in touch." He walked to his car, got in and started it.

J.D. walked to the car and said, "Clive, call me if you need me. We'll handle it. We'll handle it." Clive looked up at J.D., nodded, then pulled the car slowly out of the yard and up the driveway. J.D., Jim and Bill walked to the bottom of the driveway and watched as the car disappeared out onto the road.

CHAPTER 21

Saturday, June 26, 1:00 p.m.

Clive had driven down the dirt road and when he got to the highway he turned left instead of right toward town. He didn't know why. As a matter of fact, he wasn't sure of much of anything. He felt empty, as if he had been drained of all emotion. He was bone tired and yet wide awake. He was calm and yet his insides felt like the inside of the drink blender at Posey's Bar. He would think for a short period of time, then it seemed as if he went blank, and he would find himself on a road he did not recognize. He heard the calls come and go over the radio but he didn't hear the words. It would rain, then stop, then start again, but wet or not his wipers ran non-stop. Even the dry screech of the rubber on the windshield didn't seem to bother him. He saw a roadside rest up ahead, pulled in and parked. He sat for several minutes, the car running and the wipers jumping across the dry window. He stared out the windshield at the restrooms in front of him.

Several minutes later he was awakened from his trance

by a knock at his side window. It startled him somewhat and he turned to see an elderly man with gray hair bending down looking at him. The man was gesturing for him to open his window. Clive stared for several seconds then ran the window down. The man said in a soft voice, "Are you okay, sir? My wife and I saw you pull in near fifteen minutes ago and you ain't moved. Are you sick or hurt? Can we help you?" Clive looked into the old man's eyes, turned to the windshield, rubbed his face and looked back again. The old man repeated, "Son, are you okay?"

Clive stared for a few seconds as his mind cleared. He finally said, "What?"

The old man repeated, "Are you okay?" Clive rubbed his face again as he moved back into reality. He heard the wipers screeching across the dry window and shut them off. The old man said, "Can we help you?"

Clive forced a kind of smile and said, "No sir, I'm fine. I'll be fine."

The old man put his hand on Clive's shoulder and asked, "Are you sure?"

Clive looked up, smiled again and said, "Thank you for your concern. I guess I'm just tired. I'm okay. I don't need any help, just some sleep."

The old man said, "We'll be here for a while eating lunch. If you're hungry we got plenty. You're welcome to join us."

Clive put his hand out the window, shook the old man's hand and said, "Thank you, sir. I do appreciate that but I'm fine. Thanks for the invitation, but I need to get back to the station."

The old man backed up a step or two and said, "Don't go to the station. Go home and get some rest. You police officers need to get some rest too you know."

Clive smiled again and said, "You know, you're right. I just might do that. Tell your wife thanks for the concern and thank you for the invite. I'll be fine and you two have a nice day." He smiled again at the old man and waved to his wife then put the car in reverse and pulled out onto the highway. As he drove he thought to himself, "No matter how bad it gets we do this for people like them. Our sacrifices are justified." He came to a stop sign and recognized the route he was on. If he turned right it would take him back in the direction of Smith Falls. He thought for a second then turned left. He was now more awake and had a lot more thinking to do. He wasn't ready to head back—not just yet. He moved into a small village that he recognized, and as he drove through he waved at the local police car sitting along the road watching for speeders.

He picked up the mike and called Rose. "Rose, this is Clive." There was a pause then he called again, "Rose this is Clive, can you hear me?"

Rose came on and said, "Thank God, Clive. Are you okay?"

"Yeah, I'm fine Rose—just fine," he said, as he took a deep breath.

Rose continued, "We've been trying to get you for hours now. Are you sure?"

"Yeah, Rose, I'm fine. I'm sure. Is all going well? Are J.D. and Jim alright?"

"Yes," she said. "They are handling it but they were concerned too. They said I was to let them know when I heard from you."

Clive paused again then said, "Tell them I've got some thinking to do, and can they take over for me? I'll call back when I work it all out."

"Okay, Clive," Rose said, then asked, "Is there anything I can do?"

Clive thought for a minute then said, "Yeah Rose, there is. Call and check on Jack Duff. See how he is doing. When you find out, call me. Also we need to get to Alice's parents before the press does. I don't want them finding out that way."

Rose said, "J.D. and Alvin are handling that. There will be police at their house so no one can get close. Alvin said he knew you needed some time and he said he would take care of Alice's parents."

Clive paused again, then realized he was fighting back tears and closed his eyes momentarily then regained his composure. He said, "Rose, tell Alvin to tell them I will be there as soon as I can. Tell Bill Fry I need all he can get and I need it yesterday. Ask J.D. to hold the reigns; I'll be back as soon as I can. One more thing, have you found Brian?"

There was a long pause, then Rose came on again, "No Clive, we haven't. We put out an all-points bulletin. We can't find him anywhere."

"Did you check his apartment?" Clive asked.

"Yes," Rose said, "We used the spare key he leaves here. His apartment is a mess. It looks like he was there, but he's not now. It almost looks like someone was just in a rage. Everything off the walls, the furniture thrown all over, even the refrigerator was standing open with all of its contents thrown around the room. I don't know, I just don't know. I mean with Alice and all I just don't know."

Clive thought for a minute then said, "I've got a feeling he knows something. I can't explain why, but I do. Keep trying to find him. I hope I'm right because if I'm not and he's out there somewhere drunk... Well anyway, keep me informed. I'll call you when I can and tell J.D., Jim and Alvin I said thanks." He signed off then whispered to himself, "Brian where the hell are you and what are you up to?"

Saturday, June 26, 3:00 p.m.

Clive was still on the road only now he was alert and awake. Thoughts were racing through his mind from all directions. He would think about one thing then change to another, then think about Alice and the tears would try to come again. He stopped at a red light and put his head down on the steering wheel and whispered, "Come on. Get it together, Clive. Get it together." From behind he heard a horn and looked up to see the light had turned green. He waved to the car behind him and moved on. He took several deep breaths, shut down the car air conditioning and ran the window down. The air was warmer than he liked but it was fresh and he could smell the moisture in the air.

As he moved down one road and onto the next his mind began to settle. He found himself thinking of Alice's face and the way she smiled. He started to put thoughts together in a better order. As he began to function again, like the Clive he was used to, he looked up through the windshield to the sky and said, "Thanks Alice." He remembered the call the first morning about Jody and about seeing her body at the tracks. Then there was Wesley and then Roscoe and Bob Anderson. What did they have to do with this mess? There had been no "Forever" where they had been found. What about Bobby Rodgers and Judge Richards and Doc and now Alice? Where was the tie to all of them? He thought about his confrontation with Bob Anderson at Posey's Bar. In his mind he saw the crowd there that day, the faces he knew and the ones he didn't. He remembered people looking at them as they argued. He saw the person in the booth in the dark, and the glint or flash of something as the men's room door opened. He saw the bag containing two buttons and the white grease, the "Forever" scratched in the hood of the car at Dan's Auto Yard. He remembered the visit to the morgue and the huge handprint on Jody's face. The DNA that Bill Fry said was weird. He pictured the tire tracks in the driveway at Doc's mother's home and the hypos stuck in each of his arms. He could almost hear Jack Duff whisper in his ear, "Death travels with him." What did it all mean?

Somewhere in that mass of information was a clue, but where? He kept running the information over and over in his mind. He tried to separate, file in order then out of order. Pick each scene apart and analyze the pieces. He saw all the bodies and each time the word, "Forever." He whispered over and over, "Forever, Forever, what is

Forever?" It was close to six o'clock when he pulled the car over to the curb and put his head on the steering wheel. He was now truly exhausted, both physically and mentally. He sat there for several minutes then heard a noise. It was the rain; it had started again. He looked out the side window and then realized that he was parked in front of a church. The same church where he had attended Jody's funeral. He sat for a while and stared at the doors, as the rain came down, not hard but steady. After some time he got out of the car and slowly walked up the steps to the doors of the church. As he stood in the rain he looked down at the newspaper machine on the steps. The headline of the Saturday edition was about the killings. He turned and reached for the door handle, expecting it to be locked. It wasn't. He opened the door slowly and looked inside the dimly-lit vestibule. He stepped inside and quietly closed the door. He walked to the doorway that led to the main church room and stood there looking up the long aisle to the altar.

After several minutes he heard a voice behind him, "Sir, can I help you?" He turned and saw the pastor that he remembered from Jody's funeral. When the pastor saw Clive, he recognized him. "Sheriff Aliston, how are you? Can I help you?"

Clive paused and said, "I don't know. I'm not sure why I'm here or how I got here."

The pastor, looking concerned, said, "Sheriff, are you okay? Should I call someone?"

"No," Clive said. "I'm fine. I just need to be here I guess. Is it okay if I go inside for a while?"

"Of course you can, Sheriff, and by the way my name is Andrew, Pastor Andrew." He put out his hand, as did Clive, and they shook hands.

Clive smiled and said, "Thanks," then turned to enter. He stopped and said to the pastor, "I'm wet, I mean soaked. Maybe I shouldn't."

The Pastor put his hand on Clive's shoulder, smiled and said, "Sheriff, I don't think he'll mind," as he pointed to the altar.

Clive turned again to enter, then turned back, reached inside his coat, and unsnapped his weapon. He handed it to the pastor and said, "Hold this for me." The pastor, looking surprised, took the weapon as Clive turned and walked slowly down the aisle. He walked to the second row from the front, and stood looking up at the cross hung on the wall behind the altar. He moved into the row and sat down.

After several minutes, he felt someone put something on his shoulders. When he looked up, he saw Pastor Andrew placing a blanket on him. He looked at Clive and said, "You looked cold and I thought this might help. Stay as long as you like. I will be here for awhile."

He turned and walked back up the aisle and as he did he heard Clive whisper, "Please help me to stop this evil." Clive remained seated and almost motionless for about half an hour. He said nothing. There were no tears, no words, no prayers; he just sat and stared at the cross on the wall. His mind was almost blank except for repeating what he said earlier, "Please help me."

It was almost seven o'clock when he slowly got to his feet and, with the blanket still around his shoulders, walked slowly to the back of the church. When he reached the back vestibule, he saw Pastor Andrew neatly stacking some books on the small church library shelf. Clive didn't say anything; he just stood there and watched. Pastor Andrew looked up, smiled, and walked to Clive. Clive handed him the blanket as the pastor asked, "Sheriff, are you okay now? Have we been able to help you?"

Clive lowered his head and said, "I don't know. I think so. I feel better than I did." Pastor Andrew put up his index finger in a gesture to wait and walked to his office. He returned with a rag and handed it to Clive. Clive felt the weight and when he opened it, it was his Glock 40.

Pastor Andrew said, "I think there is a need for this—but not here. Sheriff, I do not envy you your job, not even when times are good. Certainly not now. If you need us again, please come and visit. You have friends here. Do not try to carry the burden on your own. He never meant for it to be that way." Clive and the Pastor shook hands and Clive managed a smile. They walked together to the front steps.

As Clive was about to turn and leave he looked at the newspaper machine and reached into his pocket for change then realized that the machine was empty. He just shrugged his shoulders and said, "Oh well."

Pastor Andrew again used his index finger to imply, "Hold on a minute." He went inside and returned in a few seconds with a newspaper and handed it to Clive. "Sheriff, take it. I've read it already." Clive reached into his pocket for change but the pastor said, "No need, just go home and get some rest."

Clive shook his head in agreement, smiled, shook the pastor's hand again, and said, "Thank you." He turned and went to his car. He started it and as he pulled away from the curb he looked at the church and saw the pastor waving goodbye. As he moved down the street he whispered to himself, "Thank you." Clive's first thought once on the road was to go to the station. He felt much better now—as if his strength had returned somewhat. When he reached the main intersection in Smith Falls he stopped at the red light, intending to turn left to the station.

As he waited for the light he heard the pastor's words in his mind again, "Go home and get some rest." When the light turned green he made a right turn and headed for home. On the way home he called the station and talked to the night desk. They had a message for him to call Rose Bodin at home. A few minutes later, after talking to the desk sergeant, he pulled into his driveway. He went inside and as he walked past his chair he saw the red light on the answering machine flashing. He didn't stop but went directly to the kitchen to the refrigerator, opened it, took out a pitcher of water and poured a glass. He drank the glass in three or four large gulps, the cold water actually hurting his teeth. He was about to pour another glass when one of several cans of beer caught his eye. He opened the can then noticed a Ziploc bag with several pieces of pizza in it on the same shelf. He opened the bag and took out a slice. He took a drink of the cold beer and was about to take a bite of the cold pizza when he stopped and looked at it. The question popped into his mind, how long had it been in there? He looked it over, decided it seemed okay, shrugged his shoulders and took a bite. It was stale and cold but it would do for now. He walked to the living room and sat in his chair. He took several bites of pizza and a long drink of the beer and sat quietly for several minutes. He was putting the last of the pizza in his mouth when he thought to himself, "Gotta call Rose."

He picked up the phone and as he did he saw the red light flashing again. He was going to listen to the message then decided to call Rose first. The phone rang three times and Rose answered, "Hello."

Clive said, "Rose it's Clive."

Rose said, "Clive are you alright? We all have been worried, but we didn't call you. We all figured you needed the time. Are you okay?"

Clive said, "Yes, I'm fine, tired but fine. How are things going?" Rose told him that J.D. and Jim were handling his job and that Bill Fry wanted him to call the lab tomorrow. Clive asked, "What about Alice's parents?" Rose said that Alvin Richards had gone to the house with Commissioner McCall and told them. She paused for a second or two and Clive thought he heard her crying. He asked her, "Rose are you okay?"

There was another pause then she said, "Yes, I'll be okay. We have a car there around the clock. No press or anyone else but friends and family. We thought you would want it that way."

Clive said, "Good."

Rose said, "Clive, they took it real hard. It was so unexpected. Who would ever have thought?"

Clive said, "I know, I know." He asked, "Did they tell them I would be there as soon as I can?"

"Yes," Rose said. "And I have a message from her dad." There was another pause, then Rose continued. "He said, 'Clive do what you need to do, don't let this be for nothing.' He also said, 'Don't blame yourself. She would not have wanted you to do that.'"

"Anything else?" Clive asked, now very close to being choked up himself.

"No," Rose said, "That's it. All that can be done is done. We have officers out everywhere. J.D. and Jim will be fine till tomorrow and the lab and Bill have made this the only case for now."

Clive said, "Okay Rose."

Rose added, "Clive, we'll find out who did this. We'll find out who did all of this. You will catch him, Clive. You will catch him."

Clive said, "Okay Rose, I'll see you tomorrow." He hung up the phone and sat quietly for several minutes then he looked at the answering machine and pushed the button. The automated voice said, "You have four messages in mailbox one. First message. Friday, 11:05 p.m."

There was the usual pause then he heard Alice's voice. He was about to skip over it, not sure he could listen again. He decided to let it go. "Clive, this is Alice, it's just after eleven o'clock, Friday. I need you to call my cell phone now. Clive, I know who it is. I know who's been doing it and why. We have to act fast. There are only two of us left. Clive, it's…" then there was the odd sound and the sound went dead.

Clive paused the machine and slid forward in the chair. He thought for a minute then pushed the repeat button. The message played again. When it finished he paused again then whispered, "There are only two of us left. How did I miss that? Two of who left? You Alice, you and who?" He sat and ran the list of names of the victims through his mind. Jody Miller, Wesley Dans, Roscoe Black, Bob Anderson, Judge Richards, Bobby Rodgers, Doc Watson and Alice. He thought long and hard, then he said, "Only two left, Alice and who, Alice and who?"

After a few minutes he pushed the button on the machine again. The automated voice said, "Mailbox one. Second message. Saturday, 2:00 p.m." "Clive, this is Rose. Are you there?" There was a pause then she repeated, "Clive, this is Rose. Are you there? If you're there, please pick up." There was a moment of silence then the message ended. Clive pushed pause again. He thought for a minute then realized it was when they were looking for him.

He pushed the button on the machine again, "Mailbox One. Third message. Saturday, 6:00 p.m." The pause, then Clive heard Bill Fry's voice. "Clive, this is Bill. It's about six on Saturday. Call me at the lab. I'll be here most of the night. I need to talk to you about something interesting. Call me." There was a click and Clive paused the machine again. Clive walked to the kitchen and looked at the clock above the refrigerator. The time was 8:05 p.m. He looked at his watch and the time was almost the same. He returned to his chair and then picked up the phone and dialed the crime lab. When they answered he asked for Bill Fry's extension. Several seconds passed and then Bill answered, "Crime lab. Bill Fry speaking."

Clive said, "Bill, this is Clive. You left a message."

Bill said, "Yes, I did, but first how are you doing? You didn't look too good earlier today. Well I guess most of us didn't."

Clive said, "Bill, I'm fine. Thanks for being concerned but I'm fine—at least now I am fine. I guess as fine as I can be. You said you had a message for me. Something you found interesting."

"Yes," Bill said. "I have all the items from Alice's car and around the store. I was looking them over, you know—just a first look. I came across something that piqued my interest. I'm not sure but I think Alice was trying to tell us something or maybe trying to figure it out for herself. Anyway there was a newspaper on the front seat of her car.

It was the early edition of the *Gazette*. It has a story on the front page about the murders."

"Yes, I know," Clive said. "I saw it earlier."

Bill continued, "Well, I read the story. It gives a list of murder victims and some other information, but it's the second section I'm concerned about."

"The second section?" Clive asked.

"Yes," Bill said. "At the bottom of the second section, she, I assume, circled an article with a black felt-tip pen. I found one on the seat next to the paper. Do you have a copy of the paper there with you?"

Clive thought for a moment then said, "Yes, I do as a matter of fact, but it's out in the car. Hold on. I'll go get it."

Bill quickly said, "Clive, I need to get off the line. I'll tell you where to look. You can call me back. It's the last article at the bottom, the weekly "Remember When" article. You know, about events from the past on this date."

Clive said, "Yeah, yeah, I know what you mean. Which part?"

Bill said, "The one about the accident eight or nine, maybe ten years ago. Take a look at it and call me back. I'm not sure what it means but have a look anyway. And oh yeah, at the corner of the same page is another article. I think it's associated also. She didn't circle it but it looks like she put a small arrow pointed that way."

"Okay," Clive said, "I'll call you back." He hung up then went out to the car and got the paper. He returned to his chair, opened to the second section and read the article. He then read the article in the corner, which included a photo. He then turned to the front section and read it and the list of names that was included. When he finished he sat and ran the information over in his mind. He went back to the front section, read it again and realized it was different from the other article. Before, the names of the victims were always put together in a group. This time the names were divided. Everyone that was killed with the word "forever" being present was in one list. Roscoe Black and Bob

Anderson were separate and the question was asked, "Did they actually have something to do with the other murders?" He thought again for a while then went back to the second section and read it again. It was all starting to form a picture. He strained his eyes at the photo in the corner of the page but it wasn't clear enough. It was too small. He was about to look for a magnifying glass when he remembered the last message on the machine.

He pushed the button and the automated voice continued, "Mailbox one, fourth message. Saturday, 7:30 p.m." It was just before he had come home. There was a pause then, "This is Doctor Weaver from County General, I'm calling to talk to Sheriff Clive Aliston. We met yesterday at the hospital at Officer Jack Duff's room. I'm the one who told you to leave. We are about to take Officer Duff to emergency surgery for the fracture to his neck vertebrae. He won't let us take him up until I leave a message for you. Please call my secretary Kathy at the following number and extension. Officer Duff will be fine but he was not going until I called you. Please call as soon as possible. Someone will be at that number till at least nine o'clock. Thank you." The automated voice said, "End of messages," and shut off.

Clive looked at his watch. It was 8:30 p.m. He dialed the number and waited. After the fourth ring a female voice said, "Doctor Weaver's answering service. This is Kathy speaking."

Clive said, "Hello, this is Sheriff Aliston. I received a message from Dr. Weaver about Officer Duff."

"Yes," Kathy said. "I have that message, Sir. Will you hold on please?" There was a short pause then Kathy came back on, "Sheriff, Dr. Weaver said that Officer Duff told him to tell you, 'Death travels with him.'"

Clive said, "Yes, I heard that from Jack before at the hospital. I'm not sure what he was trying to say. I guess he's still out of it somewhat."

Kathy said, "Yes, he's still in and out but he did tell the

doctor to add one more thing to the message. It's one word or name. We're not sure. He's very hard to understand in his present condition. He told me to tell you."

Clive listened, then slowly stood up. The expression on his face registered total surprise. He said, "Could you repeat that again?" He listened again then said, "Thank you so much for your time. Tell the doctor I said thank you." He slowly lowered the phone. He stood and stared at the wall for several seconds then turned and put the phone in its cradle. He sat down in the chair and then whispered to himself one word, "Lasiter."

CHAPTER 22

Paul Lasiter walked out of the mortuary prep room in the basement of his cellar. In one hand he had a large mug, in the other some old rags. He walked to the opposite wall near the bottom of the cellar steps to a large, iron door that was standing partly open. He entered, then several minutes later came out with an armful of rags or blankets that were not clean like the ones he had entered with. He also did not have the mug. He walked to the corner of the room near the washer and dryer and dropped the items in a pile near the machines. He walked back into the mortuary prep room and several minutes later walked back out and stopped in the doorway. He stood motionless for several seconds and listened as if he had heard something. He shook his head then turned and walked back into the prep room. Out in the cellar a shadow moved across the wall near the steps but there was no sound. A few minutes later Paul came out of the prep room again, turned, closed and locked the door. He walked across the cellar to a small table along the wall near the iron door. He was organizing some items on the table when he thought he heard a sound behind him. He stopped then slowly turned. He got a surprised, almost concerned look on his face then said, "Brian, what are you doing here?" Brian slowly moved out of the shadows. His hair, his uniform, his entire appearance was a mess. Paul took several steps toward Brian and repeated, "Brian what are you doing here?"

Brian stood and stared into his eyes for several seconds then spoke. "Did you really think it would all go away, Father? Did you really think the guilt could be washed away? Evil cannot be cleansed with evil."

Paul stepped back two or three steps.

Brian said, "It's really about the pain, Father. Your pain, your guilt is worse than theirs."

Brian moved closer and Paul continued to back up. He kept repeating, "Brian, Brian, wait." Paul saw a large silhouette move out from the dark shadows behind the cellar steps. The dark figure moved behind Brian as if it were following him. Paul's eyes were opened wide and his mouth dropped open as if he wanted to speak, but nothing came out.

Brian moved closer and the dark figure followed. Brian stopped just feet from Paul and said, "It is your guilt that must be cleansed."

Brian reached for his weapon and Paul yelled, "No." The huge figure raised one arm and slammed it against Brian's side, knocking him into the side of the steps. Paul stood frozen for an instant as Brian's weapon flew across the cellar floor. The huge figure reached to the floor, dragged Brian up out of the shadows and pinned him against the side of the stairs. Before Paul could speak he hit Brian again with a backhand across the face that sent Brian to the floor. Paul yelled, "No," as the figure picked Brian up and pinned him to the side of the stairs again—only this time in a strangle hold around his neck. Paul stepped up, placed his hand on the huge man's back, and yelled, "No, you cannot. He is of your blood."

Saturday, June 26, 8:35 p .m.

Clive sat in his chair, the thoughts in his head spinning like a child's top. What had transpired since Jody's death came and went in bits and pieces, flashing before his eyes like objects caught in an intense storm. He leaned forward in his chair placing his face in his hands. He took in several deep breaths as his mind began to calm. What Dr. Weaver's secretary said was so disturbing that if he had to speak he wasn't sure he could. As his mind calmed he began to run through the information they had collected: the names of each victim and where the word "Forever" was present and where it wasn't. He thought about when Brian had been around and when he was missing. He thought about Brian's relationship with Jody, where the murders had taken place, what Jack Duff had said at the hospital. He thought about Brian's reaction in the hospital room. He remembered that Alice had taken Brian back to the station from the hospital. He wondered about Roscoe Black and Bob Anderson—what had happened there. He again saw the confrontation between Bob Anderson and himself at Posey's Bar—and the crowd. The dark face in the corner and the flash of light glinting off something near that face. He remembered Brian had taken Roscoe back to the fairgrounds. So much information, so many pieces. How did they all fit?

He remembered the newspaper and picked it up again. He scanned the front page then went again to the second section and read it. The "Remember When" article was about the tragic accident on the railroad crossing near the fairgrounds some nine or ten years ago. It said that of the seven people in the car, six escaped injury but one was lost. It went on to say how tragic it was that a young person just starting out in life was taken. The short article was discreet and did not mention the name of the victim but Clive knew who it was. He had heard about it many times when he had first come to the Smith Falls Station—but how did it connect to the murders? To Brian, yes, it was his sister Victoria, but how could this involve him? Brian had been around when some of the people died. Where was the connection to it all? Why did Alice circle the article? What did the victims have to do with it all?

He moved on to the picture on the bottom corner of the page. It was small and hard to see. It was of a man standing beside a monument in what appeared to be a cemetery and the face was not clear. The article said that a group had paid for and dedicated the memorial to the victim of the car-train accident five years earlier. Clive opened the drawer of the stand beside his chair and retrieved a magnifying glass. He looked at the man's face and recognized him. It was Paul Lasiter. There was an inscription on the monument but he couldn't quite make it out. He got up and walked to the kitchen and placed the paper on the counter under the bright fluorescent light, and used the magnifying glass again. Most of the inscription was still not clear but one word stuck out like a burning brand in his mind, "FOREVER." He stood up and looked at the cabinet in front of him with an almost blank stare. He thought for a minute then looked at the paper again. He went back to his chair, sat down, and thought for several minutes. He looked at his watch and realized it was too late to call the paper. He whispered to himself, "Paul Lasiter."

Clive remembered seeing the Lasiter's Funeral Home hearse in the city the day they came to get Jody's body. He remembered the vehicle but not who was driving. He then began to think again about the confrontation with Bob Anderson at Posey's Bar. It had been the same day. He ran it through his mind again and again. He picked up the phone and called Bill Fry again. When Bill answered, Clive said, "Bill, did you read all of the article on the second page of the paper?"

Bill said, "Yes Clive I did."

Clive asked, "Did you see the picture up close?"

Bill said, "No I didn't."

Clive said, "Take a close look."

Bill said, "Hold on." There was a pause for several minutes then Bill came back on. "Clive, it's a picture of Paul Lasiter."

Clive said, "Yes, now look at the inscription on the monument."

There was silence again, then Bill said, "Clive, it says 'FOREVER.'"

Clive said, "Yes, and I just talked to a Dr. Weaver's secretary at County Memorial. They were taking Jack up for surgery and he told them he wouldn't go until they gave me this message, 'Death travels with him,' and the name 'Lasiter.'"

There was a moment or two of silence then Bill said, "Clive, surely you don't think Brian or Paul had anything to do with this?"

Clive said, "Bill, I'm not sure what I think. I've got a lot of disjointed information and I'm trying to put it all into one picture but it's a real puzzle."

Bill asked, "How much do you know about the accident that is in that article?"

Clive said, "Only what I've heard. You know, bits and pieces from Brian and a few other sources. I wasn't assigned to this station at that time, so I have no firsthand information or memory of it."

Bill said, "Well Clive, like you, I was not in a position at that time to know much about it. I wasn't on that case but I'll bet the records can be pulled. Alice wanted us to know something about this. Let me check. I'll call you back and while I'm at it I'll see what I can find out about that photo."

Clive was about to hang up when he asked one more question, "Bill, the day that I was at the morgue with you to look at Jody's body—when I was leaving I saw the Lasiter hearse coming in. Who was driving that day?"

Bill thought for a moment then said, "Well, usually it's Paul, but if I remember correctly I think he had one of his part-time drivers do the job. I never thought much about that. Why, does it mean something?"

Clive said, "I'm not sure Bill, just something I'm thinking about. Well anyway get back to me ASAP—like tonight. I got a bad feeling about this whole deal and that feeling gets worse as the night wears on."

Bill said, "I'll call you back. Just give me some time to see what I can find."

Clive said, "Okay," and hung up. He sat back in his chair and then rubbed his eyes and his face and whispered, "The pieces have got to fit. All I need to do is find the glue."

Saturday, June 26, 9:00 p .m.

Brian started to come out of his unconscious state. As he did he looked around the room, and at first all was not clear, like in a mist. He could see someone standing in front of him and another, much larger person to his right. He realized that he was seated and he tried to get up but couldn't. When he moved, his side hurt. He tried to speak, but his throat felt like someone had sandpapered it. As his eyes cleared he saw Paul standing in front of him. Suddenly there was a bright light in his eyes. He squinted and looked away but Paul turned his head back toward the light. After a few seconds Paul said, "Well, I guess you'll make it. I never intended for you to get hurt, Brian." Brian tried to speak again but nothing came out. Several seconds later Paul put a glass of water to his mouth and Brian drank. He then turned away from the glass and tried to move again. He realized then that he was tied to the chair.

He looked at Paul and said, "Father, what the hell do you think you're doing? How could you do this? All those innocent people. My God, are you insane? And Jody, why Jody? You knew how I felt about her. Why did you take her?"

Paul moved in closer to Brian, bent down and looked

into his face, "Brian, don't call me Father. I'm not your father. You're the bastard child of that whore that was my wife and Bart James." Brian clenched his teeth, took a deep breath, and screamed, "I read what you wrote. It's lies. All lies. Father, what are you saying? Mother and Bart James, are you mad?"

"Mad," Paul said. "After what happened, you call me mad. She married me but she was in love with that monster Bart. She always loved Bart. I loved her with all that was in me and she betrayed me. She was with him only months after we married and I didn't know. Not until she came home and confessed that she was with child—his child. That child is you. I am not your father."

Brian put his head to his chest, shook it back and forth and yelled, "No, no, it's not true. Father, it's not true."

Paul began to circle the chair as he continued. "Don't call me Father. You are not of my blood. I only took care of you because of her. Even with what she did, I still loved her. I always loved her. I love her still. I hate her and I love her. Try living with that."

Brian couldn't grasp what was being said. "No, no, no."

Paul stopped in front of the chair, looked into his eyes again and continued. "She confessed and asked me to forgive her and I did. I forgave her and I took you in as my own. Every time I looked at you I saw him, but I tried to love you because you were part of her. She stayed away for a long time, things got better and I thought it was over. It was the best time for me. Then Victoria came and she was mine. Mine and your mother's. She was my blood; she was our child. So I put it all behind me and I forgave her and I tried to love you as much as I could. Several years went by and we were happy, the four of us. Then he came back into our lives and her family wasn't enough. She couldn't stay away from him. I knew it was happening again but I denied it. Then I found out that she was pregnant again. Not my child but his. She tried to deny it but I knew, I knew what they had done and so did the Lord and he cursed them for it. She died of complications after the birth and I was left with their love child."

Brian screamed again, "You murdered all of them and what you are telling me now and what you wrote about us, it's lies—all lies."

Paul walked across the room to the large figure standing alone in the dark. Brian couldn't talk; he almost couldn't breath. What was he hearing; it couldn't be true. How could it all be true? Paul took the large figure by the hand and said, "Come, Maxwell, come see your brother. Show him what your mother did to you. To you and me and Victoria."

Brian watched as they walked into the light. What he saw almost stopped his heart. Standing before him next to Paul was a huge man, maybe seven feet plus. He must have weighed well over three hundred pounds. One eye was normal the other was twice its size. His nose was misshapen and his mouth was bent to one side, exposing most of the teeth on that side. One ear was just a small piece of skin on the side of his head while the other was normal. He had reddish brown hair that lay in ringlets on his forehead. He was slightly bent to one side. He smiled at Brian as saliva ran from the side of his mouth. He tried to speak but only inhuman sounds came out. Then he tried again and one word came out. It sounded like "Brother."

Brian started to scream and yell, "No, you lie. You are a liar. This isn't true. My mother was no whore and you are my father. He is not my brother. He is not my brother."

The big man started to laugh and repeated again and again, "Brother, brother, brother." Brian turned to get free but he couldn't. He moved the chair until it finally fell over on its side. Paul bent down and with Max's help set it back up again—only now it faced the other side of the room. Paul told Max to go to the corner and sit down, and the big man moved slowly back into the darkness, still repeating, "Brother, brother." Brian felt like all his strength was gone and he just sat his chin to his chest and breathed. Paul moved around in front of him, bent down to Brian, put out his hand and raised his head.

Brian, tears running down his face looked into Paul's eyes and said, "Okay Father, I guess it's my turn. You hate me so much. Get it over with. Do it now."

Paul looked calmly at Brian and said, "No, Brian. You are not one of the evil ones. You are only guilty of being her son."

Brian said, "Well Father, if not me then why the others? Why did they all have to die?"

Paul started to walk around the chair again as Max sat in the corner breathing slowly and still repeating, "Brother."

"Why?" Paul said. "Because they took from me the only thing that I had in life to love. The only part of me that could live on. They took Victoria. They took her innocence and made it an evil thing, with their alcohol and their drugs. When they had defiled her then they took her to a place where she died." Paul quickly circled to the front of the chair and grasped Brian's face in both hands and screamed. "They took a pure thing, a pure soul and they took my life and left me with Max and you. Evil must be paid back. There is a debt to be paid. Their tickets must be redeemed. This is what I have left." He turned to the wall and opened a door.

What Brian saw made his blood turn cold, and he felt himself grow dizzy as if he was going to pass out. Brian screamed as loud and long as he could, then his head snapped to one side and he began a series of convulsions, then he calmed again and just stared out in front of him, his eyes glazed and his mouth half open.

Paul screamed at the top of his voice, "Tonight the last ticket comes due. Pain will be paid in pain. What I leave them they left me. After tonight it is over."

There was a moment of silence then a damp rag was placed in Brian's face. Several minutes later Paul and Max ascended the stairs and the door at the top of the steps closed.

Saturday, June 26, 9:15 p .m.

Clive continued to sit in his chair. He would think about one part of the case, then switch to another. He tried to put sections together. He tried to think about each victim. What else did he know about them? He remembered Brian's reactions to each murder and tried to analyze them. He thought about Paul Lasiter and what he knew about him. He finally got up and started to pace back and forth across the living room. As he did, his mind went back again to the day in Posey's Bar and the argument with Bob Anderson. He kept seeing the dark face in the corner booth and the glint of light. It played over and over in his mind but why? It was about 9:20 p.m. when the phone rang. Clive picked up the phone and continued to pace back and forth. "Hello, this is Clive."

There was a pause then Bill Fry said, "Clive, it's Bill again. Well I got the information about the accident."

"And?" Clive said.

Bill said, "You're not going to believe this. I wish we had known this before. It could have saved some of those people. I mean if I'm right about what I feel now. Never mind, I'm not sure what I feel."

Clive cut in then said, "Bill what the hell is it? What did you find?"

Bill said, "Are you seated? If not I'd think you should be."

Clive said, "Bill, no I'm not seated and get on with it. Just tell me. What did you find?"

Bill continued, "The accident happened ten years ago just like it said in the article. There were seven kids involved. Six lived, one died. As you know that was Victoria Lasiter. They had been partying all night I guess. Booze and drugs—at least it's what two of them were arrested for. I mean for possession and distribution."

Clive said, "Don't tell me the kids were..."

"Yeah," Bill said. "It was Jody Miller, Wesley Dans, Bobby Rodgers, Doc Watson, Alice Shearer, of course

Victoria Lasiter, and Mandy James. Now just listen to the rest of this. From the case information that I've been able to quickly go over, this is what came down. I guess they started to party at the Shearer's family camp. You know smoking dope and drinking. I guess they thought it was an out of the way place. According to the police interviews they ran out of booze and decided to get more."

"Let me guess," Clive said. "Bobby Rodgers supplied the booze and Doc Watson supplied the dope."

"You got it," Bill said, then continued. "I guess after they got more booze they decided not to go back to the camp but instead continued the party at the newly-constructed pavilion at the fairgrounds. I guess it was near midnight when the local groundskeeper broke it up. They all scattered and ran to Wesley's car and headed out of the fairgrounds. I guess they tried to cross the tracks at the crossing near the fairgrounds but something must have happened to Wesley's car. It was stuck on the tracks and the gates came down. They all got out except for Victoria. Alice testified later that she could hear Victoria screaming until the train hit the car."

Clive said, "Did they say why she didn't get out?"

"Yes," Bill said. "I guess her blood alcohol level was so high she couldn't move. It was probably all she could do to scream. You figure, a young girl that didn't drink, you add booze and dope and the fear of being left alone in the middle of the tracks. I doubt I could move."

Clive continued to pace back and forth. He said, "Why didn't Alice realize the connection to this earlier? I mean it's not something you would easily forget. How did she even get the job at the station? I mean you don't work there if you have a record."

"I got the answer to that too," Bill said. "She was treated by a psychologist for almost six months but nothing helped until they used hypnosis."

"You mean she couldn't remember?" Clive asked.

"Yes," Bill said. "Her memory was suppressed. It wasn't

until the article in the paper and all the stress of the case that it must have finally come all flooding back into her mind. As far as the job at the station, she didn't have a record."

"What?" Clive said. "No record. How did that happen?"

Bill continued, "The only two that were prosecuted were Bobby Rodgers and Doc Watson. The police had been trying to pin something on Doc for a while and Bobby too, I guess. A deal was made. If the others testified, no charges would be filed. The others quietly did some community service and that was it. I guess they figured they were talked into what they did. None of the others had a record so I guess it was a first offense kind of deal."

"Yeah," Clive said, "And I'll bet the big money in the Miller, Dans and James families might have made a difference too."

"No," Bill said. "I don't think so. It's possible I guess but not in front of the guy who tried this case."

Clive paused for a second or two then said, "Don't tell me it was Judge Richards?"

"You got it," Bill said.

Clive just whispered, "Damn."

Bill continued, "And as for the picture of Paul and the monument. Guess who paid for that huge stone? Yeah, it was Miller, Dans and James. I guess after five years they figured they owed Paul something. I guess Paul took the gesture but didn't say much more about it. The paper picked it up and that's where the photo came from."

Clive said, "Hold on. Let me think here a second." He paused a few seconds then said, "Okay, we got Alice and her camp for the party. We got Doc and Bobby supplying the booze and the dope. Wesley was the driver and Judge Richards tried the case. What about Jody and Mandy James?"

Bill said, "Well, from what I gather Jody supplied the money for the party. I mean she did date Doc for a while. At least that's what it says here. And one more thing, guess where most of the money in the Miller family came from? The railroad."

"And Mandy?" Clive asked.

"Guess who paid for the new pavilion at the fairgrounds?" Bill asked.

"Bart James," Clive said.

"Yeah, you got the picture," Bill said, then added, "Also, Victoria was ejected from the car on impact. According to the coroner's report her body was intact and undamaged except for a near decapitation. Clive, her throat was cut." There was complete silence on both ends of the line for several seconds.

Clive sat back down in the chair then asked, "Is there any more?"

"Well, yeah, there is," Bill said. "The anniversary of the accident, it's tonight."

Clive's eyes suddenly opened wide and he took a deep breath. He thought for a second more then said, "Bill, there's only one left, Mandy James."

Bill started to say something but Clive really didn't hear him. Suddenly there were scenes in his head. It was Posey's Bar again and he could see Bob Anderson's face and Roscoe, his head hanging over his beer. There was a flash of light and there it was the dark face in the back booth again. Clive could hear a voice in the background now. It was Bill Fry and he kept repeating, "Clive are you there? Clive are you there?"

Clive closed his eyes and tried to freeze the image in his mind. Then he said to Bill, "Bill, hold on one minute. Let me think. Let me think. Hold on, hold on." His mind went back to the bar and the flash of light. The images were moving again. The flash played over and over and over in his mind. He put his hand to his forehead, squeezed his eyelids together and tried to concentrate. The flash of light came again and again and again. His head hurt as if his mind was trying to throw out something that didn't want to come. There was one clear picture of the men's room door opening and one more brilliant flash of light and there it was, the face staring back at him from out of the dark. It was Paul Lasiter and around his neck, flashing gold in the light, was a necklace that had one word on it, "FOREVER."

Clive jumped to his feet and asked, "Bill, are you still there?"

Bill said, "Yeah, Clive, I'm here. Are you alright?"

"Yeah," Clive said. "I'm here and I know now it's not Brian. You said the anniversary of the accident was tonight?"

"Yes," Bill said.

"Close to midnight?" Clive asked.

"Yes," Bill said.

Clive said, "My God, we have to move now."

"What?" Bill said.

"Now," Clive said. "Mandy is the only one left and the time's up tonight at midnight."

Saturday, June 26, 9:20 p .m.

Bart James had received a phone call at about nine o'clock from Carl Dans and another call ten minutes later from George Miller. They had all heard about Doc Watson's and Alice Shearer's deaths. They had put it all together and Bart was in a panic. He had to get his daughter at his construction company office. She had gone there earlier to get some papers for him.

Mandy had not been home in months. She had a job with an oil company and could be almost anywhere in the world at anytime. She had been awarded a new position with the company and given a bonus and a month off. The promotion had been in all the papers several weeks before she arrived home. Her father had planned a party on Sunday for her, and everyone who was anyone knew about it and was invited. She was staying in an apartment that her father kept for her on her few trips home. She was out of touch when it came to events around home and knew very little about the murders and the recent events that surrounded them.

Her apartment was only blocks away from the office and he had called and asked her to run over and make the pick-up. He needed them for a meeting Monday morning in the city. He had phoned her apartment and gotten no answer. He then called the construction office but the operator said the phone was out of service.

Mandy had left her apartment at about 9:10 p.m. to go to the office. As she got into her car she had noticed a large dark vehicle just down the block from her driveway. When she pulled out and turned the corner at the end of the block, she saw the vehicle's lights come on and pull away from the curb. Each turn she made was followed by the large dark car. She was beginning to become concerned when she stopped in front of the office and stepped out of her car. She stood and watched as the car drew nearer to her position. It wasn't until the vehicle passed and she realized what it was that she felt more relaxed. The vehicle continued to the next corner, turned right and vanished out of sight. She entered the office, locking the door behind her. She moved to the back of the building, to her father's office, and was going through his top drawer when she heard a crash that sounded like breaking glass. She stood up and stared out into the dark shop. Nothing was moving. She picked up the phone to call someone, anyone, but the line was dead. She slowly moved out around her father's desk and over to the office door. As she placed her hand on the doorknob, she looked at her reflection in a mirror on the wall beside her. With her long red hair and beautiful freckled face, she stared at the fear that looked back at her. She picked up a large heavy level that had rested against the wall, then slowly opened the office door.

Saturday, June 26, 9:45 p .m.

Bart James had raced from his home to the office, not even thinking about the police. It wasn't until he stopped in front of his office and saw the broken glass in the front door, and Mandy's car parked at the curb, that he reached for his cell phone and called the Smith Falls Police. As he talked on the phone explaining to the desk sergeant what he thought was happening, he retrieved a .38 caliber revolver from his glove compartment. The last words he spoke into the phone were, "I don't care what you want me to do, just get your damn lazy asses down here now." He dropped the phone, checked the cylinder of the revolver, and slowly walked toward the office door, leaving his car door open. He reached the door, then bent down and looked through the large hole in the bottom of the glass. The office was dark except for the small lamp in his office in the back. He reached for the knob and realized that the door was unlocked and just slightly open. He raised his weapon, then slowly pushed the door open. He entered and began to walk to the back toward the office. He saw the pieces of glass on the floor but not much else seemed to be disturbed. A few feet from his office door he noticed the large level on the floor and his office door standing open. He slowly bent down, picked up the level and looked it over. It seemed to be normal. He placed the level on a counter next to him and started to move into the office, when he heard a noise from behind. He slowly turned back toward the front of the store, then realized the view of the door was blocked by a huge silhouette. The gun was knocked from his hand and he was hit by a crashing blow to the left side of his head. He hit the counter beside him, slid to the floor, and everything went black.

CHAPTER 23

Saturday, June 26, 9:50 p .m.

Clive was already on his way to Lasiter's Funeral Home. He had told Bill Fry he would call him back, but that if he found out anything else to call him on the car radio or the cell phone. He had called the station and asked about Brian and was told that he still had not been located. He told the desk sergeant to have everyone available looking for Mandy James and Brian. He had also added that Brian's "missing" status should be treated as either a murder suspect situation, or a victim situation. He wanted J.D. to call him ASAP, and for Jim Terrell to be contacted and have people sent to the James house and Mandy's apartment. He brought his patrol car to a stop about half a block from the funeral home. He was about to get out of the car when the radio came on. It was the desk sergeant. He told Clive that the Smith Falls police had Bart James. He said that Bart's office had been broken into and that the Smith Falls police were on the way there. Clive told the sergeant to keep him informed but to call his cell phone. He would have it on vibrate to cut the noise, but if he didn't answer the call, the sergeant should leave a message. He also wanted J.D. to go to the James office and see what he could find out. He told the desk sergeant he would call back in a few minutes, that there was something he wanted to check out.

Clive hung up, put the phone on vibrate and checked his weapon. He closed the patrol car door, then started toward the Lasiter Funeral Home. He worked his way to the front of the house, hid behind a large tree and looked things over. Lights were on all over the house. Paul's private car was in the driveway. He worked his way up the driveway past the car and up to the garage door. He looked inside and saw the Lasiter Funeral Home hearse in the garage. The other side of the garage was vacant. He moved up the front steps and onto the porch. He looked at both sides of the porch, then slowly drew his weapon from his shoulder holster and moved to the front door. The main door was standing open and the storm door was unlocked. No one seemed to be moving inside. He slowly opened the door and stepped inside the entry room. To the right was a flight of steps that led to the second floor and Paul's apartment. He moved to the bottom of the steps and looked up. There was a dim light at the top of the stairs, like a night-light. He moved to the three downstairs rooms that were used as the funeral home. All the rooms were empty. In the back of the house was a kitchen that had been remodeled as a waiting room, and off to the left a small office that Paul used for the business. There seemed to be no one at home, and he was beginning to feel like an intruder. Had he figured this right? Was Paul involved or was he now in the Lasiter home illegally? He moved back to the bottom of the stairs and then decided to yell up to the second floor. He yelled once, "Paul, are you home?" There was no answer. He yelled again and got the same response. He moved slowly up to the second floor and checked each room. No one there. He came back downstairs and stood there for several minutes, thinking about what to do next. He moved back to the converted kitchen and went out a side door to the garage. He walked around the garage and the new Cadillac hearse and saw nothing unusual. He was about to leave the garage when he noticed on the cement floor a small spot of oil or grease. There was a tire track that ran through the spot as if a car had driven over it. At first he didn't pay much attention and was about to leave the garage when something told him to take another look. He walked to the track and bent down to get a closer look. There on the floor of the garage was the same track that had been in the mud at the Watson house. The tire mark with the piece of rubber missing. Paul Lasiter had been there at Doc's that night. Clive slowly stood up, feeling a lot less secure than he had earlier. He moved back to the kitchen and once again checked the downstairs rooms. He also checked the public restrooms on that floor. No one was there. He went back to the kitchen, opened the door to the cellar and flipped on the light.

He looked down the long flight of stairs to the basement. He pulled his weapon up close to the side of his face and slowly began to descend the stairs. When he reached the third step from the bottom he turned around quickly and scanned the cellar, his weapon out in front of him. The large cellar room was empty. On one wall were a washer and dryer and a pile of dirty rags or clothes. At the bottom of the steps was a large iron door, and next to the door was a small table. On the table was a large gray pewter mug. Clive moved to the bottom of the steps and reached for the iron door that was standing partially open. He reached around the door entrance looking for a light switch but found none. He backed out of the door and looked around the room looking for some kind of a light source. He saw a switch on the outside wall near the table and flipped it on. A single light bulb lit up in the center of the room behind the iron door. It hung from a twisted wire that came from an old junction box in the center of a wood beam-crossed ceiling. Clive entered and looked around the room. On one wall was a copper tube and valve that dripped water into an old porcelain bowl on a box near the floor. In the opposite corner was an old metal cot with a single mattress and a couple of old blankets. The floor was cement but had traces of straw all around. A long chain was attached to a metal ring on the wall near the cot. It was enough chain to reach almost to the door and at the end of the chain was a large, unlocked iron leg ring. A tray of partially-eaten food was on the bed. The only other item in the room was an old rocking chair that sat near the middle of the room. It faced away from the door and Clive saw something on the seat. He walked to the chair and picked up an old worn teddy bear that had most of the fur missing. The bear had on a small pink sweater and on the sweater was the single name, "Victoria."

Clive put the bear back on the chair and moved out to the main room. He saw another door at the opposite end of the room. It was standing half open and it appeared to have a lock and hasp hanging from it. He walked slowly to the door, checking the shadows under the steps as he moved. When he reached the door he realized that the lock was still locked and the hasp and ring had been pulled away from the doorframe. He raised his weapon again and slowly entered, checking each side of the room as he did. One light was on in the center, a single four-foot fluorescent bulb. It was apparently a type of night-light, so Clive looked to the wall and found four light switches. He flipped them on one at a time. As he did the room lit up and was now flooded with bright light. It was a prep room, where bodies were prepared for funerals. Steel tables were in several places in the room, the walls were lined with instruments, and shelves had jars of what appeared to be embalming supplies.

In the center of the room was a chair—or what was left of one. Pieces of rope were all over the floor and an open penknife lay near the chair pieces. Clive bent down and picked up the knife by the tip of the blade. He recognized it at once. It was Brian's. He put the knife back on the floor and started to move around the room. As he reached the back wall he realized that a set of shelves seemed to be standing away from the wall like a door that was partially opened. He walked to the shelves, raised his gun and pointed it toward them with one hand. With the other hand he opened the shelf. It was hinged to the wall and felt heavy as it swung open. When the light from the room entered the space behind the shelf, Clive almost dropped his weapon. There, facing out toward him in a glass-covered casket, was Victoria Lasiter. Clive backed up several steps as a chill ran through him. He slowly lowered his weapon and with a grimace whispered, "Oh, shit." He just stood and stared at the casket and Victoria for several seconds. He recomposed himself then stepped forward again. As he moved in closer he realized that she must have been perfectly preserved. Her face was ashen but so perfect it must have been the way she looked the day before her death. She was dressed in a white lace dress that looked almost like a wedding gown. Her hair was long and combed beautifully onto her shoulders. In her crossed hands was a single rose that appeared to be dried. The collar of the lace dress was high on her neck, but dark purple-red stitches could be partially seen. Around her neck and laying on the front of the dress was a small gold chain attached to a pendant that was one word, "Forever."

Clive continued to stare at her, almost expecting her to move at any second. After what seemed like several minutes he backed up and turned to the back of the shelf that was the door. He saw some papers tacked to a corkboard. He pushed the door to a more open position so the light from the room fell on the board. They were all newspaper clippings: one for the murder of Jody Miller, others for Wesley Dans, Doc Watson, Bobby Rodgers and Judge Richards. Each was numbered in the order of the murders. Each had several parts of the article circled in red ink. Off to the side of the board were the articles about Bob Anderson and Roscoe Black. Nothing on those articles was circled or marked in any way. There was only a single note attached to them that said, "Regrets." Below the articles was a pink slip of paper, folded in half and tacked to the board. He opened the paper and on it were two words, "Alice" and "Cabin." He stood and thought for a moment then he turned to walk out into the room. As he did his foot kicked something on the floor.

He bent down and saw the corner of a wooden box sticking out from a space behind the door near the casket. The box had a rope handle on one end and Clive grasped it and pulled the box out into the light. It was an old box that must have held bottles of chemicals at one time. He opened the lid and looked inside. Rolled in a ball at one end was a brown raincoat. Clive, trying not to touch too much, removed the coat and placed it on the floor. It had two buttons missing and a white greasy substance on the front. Inside the coat was a tag with Jody Miller's name. He returned to the box and found Jack Duff's weapon and cell phone. In the opposite corner were Bob Anderson's notepad and pen. He carefully removed the book and placed it on the floor. He flipped through the pages and found notes that Bob had written from the interview that day in Posey's Bar. In the center of the box he found some of Bobby Rodgers' porno tapes, the judge's gavel, Alice's police badge, a crisp, clean one hundred dollar bill in a money clip, and car keys probably belonging to Wesley Dans, and a gold necklace with a surfer pendant which he assumed was Doc Watson's. Each item belonged to a victim. Clive realized that Paul must have wanted Victoria to see that he was fulfilling his commitment to her for the evil he believed was done. Clive stood up and walked out to the center of the room but saw nothing else that seemed to be unusual. He stood and thought for several minutes. His cell phone began to vibrate. He holstered his weapon and answered the phone. "Hello," Clive said with normal volume, then realized he should be more careful. He repeated again in a lowered voice, "Hello, this is Clive." It was the desk sergeant from his station. He listened as the sergeant told him they had found no one at Mandy's apartment and that there appeared to be no forced entry. The Smith Falls police were at the James' home and all was okay there. He said they had found Bart James inside his shop, unconscious, and that he was being taken to the hospital for what could be a concussion. He told Clive that Mandy's car had been found outside the shop but that she was nowhere around. Clive asked if there were any signs of a struggle and was told about the broken window and that Bart had a weapon that wasn't taken. He also told Clive that J.D. had called and that he had just arrived at the James' shop and would call as soon as he could. Clive asked if Jim Terrell had been called and was told that Jim was already with Bart James and that he had also dispatched some state officers to the James' shop and the James' home, and Mandy's apartment. Clive told the sergeant that he was at Lasiter's Funeral home, and that he was to tell J.D. Ricketts that he would call him ASAP, if he didn't hear from him. He also told him to call Bill Fry and tell him to gather all the information that he and Clive had discussed. Then he added, "Tell Bill we had it figured right. He is our man."

Clive hung up, walked back to the casket and just stared for several seconds. He realized that the corkboard was at Victoria's eye level—as if Paul was trying to let her see that those who were guilty had paid. He put his hand to his forehead and squeezed as he closed his eyes. The thought ran through his mind that the pain that had created this insanity had to be tremendous. He just shook his head and said, "My God. My God." He stood there for several more seconds then lowered his hand and looked again at Victoria. She seemed so peaceful—unlike the horror and terror that her death had created. He was about to turn away when he glanced at the paper articles again. He read the circled words on Jody's article; they were, "Jody" and "Railroad." He looked at Wesley's article; the words, "Wesley" and "Car" were circled. Judge Richards' were, "Judge" and "Court." Doc Watson's were, "Doc" and "Drugs," and Bobby Rodgers were, "Bobby" and "Liquor Store." He opened the pink slip of paper and read again, "Alice" and "Cabin." He got a puzzled look on his face for several seconds, then he repeated in a low whisper, "Railroad, Car, Court, Drugs." He paused, then his eyes opened wide and he said, "Cabin." He was silent and motionless for a few seconds, then he said, "Mandy." He paused again, then added, "Pavilion." He turned again and looked at Victoria and walked up close to the glass and whispered, "You know where they are, don't you? The pavilion. My God, it's the pavilion."

He looked at his watch; it was eleven p.m. He quickly turned and ran from the room and up the steps two and three at a time. He raced through the house, out the front door across the front yard to his car. He started the car and pulled forward across the center of the street. He backed up so fast the rear wheels jumped the curb and ran onto the grass in the yard. He slammed the car into drive and mashed the gas pedal to the floor. The rear tires dug in and threw grass, sod and dirt in every direction. When the wheels jumped off the curb onto the street they squealed and smoked for twenty feet as the car swerved back and forth on a dead run to the highway. When he reached the main road he snapped on the red lights on the roof and pulled out onto the road in the direction of the fairgrounds. He picked up the mike and called the desk sergeant, "This is Clive, come in."

There was a pause, then the sergeant answered, "Yes, Clive. Go ahead."

"Patch me through to J.D. Ricketts as fast as you can." He waited and as he did he whispered, "Come on, come on."

The radio crackled and J.D. said, "Yes, Clive. It's J.D."

Clive said, "J.D. call me on my cell phone. I don't want this over the radio."

J.D. started to interrupt about what they found at the James' construction office, when Clive cut in. "J.D., I need you to call me now. The cell phone. Call my cell phone. Mandy's life depends on us now." Clive threw the mike to the seat and took his phone off his belt and waited as he drove at high speed down the highway. Several seconds later his phone rang, "Yes, J.D.," he said. J.D. started to ask what was going on when Clive interrupted again, "J.D., listen. We don't have time. You need to listen to me now. I know who it is. It's Paul Lasiter and he has Mandy."

J.D. said, "Paul, who?"

Clive said, "Paul Lasiter, Brian's father. I don't have time to explain, just listen. He has Mandy and this whole thing is over at midnight. She has less than an hour to live. We have to move now so just listen. Call Jim Terrell and Alvin Richards and tell them to cover the James' home, office, and Mandy's apartment just in case I'm wrong. I want you to come with me. We have to stop this before it's too late."

"Stop what and where?" J.D. said.

Clive repeated, "J.D. listen to me. I want you to get to the fairgrounds as fast as you can. Do you know where they are?"

"Yes," J.D. said.

Clive asked, "Do you know where the large gazebo-style pavilion is at the top of the hill?"

"Yes," J.D. said. "I know where it is."

"Good," Clive said. "Do you think you can find the back road onto it?"

"No, Clive. I'm not sure of that," J.D. said.

"Okay," Clive said. "I'll take the back road in. You take the front and no lights or sirens. Park at the bottom of the hill. We scare him and he'll kill her before we can move in close enough to stop it."

"To stop what?" J.D. asked again.

Clive said, "J.D., you gotta trust me on this one. Just get there and cover the front. I'll move in around the back. No lights, no sirens and no other back up. We make too much noise and she's finished. If you see anyone at the pavilion, do not move in on your own. There is probably more than one perp here. Just lay back until I can move up the hill through the woods. I know that area and I think I can get close enough for a clear shot if I have to. Repeat, do not move until you see me."

J.D. said, "You got it, Clive, and be careful."

Clive ended with, "I'll be there in ten minutes, so get a move on now. You're closer than I am at your location –so, like I said, give me time to move in." Clive shut off the phone, stuffed it in his coat pocket and pushed the gas pedal even harder.

Saturday, June 26, 11:30 p .m.

Clive pulled off the main highway and turned off all his lights except for the fog lights. He traveled a one-lane dirt road to the back side of the hill where the pavilion stood. As he got closer to the path that led up the hill to the pavilion, he shut off the fog lights, killed the engine, and rolled to a stop at the side of the dirt road. The creek was close to the fairgrounds near the hill, and a thick fog hung in the air. Clive took a small mag-light flashlight out of the glove box, snapped it on, and stepped out of the car. He did not close the door but instead gently pushed it until it clicked. He took out his weapon and checked it, then pulled the slide placing one round into the chamber. He walked slowly to the path at the bottom of the hill. He shut off the light for several seconds and looked up toward the top of the hill scanning for any light. There was none. He snapped the flashlight back on and started up the path toward the top. As he moved he whispered, "Mandy girl, I hope I got this figured right."

He moved up the path fifty feet at a time. Each time he stopped he shut off his mag and checked for any type of light at the top. As he came closer to the top of the hill he saw a dim glow of light coming through the fog. He shut off his mag-light and put it in his pocket. He moved slowly as the fog began to thin out. It was now a thick layer along the ground that almost gave him the feeling that he was in an old horror movie set on the Scottish Moors. As he came close to the end of the path and the woods, the pavilion came into view in the distance. The fog hung low to the ground all the way across the clearing. It made the pavilion look as if it was an evil-looking castle at the edge of a dark swamp. He saw what appeared to be a large, dark car parked in the fog near the pavilion. He bent down, trying to use the fog for cover and started to move toward the vehicle. He could see a dim light behind the car—the same dim light that he had seen through the fog on the pathway up the hill. The light moved out from behind the vehicle and Clive got down on both knees, using the fog for cover. A lone man carrying what appeared to be a gas or Coleman lantern walked slowly toward the pavilion through the fog. As he moved toward the pavilion the light from the lantern shone on the vehicle. It was an old dark or black hearse. The man walked slowly up the steps to the pavilion deck. As he reached the deck floor the lantern lit up the entire deck area. Clive slowly stood up in a crouching position. As he started to move again he saw in the center of the pavilion, hanging upside down by her feet, Mandy James, bound and gagged.

Saturday, June 26, 11:50 p .m.

Clive moved low and slowly toward a large oak tree that was between him and the pavilion. As he grew nearer to the tree he could hear bits and pieces of what sounded like a one-sided conversation. He heard something about a loss of innocence and about evil, and how it could not just go away. When he reached the tree he leaned against the back side and looked around at the pavilion about seventy-five feet away. He took his cell phone out of his pocket and called the desk sergeant. When he answered he whispered twice, "Send backup to the fairgrounds pavilion now. I need backup now." He closed the phone and put it back in his pocket, then looked to his right to the hearse sitting in the fog with the back door standing open. There seemed to be no one else around. He looked again to the pavilion and realized that leaning against the steps, was an open empty casket. He moved back against the back side of the tree, closed his eyes and grimaced at the thought that Mandy must have been taken there in the casket.

He opened his eyes again when the thought hit him. "Paul couldn't have moved that casket himself." He quickly turned and looked behind him toward the woods, then to his right and left. He again looked at the car, trying to see if someone was inside. No one there—only the hearse and the fog. He looked around the tree again toward the pavilion and saw Paul Lasiter grasp Mandy by the hair.

Paul turned her face toward his, and Clive clearly heard him say, "Mandy, it's not about the pain. It's about the fear, the terrible fear. She was trapped like you and alone, unable to move because of the poison you all fed her. She saw death coming just as you shall see it, and now it is your time. Your ticket must be redeemed. The debt must be paid in full. You are the last of the evil. Those left behind will feel pain. I take your sin from you and set your spirit free. Your soul is now redeemed." Paul raised Mandy's upper body by the hair on the back of her head and tilted her head back, exposing her neck. He raised his hand and Clive saw the glint of silver in the light of the lantern.

Clive yelled, "No," and stepped out from behind the tree, his weapon raised and pointed at Paul. Paul lowered the scalpel and turned toward the sound of the voice. Clive stood in front of the tree and yelled, "Paul Lasiter, this is Sheriff Aliston. Drop the weapon." Paul lowered Mandy but still held onto her hair. He placed his hand and the scalpel above his eyes trying to see into the dark beyond the edge of the pavilion. Clive continued, "Paul, I said drop the weapon. Drop to the floor and put your hands behind your head." Paul lowered his hand as he now saw Clive step several feet toward him in front of the large tree.

Paul stood and faced Clive, Mandy's hair still in his hand. "Sheriff, you have no part in this. This evil is not for you to protect. The debt must be paid, the evil must end."

Clive stopped, his weapon held out in locked arms. "Paul, put the weapon down and let the girl go. Enough blood has been spilled. This will not bring Victoria back."

Paul raised the blade high in his right hand, waving it in the air over her head. "Clive Aliston, you have no right to tell me about innocent blood. It was not your blood or your flesh that was defiled and slaughtered. I am the judgment and the redeemer. This final evil must be laid to rest so that all the spirits can cross over. Enough of your interference. It ends now." Paul turned again to Mandy, his hand now raised in the air.

Another voice came from the other side of the pavilion. "Paul Lasiter, you heard the man. Drop the weapon now." Paul turned to his right as J.D. Ricketts came up the steps on the other side of the pavilion, his weapon also raised. Paul did not attempt to lower his hand. He just stared at J.D. J.D. repeated, "Lower the weapon."

Paul yelled, "The protectors of evil now come from all sides. So be it, it is over." Paul raised his right hand even higher and raised Mandy's head in his left at the same time. As he started the downward motion with the blade, J.D. fired. The bullet hit Paul in the right lower arm. The blade dropped to the floor as Paul spun around and fell to his knees. J.D. stood at the edge of the pavilion deck, his weapon pointed down at Paul.

Clive was about to move toward the pavilion when he heard a noise to his left. Out of the brush at the edge of the woods, not thirty feet away, stepped Brian Lasiter. His weapon was raised in the direction of the two men on the pavilion deck. He stepped forward and as he did he yelled, "No," and fired a shot toward the men. The bullet hit J.D. Ricketts in the lower right leg, dropping him to his knees and against the pavilion rail. Clive turned toward the pavilion as J.D. fell. Brian fired a second shot that hit the railing beside J.D.'s head, splintering the wood in all directions.

As Clive turned again to Brian he saw him step forward again in an attempt at a third shot. Clive yelled, "Brian, no." Brian turned toward Clive for an instant, the gun still pointed toward J.D. The look in Brian's eyes almost turned Clive's blood cold. It was a look of pure insanity. Brian slowly turned back toward the pavilion and aimed. Clive turned quickly toward Brian while yelling, "No," again and fired a shot. The bullet hit Brian in the right shoulder, spinning him around and knocking him back into the brush and fog. Clive turned to move toward Brian when a huge hand grabbed him from behind. He was dragged backward and slammed into the trunk of the big tree. His gun dropped to the ground and he started to slide down the trunk while trying to catch his breath. An instant later a huge silhouette was before him. A huge hand reached down and grasped the front of his shirt and picked him up, raising his feet off the ground. He reached out with his left arm to try and fight back but he was again slammed into the tree. His arm was pushed back against his chest and he felt the bone in his lower arm snap. Pain shot up his arm and into his shoulder and to his neck and came out as a loud scream.

Brian stood up out of the fog and staggered toward Clive. He yelled, "Max, no." Clive felt himself sliding down the tree to his knees, as Brian yelled again, "Max, no." Clive, still reeling from the pain, looked up to see a huge grotesque face looking back at him. The big hand came again only this time around Clive's throat in a grip like a vise. Brian continued to stagger toward Clive his gun raised and yelling, "Stop, Max, stop."

J.D. had managed to get to his feet by using the railing. He looked at Paul who was still on his knees his head turned to the floor. He looked out at Clive and saw Brian moving toward Clive his gun raised. J.D. raised his gun and pointed it at Brian yelling, "No," and fired. At that same instant Brian turned toward the pavilion. The bullet struck him at the hairline on the left side of his forehead. Brian staggered back two steps then fell forward into the fog.

Paul Lasiter had gotten back on his feet and, with his bloody right hand, had reached into his waistband and pulled out a revolver. J.D. turned just in time to see Paul raise the gun and fire. The bullet hit J.D. in the center of the chest, knocking him back down the steps to the ground. As Paul fired, he yelled, "Max." Max, seeing Brian fall and hearing Paul yell, dropped Clive to the ground. Clive, even while pinned to the tree, had seen J.D. fall backwards. When Clive hit the ground his right hand hit something cold. It was his weapon. He fumbled with it at first but then got it into his hand and started to rise up out of the fog. Max had started to walk toward Paul as Clive stood up. Clive looked toward Paul and saw him raise his gun. Paul fired and the shot hit the tree next to Clive's head. Clive slowly raised his right arm and took aim at Paul. Paul fired a second shot and missed again. Clive squeezed the trigger and his weapon fired. Paul fired a third shot at the same instant. The bullet from Paul's gun hit Clive in the upper left thigh at the same instant Clive's bullet hit Paul in the center of the forehead. Clive fell back against the tree as Paul staggered forward and crashed through the pavilion rail to the ground. Max, seeing Paul fall, ran to the pavilion, reached into the thick fog and picked up Paul. He held Paul close to him as he moved back toward Clive. Clive, in almost unbearable pain, managed to sit up against the tree, his head just barely out of the fog. Max moved closer, still holding Paul in his arms. When he was within ten feet Clive raised his gun. Max stopped, looked at Paul and said "Papa, Papa." Max slowly lowered Paul to the ground, stood up before Clive, raised his fists into the air and screamed. He moved toward Clive with a look of a wounded animal on his face.

Clive yelled, "Max, no. Max, no," but Max moved in closer. When he was only several feet away, Clive fired. The bullet hit Max in the left shoulder, driving him back two steps. Max stopped, looked at his shoulder and touched it with his right hand. When he saw the blood he raised his head to the sky and screamed. He turned, ran toward the woods and disappeared in the thick fog. Clive listened as the screams echoed through the valley then slowly faded. The entire area was now quiet except for the whimpering that came from the pavilion deck from Mandy's taped mouth. Clive managed to get to his feet, his left arm hanging at his side, throbbing with pain. He looked down at his left thigh. The blood ran down the front of his pants to his shoe. The part that seemed funny to him was that there seemed to be no pain in his leg. It felt almost numb. He stood, weaving back and forth for several seconds then he moved toward Brian. When he reached him he fell to one knee and checked his pulse. After several seconds he got up again and started to move toward the pavilion and J.D. He had only gotten a few feet when a wave of dizziness came over him. He stopped then staggered backwards into the tree again. He felt weak, almost unable to move. He slid down the tree again into a sitting position. He put his weapon on his lap and stared out across the fog to the pavilion. Off in the distance he could hear the bell from the old Smith Falls Methodist Church as its ring echoed through the fog covered valleys. It was midnight on June 27. Clive took a deep breath and then all seemed to go dim and then black. At the bottom of the hill, coming from almost every direction, was the sound of sirens. Flashing red and blue lights cut through the dense fog.

CHAPTER 24

Tuesday, July 6, 12:45 p.m.

Ten days had passed since the events of that night at the pavilion. Clive had been in the hospital and had undergone one surgery for the bullet wound to his left leg. His arm was in a cast and he felt bruised and beaten from head to toe. Mandy James had been saved and was now undergoing counseling for the nightmare she had lived through. Paul Lasiter was dead, killed instantly by the shot Clive had fired at him to protect Mandy and himself. Another death was not what Clive had wanted. It left a huge gap in the information about why all the murders had happened. J.D. Ricketts had died of his wounds, and Clive was taking that very hard. They had started out as competitors—almost enemies, but in a short period had come to respect each other very much. They had not been together for very long, but Clive would always count him as a good friend. Max had been wounded and a blood trail had been followed into the woods, but it soon disappeared, as did Max. No trace had been found of him—at least not up to the present time. People believed that he ran off and died of his wounds and that his body would be found sooner or later. Clive wasn't so sure.

Brian Lasiter had suffered two wounds: one to his shoulder, the shot from Clive's gun; and a second to the head, the last shot fired by J.D. Ricketts before Paul had killed him. Brian had undergone two surgeries and was in a coma in a well-guarded room at the hospital. He was probably the hardest part of it all for Clive to accept. He had been a good kid, and an even better cop. He did have his downfalls but Clive had a lot of faith in him and had felt that he would have someday taken his place or even more. Brian was being held on several charges, including attempted murder of an FBI agent. He was to stay at the hospital until he regained consciousness. If he did, he would be transferred to the maximum-security hospital at the prison to await trail. Jack Duff had recuperated well and was sent home about three days after Clive had entered the hospital. They had talked on the phone but had not yet seen each other. It was just past lunchtime and Clive had just finished eating. He had been joined for lunch by his wife Kathryn and daughter Amanda, who had flown in from Mississippi when they had received word of what had happened. He was also being visited by Bill Fry, and Rose Bodin, who had temporarily taken Alice Shearer's place at the station. They were all deep in conversation when Clive, who was about to put a last piece of pie in his mouth, looked toward the door when he heard a knock. The face he saw shocked him into dropping the fork and pie to his lap. There, standing in the doorway, was a man who looked like Paul Lasiter. Everyone in the room turned to the doorway and stared. There was a moment of silence then the man spoke. "I'm sorry. I hope I'm not interrupting anything important?" No one responded, they just continued to stare. After several seconds of continued silence he spoke again. "May I come in?"

Clive, realizing he had dropped the pie, turned and

reached for a napkin but his wife Kathryn stood up and said, "It's okay, I'll get it."

Clive turned again to the man and said, "Yes, please come in."

The man walked to the side of Clive's bed and put out his hand. "My name is Robert Lasiter. I am Paul's brother."

Clive, staring intently at the man, said. "Twin brother?"

The man smiled and said, "Yes I am. Not many people knew that Paul had a brother—let alone a twin. I know seeing me now must be a shock to all of you."

Bill Fry let out a sigh and said, "I think shock may be a little too mild a description."

Robert walked to each person, shook hands, and said hello. He then returned to the side of Clive's bed. "As I said, I hope I'm not interrupting anything, but I have come a long way and I think we need to talk."

Rose and Bill got up and tried to excuse themselves but Clive said, "Sit, sit. You don't need to leave." He looked up at Robert and said, "This is my wife Kathryn and daughter Amanda. Bill is the coroner and Rose is my secretary. Anything you have is okay to say in front of them."

Robert reached into his sport coat pocket and retrieved two tapes and a small tape recorder and placed them on the bed beside Clive. "Well, I guess I better start with me. As I said, I am Paul's twin brother. I have lived in Germany for several years now. I work for an American firm there and have not been home or seen my brother in several years. We were very close as children but we grew apart in later years, I suspect because of his situation. It's that situation that I am here to talk to you about. Most of what you need to know about what Paul did is on those tapes. I know I should have turned them in but I heard about what you have been through and what losses you've suffered and I guess I thought you had the right to hear them first. All I ask is that as you listen to the tapes you try to understand what that man had lived through. It in no way justifies what happened but I feel his story—the whole story—

needs to be understood."

"When did you get these?" Clive asked as he picked them up and looked at them.

Robert began to walk back and forth in front of the door then began again, "As I said, I live in Germany, and I received those about four days ago. I let them sit for two days before I got around to listening to them. Now I wish I had listened sooner. I could have saved some lives, maybe. They are the complete story of what happened to Paul and why he did what he did. I think when it was over he wanted the world to understand. It lets you look into the mind of a man who lived in emotional pain. Pain caused by what he saw as an evil. That evil ate away at him and took all that was good in his life. In his mind he was convinced that he was given the job of avenging angel and redeemer all wrapped into one. I know what he did was wrong. He saw it as right, and his mind led him down a path to a dark pit that was too deep to crawl out of. I'm not sure that if it had happened to me, I could have endured it. I know that after hearing these, you will realize that Paul was insane. I'm not asking for you to forgive or accept what he did. All I'm here for is to be the one person who speaks for him, him and Max. I'm here also to thank you for all you did and tried to do to stop him. If I had known about this sooner I would have put a stop to it myself. I'm also here to see Brian. I understand he is in a coma and he probably won't even know I'm here."

Clive set the tapes back on the bed then looked up at Robert. "Brian is in a room with guards, but I'll try to get you in to see him. Have they told you anymore about him?"

"No," Robert said. "They haven't. I came to see you first. I really would appreciate seeing him even if he has no idea that I'm here. I owe Paul that much. I also will pick up any bills that insurance does not pay. One more thing before I leave. Please try to forgive Brian. His life was not easy either and I would guess that when he found out the truth about Paul his mind snapped also."

Clive, with a puzzled look on his face, asked, "How would Brian have found out all of this? Paul sent you the tapes."

Robert stopped pacing and stopped at the side of Clive's bed. "The tapes are recorded from a log book or diary that Paul wrote. I guess it is as detailed as the tapes but I don't know where the book is. I already checked and I'm being told that a search of all Paul's property has not turned it up. He may have destroyed it, but he may also have given it to, or sent it to someone else—maybe Brian."

Clive turned to Bill Fry and said, "Maybe we know now why Brian disappeared."

Robert reached out to shake Clive's hand and said. "If Brian never comes out of this we may never know for sure. Well, I leave you all to your conversation. I will be at the Holiday Inn in town for the rest of the week—or longer if you need me."

Clive said, "Thank you."

Everyone got up as Robert was leaving. As he reached the door he turned and said, "Clive, as you listen try and understand. It's all I ask, try and understand." Robert waved and said, "It was nice to meet you all." He smiled and walked away. Clive's wife and daughter and Rose stayed for about half an hour longer, then left to give Clive time to listen to the tapes and rest.

Clive asked Bill Fry to stay and listen also. The tapes lasted for almost an hour and as they listened you could almost feel the pain in the voice of Paul Lasiter as he spoke. The tape started out years before, Paul explaining how he and Lynn had met. He told of being friends with Carl Dans, George Miller and Bart James as young men. Lynn had been Bart's girlfriend before she dated Paul, and it wasn't until after Paul and Lynn were married that he began to realize that she still had feelings for Bart. He tried to put that in the back of his mind, hoping that she would get over it and begin to love him. He knew that she started seeing

Bart again behind his back but he would not let himself believe it. She was his wife and Bart was his friend. He tried to convince himself that it was all in his mind, until the day Lynn came to him and told him she was pregnant and the child was not his. He said he felt he could have killed them both then but he loved her too much. He buried his feelings and took her back, and when Brian was born he tried to love him also but it wasn't easy.

For several years all seemed to be okay. They even had a child of their own: his pride and joy, a beautiful little girl they called Victoria. Life was good again. He was in business for himself, he had a beautiful child and a wife he loved and he had Brian. When Victoria was only two years old, the old flame for Bart seemed to grow in Lynn again. Paul knew what was happening but again he tried to deny it. As the affair continued it also became harder and harder to look at Brian. Paul could not stand to be around him. Paul knew that at times Brian felt neglected and almost shunned and he felt bad about that also.

After almost eighteen months of seeing Bart again, Lynn became pregnant a second time to Bart. She never told Paul that this child was Bart's but Paul knew. He and Lynn had not been together in many months. Once again he tried not to think about it but his world ended the day of that birth. It had been decided that the birth would be at home and a midwife was hired. The labor was extremely difficult and in the end Lynn gave birth to twins. The one twin was stillborn and Lynn began to hemorrhage just after the birth had ended. The second twin was Max and when Paul and the midwife saw him they cleaned him up and took him away. An ambulance was called but they did not get Lynn to the hospital in time. Paul paid the midwife to keep quiet and he kept Max out of sight until he could take him away. Several days later Paul took Max to an out-of-state facility for such cases and left. How he got past all the legal paperwork was anyone's guess but Max somehow remained a secret. Paul paid the midwife on several occasions until her death about five years later. For a time, Paul was the only one who knew that Max existed. It was kept even from Brian and Victoria. Paul's life crashed down around him. His wife, the woman he loved, was dead. His first child, Brian, the one he had tried to love, wasn't his. Now he had Max, a genetically-defective child that he felt must have been a punishment placed on him for not taking care of the problem of his wife's infidelity before. The only bright spot left in his life was his beautiful Victoria.

Years passed and Paul raised Brian as best as he could, but each time he tried to draw closer to him he would see Bart. Victoria was the center of his life and he knew it hurt Brian, so he tried to make up for it in other ways—like money and college. As Brian grew older, he grew further away from Paul and Victoria grew closer. Paul said that one thing he did know was that Brian and Victoria loved each other. He was grateful that Brian didn't take out on his sister his feelings about his father.

On Victoria's sixteenth birthday, Paul bought her a necklace. A small gold chain and the one-word pendant, "Forever." It signified to Paul that his love for his wife now belonged to Victoria and always would. She wore it always. Brian entered college and he and Paul grew even further apart. Paul was at his graduation but that didn't go well, and after that they drifted apart even more. The money that Paul paid out for Max was beginning to take its toll on him and he finally had to bring Max home secretly. He worried about what Victoria would think, but she loved him almost immediately. Max was confined to the house and finally the cellar room. He would get excited and at times hurt himself or even Paul. Paul and Victoria kept Max a secret from everyone—even Brian, who was never around. Victoria would spend long hours in that cellar room, reading to Max as he held that old teddy bear that she had given him.

Victoria, at the age of seventeen, almost eighteen, began to look for friends outside the family. She spent more and

more time away from Paul and Max. Then that horrible
night happened just before the Fourth of July. There was
the party and the drugs and the booze and those terrible
friends that Paul disliked. It all ended that night at or just
before midnight on the 26th of June. Victoria was gone and
so was Paul's life. The parents of the other kids felt that
they owed Paul something and they bought the huge stone
for her grave but it was too late. Victoria was no longer in
the grave. She was again with Paul and Max. Paul would
watch those who were involved that night from a distance
and kept asking why their lives should go on. Why do they
not pay for what was done? Victoria was the innocent and
they were the evil. They, their parents, his ex-friends and
that horrible judge were the evil.

A grievous sin had been committed and he was
convinced that he had been given the task of making it
right—he and Max. He created a plan in his mind and he
confided in Victoria, who was now with him forever. In his
notes he said they had conversations and she would tell
him what she thought. It all came together when he
realized in his mind that he was chosen to save the souls of
the children who had caused Victoria's death. He must
redeem their tickets of life that were stained with sin. In
their deaths, their fear would cleanse them and the gates of
heaven would open again. He had to save them; he had to
punish their parents the way he had been punished, and
send their souls to eternal damnation. The money, the
drugs, the booze, the fast cars, and the corrupt judge, were
all part of an evil that must go.

The tape went on for several more minutes but Bill and
Clive had heard enough. Bill sat back in the chair and let
out a sigh, "My God, Clive, what that man lived through.
Could you have endured it? I'm not sure I could." Clive
placed the tape back in the case and handed the bag to Bill.
"Take this to Jim Terrell and tell him to make sure he's
sitting before he listens to it." Clive didn't say much more
about the tape. He told Bill he was tired and that he

thought he would take a nap. They talked a few minutes longer then Bill left and Clive slid down into the bed and pulled up the blanket. He turned slowly to his right side and stared out the window at the now-cloudy sky. It was getting dark and a summer storm was coming. Rain started to cover the window.

Tuesday, July 13, 2:00 p.m.

Clive had responded well enough to therapy to be sent home. He filled out the papers and was being wheeled out of the hospital to his wife's rental car when he asked to see Brian. Brian had come out of the coma three days before but had not spoken a word. He just sat in bed or in a chair in the corner of the room and stared at nothing. Clive told the nurse to wait out in the hall after she wheeled him into the room. Brian was in the corner chair near the window, in a robe and pajamas. Clive sat and stared for several minutes at him as he sat and stared back, his head in a large white bandage and thick padding at his shoulder. Clive reached out and placed his hand on Brian's but Brian didn't move his hand or his eyes. "I'm sorry buddy," Clive said as tears started to well up in his eyes. "I'm sorry. I didn't know or understand and I'm sorry I had to shoot when I did. Why didn't you come to me when you knew? I could have helped."

Brian stared past Clive. Clive sat quietly for several more minutes then whispered, "What's going on in that mind? What do you know?"

He called for the nurse several minutes later and he was wheeled out of the hospital and to his wife and the waiting car. As the car pulled away from the hospital entrance a lone tear rolled down his cheek, and he slowly turned and looked out the side window.

Friday, July 23, 9:30 p.m.

Brian was still not talking or moving but was considered

well enough to move to the prison hospital. He was taken from his room in a wheelchair by two officers from the prison to a loading dock at the rear of the hospital where a prison ambulance was backed into the ramp. He was being moved at night to prevent any press or media attention. Across the street in a large grove of trees at the opening of a tunnel that allowed the creek to pass under the road, a pair of eyes watched as Brian was being brought out. One of the officers wheeled Brian down the ramp to the open doors of the ambulance, while the other signed papers on a clipboard at the back entrance door of the hospital. The officer placed Brian in the ambulance, locked the wheelchair in place, and strapped Brian into the chair. He placed handcuffs on Brian and leg restraints, which were fastened to the floor. Brian sat and stared at nothing.

When the officer had finished he got down on one knee in front of Brian and said, "Brian, sorry about this, buddy." He placed his hand on Brian's for a moment then smiled and got up and closed and locked the doors. He walked down the steps at the side of the ramp to the ground, stopped, put his hand into his pocket, got the keys, and continued to the front of the ambulance.

The officer at the door of the hospital signed the last paper, said, "Thanks," and was about to turn toward the ambulance when he thought he heard a thud. He stopped and listened; the nurse with the clipboard went back into the hospital. He slowly walked to the back of the ambulance tilting his head to one side to listen. He stopped at the back doors of the ambulance and checked the lock then yelled, "Kevin, Kevin, what's up buddy?" He turned to walk to the steps at the side of the ramp when something smashed into the back of his head and he fell to the floor and rolled to his back. He looked up through what seemed like a thick fog and saw a silhouette above him then all went black.

EPILOGUE

Friday, September 26, 1:00 p.m.

It had been three months since that night at the pavilion and two months since Brian had escaped. All attempts to find Brian and Max had ended with very little success. Clive had been back to work for about a month on a part time basis. He had been in touch with his wife and daughter much more now than in the past and was planning a visit to Mississippi to see them in the next two weeks. Jack Duff was back to work and in good health again. Rose was still part time at Alice's old job but she didn't want it full time so there was an open position. The storm that hit that night when Jack Duff was hurt had produced a tornado according to National Weather Service but a lot of damage had been repaired. The funerals were over, but the case was still open. The town was slowly getting back to normal but like Clive, most knew that life in Smith Falls was never going to be exactly the way it was.

Clive was sitting in his office, his chair turned to the window, staring out into what was turning out to be a very nice fall afternoon. After several minutes he turned back to his desk, picked up a pen, and opened his drawer to retrieve some papers. He saw in the front right hand corner a box of unopened cigars and he picked them up. They had been given to him by Brian months before. He sat and thought for a moment, then put the pen back on the desk and placed the cigars in his pocket. He closed the drawer then turned his chair back to the window for a few seconds. He got up slowly from his chair, picked up a cane that hung on the side of his desk and then spun the chair in circles and walked to his office door. He turned at the door and looked back at his desk, then shook his head as if to say, "No," and left the office. He stopped at Rose's desk and asked. "Do I have anything pressing? Or is there something you need me to do?"

Rose thought for a moment then said, "No Clive."

Clive smiled and said, "I'm tired. I think I'll head home. If I'm needed, call me. Just make sure it's important."

Rose said, "Okay Clive." They both smiled and Clive turned and limped slowly out of the station to the front steps. When he got to the top step he paused and looked around at the beautiful sunny day and took a deep breath. The smell of fall was in the air and he felt good for the first time in a while. He slowly walked down the steps and across the parking lot to his patrol car. He was about to get in when he looked past the car to a park bench on the grass near a big tree. He closed the car door, limped slowly to the bench and sat down. He placed the cane on the back of the bench and sat and looked up at the tree and the sky and felt the warm sun on his legs. He took a deep breath again. It felt good to relax, and the air smelled crisp and clean. After several minutes he remembered the cigars, took the box out of his pocket and looked at it. A picture of Brian's laughing face flashed through his mind. Clive slowly opened the cigars and took one out. He placed the rest of the box back in his pocket. He removed the wrapper from the cigar and then rolled the cigar through his lips, wetting the outside cover. He reached into his pocket, took out a lighter and lit the end until it glowed orange. He put the lighter away then sat back and took a long drag on the cigar then slowly blew out the smoke.

He was about to take a second drag when he saw a young boy coming across the parking lot on a bicycle. The boy pedaled up to Clive and stopped. Clive lowered the cigar and asked, "Yes, son. Can I help you?"

The young boy slowly looked him over then asked, "Are you a sheriff?"

"Yes," Clive said. "I am. Can I help you?"

The boy paused again for a second then asked, "Is your name Clive?"

"Yes," Clive said. "I'm Clive Aliston, the sheriff here. What is it that I can do for you?"

"Oh nothing for me," the boy said as he reached into his back pocket. "I have something for you. I got five dollars to give you this." He handed Clive a sealed white envelope. Clive put the cigar in his mouth and bit down to hold it in his teeth. As he opened the envelope the boy turned his bike and started to pedal away. When the envelope was open Clive took out a scrap of paper and started to open it. As he did, something fell out onto his lap. He picked it up. It was a gold chain with a one-word pendant attached, "Forever." He turned back to the scrap of paper and continued to open it. Scrawled across the paper in large uneven letters was the message, "Their tickets must be redeemed." Clive stood up, the cigar dropped from his mouth and he looked to where the boy had been, but he was gone.

Out Now...

Another Clive Aliston Novel

C. William Davis III

Bill Davis plans to continue his Clive Aliston series along with two other full length novels. Since retiring from the industrial electrical and aerospace electronics field, where he did work for the government aerospace and space programs, Davis has focused on his lifelong interest in literature and writing.

A long-time resident of Brackenridge, Pennsylvania, he graduated from Har-Brack High School and earned a degree in Aerospace Electronics from A.T.I. in Pittsburgh.

He has been married to his wife, Linda for forty years and has two children and three grandchildren.